DEADLY
GOLD

DEADLY GOLD

KEN BAYSINGER

Published by Yorkshire Publishing
3207 South Norwood Ave.
Tulsa, Oklahoma 74137 USA
918.394.2665
www.yorkshirepublishing.com

Book design copyright © 2017 by Ken Baysinger. All rights reserved.
Cover design by Maria Louella Mancao
Interior design by Richell Balansag and Ken Baysinger
Spanish translations by Kirsten Sabata

Published in the United States of America
ISBN: 978-1-947491-99-1

1. Fiction / Mystery & Detective / General
2. Fiction / Mystery & Detective / Private Investigators
15.09.18

Remembering
Elizabeth Lynn Dunham,
who deserved better

A note from the author:

Deadly Gold is the second book in the Corrigan Mystery Series. It is strongly recommended that you read *El Camino* first, because much of this book is a continuation of the story that begins in *El Camino*. If you read *Deadly Gold* first, you will know the outcome of *El Camino* before you read it.

Thank you for reading my Corrigan Mystery Novels.

Ken Baysinger

Prologue

Canemah, Oregon

The tiny community of Canemah (pronounced Cah-**nee**-mah) lies on the east bank of the Willamette River, on the southwestern fringe of Oregon City, the first town incorporated in the Oregon Territory. In the Chinookian language, *canemah* means "the canoe place." Located at the brink of Willamette Falls, Canemah was the upstream terminus for the long, difficult portage around the falls. Many of the early river travelers simply put their canoes in storage at Canemah and obtained new ones below the falls to continue downstream.

The last tribal inhabitants of Canemah were Calapooyas, but their village was wiped out by the neighboring Clackamas and Clough-we-wallah tribes in the early 1800s. When the first white settlers arrived, they found the site vacant. By the time Absalom Hedges arrived in 1844, the prime real estate adjacent to the falls had already been claimed by Dr. John McLoughlin, so Hedges had to take second choice.

He chose Canemah, and in 1849, he platted the town he called Falls City on the site. Hedges was enough of a visionary to see that all commerce up and down the river hinged on the portage around Willamette Falls, and his new town quickly became a major port on the river. But his name for the town didn't stick since everyone already knew the place as Canemah.

For twenty-five years, Canemah prospered, despite having been swept completely away by a flood in 1861. But the opening of the Willamette Falls Navigation Locks in 1873 did what the flood couldn't do—it rendered Canemah economically irrelevant. Still, the town remained home to many of the steamboat captains who worked the upper Willamette River, and many of their homes still stand, which is why Canemah has been declared a National Register historic district. The railroad came through Canemah in the 1880s, running along the riverbank, effectively separating Canemah from the Willamette River. That rail line has been in continuous use ever since, and it is now the Union Pacific's main line from Oregon to California.

Then in the 1890s, the first hydroelectric generating plants were built at Willamette Falls. To stabilize the water level feeding the turbines, the power company built a low dam across the brink of the falls. Doing this required the purchase of all of the riverbank property that would be affected by the raised water level above the falls.

The docks and wharfs along the waterfront were torn down or abandoned, and Canemah ceased to be a river port. As rail traffic increased, the noise and soot from the trains made Canemah a less desirable place to live, so it degenerated into a low-rent district.

The railroad eventually bought up all of the property facing the river, with the long-term objective of using the land to straighten out an inconvenient curve in the rail line. In the meantime, they made rentals of all the homes adjacent to their right-of-way, and so things stayed until the early 1990s. By then, Oregon City was becoming increasingly conscious of its unique place in history and had passed a series of laws protecting historic structures, including those in Canemah, which had been annexed into Oregon City in the 1930s.

A commercial diving company owned a parcel of land on the downstream tip of Canemah, and when they wanted to expand, they approached Union Pacific about buying some of their property. The railroad, realizing that the historical protection granted to the houses they owned would make it difficult and expensive, if not impossible, to ever tear down the structures to re-route the rails, agreed to sell to the dive company, with just one stipulation—they had to buy it all.

The dive company agreed and purchased all twenty parcels in one lump. Keeping the parcels they needed, they offered to sell the remaining properties to employees at bargain prices. The rest were sold on the open market. Most of the properties have been resold once or twice since then, but a few are still owned by the people who originally bought them from the dive company. A couple of new houses were built on vacant lots, and all of the old houses—some dating back to the 1860s—have been renovated or restored as Canemah regains its community dignity and eclectic appeal.

Several years ago, the property owners joined together and bought the power company's strip of land along the waterfront and have since been re-connecting Canemah with its riverfront heritage. The recreational opportunities associated with that have provided further incentive for improvements to the adjacent homes.

One old home in particular received a total makeover in 2013. During the early stages of the project, workers discovered a stone-lined water well beneath the concrete slab in the basement. Before laying the new floor, the well was searched for historical artifacts, but disappointingly, nothing was found. Once again covered beneath a concrete slab, any secrets the old well may contain will have to wait for future archeological study.

Friday, October 12

I was startled from a sound sleep by a crashing sound at my door. My comatose state grudgingly yielded to awareness, and I recognized a woman's voice, highly agitated, behind the loud knocking.

"¡Ayúdame! ¡Ayúdame! Mi gallo desapareció. Alguien se me ha robado. Es crítico que me ayude—¡alguien robó mi gallo!"

While groping around for my pants, I glanced at the digital clock on my dresser. Christ, it wasn't even seven o'clock yet.

"I'm coming! Hold on!" I shouted as I pulled on my jeans.

"¡Señor Corrigan, de veras necesito su ayuda! ¡Mi gallo desapareció y necesito su ayuda! ¡Hay un ladrón que tomó mi gallo! ¡Por favor! ¡Por favor!"

I got the "por favor" part, but that was the extent of my Spanish language skills.

The early morning light blasted me in the face as I opened the door. Squinting against the brightness, I found a short, middle-aged woman with a crazed look on her face jumping up and down on my porch.

Her screaming continued, "No lo oí esta mañana, y cuando salí de la casa encontré su jaula abierta y nos dejó para siempre! ¡Alguien lo tomó! No ha salido por sí mismo. ¡Alguien lo ha matado!"

I held up my hands in surrender. "No habla," I said, "No habla." Okay, so I did know another Spanish phrase. But that was definitely it.

"Venga conmigo y le puedo mostrar a usted. Venga conmigo, señor. ¡Por favor!" she cried, taking my hand and tugging me toward the street.

I recognized her as the matriarch of a Nicaraguan family who lived a block and a half up the street from my place. "Señora Valensueva," I ventured, "please, do you speak any English?"

"Quiero contratarle a usted para investigar. Necesitamos encontrar me pobrecito, mi gallito ¡Ándale! ¡Alguien le tomó!"

I took that to mean no. She continued tugging, but I managed to stop her from pulling me into the street.

"Wait," I pleaded, "I have to get my shoes. And a shirt. Just hold on!"

I gestured down at my bare feet, and for the first time, I saw a glimmer of comprehension.

"Sí, Señor Corrigan, vaya usted para los zapatos y después vamos para buscar el ladrón que tomó mi gallo. ¡Dios mío! ¡Ojalá que no le haya matado!"

While Señora Valensueva danced around impatiently on my porch, I found the previous day's t-shirt on the floor and quickly determined that it didn't smell bad. Well, not *too* bad, anyway. I pulled it over my head and found my Tevas, one under the bed and the other in the bathroom—right where I'd left them.

Hopping on one foot while tugging my Teva onto the other, I made my way back outside. Señora Valensueva grabbed my arm and dragged me out to the street, pulling me in the direction of her house. This was a hell of a way to start the day.

A block ahead, Señora Valensueva's teenage daughter, Rosita, suddenly appeared. I knew her name because she often made the rounds in the neighborhood, socializing with anyone she encountered. To say that she had an outgoing personality was like saying Shaquille O'Neal is tall. Rosita had always struck me as being like a freshly shaken bottle of soda, a perpetual stream of words bubbling from her mouth.

But even from a hundred yards away, I could see that her usual effervescence had been supplanted by something else. Upon seeing her mother, Rosita threw her hands in the air and ran toward us.

"Lo encontré está muerto. Alguien lo mató. I found heem. Julio is dead! Someone murdered heem!" she cried as she ran toward us.

As mother and daughter fell into each other's arms, their eyes overflowing with tears, I tried to make sense of what I'd just heard.

"Murder," I repeated. "Did you say someone was murdered? Who is Julio?"

I finally had to take Rosita by the arm and shake her loose from her mother.

"Have you called the police?" I asked.

"No, Señor Corrigan," she wailed. "Police, they do notheeng."

She turned back to her mother and cried, "Julio ha sido asesinado. Someone keeled heem!"

I tried to regain Rosita's attention. "If someone has been murdered, you have to call the police! Who has been killed? Who is Julio?"

I grabbed Rosita by the shoulders and forced her to look at me. "Who is Julio?"

"Julio es nuestro gallo," she cried. "Julio ees our rooster."

I tried to make sense out of that. "Wait. Are you saying that Julio is just a chicken?"

That caused Rosita to wail even louder. "No ees cheeken! Ees rooster! And someone keeled heem!"

"Okay, okay. Julio is a rooster," I repeated, just to make sure that I was hearing this right.

"Si. Yes. Julio ees rooster," she cried. "Julio era un gallo. Era un gallo!"

That made both Rosita and her mother break into another round of wailing. I was starting to get the picture. They really liked their rooster.

With some effort, I again got Rosita's attention. "You said that you found Julio. Where is he?"

With a shaking hand, she pointed toward a mass of blackberry brambles on the other side of the railroad tracks that ran parallel to the street. As we walked closer, I noticed a few orange and black feathers lying on the ground. There were feathers on the railroad right-of-way too. I motioned for Rosita and her mother to stay on the road while I ventured across the railroad tracks.

Sure enough, there among the overripe blackberries lay a large rooster, his neck forming a decidedly unnatural right angle. Julio was dead. There was no doubt whatsoever about that. Old Julio was as dead as a door nail. And someone was going to catch the Dickens over it too.

I shook my head as I walked back across the tracks, confirming what Rosita had observed. Someone had indeed killed Julio.

"Do you have any idea who—" I started to ask.

"It was heem!" Rosita shouted. "Heem!" She gestured toward the gray house on the other side of Valensueva's fence. "It was Señor Carlton!"

Señor Carlton was Carlton McDermitt, an oddball character who lived next door to the Valensuevas and kitty-corner from his ex-wife, Jill. Carlton had once owned a waterbed store, but when that business went belly-up, he opened a small used car lot that specialized in vehicles that no self-respecting car dealer would touch.

Three years earlier, on the day I moved into my little home/office down by the Willamette River in the historic town of Canemah, I watched a man swim about two hundred yards out to the middle of the river to a small inflatable raft that was anchored there. It was Carlton McDermitt. He pulled out a pocket knife, cut the anchor line, and began swimming the raft back toward shore.

"Hey, where do you think you're going with that?" someone shouted to him.

Carlton ignored him and kept swimming.

"What the hell are you doing?"

"I'm claiming salvage rights," Carlton shouted back.

When he got to shore, he was met by the guy I came to know as Big Dan. Dan Barlow was big, but he seemed a lot bigger than he actually was. Dan was a commercial diver, and I'd heard that he'd been a Navy SEAL a few years back. Nothing I could see ever led me to think otherwise.

But here's the thing about Big Dan. I once noticed that he routinely left things of value out in the open on his dock—things like water skis, scuba gear, even ice chests full of beer. I wondered aloud if it was safe to leave things like that out in the open. Dan said nobody had ever bothered anything of his. I asked why, and all he said was, "Because they're scared of me."

It seems Big Dan had anchored the raft out in the river as a target for golf balls that he and his friends whacked from his dock. With every miss, they contributed to a growing cash pool that would go to the first person who landed a ball in the raft. What prompted Carlton to claim salvage rights on Big Dan's raft was a mystery. Clearly self-preservation was not high on Carlton's list of priorities. Next to Big Dan, Carlton looked like a wet Pomeranian alongside a bull Mastiff. I could see Carlton re-thinking his salvage project.

Big Dan set Carlton straight on salvage rights. "There is no such thing as a 'salvage right' on inland waters. Even if you were to raise a sunken vessel from the bottom of the river, the vessel would still belong to its registered owner. The most you could do is to negotiate a salvage fee with the owner."

Even I knew that. But I admired Big Dan's restraint in treating the event as a "teachable moment" instead of rearranging Carlton's major body parts. And that was my introduction to the "Señor Carlton" who was behind the current uproar.

I wanted to offer some kind of consolation to the grief-stricken Valensuevas, so I said to Rosita, "Tell your mother that I will bury Julio for her. And then I'll go have a talk with Señor Carlton."

Rosita said, "You wring hees neck, like he deed to Julio!" Then she turned to her mother and translated what I had said.

From the string of words that then came from Señora Valensueva, the only one I picked up was *bastardo*, and I heard it several times during her sustained diatribe.

When she finally ran out of things to say about Señor Carlton, she took my hand and looked sadly into my eyes. "Usted va a capturar ese serpiente cascabel sin vergüenza que mató a nuestro Julio. No es como podemos reemplazarlo con otro gallo. ¡Era de la familia!"

I looked to Rosita, and she translated, "She wants you to break Señor Carlton's arms and legs."

I followed them back to their house and again assured them that I'd have a talk with Carlton. In one sense, I understood why he would want to do away with the rooster, which had the annoying habit of announcing sunrise to the entire neighborhood at ungodly early hours.

I walked around the block to Carlton's side porch and rapped on his door.

"Top 'o the mornin' to ye," Carlton exclaimed, using the pseudo-Scottish accent that he frequently affected because he thought it made him seem more erudite. He twisted the end of his handlebar mustache while he spoke, and the total effect was to make him seem like a complete jackass. "What brings ye out on this fine day?"

I got right to the point. "Señora Valensueva thinks that you killed her rooster."

With a look of smug satisfaction, Carlton said, "Aye, laddie, this was indeed a quiet mornin'. The first time in months I've slept past the breakin' of the dawn. May the old cock rest in peace."

"So you really did kill him?" I could never be quite sure that I was correctly translating Carlton's words.

"Aye. That damned rooster's been awakin' me up at the crack of dawn every-day for six months. So I snuck over there last night and wrung his neck." The fake accent faded away. It required a higher level of focus than he could maintain for very long.

"Well, I hate to say it, my friend, but you'd better think about getting Señora Valensueva a new rooster, because if you don't, she's going to call the cops."

"Oh hell, that would just get the INS out here. Would she want that?" Carlton exclaimed. "They find out she doesn't have a green card, she's gone. Back to Mexico."

"Nicaragua," I corrected. "She's from Nicaragua, not Mexico, and I'm pretty sure she's legal."

Carlton shrugged it off. "Nicaragua, Mexico—it doesn't matter. Those people are all alike."

"Well, you'd better get things straight with her. I gave her Officer Durham's card. If the señora doesn't hear from you within the hour, you'll be hearing from Officer Durham."

So here it was, not yet seven thirty in the morning and I'd already solved a major crime. I walked back to my cottage feeling the sense of satisfaction that comes only from setting things right. It remained to be seen whether or not Carlton would uphold his end of the bargain.

Typical for early October, it was still comfortably warm, though a few of the maple trees were starting to change color. The morning sun was just reaching the river, erasing the thin fog that hung over the glassy smooth water. I went inside and pulled the chain that switched on the little neon sign in my front window: Discreet Investigations.

"What was that all about?" asked Kim Stayton as she fluffed her wet blond curls with a towel.

I said, "Rosita found a body in the brambles alongside the railroad tracks."

Seeing Kim's startled expression, I hastily added, "Rosita said his name was Julio—and he was clearly the victim of fowl play."

Tossing the towel aside, Kim grabbed her uniform from the closet and quickly started getting dressed. "Have you notified OCPD?" she asked, referring to Oregon City Police Department.

"There's no need," I told her. "I already solved it."

Deputy Stayton stopped dressing and gave me a cold stare.

"Julio was Rosita's rooster. Carlton wrung his neck last night," I explained.

"You turd!" she exclaimed as she threw a shoe at me.

I fielded it like Derek Jeter grabbing a belt-high line drive.

"Now I can take the rest of the day off," I bragged. "I have a one-murder-a-day rule."

Even as I spoke the words, I became aware of the sound of a boat coming down river, a fairly unusual occurrence this early in the morning. Looking upstream, I watched a battered, old tugboat lumbering toward us and recognized it as Captain Alan's *Misty Rose*, a common sight all up and down the river. Alan's family had deep roots in West Linn and Oregon City, and Alan was known to many as the Old Man of the Willamette.

Alan lived aboard *Misty Rose* with his dog, Cinnamon, an undocumented mix of Irish setter, yellow lab, and golden retriever. He bought gas, groceries, and booze with whatever money he could earn doing odd jobs along the river anywhere from Corvallis to the Columbia. I think it very unlikely that anybody alive has more knowledge of the Willamette River than Captain Alan.

Misty Rose was a steel-hulled thirty-two-foot tug of questionable seaworthiness, powered by a 1951 Chrysler Hemi. The pilot house was a rickety plywood box set amidships, with a sloping roof over the engine compartment forward of that. There was a two-burner propane hotplate in the pilot house that served as the galley, and the sleeping accommodations consisted of an old steel army cot wedged alongside the engine. It is best to avoid questions regarding sanitation.

Somewhere up along the shores of the Yamhill River, Alan had an old travel trailer, with its wheels removed, sitting on a barge next to a corrugated metal shed filled with an assortment of tools and greasy parts from all manner of mechanical equipment. This served as his home base, and he kept an old red Toyota pickup truck parked at the end of the dirt path that led down to the riverbank. Whenever he had a few weeks worth of money saved up, he'd take *Misty Rose* up the Yamhill and tie up at his barge. From there, it was a short drive to Lumpy's Tavern in Dundee, which would be Alan's headquarters until the money ran out and he had to go back out onto the river.

The past few weeks, Alan had been salvaging sunken logs from the river half a mile upstream from Canemah. As he explained it to me, the mills used to tie up huge rafts of logs there, and frequently they'd have so many logs in the water that some would be forced beneath the surface. Over time, they would become waterlogged and sink. Nearly a century later, many of the submerged logs are still there. These are old-growth timber, and their lumber is highly prized at salvage mills. Alan told me that a single log could be worth over a thousand dollars.

When he spotted me on my porch, Alan urgently waved me down to the beach. I hurried out onto my dock just as Captain Alan brought *Misty Rose* alongside.

"Is your little deputy-sheriff friend here?" Alan asked while he tied up the boat.

I said, "Yeah, sure. What's up?"

"I have something she needs to see!"

Taking Alan at his word, I pulled out my phone and touched speed-dial number 1. When Kim answered, I said, "We need you down here on the dock, babe."

"You have another dead rooster?" she asked.

Looking over at the afterdeck of *Misty Rose*, I said, "It's bigger than a rooster."

Minutes later, Kim appeared in full uniform but with still wet hair. She took one look at what Alan had brought in and pulled out her portable VHF radio.

"Dispatch, this is Marine Unit 1," she said.

"Go ahead, One."

"Notify Jamieson that we need HVCU on Water Street in Canemah, just west of Jerome Street. On the dock at Corrigan's place—he'll know where that is. A tugboat operator just brought in human remains rolled up in a piece of carpet. Did you get all that?"

"Affirmative. Human remains at Corrigan's dock on Water Street."

Larry Jamieson was still in charge of the Homicide and Violent Crimes Unit, despite his recent appointment as acting sheriff following the arrest of his predecessor on charges of racketeering and obstruction of justice. HVCU investigates all major crimes in Clackamas County.

While we waited for the posse to arrive, I snapped some photos with my phone. I carefully avoided touching anything that might contain trace evidence.

Within half an hour, Water Street was filled with sheriff's office vehicles of all description. Two crimescene technicians were standing on the afterdeck of *Misty Rose* discussing how to best preserve whatever evidence might be present.

A young deputy took notes while Alan explained, "I was tied up to a dolphin, up where they used to tie up log booms."

Looking confused, the deputy asked, "Wait, did you say dolphin—are there really dolphins in the Willamette?"

Kim interjected, "He's not talking about Flipper—a dolphin is a cluster of pilings all attached together."

As senior deputy on the sheriff's Marine Unit, Kim was more than familiar with nautical terminology.

Acting like he understood, the deputy interviewing Alan nodded.

"Just before dark last night," Alan continued, "I pulled up two big old logs. It was too late to do anything with 'em, so I just tied them off for the night. This morning, I was attaching floats to the logs when I found this roll of carpet snagged on my cable.

"It was all tied up in cord," he explained, "but when I pulled it up on deck, the cord came loose. The carpet unrolled, and that's when I saw…that. As soon as I could get my logs secure, I hightailed it down here.

The skeletal remains lay in a muddy puddle on the unrolled carpet, together with a rusty ten-pound cast iron anchor. A few of the bones were still connected together, but mostly they lay roughly in the shape of a body. The tattered remains of a pair of red shorts and flower-print short-sleeved top suggested that the victim had been female and she had died in summertime. I looked closely at the carpet, judging by its fiber and mauve color that it might be fifteen or twenty years old. There probably was more to see, but this wasn't my investigation.

A pathologist from the medical examiner's office bent over and looked closely at the skull and the clumps of medium-length brown hair that lay around it. She dictated into a recorder, "Victim appears to be a Caucasian female, about thirty years old. Possible head trauma. Been in the water a long time—probably ten years or more. We'll know more when we get the remains to the lab."

"Does that mean we're clear to move the remains?" asked the crime scene technician I recognized as Carrie Silverton.

"The sooner the better. I don't want them to dry out," the pathologist replied.

Silverton retrieved a large polyethylene tub from the dock and poured two gallons of distilled water into it. She knelt down next to the skeleton and, with gloved hands, started carefully transferring the bones into the tub.

The other CSI tech, David Elkton, commented, "You know what I'm thinking?"

Without waiting for an answer, he said, "Dennis Tyler Lawen."

Dubbed "the Carpet Bagger" by the news media, Lawen had been convicted of killing two women in Salem during the early part of 2000. In both cases, he had rolled up the victims in pieces of carpet and dumped them into the Willamette River. He had worked as a carpet installer, and Salem Police had tracked the carpet remnants back to him.

Another body rolled up in carpet had been found in the Santiam River a couple of months earlier, and even though Lawen was never charged in that case, it was broadly assumed that he was responsible; and there had always been speculation that he had been involved in other cases, where bodies were never found. If it turned out that this girl had worked the streets in Salem and disappeared around 1999 or 2000, there would be little doubt.

I turned to Alan and said, "Looks like it'll be awhile before they're done with your boat. Want to come up to the house for a cup of coffee?"

"Appreciate the offer, but I think I'll just go up to Mike's place and see what he's doing."

Alan's brother, Mike, lived in an un-restored nineteenth century house on the high side of Third Avenue, just a couple of blocks away. Mike was a retired welder, who decorated his yard with "artwork" that he created with his cutting torch and arc welder. Although severely impaired by past injuries and alcoholism, Mike was an easy-going guy who got along with just about everybody.

As Alan started off in that direction, followed closely by Cinnamon, there was a sudden rustling in the bushes next to the path, followed by a streak of yellow and a scream that sounded like a hawk descending on its prey.

But it wasn't a hawk. It was my excessively large yellow-striped tomcat, DC, who planted himself in the center of the path, directly in front of Cinnamon. This was the DC's idea of fun. Even though the dog was five times his size, DC stood his ground with ears laid back and a defiant expression on his cat face.

My relationship with DC began a few months after I moved down by the river. I was on the beach taking measurements for a new stairway down to my dock when I glanced out at the river and spotted a wide-eyed yellow cat clinging to a scrap of lumber drifting downstream on the early-spring current. I heard a pathetic yowl and decided that I couldn't just watch the helpless animal float by.

Leaving my jacket, shoes, and phone on the dock, I dived into the frigid water and swam out to the beleaguered animal, who was about forty feet off shore. As soon as I reached for him, he abandoned his inadequate float, climbed up my arm, and attached himself to my head. I probably should have anticipated that, but once he grabbed hold, there was nothing to do but swim to shore as quickly as possible.

The current carried me past Daryl Tiernan's dock, and it was only with great effort that I was able to reach Kaylin Beatty's dock thirty yards further downstream. There was no ladder, so I worked my way along the edge of the dock until I got into shallow water where I could wade ashore, still wearing the cat on my head, his long wet tail draped across my shoulder.

Having seen me frantically swimming toward shore, Kaylin came running down from her house.

She took note of the cat and commented, "You look like Davy Crockett with a catskin cap."

The cat, who would forever after be known as Davy Crockett, shortened to DC, held on until I climbed up the riverbank to the safety of dry land. I touched my forehead, where the cat had sunk his claws in to my scalp, and my fingers came away red with blood. The cat was trembling, perhaps from fear, perhaps from the cold, or perhaps from hunger—most likely from all three.

He took a few wobbly steps before tipping over in an exhausted heap. I scooped him up and carried him up the beach toward my place, where I retrieved my shoes before attempting to cross the railroad grade.

Kim looked up from the newspaper when I walked, still dripping, through the door carrying the waterlogged cat.

"What the hell?" she exclaimed, glancing from the puddle forming at my feet to my chattering teeth and scratched forehead.

She dropped the paper, jumped to her feet, and rushed toward me. She took the cat from my arms and hurried to the bathroom for a towel to dry him off.

In a mirror on the wall, I saw my reflection. I had little rivulets of blood trickling down from my scalp, and my skin was pale and had a bluish tinge.

"Crockett," I called to Kim. "His name is Davy Crockett."

Over the next year, DC grew into one of the biggest domestic cats I've ever seen. He declared himself to be a citizen of the world and put himself in charge of Canemah. He knows and uses every pet door in the neighborhood, helps himself to cat or dog food wherever he finds it, and occasionally leaves behind a token of his gratitude in the form of a hapless rodent whose entertainment value had expired.

DC's decision to toy with Cinnamon was typical. Any animal that encroached on his territory was, in his mind, a target of opportunity. The only time his bravado had failed him was when he took on a pair of

Canadian geese who not only faced him down but actually forced him to retreat to his hiding place under my front porch.

This time, it was Cinnamon who backed down. She dropped her head in submission and slowly backed away, while DC sat down and started licking his paw—his way of demonstrating his utter distain for the affairs of dogs.

Alan stepped over DC, while Cinnamon took a wide detour around the cat. As they walked off in the direction of Mike's place, I went inside to get my past-due first cup of coffee for the day.

My assistant, Martha Hoskins, was on the phone, explaining, "I'm sorry, but I don't know anything at all about what's going on down there. You'll have to contact the sheriff's office."

After she hung up, Martha said, "The reporters must have picked up your name on their scanners, and that got 'em all excited."

I said, "Yeah, I'll bet. They're hoping the dead body is mine."

"Oh, they're not that bad," she said.

"Yes, they are. They're opinionated, vindictive, incompetent—and predictable too. I'll bet you a Jackson that they use the word *horrific* in the first paragraph."

"No deal," Martha agreed. "That's their favorite word. Of course, they'll use it. But I still think you're being too hard on them."

3

Saturday, October 13

Alan's "horrific discovery" was front page news the next day, in a story that said the victim had been a female, aged twenty-five to thirty-five, and had been in the river for at least ten years. These facts led the reporter to express the obvious conclusion that the Carpet Bagger was almost certainly responsible. They included a list of Salem prostitutes who had gone missing in 1999 and 2000, speculating that "the girl in the carpet" was one of them.

Because it was Saturday, I gave myself the day off to work on the Project—an 1885 fishing schooner that I was restoring. Three years into the Project, I hadn't yet reached my first-year goal of turning it into a live-aboard yacht. To anyone contemplating such a project, I'd strongly recommend you seek immediate help from a mental health professional.

Annabel Lee was moored at a private dock in West Linn, below Willamette Falls. In three years, I'd managed to install all new plumbing, a gas-fired hot water heating system, and several miles of electrical wiring. I was currently engaged in the extremely tedious process of connecting the rough wiring to the various circuit panels, fixtures, and devices throughout the ship, starting with the five-kilowatt diesel generator that I was going to install in the engine room.

The crate containing the generator had been delivered by barge the week before. I lifted it off the barge with the small cargo crane attached to the aft mast and deposited it on deck next to the main gangway hatch. It took all day and a considerable amount of help from my neighbor, Bud Tiernan, to wrestle the 360-pound machine down two levels into the engine room.

"How're you doing with your remodeling project?" I asked Bud while we worked.

"I was doing fine until Leonard Butts showed up yesterday," he said.

For the past few weeks, Bud had been engaged in a major renovation project on the dilapidated shack he occupied behind his son's house. His latest improvement had been to start rebuilding the roof, and if he hadn't come down to help me move the generator, he'd have been home tearing off the rusty, old corrugated tin roofing.

Bud's shack had been a greasy workshop when his son, Daryl, generously offered to let him live there rent-free sometime before I moved into the neighborhood. Bud had scabbed together some scraps of lumber to build a partition across the middle of the shack and moved all of the tools and most of the junk to one side. The side he occupied was about half a notch better than living under a freeway overpass.

I asked, "Did Butts offer to supervise the project?"

Bud growled, "That meddling bastard can't keep his nose out of anything. He tried to tell me that the building is some kind of historical landmark and can't be improved without his permission."

I couldn't help chuckling. Leonard Butts was the self-appointed neighborhood busybody. Over the years, he had managed to alienate just about everybody in Canemah by criticizing and interfering with anything that he considered to be a violation of the neighborhood's historical purity. The sound of a power saw would draw him from three blocks away, and a person couldn't pound a nail without Leonard Butts stridently insisting that some priceless part of history was being destroyed.

"Historical landmark?" I asked. "What kind of historical landmark could it be? I thought it was just an old garage."

"That's all it ever was. But Leonard Butts—he *deserves* his name! He tried to tell me that the building used to be the Canemah fire station, and he's going to try to get the city to stop me from fixing it up."

"He has his old buildings mixed up. The old firehouse is Red Harper's garage," I said.

"I told him that, but he wouldn't listen—got right up in my face and said he'd have my place red-tagged by the end of the day."

"On what grounds could he possibly get the city to issue a stop work order?"

"He says that I can't replace the old shake roof with composition shingles. According to him, that violates some preservation law."

"But it doesn't *have* a shake roof," I pointed out.

"Oh, he says there's cedar shakes underneath the tin."

"How could he possibly know that?" I wondered.

"I asked him that very question. He says that he's seen it in old photos of the firehouse."

"If he's banking on *that* to shut you down, you have nothing to worry about," I assured him. "I've been inside Red's garage, and I've seen the lettering stenciled on the inside walls that prove it was the firehouse."

"Butts!" Bud growled. "More like a big hemorrhoid—a major pain in the ass!"

We were interrupted by the big blue hydrojet from Portland rumbling past with a full load of sightseers. They paused at the entry to the locks, and we could hear the operator speaking over the loudspeaker. "The Willamette Falls Locks are the oldest multilift locks in the United States. They were opened on January 1, 1873, and have been in continuous operation ever since. There are four chambers, and upstream passage takes about forty minutes."

From there, they idled up into the pool beneath the falls, before turning and coming back past us. We waved, and all the people onboard who weren't taking pictures of *Annabel Lee* waved back.

"Hey, I saw Captain Alan was still tied up at your dock this morning," Bud said when the noise subsided.

"Yeah, I guess he spent the night up at Mike's place," I said. "He's planning to go back and get his logs today."

"People shouldn't wear carpet when they go swimming."

"No, I suppose not."

My need for Bud's help was over, but he was content to hang around and drink my beer for the rest of the day while I bolted down the generator and started connecting its cooling system to the already installed heat exchanger. I briefly considered asking if he wanted to start connecting the wiring, but good sense prevailed, and I kept my mouth shut. Not that I figured Bud wasn't a competent electrician; it was just that I'd never be completely able to trust his work after three or four beers.

4

Wednesday, October 17

I took a few minutes to read the morning paper before starting my day's investigative work. The big news was that in the pocket of the victim's shorts, investigators had found a few coins, including a 2000 penny. That set the time of the crime no earlier than when that coin went into circulation, presumably early 2000.

That, coupled with the fact that the victim had been wrapped in carpet, suggested that she almost certainly had been a victim of the Carpet Bagger, who had been arrested in July of 2000. The window of opportunity for Dennis Lawen to have committed the murder was admittedly tight—January to July—but rolling up the victim in carpet was a pretty distinctive calling card.

On the other hand, there had never been any indication that Lawen had gone outside the Salem area to commit his crimes, and it was difficult to imagine how a body wrapped in carpet could have gotten fifty miles downstream. However, I didn't get a chance to ponder the question.

"¡Señor Corrigan! Señor Corrigan! ¡Ese maldito gallo es el diablo! ¡Él le ataca a nuestro perro! ¡Que barbaridad! ¡Tienes que ayudarnos!"

I jumped up from my desk and looked out the front window to see Señora Valensueva running up Water Street waving her arms in the air and screaming.

"¡El gallo es vicioso! ¡No deja que nadie consigue cerca de él, y ahora está atacando a nuestro perro precioso! ¡Traiga su pistola y dispárarle! ¡Él es el mismo diablo!"

As I rushed outside, Señora Valensueva ran headlong into me, nearly bowling me over. I had no clue what had gotten her so agitated, but there was certainly no way to ignore her. She grabbed my arm and started pulling me up the street.

"What is it?" I asked, knowing the futility of trying to make her understand English.

"¡Ese gallo va a matará a mi perro! ¡No puedo acercarme a él. ¡Hay que detenerlo! ¡Es loquismo!"

"Okay, okay, I'm coming!" I told her.

As we neared the alley leading to the señora's house, I heard a cacophonous of blend of screeching, yelling, barking, and whining. The sight that greeted me was even more chaotic than the sound.

Amidst a cloud of dust, Rosita Valensueva was rolling on the ground clutching the feet of a huge black-and-white rooster, with his neck feathers fluffed out and eyes bulging. Even while Rosita tried to hang on, the rooster kept lunging at the Valensueva's poor old beagle cowering in a corner next to the porch. The bird got loose and charged the beagle, who took off running in circles around the yard with the rooster in hot pursuit.

"¡Cójalo! ¡Cójalo! ¡Ese Diablo va a matar a mi perro! ¡Señor Corrigan, necesitamos capturer ese gallo antes de que mate a alguien!"

Rosita tried desperately to grab the rooster as it shot past her, but all she got was a fistful of black feathers. The beleaguered beagle howled as he frantically tried to evade the rooster.

"Rosita, do you have a fish net?" I shouted.

She screamed in terror as the rooster suddenly turned his attention from the dog to her. Swinging a broom, Rosita swatted the rooster to one side, but the enraged bird jumped to his feet and charged again.

"¡Ese bastardo Carlton hizo esto! ¡Nos trajo ese gallo diablo. ¡Lo hizo a intencionalmente!"

Hearing "bastardo Carlton," I immediately understood the situation. No longer concerned about the welfare of the rooster, I picked up a baseball bat that was lying on the ground and vaulted over the fence into the backyard. Once in the arena, I poked at the rooster, trying to turn his attention from Rosita to me.

Bad idea. The bird came at me like a cyclone, flying up past my face, leaving long scratches on the side of my neck. I took a swing at the bird as it turned to make another charge, but all I got was tail feathers.

"¡Mátele, Señor Corrigan, antes de que él le mate! ¡Cójalo! ¡Cójalo! ¡Dios mío! ¡Híjole!"

As the bird gathered himself for another run at me, I tried to guess the height and speed of his attack. Like Ichiro awaiting a fastball, I held the Louisville Slugger high and ready. The bird lunged, I swung, and with a gratifying *thunk*, I connected.

The bird sailed through the air, over the fence, into Carlton's yard. I was pretty sure we'd seen the last of that rooster.

"¡Usted lo hizo! ¡Muchísimas gracias, Señor Corrigan! ¡Tienes el diablo gallo!" Señora Valensueva shouted.

Rosita ran over and picked up the beagle, inspecting him for damage.

"Señor Carlton brought thees rooster here," Rosita said to me. "Eet is the meanest bird I have ever seen!"

Señora Valensueva handed me a tissue, and I dabbed at my scratches. I wondered if that bird knew how close he had come to my carotid artery.

"¡Carlton es un culo, y deseo que gallo que destruya los ojos de él!" Señora Valensueva told me.

Whatever she'd said about Carlton, it didn't sound like a compliment.

"I'll go have another talk with Carlton," I told Rosita, who quickly translated for her mother.

"Gracias, Señor Corrigan. Pienso que Carlton lleve el gallo muerto y lo meta por su cula."

I walked around the block and pounded on Carlton's back door. He peeked out through the curtains before opening the door and did not offer any kind of greeting. I assumed that he'd been watching the battle from his window. He started to speak, but I held up my hand.

"I don't want to hear anything you have to say," I told him. "I'm just going to tell you how this is going to go down. I'm going to take Señora Valensueva to the farm store and let her pick out whatever rooster she wants. I don't care what it costs. Then I'm going to come back here, and you're going to reimburse me for my expenses, including my time."

Carlton sputtered, "You can't make me pay for another rooster. I already bought her one, just like I said I would."

"Don't press your luck, Carlton," I told him in the most menacing voice I could muster.

I think he got the point because he laughed nervously and said, "It was all just a little prank. Those people don't have a sense of humor."

"Neither do I, Carlton," I said, dabbing at my scratches.

As I walked away, I looked back over my shoulder and saw the rooster, still lying where he landed when I knocked him out of the ballpark. A home run for Ichiro.

It was the time of year when any nice day might turn out to be the last one until spring. With the afternoon temperature in the upper seventies, I felt that I had a moral obligation to go out on the river. The surface of the water was like polished glass, and when I pushed the throttle forward, my old Tigershark shot up to fifty-five miles an hour in about eight seconds.

Skimming across the water, I zipped past the old Oregon City Marina, which stood on pilings out over the river. Moments later, I passed Bernert's Landing, where five months earlier, a Chevy El Camino was pulled from the river. As I sped past the mouth of the Tualatin River and the mansions built for a couple of local basketball stars, I spotted *Misty Rose* parked along the east bank.

Pulling back the throttle, I eased over to say hi to Captain Alan. Cinnamon came out of the deck house, wagging her tail and barking happily, and a second later, Alan poked his head out.

"Hey, Corrigan," he said as I pulled alongside and cut the engine.

"Still pulling up logs?" I asked.

"There's still more down there," he said, "but I've been taking it easy—wouldn't want to empty out my 'savings account' all out at once."

"What do you do with them after you pull them up?" I asked.

He pointed to a tall yellow crane with an osprey's nest perched on the tip of its boom. "They'll pick 'em up and set 'em on a log truck. I sent a load to the mill this morning. I'm just waiting around 'til they get back with my money, so I can get my scuba tanks filled. Then I'll go down and get some more logs."

Still making conversation, I asked, "This isn't where you pulled up the carpet, is it?"

"No, that was down toward your place—on the west bank, a ways past the boat ramp," he said. Then he snapped his fingers and said, "Hey, I've got something here for your deputy friend."

He stepped into the pilot house and returned with a torn scrap of carpet. "I don't know if this is anything the sheriff would want, but it's the piece that tore off when I pulled the carpet roll loose from the cable that snagged it," Alan said.

He handed me the ragged little piece of carpet, and I turned it over in my hand. Since the CSI techs already had the eight-by-ten-foot carpet that the body was wrapped in, it didn't seem like they'd have much need for this scrap. On the backing, I could barely make out the markings, "Tahoe® 28 oz."

"I'll pass it along," I promised. "You heard what the newspaper had to say?"

He shook his head, so I told him what I'd read in the *Chronicle*. During that monologue, we watched a blue log truck, with its empty trailer stacked on the back, pull in and park next to the crane.

"There's my paycheck," Alan said happily. "I better go git it while the gittin's good."

Alan gave my boat a gentle push away from *Misty Rose*, and as I started the engine, he turned and hurried up the narrow plank to shore, followed closely by Cinnamon. I stashed the carpet scrap under the seat and pushed the throttle forward. I went upriver to the place called Wattles Corner, where the river makes an abrupt hairpin turn. I slowed down enough to ease the boat into a wide circle in front of the perpetually unfinished mansion that the former Hollywood Video mogul abandoned after a particularly contentious dispute with the county.

I aimed the boat back downstream and gave it full throttle. A speed that would be commonplace in a car on the highway is surprisingly exhilarating on the water. At this speed, my lightweight boat skimmed over the water with almost no wake, which is what makes it such a great ski boat. When I got back to my place, I saw someone standing on my porch.

It turned out to be Jill McDermitt, Carlton's ex-wife.

"I've about had it with Carlton's stupid antics. I can't take it anymore," she announced when we got inside. "You know what he's doing now?"

Without waiting for an answer, she continued. "After I put the trash cans out, he sneaks over in the night and digs through my garbage!"

"Any idea why he'd do that?" I asked.

"Same reason he bought the house almost next door! Because he's a nutcase!"

"It sounds like he's a stalker," I commented.

"Call it what you like. I want him gone."

The way she said it made it sound like she wanted a hit man.

"What is it you'd like *me* to do?" I asked cautiously.

"Get the police to scare him. Find a way to make him move away. I don't know."

"I could help you compile documentation to take to court for a restraining order," I suggested.

"I already *have* a restraining order. But since he lives so close, it doesn't mean anything. He's not supposed to even go to my side of the block."

"But if he's raiding the trash cans, he's violating the restraining order, isn't he?"

"Of course he is! And that's not all. He goes into my house when I'm not around."

"You need to have the locks changed," I said.

"I've done that! Not once but twice. But he gets hold of the kids' keys and makes copies," Jill explained.

Jill and Carlton had two teenage children and shared custody, an arrangement that obviously wasn't working out. A few weeks earlier, Carlton had bought his son, Patrick, a little minibike and encouraged him to ride it around and around the block past Jill's house, after having coached him in the removal of the muffler—post-marital warfare at its best.

As though reading my mind, she said, "What's more, he's trying to turn Patrick into a juvenile delinquent, giving him that damned motorbike. And he takes him down onto *my* beach and smokes pot with him!"

"Well, it's pretty clear that he's not just violating the restraining order," I said, "He's engaging in criminal activity. If you really want to bring the law down on him, you'll need to assemble proof. I can give you some suggestions, if that's what you want to do."

"Oh, I don't know…I don't want to put the father of my children in jail—I just want him to leave me alone."

"The tangible threat of prosecution might make a pretty strong argument for leaving you alone," I suggested.

"That sounds a bit like blackmail," she objected.

"Oh heck no, it isn't blackmail. It's extortion. But it's obvious that court orders don't work. A little bit of extortion just might be the best way to make him back off."

"What if it just makes him mad? Wouldn't that make things worse?"

"If you really believe that, you should forget about trying to change his behavior and do what you can to get him locked up."

Jill threw her hands up in the air. "I just don't know what to do!"

Tapping my finger on the desk for emphasis, I said, "At the very least, you need to assemble documentation of everything he does. Keep a detailed log. Shoot pictures or video. Get written statements from witnesses. Even though you may not want to pursue it now, you need to be fully prepared to have him prosecuted."

"But I can never catch him in the act," Jill objected.

"One thing you could do is have some security devices—including cameras—installed in and around your house. If you want, I can help with that. I could also do some online investigation into what Carlton is doing that you may not know about."

There was an uncomfortably long pause before Jill said, "That's probably the way it'll have to go, but I need to think it over."

"Don't think too long," I advised.

5

Monday, October 22

The voice on the phone asked, "Is this Corrigan, the private eye?"
I hate the term "private eye," and I never use it.

"I'm Corrigan," I answered. "What can I do for you?"

"My name is Dennis Lawen. You know who I am?" he asked.

Attempting to conceal my shock, I said, "Yes. I know who you are."

"I read all about you in the newspapers. I hear you're a standup guy."

"What can I do for you?" I asked.

"They're saying I killed that woman they found in the river," he
said. "I didn't do it. I want you to prove it."

"You understand that it is a lot easier to prove that someone *did* do
something than it is to prove that someone else *didn't* do it," I said. "It is
almost impossible to prove a negative."

"You're the guy who brought down that senator, ain't ya?" he asked.

"Yes, but—"

"Then you're the guy who can find out who did this broad," he said.
"And it sure as hell wasn't me!"

"Do you have the ability to pay for a private investigation?" I asked,
getting straight to the heart of the matter. "I don't work for free."

"Yeah. Listen, I have plenty. Money's no good in here—it cost me
four packs of smokes to make this phone call, ya know what I mean? But
I have plenty of money."

This was shaping up into a real tar baby. I could see myself getting
stuck in an impossible situation, doing an investigation for a convicted
murderer who probably had nothing to pay me with.

"Tell you what," he said. "You come down here tomorrow. I'll give
you the whole story and pay you five hundred bucks, cash. Then if you

take my case, I'll spot you ten grand up front. Even if you don't take the job, you keep the five bills for your trouble."

"You can't possibly have that kind of money where you are," I challenged.

"No shit, Sherlock!" he agreed. "You can meet my attorney before you come here and get the five hundred from him. Then if we make a deal, he'll give you the ten grand. What do you say?"

Common sense was screaming at me to walk away. And yet my curiosity was aroused. Or maybe it was simple greed.

"Okay, what time?"

The next day, at ten forty-five, I met Lawen's attorney in Salem, at Denny's Restaurant on Market Street next to Interstate 5. He introduced himself as Walter Brooks.

"Just so you know, I advised my client not to do this," Brooks told me. "He hasn't been charged with this thing, and he never will be. They don't have a case, and I told Lawen not to waste his money."

"So why does he want to do it?" I asked.

"He thinks his good name is being tarnished by the accusation," the attorney said. "Go figure."

He handed me an envelope, and a quick glance inside confirmed that it contained five new hundred-dollar bills. "I'll give you the ten grand after we meet with Lawen."

"Assuming I take the case," I reminded him.

"You'll see," he said simply.

Half an hour later, we were escorted to the visiting area at the Oregon State Penitentiary. Lawen was brought in, and the three of us sat down at a table. The table top was imitation dark walnut, and the scratched and chipped plastic laminate was peeling loose from the particle board underneath.

I'd never seen a photo of Dennis Lawen, so I didn't know what to expect. But in my imagination, I'd conjured a vision of a tattoo-covered weight lifter with a shaved head. In reality, he was about five foot six and couldn't have weighed over one-thirty. He looked more like computer nerd than a convicted serial killer.

"You got your money?" he asked.

Both Brooks and I nodded.

"Mr. Brooks has told me—and you as well—that you'll probably never be charged with the West Linn murder unless they somehow establish a connection between you and the victim," I told Lawen.

He answered, "So everyone in the world will believe forever that I killed the broad and got away with it? They can't say when she was killed, so I can't prove I was someplace else at the time."

"Does it really matter what people think?" I asked.

"Hell yes, it matters!" he said, slamming his palm on the table, drawing a stern look from the guard. "I told my momma that I did those two hookers, but I promised her that I didn't do no others after that. I don't want my momma thinking I lied to her."

I noted how neatly his claim of innocence excluded the girl who had been found *before* the two he had been convicted of murdering. To me, his careful wording was as good as a confession.

I said, "I have to warn you that I think there's very little chance that I'll be able to prove you didn't do it. Like I said on the phone, about the only way I can prove that will be to prove that someone *else* did it. The police haven't identified any suspects. What makes you think I can?"

"The cops aren't gonna look for anyone else," Lawen said. "They've zeroed in on me and consider it a waste of time looking any further. But you...you busted that old Devonshire thing wide open and put a US senator in jail. So I figure you're the best guy for the job."

At that moment, I had not the slightest idea where to even begin this investigation. In spite of myself, I said, "I'll see what I can find out. But the minute I feel like I'm wasting my time, I'll quit the case and give you back whatever part of the ten grand I haven't earned. Is that satisfactory?"

We shook hands and closed the deal. Outside the gates, Walter Brooks handed me a fat envelope. I glanced quickly inside and confirmed that it contained a bundle of currency, which I didn't bother counting. I scribbled out a receipt and handed it to Brooks, tucked the envelope under my arm and headed back to my car.

Driving home, I contemplated how I might approach the investigation. There really wasn't much I could do unless or until the victim was identified. But I found it ironic that I was again trying to solve the murder of a victim whose body was pulled from the Willamette River many years after her death.

I needed to look at Dennis Lawen's case files and see how he left his victims. Lawen had been prosecuted in Marion County, so I put in a call to Kevin Fox at Salem PD.

"Hey, Corrigan, I thought we agreed that if I ever wanted to hear from you, *I'd* call *you*," Fox growled when he came on the line.

"Yeah, but that was before my investigation made you a superstar," I offered.

"So now I should be your humble servant?" he asked.

"You'll *never* be humble, Fox," I answered.

"So what's this about?" he asked, getting down to business.

"You hear about 'the girl in the carpet' up here?"

"How are you involved in that?' he pressed.

"For one thing, I was there when they unrolled the carpet and found the remains. It happened right at my dock," I explained.

"How'd that come about?"

"Just lucky, I guess. I know the tugboat driver who fished the carpet out of the river, and mine was the nearest dock." I neglected to mention that Captain Alan also arrived there expecting to find Deputy Stayton. That would still be a touchy subject for Fox.

I continued, "Then I got a call from Dennis Lawen, wanting me to prove that he didn't do it."

"You're working for Lawen?" Fox almost shouted. "That little weasel makes me sick!"

"I'm sure you know him better than I do," I conceded. "Look, I have no intention of doing anything that would jeopardize his convictions. He doesn't even want me to. He just doesn't want this one pinned on him. He thinks it would hurt his momma's feelings."

"I'm gonna puke," Fox said.

"Well, here's the deal," I said. "I want to see the file on your old investigation, just to compare his MO with what we know about the West Linn case. If there's a match, I'll let you know. If not, then maybe Lawen's momma gets a break."

Fox sighed deeply and said, "I can't think of a single good reason why I should do you a favor like that. But what the hell. Maybe it'll make you feel indebted to me, and maybe you'll do me a favor in return, like staying the hell out of my life!"

"I knew I could count on you, Fox."

The afternoon rain ended Kim's river patrol early, so we found ourselves lounging in my living room/office, talking about the events of the day.

"My new client is Dennis Lawen," I said.

"So you met him today?" she asked.

"Yeah, Lawen and his attorney. He handed me ten thousand dollars in cash. It's hard to say no to that."

"Anybody home?" asked the voice from the front porch.

"Depends," I said. "If you're with the IRS or the county assessor's office, nobody lives here and the former residents haven't been seen for months."

Kaylin Beatty pulled the screen door open and said, "Nope. It's just your friendly neighborhood real estate agent."

"Come on in," I said unnecessarily since Kaylin was already inside. That kind of thing happens when your front room is also your business office.

"Glass of wine?" I asked.

"Oh no, thanks," she said. "I can't stay. I just wanted to let you know that I've sold the Dexter's house."

"That was quick," Kim observed.

Kaylin said, "Well, after all of the excitement down here over the last few months, Dexters just wanted to get out, so they offered it at a bargain price."

I felt uncomfortable about my role in "the excitement" that had driven Duane and Sharon Dexter to feel the need to move out of Canemah, but Kaylin continued.

"They found a place in Milwaukie that they really want, so they were willing to deal."

"So tell us about our new neighbor," I said.

Kaylin answered, "It's Barry Walker."

"Same guy who's been doing all the work on the old Draper House?" I asked.

Kaylin nodded. The Draper House was the oldest structure on the Canemah riverfront. Like most of the historic properties, it had a white placard on the front porch identifying it as the George Draper House, circa 1886. It was about a hundred yards upriver from my place, next to the vacant lot where Rosie Bly lived in her travel trailer.

Walker had been conducting a major renovation on the old house for the past six months.

"What's he want with another house?" Kim asked.

"As far as Barry's concerned, the Draper House is an investment. When's he's done fixing it, he's going to sell. But the Dexter's house is where he's going to live," Kaylin explained. "He has boats and jet skis that he wants to dock there."

I said, "Well, it'll be nice to have another boater in the neighborhood."

"Things are changing fast down here," Kim commented after Kaylin left.

"I've thought for a long time that the Dexters were probably going to move out," I said.

"You think it was because of what happened last summer?"

"Not really," I said unconvincingly. I didn't want to think that the fallout from my investigation of the Mendelson-Devonshire case had driven the neighbors out.

"It always struck me as odd that they lived on the riverfront but had no interest at all in the river. They never even ventured across the railroad tracks."

"I think we'll probably see Jill McDermitt moving out pretty soon too," Kim commented.

Surprised, I asked, "What makes you say that?"

"Oh, you're not keeping up on your neighborhood gossip. Jill has a new friend, and from what I hear, they're getting pretty thick."

"You mean that tall guy? You actually think he's going to take her away from all this?"

"That's the guy. I heard he played pro basketball in Europe. Anyway, I'm sure you've noticed that his car's been parked overnight at her place a lot lately."

"Oh sure, but that certainly doesn't mean they're about to get hitched," I said, carefully *not* pointing out that Kim's sheriff's office Explorer spends quite a few nights on *my* driveway.

I think Kim read my mind because she abruptly changed the subject. "So tell me about your new client."

I held up the bottle, my way of asking if she wanted more wine. She nodded, so I split the remaining pinot noir between our two glasses and went back to discussing Dennis Lawen and the girl in the carpet.

6

Thursday, October 25

At first, I thought I'd misunderstood. "I'm sorry, Mr. Corrigan, but your card has been declined."

"That has to be a mistake," I said to the Home Depot clerk. "There's at least twenty-five thousand dollars in that account."

"I ran it twice, and it was declined both times," she said.

Is there anything in life more embarrassing than having your debit card rejected while ten people wait in line behind you?

"Do you have another card?" the clerk asked.

With a sigh of resignation, I pulled out the credit card that I rarely used and which had a zero balance. To my utter dismay, it too was rejected. Even though the purchase was only twenty-four dollars, I wasn't carrying enough cash to pay for it.

"Maybe someone stole your identity. That happens sometimes," the clerk suggested helpfully.

"It has to be something like that," I quickly agreed, mostly for the benefit of the spectators.

I left my little pile of electrical parts on the counter with the promise that I'd be back in half an hour once I got things straightened out at the bank.

I was wrong.

"Your accounts have been frozen," the bank teller politely informed me.

"Frozen?" I asked, "Frozen how, and by whom?"

"I don't have that information. You'll have to talk to the manager."

After an uncomfortably long wait, I was invited to take a seat in front of the branch manager. She had a folder open on her desk. She handed me a sheet of paper, and even before I had my hand on it, I could see the IRS logo in the upper left corner.

"Your accounts have been frozen by order of the Internal Revenue Service."

"But why? How?" I sputtered.

"They don't give us the reason, but we are obligated to comply with their order."

"And this applies to *all* of my accounts?" I asked, already knowing the answer.

I gave up any notion I had of returning to Home Depot for the parts I needed to finish wiring the gauges for the new generator on *Annabel Lee*. Instead, I went home and called Bill Cheshire, my accountant.

"They *do* have the authority to do that," he said in answer to my question. "But they're supposed to give you prior notification. For that matter, they should have notified me as well since I'm your accountant of record and represented you through your audit."

"I haven't heard *anything* from them," I protested.

"I'll call them and find out what's going on," Cheshire promised, "and I'll get right back to you."

While I waited for that call, I mentally went through my options. All of my money was in the bank. Aside from the small amount in my wallet, the only cash I had was the ten thousand dollars from Dennis Lawen. I started mentally calculating how long that might last, *assuming* that I would continue working for him—and that was far from a sure thing.

"They put me on hold for nearly an hour," Cheshire said when he finally called back. "I ended up talking with Mattie Otis."

Otis was one of the auditors who had visited my office two months earlier in an unsuccessful attempt to find tax-code violations. The memory of her condescending arrogance made me grit my teeth to stifle the outburst that was threatening to explode.

Cheshire continued, "Her explanation for freezing your bank accounts is that you have unpaid tax liabilities along with penalties and interest."

"But I *paid* what they said I owed for the home-office deductions they disallowed!" I protested.

"This isn't about that," he said. "It's something that came up in the audit of the expense documentation we gave them."

I said, "I thought it was pretty complete."

"So did I, but Otis says that you failed to provide a bank statement. And she says that she sent you multiple letters requesting the missing statement."

"I never got any letters from her or anyone else at the IRS!"

With a sigh, Cheshire said, "That's probably because she sent them to an address on Newell Ridge Drive."

"Newell Ridge? That's *Marie's* address!" I said, a lot louder than I'd intended, even as a clear picture of what had happened formed in my mind.

"Your ex-wife? Wouldn't she have forwarded them to you?"

"She'd *never* waste her valuable time forwarding anything to me—especially not if she saw the IRS return address on it."

"Well, the first thing you'll have to do is find out what she did with them. If she threw them out, get her to say so in writing. If she still has them, get her to say so in writing. We're fighting an uphill battle here, and we'll need everything you can get.

I just groaned. Talking with my ex-wife was near the top of my list of things I never want to do.

Marie Colton has the thickest, most beautiful head of hair I've ever seen. In fact, everything about my ex-wife was beautiful—except her attitude. But it's the hair you notice first. Reaching luxuriously down to the middle of her back in a wide cascade of ebony curls, Marie's hair instantly and simultaneously ignites jealous hatred among women and lustful passion among men.

On the other hand, trying to carry on a civil conversation with her is a skill that has eluded me for most of the past seven years. Of course, it wasn't always that way—and I know exactly when it changed. I have a pretty good idea why too. Marie's attitude—at least toward me—makes pit vipers, hornets, and wolverines seem like cuddly pets. I once knew a guy who referred to his wife as the Barracuda, but she was Shirley Temple next to Marie.

The turning point in our relationship coincided with my decision to resign from my job at Pacific-Northern Mutual Insurance, where I'd worked since a week after graduation from the University of Idaho. They hired me as a "specification writer." I didn't exactly know what that meant, but I pretended I did and got the job.

It turned out that I was pretty good at it, even though I didn't particularly like the work. I watched the internal job postings, and when something came up in the company's fraud-investigation department, I put in my application. My career progressed from writing investigation summaries to conducting investigations.

Investigation was a job I liked doing, and I was good at it, but the corporate environment was something I was never able to embrace. It seemed that there was always someone who was a walking demonstration of the Peter Principle in a position to make my job unnecessarily difficult. While some people are able to see that kind of situation as an intellectual challenge, I just get pissed off.

The pay was good and got better each year at performance-review time. That's what made me tolerate fifteen years of daily aggravation at the hands of Mr. Peter Principle, but eventually my self-respect forced me to turn in my resignation.

"You did *what*?" Marie demanded angrily.

"I submitted my resignation," I said.

"I heard you!" she yelled. So I didn't say anything. "Well?" she demanded.

"Well what?"

"You know what! How in hell are we going to pay the bills?"

"We're not short of money."

"Our savings won't last forever, and you know it!"

"I'm going to get a private investigator's license."

"Well, that's just great! You're going out to play Magnum, and I'm going to have to figure out how to buy groceries!"

"Marie, we could go for two years without income if we had to—"

"And then what, huh? Then what? Food stamps? Free cheese? What!"

"I'll be making money long before you'll qualify for free cheese."

"I suppose you expect *me* to get a job?"

"If you want to."

"So you can go out and play cops and robbers? Like hell I will!"

From there, it just went downhill. It took me three months to get my license and another two months to get my first job as a private investigator, ironically hired by my replacement at Pacific-Northern Insurance to do investigations that he couldn't figure out. And Marie was unimpressed.

"If you hated the job so much, why are you working for *them*? What have you accomplished other than burning through half our savings?" she demanded.

"If you don't understand the difference," I said, trying to keep my voice calm, "I can't explain it to you."

Day after day, Marie criticized my decision to be self-employed. She could always find something that had to be replaced or repaired—often with greatly exaggerated urgency—and then groused about the cost of doing what she demanded. She found fault with every aspect of my business and vented her annoyance at every opportunity.

Seventeen months after quitting my job, I reached a benchmark. My monthly net income as a private investigator for the first time exceeded what I made as an employee of Pacific-Northern. But Marie didn't change her attitude. She railed about the lack of security, she whined about the hours I spent on the job, and she complained about every nickel I spent.

But what really burned me out was her ongoing effort to sabotage my business. She absolutely refused to answer my phone, and then she'd "accidentally" erase messages from voice mail. She would be snotty to anyone who came to the office, and she loved to tell anyone and everyone how hard I'd made her life.

I think that she just got herself worked into such an internal turmoil in the first few weeks that she was not able to change her attitude, even after I was making more money than I had ever made on somebody else's payroll. Worse, while these detriments to being married to her escalated, the benefits of being married to Marie diminished until eventually there were none. That was six years ago.

The one big break I got from her was when—four months after our divorce—Marie married the new car-sales manager at a nearby Pontiac dealer. That got me off the hook for support payments, but for Marie, it didn't work out so well. The car business went into the toilet; the government took control of General Motors and promptly closed the Pontiac division and all of its dealers.

Marie's second marriage lasted less than two years, and the last time I talked to her, she made it clear that it was somehow *my* fault—despite the fact that I'd bought my new Yukon from her husband just before the bottom fell out at GM. She couldn't stand the disgrace of being married to an unemployed car salesman, so she ditched him and got herself a job at Walmart.

When I called her on the phone and asked if she had received letters for me from the IRS, she laughed maliciously. "I always *knew* you'd get in trouble over taxes," she gloated.

"Thank you for your warm concern," I responded.

"I don't even know where those letters are. I might have tossed them out."

I doubted that. Marie was, if nothing else, a meticulous record keeper.

"I'll come over and get them this evening," I told her.

"Corrigan, I have a date tonight!" she complained.

I doubted that too, but I said, "I'll come over before your date. Just tell me what time."

"Why the big rush? Can't you wait until tomorrow?"

"Let's just make it six thirty."

7

Friday, October 26

There were four letters from the IRS. Marie had kept them in the drawer, "intending" to forward them to me. Sure.

The first letter advised me that I had failed to provide my bank statement for April 2006. The second letter, dated two weeks later, threatened to disallow all of that year's deductions should I fail to produce complete documentation. The third letter informed me that because of my failure to respond to the first two, I would have to pay $4,871 in taxes, plus $27,946 in penalties and interest. The final letter was the one informing me that my bank accounts would be seized if I failed to pay up.

When I delivered the letters to Bill Cheshire, he said, "I think you're going to need legal help to challenge this."

"Don't I have some kind of automatic appeal? Even convicted murderers get an automatic appeal."

"As far as the IRS is concerned, they gave you every opportunity to defend your position. You didn't do it, so their decision is final."

"But I didn't get their letters!" I protested.

"I know that, but as an accountant, I have no recourse. And your only recourse will be in tax court."

He handed me a business card for Leo Gilchrist. I knew the name because he'd campaigned for a seat on the city commission. I hoped he was better as an attorney than he was as a campaigner because he had been soundly defeated at the polls.

I met him in his office on High Street at the top of the Oregon City Municipal Elevator, which the city calls the world's only vertical street, a claim that is debatable, given that the elevator is for pedestrians, not cars.

"This could be difficult to win," Gilchrist told me.

"Why?" I asked, letting my frustration show. "The whole thing is their mistake—they've had that bank statement all along."

I showed him the copies of the bank statements I'd turned in during the audit. There were statements dated March 31, May 1, and May 31. The "missing" April statement was the one dated May 1 since April 30 had fallen on a Sunday. It was too stupidly simple to have been an honest error.

"I'd have pointed that out to them if they hadn't sent their letters to the wrong address!"

"I doubt that any of that was a mistake," Gilchrist said. He paused to let that soak in. "The IRS has a track record. You can bet every nickel they haven't already taken from you that this whole thing is being done on orders from Alan Blalock.

"But Blalock's in jail," I objected.

"He's still a US senator. And he has a history of using the IRS against his enemies. Remember, he was at the heart of that whole IRS scandal last spring. He wrote letters to IRS agents requesting audits on Tea Party organizations during this year's election campaigns."

"I remember that, but do you really think he told them to do this to me?"

"You already have the phone records showing that Blalock's hatchet man, Richard Elgin, called the IRS immediately after a call from Blalock. And he also called the state about your investigator's license. Do you really have any question about the purpose of those calls in light of what happened in their aftermath?"

"Hell no, but he was trying to stop my investigation. That's all over now. What does he have to gain by ordering harassment now?"

"How about revenge? How about damaging your credibility in anticipation that you'll be a prosecution witness in his trial?"

I rubbed my eyes. "He's a murderer, damn it. A pedophile and a murderer. Why would anybody—in the IRS or anyplace else—do anything for him?"

"It isn't necessarily about Blalock anymore, and it isn't even about you. It's about the machine. Word will get around. They want people to see what happens when you mess with the machine. Intimidation is a powerful weapon."

"Okay, okay. I get it. Where do we go from here?"

"First, we'll have to file suit against the IRS. We can clearly show their negligence in sending the letters to the wrong address. They might be able to convince the court that it was an innocent mistake, but they'll never be able to prove it was anybody's fault but their own.

Once that's done, we'll be able to challenge the substance of their claim about the bank statement. Again, the best they'll be able to do is claim that it was another innocent mistake. But the result will unquestionably be in your favor."

"That's all good news," I said, "so why do you say this might be difficult to win?"

"Well, the problem is timing. It's possible that they could stretch this out for months, just to get onto the docket. Then the IRS will make motions for postponements at every turn. There's almost no limit to how long they can drag it out."

"But I can't do business without my bank accounts!" I said.

"The only way you can get your bank accounts back is to payoff the tax lien. How much are you short?"

"Not that much—maybe five grand. The thing is, I don't *have* five grand."

"You can raise five thousand dollars. Just about anybody can. Until you do, you'll have to do business in cash. You won't even be able to cash a check."

Over dinner, Kim asked, "How'd your day go?"

"Just a normal day," I said. "Marie failed to forward a few letters from the IRS, so they seized my bank accounts and took all of my money. How was yours?"

"What are you talking about?" she asked, concern showing on her face.

"It's true. I don't yet know what it's going to take to get it straightened out."

"But how can you operate without your bank accounts?"

"I'll just have to operate on a cash-only basis. It's a good thing Dennis Lawen paid me in cash. That's all I have to work with now. Let's talk about something else. Anything else."

Kim said, "Okay. Well, did you hear that they identified the 'girl in the carpet' this afternoon? Her name was Tara Foster, aged twenty-nine when she disappeared in June of 2000."

"Was she a prostitute from Salem?" I asked.

"Not even close. By all accounts, she had a good job and owned a condo in Charbonneau, across the river from Wilsonville. No idea how she might have crossed paths with Lawen."

"Maybe she didn't."

"Until Captain Alan fished her out of the river, her disappearance had been written off as a probable suicide. Friends said she'd been despondent following a recent divorce."

"Well, now we know *that* didn't happen," I said.

"Which brings up a question—does Jamieson know you're working the case for Dennis Lawen? It *is* an open investigation," Kim reminded me.

"Not yet. I really doubt that I'll find anything. I'll most likely end up giving Lawen's money back. But if I do find something that warrants a longer look, then I'll call Jamieson."

"It does look pretty straightforward. The timeframe fits, and Lawen's the only guy I ever heard of who rolls his victims up in carpet."

"Is that the way Jamieson sees it?"

"There isn't any *other* way to see it, is there?"

"Lawen doesn't want his good name tarnished by an assumption of guilt that can't be proven."

"But he already has two murder convictions. How can he be bothered by this one?"

"Don't ask me. That's a question for Dr. Phil. But I do recall that even Ted Bundy got indignant when people tried to pin murders on him that he hadn't admitted doing."

"So what's next?"

Thinking aloud, I said, "The starting point will have to be the newspaper archives. Stories written at the time Tara Foster disappeared will have names of people who knew her. With that, I can track them down and see where that leads. I'll send Martha downtown next Monday. She spent a good deal of time in the archives at the *Chronicle* during the Devonshire investigation. She knows how to find whatever was printed about Foster's disappearance."

We were just finishing dinner when I got a call from my regular attorney, William Gates, who stopped using the nickname Bill when Microsoft became a household name. In addition to handling my normal legal affairs, Gates is also a client for whom I do a lot of work. He is on retainer—that is, he pays me a monthly fee that guarantees my availability for any investigation he needs on a moment's notice.

"I have a note that you called earlier," Gates said.

"I did," I confirmed. "I'm having some trouble with the IRS, and they've taken over my bank accounts."

"For that, you don't need me. You need a tax attorney," he said.

"Yeah, I'm on that, but I need you to do me a favor." Without waiting for his response, I continued, "With my bank accounts seized, I'd like you to pay me in cash instead of checks."

"No problem. I'll need you to sign for it, of course. You know, I was going to call you tomorrow. I have something for you to work on."

The upshot was that I would spend much of my time for the next three weeks working for Gates, tracking down victims of apparently fraudulent foreclosures by the defunct Northwest National Home Loan Corporation.

It was my opinion that the investigation should have been carried out by the state attorney general's office, but key members of the NNHLC board of directors had contributed heavily to the attorney general's most recent reelection campaign, and the AG's office had publicly announced that there had been no criminal malfeasance involved. Meanwhile, NNHLC had been purchased out of insolvency by the American Global Banking Group of New York.

Gates was suing them for release of documents listing the names of people whose homes had been foreclosed by NNHLC, but pending a ruling on that case, he put me to work identifying victims through other channels. Though not particularly difficult, the task was tedious and time consuming. To complicate matters, many of the victims, embarrassed about having been unable to keep up on their house payments, were reticent to talk about the matter.

8

Tuesday, October 30

Martha brought in copies of everything she'd found regarding Tara Foster on her field trip to the *Chronicle*. It was a disappointingly small stack of paper, including a photograph, which I pinned to the corkboard next to the photo of her remains. Newspaper coverage at the time of her disappearance described Tara Foster as "emotionally fragile," saying that she had been receiving treatment for chronic depression for at least a year.

The authorities, at the time, believed she had made herself disappear, either by running away to a new life with a different identity or by committing suicide in some obscure place where her remains would never be found. She had been unremarkable in life, so her disappearance was equally unremarkable.

There had apparently been no criminal investigation at all. The Wilsonville Police had no evidence to suggest criminal activity, so they treated the disappearance as a simple missing-person case. Tara Foster simply vanished and was forgotten.

I was surprised to learn that she had been assistant to the administrator at the Museum of the Oregon Territory. The museum was only half a mile from my doorstep. For the first time, it made some sense that her body was found nearby. Someone at the museum reported her missing on June 15, 2000, after she'd missed three days of work. They'd tried to phone her, but nobody answered, so they called the police.

Nowhere could I find anything to even hint that she had ever worked the streets, in Salem or anywhere else. Nevertheless, since she had been found rolled up in carpet, the media—and just about everybody else, including me—had jumped to speculation that Tara Foster's murder had to be the work of the Carpet Bagger.

When the mail arrived, it included a package from Kevin Fox containing the file on Dennis Lawen. It wasn't big, but it was very revealing. Lawen was thirty-five years old at the time of his arrest. He'd been born out of wedlock and raised by his mother, who never married. Nor had Lawen. Instead, he had lived his entire life with his mother.

In April 2000, a prostitute named Ashley Walton was reported missing by a friend, assumed by police to be a coworker. Four days later, her nude body was found rolled up in a piece of carpet floating in the Willamette River north of Salem. She had been strangled, and a piece of polyester twine identical to the binding around the roll of carpet was left tied around her neck.

Less than a month later, another body was found two miles upstream from where Ashley Walton was found. Like Ashley, this victim was nude, with polyester twine tied around her neck, and she was rolled up in carpet. She was subsequently identified as Erin Murphy, a sixteen-year-old runaway from Portland.

Analysis of the carpet revealed that both pieces were low-end products, apparently brand new but different from one another. This led to speculation that the perpetrator was someone in the carpet or home construction business. While canvassing carpet outlets, police ran across Dennis Lawen, an independent carpet installer known for his use of cheap, low quality products. Two of his recent jobs matched the carpet remnants used to wrap the victims.

Under interrogation by police, Lawen confessed to the killings, asserting that both girls had been "nothing but a couple of whores standing by the side of the road." His reason for killing them was that they were nasty and evil. He subsequently tried to recant his confession and entered a plea of not guilty at trial. The jury deliberated for about two hours before pronouncing him guilty.

The Santiam River victim, who was never identified, had also been rolled in new carpet bound with polyester twine. But the authorities had been unable to match the carpet with anything Lawen had installed, so he was never tried for that murder, even though police were sure he did it.

"What do you think?" I asked Martha, after she glanced through the Lawen folder.

"Lawen's still the only killer who rolls his victims in carpet before dumping them," she said.

"True," I said, "but this might be a copycat."

"Why do you say that?" she asked.

"Some things are different. For one thing, all three of the Salem victims were nude. Foster was wearing a short sleeved top and shorts. The other three had polyester twine around their necks," I explained. "Our victim didn't."

I pointed at the photo of the skeletal remains on the deck of *Misty Rose*.

I continued. "I don't know what Foster's carpet was tied up with, but it wasn't polyester twine—it looked more like the cotton cord from a curtain rod."

"So you think Lawen might be telling the truth?" she asked.

"I sure can't rule it out," I said.

Ten minutes later, I had Larry Jamieson on the phone.

After exchanging pleasantries, I said, "The reason for the call is to let you know that I've been hired to look at the Tara Foster thing."

"You think there's anything there?" he asked.

"I don't think it's as clear-cut as the newspapers say," I said. "There are some things that don't match Dennis Lawen's MO."

"Let me explain the situation," Jamieson said. "We're spread thinner than the mayonnaise on a cheap ham sandwich. I have half of our detectives working full time making sure that the Alan Blalock prosecution doesn't fall apart, and we have others tied up on the thing with Richard Elgin. I have nobody left to work this case."

Just a few weeks earlier, Senator Alan Blalock had been arrested for the 1980 murders of Jessie Devonshire and Randy Mendelson. Those arrests were a direct result of an investigation I had conducted for Randy's mother after the victims' bodies were found in the Willamette River. Richard Elgin was in jail in Salem, charged with the murder of Jessie's stepfather, Wilson Landis Devonshire. Both Elgin and Devonshire had participated in the cover-up of the 1980 murders.

"So how are you handling the Foster thing?" I asked.

"I've assigned the case to a detective, but it's so far down his priority list that I don't expect him to get to it for weeks—maybe months," Jamieson explained.

"Where does that leave me?" I pressed.

"Tell you what. If you want to keep working the case, I'll let you look at everything that develops through forensics. In exchange, I expect you to keep my detective informed of everything you're doing, and I don't want to read about any of this in the newspaper," he said. "Report to Michael Wheeler by email—I don't want him wasting time on the phone with you."

"Has Wheeler seen the file on Dennis Lawen?"

"No. Like I said, this is so far down his priority list I don't want him spending any time on it. It would take him off more important work," he said.

"Okay," I said, "I have the file, and based just on what I've seen, Tara Foster doesn't fit. It looks more like a copycat."

"I'll have someone get you the pathologist's report and whatever comes from CSI. I'm happy to let you do our work for us. Just don't screw it up," he concluded.

9

Tuesday, November 20

Two days before Thanksgiving, I looked up from the morning paper to see a house floating lazily downriver toward my place. In the time it took to get out the door and across the railroad tracks, several facts registered in my mind. The floating structure was a houseboat that had, until this morning, been a part of the moorage just upstream from my place. It had been vacant and for sale for most of the past three years. Now it seemed to be headed for the falls, a quartermile downstream.

Just as I was starting to pull out my phone to call 911, Carlton McDermitt in an old jon boat appeared from behind the houseboat. Getting out in front of the houseboat, he then maneuvered his boat back upstream against it. He gunned the ancient Scott-Atwater outboard motor, sending up a plume of blue smoke and churning the water into a white froth.

The houseboat gradually slowed to a stop, and Carlton eased off the throttle. He re-positioned his boat against the near side and nudged the houseboat further out from shore to avoid a collision with the dock belonging to Daryl and Bud. Once clear, Carlton repositioned again. As soon as he got past Kaylin Beatty's dock, he pushed the old houseboat up against the shore in front of Jill's house.

Scrambling out of his boat onto the houseboat's deck, Carlton grabbed a thick line and leaped ashore. He hurriedly wrapped the line around a maple tree and tied it off with a double half hitch. Then he scrambled back and grabbed his jon boat before it drifted away and dragged it up onto the shore.

"What's this?" I asked Carlton.

"Well, laddie, I won the auction," he said, again affecting his phony accent. "Got it for a mere five hundred quid."

"What's a quid?" I inquired.

"Dollars, laddie, dollars," he said happily.

I had looked at the old houseboat when it first went up for sale, and I decided it wasn't worth the twenty-five-thousand-dollar asking price. Its floatation was so bad that one corner of the kitchen had two inches of water on the floor. There was structural rot in the lower part of the walls, and some of the interior walls were black with mildew.

"Good deal," I told Carlton, who completely missed my sarcasm.

"That's not appropriate for this neighborhood," I heard someone say.

I turned to see Leonard Butts standing on the railroad grade..

"Mind your own business," Carlton told him.

"Preserving the neighborhood is *everybody's* business. Canemah is the only National Register Historic District in all of Clackamas County," Butts said, reciting his mantra.

He emphasized his point by jabbing what looked like a small baseball bat toward the old houseboat. It was actually a fish club—a weighted metal bat that fishermen use to kill large fish as they are landed.

"Get that thing out of my face!" Carlton demanded. "Why do you carry that thing around, anyway?"

"I carry it when I walk my dogs, in case of an attack by strays."

Carlton looked around. "You aren't walking your dogs."

"It's none of your business why I carry it," Butts told him.

That was when Carlton's ex-wife beat her way through the blackberry brambles, followed closely by their teenage kids, Patrick and Colleen.

"Just exactly what are you doing?" Jill demanded.

"Just tying up my houseboat," Carlton smugly told her.

"Well, you can't tie it up here!" she exclaimed.

"Can and did," Carlton proclaimed with finality.

"Well, get it out of here," Jill ordered. "I'm not going to let you park it here."

"The judge gave you the house. He didn't say anything about the beach," Carlton informed her. "I have as much right to it as you do."

Jill answered, "The beach is part of the property!"

"Not with the railroad tracks in between. Besides, what do you care? You don't ever come down here," Carlton argued.

Jill looked toward the heavens and asked, "Why me?"

By this time, others, including Kaylin Beatty, had arrived down by the houseboat.

"I'm not taking sides here," Kaylin told Carlton, "but the beach easement is legally attached to the house. It can't be separated."

"I've never yet seen anything that can be *done* legally that can't be *undone* legally." Carlton retorted.

"You'd better talk to your attorney about that," Kaylin suggested.

"I don't need an attorney to tell me what's mine," Carlton said.

"Sounds to me like you do," Jill told him.

Carlton declared, "Possession is nine-tenths of the law, and I now possess this riverbank."

About then, an Oregon City Police cruiser came to a stop on Water Street. Officer Jeffrey Durham joined the group on the rocky beach.

"Would somebody please tell me what's going on here?" Durham asked.

Carlton gulped but didn't get any words out.

Pointing at Carlton, Jill said, "He brought this derelict in and thinks he can keep it here."

"You can't keep this thing here," Durham told Carlton.

"I'm as entitled to this beach as she is," Carlton objected.

"That doesn't matter," Durham answered. "You need a permit from the Corps of Engineers, a lease from the Department of State Lands, and approval from the city. If you don't have all of those, you're going to have to remove it."

"It's just temporary," Carlton whined. "I need it here so I can fix it up and get it ready to live in."

"I'm going to notify Code Enforcement," Durham said. "They'll tell you exactly what you can and can't do."

"He can't park that shit pile here!" Jill insisted.

"Why did you move it out of the houseboat moorage?" I asked Carlton.

"They wanted me to pay the past-due rent, and that wasn't my responsibility," Carlton answered.

"How much was past due?" I asked.

"Well, seven months, at $150 a month," Carlton exclaimed. "Over a thousand dollars!"

"Quid," I corrected.

Carlton acknowledged my quick sense of humor by giving me the finger.

"So for a thousand bucks you abandoned the moorage?" I asked in amazement.

"I figured I could tie up here, and it wouldn't cost me anything—and no monthly rent, either."

Jill told him, "Well you'd better push it right back up there because you can't keep it here!"

"There's no way I can take it back upstream," Carlton protested. "That little boat doesn't have near enough power. Besides, those assholes up there won't let me back in."

Officer Durham simply shook his head. "I can't write a ticket for code violation, but I am going to write a citation for willful littering. And you, Mr. McDermitt, had better find a way to get that pile of trash out of here."

"Does this kind of thing happen often around here?" asked a new arrival.

"Not often. Barry, let me introduce you," Kaylin said. She turned toward the largest part of the gathering and announced, "Everyone, meet Barry Walker. He's just purchased the Dexter's place."

"Welcome to the nut farm," Bud said. "We grow all kinds."

"Hang it in your ass, you old fart," Carlton grumbled.

"Lighten up, Carlton, I didn't mean nothing," Bud said.

I heard Patrick and Colleen snickering at their father's entertaining repartee.

"What do you do for a living?" Jill asked Barry.

"Little bit of everything," he said. "Investing, real estate, whatever makes a buck."

Rosie Bly said, "I hope you're not a crazy person. We don't need another crazy person."

Red Harper, who was looking at Leonard Butts, nodded in agreement. "And we don't need no more busybodies, either."

Butts said, "The riverbank is public property."

Kaylin looked helplessly at Barry and said, "I told you it was an eclectic neighborhood."

Rosie looked suspiciously at Kaylin and asked, "What's that mean, eclectic?"

"Just like this," she said with a sweeping gesture.

"Did she say 'electric' neighborhood?" Red wanted to know. "What's an electric neighborhood?"

It's always nice to start the day with a neighborhood social function. I really hated to leave, but I had work to do.

10

Monday, December 10

Because of the low priority the sheriff's office had given the Tara Foster case, it took weeks to get the reports back from the state lab on the evidence. After several email exchanges with Deputy Wheeler, he finally let me know that the reports were in and he was sending me everything I'd need to determine whether or not Dennis Lawen had anything to do with the death of Tara Foster. A courier service delivered to my office a fat envelope containing copies of the pathology report and the crime scene evidence analysis.

Looking first at the crime scene evidence, because it was the thinnest file, I found detailed descriptions of the bones, clothing, carpet, and the few other items collected. There was a full set of photographs documenting everything found.

The sheriff's office criminalists had written a summary report stating that the victim had died as a result of skull fractures and brain injuries resulting from blunt-force trauma. There was no mention of any kind of twine or rope found with the body, suggesting that the victim had not been tied. That too was different from the three other victims, all of whom had been bound and strangled using polyester twine. So that was another point in Lawen's favor.

The cord used to bind the roll of carpet was described as a braided cotton cord consistent with what would be used on a curtain rod. The cotton had deteriorated over the years and broke while Captain Alan was handling the roll of carpet. Lawen had tied his carpet with the same type of polyester twine that he used to strangle his victims, which can last almost indefinitely underwater.

Next, I turned my attention to the pathologist's report. Once I beat my way through all of the medical jargon and translated it into real English, what I found was that this case looked nothing at all like Dennis Lawen's work. There were two distinct injuries to the skull. In the left temporal region, there was a depression fracture described as nonfatal but possibly rendering the victim unconscious. The fatal injury was to the back of the skull, which was shattered, most likely causing instantaneous death.

It was easy at that point to conclude that Dennis Lawen didn't have anything to do with Tara Foster's death. But would that conclusion be enough for my client? The evidence *indicated* that he had not been involved, but it didn't—indeed couldn't—*prove* his innocence. Time to call Lawen's attorney.

After confirming that Walter Brooks was bound by the rules of client confidentiality regarding anything I told him, I outlined everything I'd found out.

"On the basis of the evidence," I told him, "I am convinced that your client had nothing to do with Tara Foster's murder."

Brooks asked, "Does that mean that Lawen will be publicly dismissed as a suspect?"

"I doubt it," I said. "The sheriff's office has never so much as mentioned his name. All of the speculation about Lawen's possible involvement came from the media."

"In that case, are you going to share what you've found with the media?" he asked.

"I can't do that," I told him. "The only way the sheriff's office would let me see their files was with my promise not to reveal anything in them with anyone—especially the media."

"Okay, then I guess I'll have to contact Lawen and see what he wants to do," Brooks said.

"And you understand that you can't tell him about any of what I've told you," I repeated.

"He won't be satisfied with that," Brooks speculated.

"Be sure that he understands that the only thing I can do from here is to actively investigate who is actually responsible for Foster's murder. And I'd say that it's extremely unlikely that I'll ever be able to find enough to get anyone indicted, if that's what Lawen expects."

"I understand," he said. "Such is the world we live in."

Hearing footsteps on my front porch, I wrapped up the phone call and went to the door. Bud hastily ushered himself inside, accompanied by DC, who shot between Bud's legs and plopped down next to the pellet stove.

As he stepped over the cat, Bud observed, "It's kinda cold out there."

"I heard they're forecasting twenty-five degrees in Portland," I said, while going to the kitchen to get a pair of MGDs out of the refrigerator.

"How about a beer?" I asked rhetorically.

Without waiting for an answer, I handed one to Bud and snapped the other one open for myself.

"Got that wiring job on your boat finished yet?" he asked.

"No, that's a long-term project," I told him. The truth was that I hadn't done any work on *Annabel Lee* since the IRS seized my bank accounts.

"Carlton asked me if I wanted to help him fix up his houseboat," Bud said.

"I think it's beyond help," I said.

"No, he says that once he gets some more floatation under it, the rest won't be bad. He says he's going to live on it and rent out his house. That sounds pretty good."

"Well," I said, "first he needs to find a place to moor it—and I don't know where that'll be."

"He says he can have it towed upriver, outside the city limits, and find a place to tie it up," Bud explained.

Skeptical, I said, "We'll just have to wait and see how that works out."

"He's hooked up water and electricity, and I just helped him carry some propane tanks down to it," he said.

"How on earth did he get power and water?" I asked.

Bud quickly said, "Oh, it isn't a permanent hookup. He just ran a garden hose and extension cord under the railroad tracks and connected them to Jill's house."

"And Jill let him do that?" I wondered.

Bud shrugged. "I don't think he asked."

"What about sewage?"

"Into the river, I guess."

Looking downstream, I could see lights on in the windows of the houseboat, which completely blocked my view of the falls and paper mills below.

11

Tuesday, December 11

I was greatly relieved when Walter Brooks called back and told me that Dennis Lawen wanted me to stay on his case, since I had already spent a large chunk of his ten thousand dollars to pay off the IRS lien and regain access to my bank accounts and credit cards. But with no money left in my business account, I was spread pretty thin. If Lawen had decided to drop the investigation, I'd have had to borrow money against my new Yukon to reimburse him for the unearned portion of the money he'd given me.

The basic question was simple. If Dennis Lawen didn't do it, how might I find out who did? I could think of only two places to look for ideas. One would be to interview everyone who knew Tara Foster during the last year of her life. Martha had compiled a list of everyone mentioned in the original investigation into her disappearance and in the media coverage of it, but tracking down witnesses more than twelve years after the crime was going to be a slow process.

The only other place to look was the physical evidence. I went back to the Tara Foster folder and took another look through pages of notes and photos. Studying the photos, I gazed at what remained of Tara Foster, who had once had friends, dreams, loves, and ambitions, lying on the stained mauve carpet on the deck of the old tugboat. As I stared at the photo, something caught my eye.

The edges of the carpet appeared to be not rough cut but neatly finished with bias tape. It struck me that this wasn't a remnant or scrap. It was a piece that was tailored for a specific installation. Looking closer, I noticed that a chunk of carpet was missing down near one corner.

That's when I remembered that Captain Alan had given me a scrap of carpet. I'd stuffed it down under the seat in my ski boat and forgotten all about it. I went out to my garage where the boat was stored for the winter and poked around until I found what I was looking for.

"What's this?" Martha asked when I showed her the carpet scrap.

"It's a piece of Tara Foster's carpet," I said, pointing to the photo showing where the scrap had originated. "The brand name is printed on the back, Tahoe. See what you can find out about it."

While Martha worked on that, I went to the sheriff's evidence room and asked to see the carpet. It took some time for the deputy in charge to clear it with higher authorities, but she finally allowed me to take a look. She stood by watching everything I did, as I photographed and measured the carpet.

It was basically rectangular in shape, but one of the long sides was curved in a gentle arc so that the rectangle was about six inches wider in the center than at the ends. I noted the damaged area, which appeared to be the right size for the torn scrap that Captain Alan had given me. The bias tape sewn around the outer edges of the carpet showed professional stitching and high-quality workmanship. Clearly, it was not an amateur job.

Over dinner that evening, Kim asked, "Are you getting anywhere with the Lawen investigation?"

"We've taken another look at the carpet the body was wrapped in," I said. "Turns out that it's a marine-grade carpet."

"Boat carpet?" she asked.

I explained, "It seems obvious now. The shape of the carpet shows what it was made for—basically rectangular but with a convex curve on one side. I think it came from the aft deck of a good-sized boat, a cruiser. Put that together with the anchor wrapped up with the body, and I'd guess that the killing took place right there—on the carpet."

"A ten-pound anchor comes from a pretty small boat," Kim said.

"The carpet came from a boat big enough to carry a dinghy. The anchor probably belongs to that," I said. "He killed her and then made a burrito out of the carpet and the body, adding the anchor to make it sink. He tossed it over the side, and twelve years later, Alan snagged it with a frayed cable."

"Definitely not Lawen's style," Kim observed. "What's next?"

I said, "I have two things to look at. We're trying to find out who sells that carpet locally—or rather, who did fifteen years ago—and if we get exceptionally lucky, we might be able to find out who bought it. We're also looking at boat plans, hoping to find out what boat the carpet might fit. It was professionally fitted. If we can find out what boat it fits, we can check registration records for 1999 and 2000. We might find a killer."

"Does Wheeler know about all this?" Kim asked.

"Not yet," I said. "The only thing we know for sure right now is that it's marine carpet. All the rest is speculation. I'd like to know more about it before we start wasting his time."

The next morning, Martha managed to talk with someone at the company that manufactured the carpet. She determined that Tahoe was a premium marine-grade product line that was still manufactured, although the mauve color had been discontinued many years ago.

"That color was made between 1984 and 1996," she said. "They're going to email a list of retail outlets in the area that sell Tahoe carpet."

"Good. While you wait for that, start compiling a list of every upholstery and carpet shop that works on boats and was around when that carpet was being sold."

"So you're really sure it came from a boat?" she asked.

"The shape of the carpet and the fact that it is a marine-grade product indicate that it was installed on a boat. And the size of it suggests that it was a pretty big boat," I said.

She asked, "Wouldn't the carpet have been installed by the boat manufacturer?"

"I've been thinking about that. If the carpet were shaped to fit in the salon or other interior space, you'd probably be right," I said. "But the curved edge means that this piece came from the aft deck, and that part of a boat is rarely carpeted."

"Why is that?" she wondered.

"For one thing, it's exposed to the weather. Besides, on most cruisers, the engines are located beneath the aft deck, and there are lift-up hatches to give access. Putting carpet over the top would impede access to the engines, so boat manufacturers don't do it," I explained.

"So you're thinking that a boat owner decided to embellish his boat by adding carpet where the builder hadn't," she speculated.

"I think that's the most likely explanation. But then again, if it's an aft-cabin model, it's *possible* that carpet may have been installed by the manufacturer, in which case, our guy might have gone back to the boat builder for a replacement after he tossed this one overboard," I said.

"This isn't making it any easier," she protested.

"I'll focus on boat builders," I said, "and you focus on aftermarket possibilities."

"What about marina records?" Martha asked, changing direction.

"That could get us somewhere. Our carpet is ten and a half feet wide. That means it came from a boat with at least an eleven-foot beam. A boat that big lives in the water. It's too big to tow to and from the river when you want to go boating. So either the owner leases moorage space at a marina, or he owns riverfront property.

"Kaylin Beatty can get us a list of all the residential riverfront properties on the Willamette between the Columbia and Yamhill Rivers. I've asked Deputy Wheeler to request the Marine Board to send a list of all registrations for boats over twenty-six feet in 1999 and 2000. When I get that, I'll cross-check. There can't be more than a handful of boats on the Willamette big enough for our carpet," I explained.

"How many marinas are there where the boat could be moored?" she asked.

"Above the falls, there's only one—at Wilsonville," I said. "Below the falls, there's quite a few, especially if you include those out on the Columbia. Our guy could have come up through the locks, so we might have to check them all, but we'll check Wilsonville first. It's only half a mile from where Tara Foster lived, so that's the most likely place."

For the next week, we gathered all of the information we could find that might help identify the boat where our carpet had originated. While the rest of humanity was occupied with Christmas shopping, office parties and decorating, Martha and I narrowed our search.

Working on the aft cabin theory, I was able to identify a few boat builders who put Tahoe carpet in their aft cabins in the eighties and nineties, but none had the distinctive curve that our carpet had. Unfortunately, a number of prominent boat builders—like Tollycraft, to name a big one—had gone out of business. Information on them was available only through their various owners' clubs.

I joined a dozen different boating forums on the internet and posted photos of our carpet, asking if anyone could identify what model of boat it might have come from. Nothing had come from that, but I was still trying to keep the conversations alive.

12

Monday, December 17

The sheriff's office sent me a print-out from the Marine Board listing all boats that were registered in Oregon in a four-year window centered on January 1, 2000. For some reason, the Marine Board would not provide an electronic copy, so Martha won the task of manually going through page after page of data and identifying boats that were the right size and location.

If not myopic at the start of this project, certainly Martha would be before its completion. Whenever she needed a break from that tedious task, she switched to phoning upholstery and carpet shops. She found several that sold Tahoe carpet but none that could remember making a piece like ours. The more hours we spent on this case, the closer we were to reaching the end of Dennis Lawen's ten-thousand-dollar budget.

Determined to keep from losing any more money to the IRS through the bank, I resolved to do business as much as possible in cash and use the bank for only those things that couldn't be done any other way. When it was time to write Martha's paycheck and pay the payroll taxes, I'd deposit enough cash to cover the checks. My real "bank account" was cash in the safe under my bathroom floor.

"I think you should brace yourself for some negative publicity," Leo Gilchrist advised. "Now that I've officially filed suit, it's just a matter of time before the press starts in on you."

"Does the newspaper really have time to watch the tax-court proceedings?" I asked.

"They don't need to. Someone in the court will call a friend, and pretty soon, a press release will show up at the *Chronicle*, no doubt from an organization called Concerned Citizens for Universal Fairness, or some such thing, accusing you of tying up the courts with your frivolous lawsuit."

Two weeks later, I was reading the Sunday paper and sipping a cup of fresh coffee when I opened the editorial section.

The Fragile Case Against Senator Blalock
Tibbett Gaylord

If you listen to right-wing talk radio, though I can't imagine why anyone of normal intelligence would, you might believe that Oregon's senior senator, Alan Blalock, is a criminal on par with Ted Bundy or Gary Ridgeway. The neocons love to make accusations but seldom can back them up.

It's been nearly three months since Alan Blalock was charged with the killing of Jessie Devonshire and Randy Mendelson, and we've all had ample time to review not just the evidence against him but also the character of his accusers. You would, of course, expect the likes of Rush Limbaugh and Lars Larson to embrace any accusation against a progressive public servant like Senator Blalock, but what is remarkable about this case is how very little actual evidence there is.

And what is more troubling than the paucity of evidence is the nature and source of the so-called evidence that does exist. There are audio recordings that supposedly were made during the cover-up of the crime scene, but the authenticity of the recordings is in question. With today's computer technology, it would be a relatively simple task to replicate the voices of anyone. So the validation of the recordings as evidence relies almost entirely on their provenance.

And that's where the case is not just weak, but so remarkably weak that it is hard to imagine how it could even support an indictment. You see, the recordings were "discovered" in the Salem home of the late Supreme Court Justice Wilson Landis Devonshire, by a private investigator from Oregon City. That investigator, one March Corrigan, orchestrated a coup d'etat in the Clackamas County Sheriff's Office last October, with the enthusiastic support of the purveyors of hate speech on right-wing talk radio.

We have now learned that Corrigan, who recently was forced to pay over thirty thousand dollars in delinquent taxes, has filed a lawsuit against the IRS, claiming that he was targeted for audit simply because of his accusations against Senator Blalock and other respected leaders.

It isn't enough that Senator Blalock, District Attorney Roger Milliken, and Sheriff William Kerby are going to have to defend themselves against serious felony charges based entirely on questionable evidence that all came from March Corrigan, now they are accused of using the IRS and other government agencies against Corrigan.

It is hardly a surprise that the extra-chromosome types on the extreme right would jump on the bandwagon, given that the main target of the fanciful accusations, Senator Blalock, has been reviled by the neocons to the same degree that he is venerated by most of his constituents.

This new lawsuit by Corrigan is nothing more—or less—than an attempt to contaminate the potential jury pool and make it impossible for Senator Blalock and the others to get fair trials, should the shaky cases actually make it to court. It's time for someone to say enough is enough. This goes way beyond the arena of civil debate. It is an open assault on democracy.

Free speech is a wonderful thing. It is what has made our nation great, and you will find no argument here in favor of any abridgment of free speech. But with every freedom, there comes a responsibility. For freedom of speech to work, thinking people must recognize that there are some who would abuse that freedom through the use of half-truths, innuendos, or outright lies.

Nevertheless, for the sake of pushing a political agenda, there are some who would have you believe not only that the official conclusion in the investigation of the murders with which Senator Blalock has been charged, and reaffirmed in repeated subsequent investigations, was somehow incorrect but also that there exists a massive conspiracy to conceal the "truth."

In disgust, I threw the newspaper in the general direction of the waste-basket.

"You need a lesson in how to make airplanes," Kim observed.

"No, I need my blood-pressure medicine," I snapped.

"You don't take blood-pressure medicine," she reminded me.

"Tibbett Gaylord! That pious bastard is excoriating me with the accusation that *I'm* the criminal and people like Blalock are saints. And then he accuses talk radio of doing the very things that he himself is doing! It's the sanctimonious *Tibbett Gaylord* who's using lies, innuendo, and half-truths!"

"I'm going to have to keep the editorial section away from you."

"It isn't just the editorials. You know as well as I do that Portland's television and radio stations have a long-standing habit of regurgitating whatever the *Chronicle* publishes. This crap will be all over town tomorrow."

"Don't let it get to you. They're just expressing their opinions, same as you."

I exploded. "I am *not* expressing *opinions*! I'm presenting *indisputable facts*! And they aren't expressing opinions either. They're *blatantly lying*!"

I caught my breath and saw the startled expression on Kim's face.

"Sorry," I said quietly. "Crap like this gets to me."

"Do you really think that people will believe them?"

"Kim, you know as well as I that many people will. It's clear now what the strategy is. Blalock's cronies in the media are going to challenge the hard evidence by attacking me. The defense will be built on discrediting me. Until now, I didn't have a clear picture of how they're going to do that, and it isn't going to be pretty."

"I think you should take some time off. Go someplace nice, relax, and get away from all this for a few days," she suggested. "They say Cancun is nice this time of year."

"I'll bet it is," I acknowledged grudgingly.

"Give yourself some time to go fishing—"

"I don't fish."

"Well, diving then, or just sitting on the beach enjoying tropical fruit drinks."

I considered that. "It'd be a great place to go for a honeymoon."

The eye roll that greeted my suggestion told me that the conversation was going no further in that direction.

13

December 31, 2012

It was just before midnight when we were startled by the sound of a mortar being launched. We looked out the window, in the direction the sound had come from, in time to see a smoke trail arc out over the river. With a loud boom, the mortar exploded, sending an incendiary shower raining down on the water.

"Happy New Year," Kim said, raising her champagne glass. "I wonder who's providing the fireworks."

In answer to her comment, two more mortars were blasted out over the water. We walked out onto the front porch for a better view, and then we could see that the fireworks were being launched from the area above the beach, either from the railroad grade or Water Street. We sat down and watched for several minutes as the show continued.

The launch of the last mortar was followed immediately by loud shouting and cursing. A cloud of black smoke started rising from the roof of Carlton's old houseboat. Kim and I hurried out to the street and ran down toward the place where Carlton was running back and forth waving his arms and shouting for someone to call the fire department.

Kim was already on it, using her portable VHF to bypass the 911 switchboard and go straight to the dispatcher. Meanwhile, neighbors poured out of their houses and gathered on Water Street to watch the rapidly growing fire on the roof of the houseboat. Burning asphalt shingles sent flaming streams of melted tar down off the roof onto the decking below, as the thick, black cloud of smoke rose straight toward the sky.

I spotted Carlton's kids trying hard to make themselves invisible. Kaylin Beatty and Jill McDermitt were standing together, laughing. I approached them and asked what happened.

Through tears Jill said, "The genius bombed his own houseboat!"

I looked to Kaylin for further explanation.

"Carlton set up his fireworks on the railroad tracks," Kaylin told me. "He knocked one of them over trying to get away after he lit the fuse, and it launched sideways. It hit the dormer and started the roof on fire!"

Sirens announced the approach of fire engines coming down Highway 99, while the fire continued to spread and McDermitt ran around waving and screaming.

"Hey, Carlton," someone shouted, "you didn't tell us you were going to have a cookout!"

I turned around to see Big Dan walking up Water Street. Bud came around from the alley, joined by Rosie in a ragged housecoat, carrying a freshly topped-off glass of her fortified wine. Barry Walker came out and joined the impromptu block party.

"That's one way to clean up the neighborhood," Barry commented.

"Burn, baby, burn," Red Harper cheered.

It took the firefighters longer to connect their hoses than it took to knock down the fire. Unwilling to string their hoses across the railroad tracks and risk derailing a train, they shot a huge rainbow stream of water from the street, over the railroad and beach, and onto the houseboat.

As soon as the visible flames were extinguished, a team of firefighters armed with ladders and axes scurried down the embankment to the beach. One fireman started chopping away at the wall adjacent to where the fire had been burning on the deck, while others set up the ladders and started climbing to the roof."

"Hey, wait! What are you doing?" Carlton screamed.

He pushed his way past police officers, paramedics, and firefighters trying to get to the beach.

"You can't do that!" he continued to shout. "That's private property!"

By this time, a firefighter on the roof was firing up a gas-powered circular saw, which he used to cut a large hole in the roof. Other firefighters carried a portable water pump down to the houseboat. Smoke drifted up from the hole in the roof.

"You're going to have to pay for this," Carlton shouted. "You're doing more damage than the fire."

A firefighter yanked the cord on the water pump, and it started up with a roar. A hose was passed up to the men on the roof, and they poured water into the hole until the smoke and steam stopped. By then, soot-laden water was flowing out from under the front door on the main level.

With the fire well and thoroughly drowned, the firefighters started lugging their equipment back up onto Water Street, where the crowd of spectators gave them a round of applause.

Carlton was, by this time, engaged in conversation with Officer Durham, trying to explain what had happened.

"So let me get this straight," Durham said. "You were illegally trespassing, and you fired off illegal fireworks that torched your illegal houseboat. Does that about sum it up?"

"Everyone buys illegal fireworks," Carlton groused.

"I can't quite decide where to start writing citations," Durham told him.

Rosie raised her glass and said, "Here's to you, Carlton!"

Bud speculated that Carlton might need some more of his help. Once the show was over, people started heading back home. Rosie had it right—all in all, it had been a memorable way to start the New Year, though I don't suppose Carlton saw it that way.

Welcome to 2013.

14

Monday, January 7

Snow fell during the first few days of January, followed by rain that turned the snow on the ground first into a sheet of ice and then into a mess of slushy puddles. The foul weather matched my mood. The IRS problem was no closer to resolution, a barrage of hate mail and anonymous phone calls followed Gaylord's slanderous editorial, and the Tara Foster investigation had all but stalled.

It's always tough to get anything done during the holiday season, with too many people taking time off, including many who are still supposedly at work. Martha was still plodding through the seemingly endless printout of boater registrations, while I tried to contact people who knew Tara Foster during the last year or two of her life.

But true to form, the holiday season had made it next to impossible to talk with anyone. I'd left a dozen or more voicemail messages, and I learned very little from the few people I'd actually reached. By all accounts, though, Tara Foster had been a nice person, a bit withdrawn, but definitely not suicidal.

I took time to write up a summary of my progress for Walter Brooks. I again emphasized that he couldn't share any of the specifics with his client, which I knew would not sit well with Dennis Lawen. I wrote an updated invoice totaling $8,250 for my work to that point and enclosed it with the redacted progress report. As a matter of form, I added a note again asking if his client wanted me to continue the investigation, crossing my fingers in hopes that he would.

When I carried the letter out to my mailbox, I was met by Jill McDermitt.

"I was just coming to see you," she said. "Something has to be done about that idiot!"

"Carlton?" I asked, knowing perfectly well who "that idiot" was.

"He refuses to get that wreck of a houseboat out of here, even though it's completely uninhabitable now."

"I heard he moved back into his house. What did he do about the guy he rented it to?"

"You'll love this. That guy was a registered sex offender, and Carlton knew it when he rented to him. So when he wanted him to move out, he made an anonymous call to the police, claiming that the guy was bothering kids in the neighborhood. And now he's actually bragging about doing it!"

"Sounds like he did us all a favor with that," I observed.

"But he's the one who brought the creep here in the first place!" Jill complained.

"Good point," I conceded. "What I don't understand is why Carlton wants to hang around here in the first place. No offense, but most guys don't want to be anywhere near their ex-wives."

"It isn't about me. Or the kids. It's about the house. He's obsessed with the house," Jill said.

"I don't understand. Why would he be obsessed with your house?"

Jill took a deep breath and asked, "You ever notice the little historical home sign above the front door?"

"The Jeremiah Applegate House," I quoted.

"Jeremiah and Rebecca Applegate were Carlton's great-great-grandparents. He expected the divorce court to award the house to him on that basis. But when the judge gave it to me, Carlton kind of went off the deep end."

"Wait. Let me understand this," I said. "That house has been in Carlton's family since the nineteenth century? I thought that Union Pacific had owned everything on Water Street."

Jill said, "Oh, they did. The dive company bought it from the railroad in 1993, and Chuck Hampton bought it from them."

I was acquainted with Chuck, who was a "flipper" long before flipping houses became fashionable. He kept his eyes open for any kind of derelict house—burnouts, meth houses, vandalized houses, abandoned and trashed houses—anything he could buy dirt cheap.

Then he'd rehabilitate them, shine them up, make them look respectable, and sell them for a tidy profit. His laborers often lived in the houses where they were working. Chuck paid their wages, sometimes with drugs and other times in cash from a fat roll of bills that he always carried in his pocket. I once watched him peel off a thousand dollars and hand it to Kaylin for earnest money on a house he wanted to buy, and it didn't even make a noticeable dent in the size of his money roll.

Jill continued, "Carlton didn't even know the place existed, let alone that it had any family connection. Not until someone at the historical society told him."

Confused, I asked, "And then he bought the place?"

"It took a couple of years, but he was adamant about getting it back into the family. So when Chuck built the new house next door—now Kaylin's house—he sold the Applegate house to us.

Everything was okay for a while, but then Carlton starting finding things that he had to fix, even though I couldn't see anything wrong. He blamed it on Chuck Hampton, saying that he did things all wrong. It turned into an obsession. I don't think there's a wall anywhere in the house that Carlton hasn't torn apart and patched to fix the plumbing, wiring, or some damned thing."

"That does sound a bit eccentric," I commented.

"Do you know that we lived there for over fifteen years, and during that time, he *always* had a wall or ceiling torn open somewhere in the house? Honestly, it's one of the reasons I got the divorce," Jill explained. "I just couldn't stand it anymore."

"Still, none of that explains why Carlton would want to live right next to your place," I noted.

"He's nuts! Don't you see that?"

I'd thought that from the first day I'd met him.

"So what's he planning to do about *that*?" I asked, indicating the fire-damaged houseboat with a blue tarp nailed over the hole in the roof.

"I wish they'd just let it burn. Now he says he can sell it for salvage. He claims that the float logs alone are worth more than he paid for the whole houseboat."

"That might be true if they weren't half-waterlogged."

"Meanwhile, the city is tacking on a hundred dollars a day to his fine," Jill told me, "though I can't imagine how they'll ever collect from him."

"Well, I'm sure they'll find a way to make him get it out of here," I assured her.

I went back to work on the Tara Foster leads. I finally found a promising lead on the carpet. There was a place called Bentley's Manufacturing, a shop that specialized in boat upholstery, located on Highway 99, just south of Milwaukie. They did sell Tahoe carpet and, more importantly, identified the photo of our carpet as looking like their work. Nobody at Bentley's that day could actually remember the specific project, but they offered to let us look through their invoices.

"Wouldn't it be nice to get out of the office for a few days and do some field work?" I baited Martha.

"*Anything* would be better than this," she said. Sometimes Martha can be wonderfully naïve.

"I've found a shop that might have fitted our carpet and finished the edges," I said. "If we can get the job ticket, we'll have our boat *and* its owner."

"That's great," she said enthusiastically. "When will they have it for me?"

"Uh…well, they won't," I hedged.

"Then how?" After a pause, she answered her own question, "Oh. I get it. I have to find it."

"But you said it yourself, *anything* would be better than what you're doing," I reminded her.

I gave her the address and promised to work on the Marine Board printout while she was gone. She hopped into her Subaru and drove off, and I went back to the boaters' forums on the computer. I logged on as "Idaho Vandal" and found some new responses to a thread.

MOBY DICK: Dude, why are you trying to find the boat? That carpet is trash. He ain't gonna want it back. Just throw it away.

IDAHO VANDAL: It isn't as bad as it looks in the picture.

MOBY DICK: Looks like crap.

IDAHO VANDAL: I just want to know what model boat it fits.

GOPHER BROKE: I'd say it came from a big cruiser.

IDAHO VANDAL: Do you have a specific model in mind?

GOPHER BROKE: Like a big Sea Ray or Bayliner.

IDAHO VANDAL: Thanks.

I'm not sure that Martha's project was more tedious than this. But I diligently kept at it, moving from one forum to the next, responding to any posts, trying to run across anyone who could give me a lead. Once I'd made the rounds of the boaters' forums, I switched to the massive Marine Board printout.

The registrations, of course, listed each boat's manufacturer, model number, and length, but not its beam. I felt I could automatically eliminate all boats under twenty-six feet in length because it was extremely unlikely that any would have the eleven-foot beam needed to accommodate our piece of carpet.

Whenever I identified a boat that was long enough, I would Google the manufacturer and model number. That usually led to used boats for sale somewhere in the world, and the descriptions included a beam measurement, along with photos. Sometimes the photos could eliminate a boat if it was apparent that the aft deck area was a different shape than our carpet.

I found that I could screen about five hundred registrations per hour. In 1999, there were one hundred forty-five thousand boats registered in Oregon, so I was looking at a three hundred hour, or seven week, project. The thing that was galling about the whole thing was that the Marine Board could have used their computer—or given me the data so I could use my computer—and cut the job by at least ninety percent. But no, the bureaucracy was completely unable to provide that level of service.

So I plodded through the pile of paper, and gradually a list started to take form of boats that might possibly have once had a mauve carpet on the aft deck.

Martha came back after four days spent screening invoices at the upholstery shop and dropped a sheet of paper on my desk.

"The good news is, this could be our guy buying our carpet," she said. "The order was placed on April 30, 1996, for a custom-shaped piece of 28-ounce Tahoe in mauve, with color-matched edge finishing. Carpet size is shown as 126 x 74 inches, same as ours. The sketch looks exactly right."

Whenever anyone says "The good news is," you can be sure that there's bad news coming. I didn't have to ask.

"The bad news is that all there is on the invoice is a first name—John—and a phone number. He paid in cash," Martha explained.

"I don't know how far we're going to get with a thirteen-year-old phone number," I said, "but give it a shot. I guess when we start going through the finalists on our boat registration list, we can give special attention to boat owners named John."

15

Friday, February 1

Cold weather persisted throughout January, so when the thaw came, it was a welcome relief. The snow started melting, and the river started rising, and there was talk of flooding on many of the local rivers, including the Willamette. For two days, we watched the river rise, and when it finally reached its crest, the gauge read sixty-six feet, officially establishing this as a "minor" flood.

Still, it was the highest water on the Willamette since February of 1996, and the entire Canemah waterfront was submerged, with water lapping at the base of the railroad grade. There was a loud crack that sounded like a gunshot, followed quickly by two more, sending DC running to the bedroom to hide in the closet until he was sure the threat was over.

"What the hell was that?" I asked Bud.

He'd already put down his beer and raced to the window, looking downstream.

"I think it's coming from Carlton's houseboat," he said.

We rushed down and joined a small group on the railroad grade looking at the fire-damaged old houseboat. Carlton had secured it with a heavy line tied around the trunk of a tall cottonwood tree. As the river rose, the line failed to climb the tree trunk. Instead, it had gone increasingly vertical, pulling the houseboat closer and closer to the tree.

The line was about a foot shorter than it needed to be. The upstream edge of the float was under water, and the whole houseboat was shuddering with the tension on the tie up line. Water piled up against the wall, putting additional strain on the line. There was another loud crack as a stringer broke under the strain. Suddenly there was a ripping sound, and the houseboat swung away from shore, leaving behind a single float log, which remained attached to the tie up line.

The swift current pulled the lopsided houseboat out toward the middle of the river, where the water raced by at a rate of a quarter-million cubic feet per second. Once in the main flow, it took only a few seconds for it to reach the brink of the falls, now more than ten feet underwater. The falls had turned into a mile-long flume racing between the vertical rock walls of the riverbanks.

With an explosive shattering of wood and glass, the upstream edge of the houseboat dipped under, and as a thousand tons of water crashed against it, the entire wall collapsed, bringing down the roof. In less than five seconds the houseboat was gone, pulverized into a mass of splinters.

"Well, that was convenient," Jill observed happily.

"Where's Carlton?" I wondered.

"Good heavens!" Kaylin gasped. "He wasn't on board, was he?"

"I should be so lucky," Jill said. "No, he abandoned ship after the fire. I think he's been staying in the emergency shelter at the VFW hall because his plumbing froze up before the flood."

"Well, at least you won't have to worry about him living in your front yard," Kaylin commented, gesturing toward the lone float log still tied to the cottonwood tree.

The excitement over, I walked back up the railroad grade, now only about six feet above the water level—which was thirteen feet higher than its normal summer level. The trains had stopped running when the water got high enough to present a threat to the roadbed. Liquefaction is the process where vibration causes wet soil to become liquid, and a freight train creates more than enough vibration to trigger the process. The result wouldn't be much fun.

Kim had spent the day with Sammy Cushman on their patrol boat at the West Linn boat dock, watching for runaway docks and boats coming downriver. When they'd spot one heading their way, they'd run out and get a line on it, then tow it in. By evening, they had three docks and a small boat tied to the transient dock.

"We're wrapping it up here," Kim told me on the phone. "Even if a burning boatload of puppies and handicapped children floated by, it'd be too dangerous to go out and chase it in the dark. There's an unbelievable amount of junk in the water."

"My world famous lasagna is in the oven," I told her.

"I'll be there in half an hour. Don't start without me," she said.

By Monday, the river level was slowly going down, leaving behind a thick layer of silt and trash ranging from mismatched sandals to bottles of all description, with a generous littering of plastic foam chunks. A railroad-inspection crew drove slowly down the tracks in a pickup modified to ride the rails, but apparently they hadn't yet deemed it safe to allow freight traffic to resume.

We'd been lucky in Canemah. Except for the loss of Carlton's houseboat, everyone's docks had survived the flood, along with the few boats that had been in the water. Some of the little storage sheds and beach shacks had been swept away, along with chairs, picnic tables, barbecues, and anything else that hadn't been carried to high ground before the river came up. But on the whole, damage was minimal.

"Any idea when you might be able to move back onto the boat?" I asked Martha.

Since the previous summer, Martha had been living aboard a thirty-foot Sea Ray cruiser tied-up at Daryl Tiernan's dock, but when the river started to rise, she moved into a little studio apartment on the lower level of Kaylin Beatty's house.

She said, "I'm in no hurry. Kaylin's little apartment is pretty comfortable. In fact, I asked Kaylin about renting her apartment for the long run."

"What did she think of that idea?" I asked.

"Actually, I think it's going to work out. It'll cost a lot more than renting the boat, but Daryl's going to be installing new engines in it pretty soon, and then he'll want me to move out anyway."

"I don't know," I commented. "It'd double your commute time."

"Yeah, all the way up to two minutes. I guess I should think about that."

16

Tuesday, February 19

I heard footsteps on my porch immediately followed by frantic knocking at my door.

"Corrigan, are you there?" called a familiar voice.

Kaylin Beatty, dressed in a plumb-colored fleece robe, stood on my porch, trying hard to suppress a grin.

"You'll have to see it to believe it." She laughed. "Carlton fell through the roof of Jill's garage!" She could hardly talk between bursts of laughter.

I asked, "What was he doing on the roof of Jill's garage?"

"You just have to see it!" Kaylin giggled.

I hurried with Kaylin down Water Street to Jill's house and then turned up the alley to her garage. There we found Carlton, visible only from the chest up, poking through the cedar shake roof of the garage.

"Help me get out of here," Carlton begged. No phony accent.

I asked Carlton the same question I'd asked Kaylin. "What on earth are you doing up there?"

"Don't ask stupid questions," Carlton pleaded. "Just get me out of here."

Obviously, he had stepped on a soft spot on the old cedar roof and dropped through to his armpits. Then the broken edges of the hole clamped him in place, like the Chinese finger traps we used to play with as kids, so that he couldn't pull himself out.

"Honestly, Carlton, I don't see any way to help you," I said.

Carlton demanded, "Go into the garage and find a ladder or something to put under my feet!"

"Shouldn't we ask Jill before going into her garage," I suggested.

"Forget it!" Carlton cried. "She already left for work. Just try the door!"

I found the garage door locked, so Carlton suggested that I break a window.

"I can't break somebody else's window," I told him.

Carlton saw me pull out my phone. "What are you doing?"

"I'm calling the fire department."

"No!" Carlton pleaded. "Don't call the fire department!"

"Why not?" I asked.

"It's too embarrassing," he whined.

"I don't know how else you're going to get out of there."

"Can't you just come up here and pull me out," he begged.

"Carlton, the roof didn't hold *you* up. What makes you think that it would hold *both* of us?"

"I just stepped in the wrong place," he whined. "As long as you just don't step between the rafters, you'll be okay."

"Sorry, Carlton, I'm self-employed. I can't afford to get myself hurt," I told him as I dialed 911.

Throughout the whole exchange, Kaylin gurgled with suppressed laughter. Barry Walker was attracted by the unusual early-morning activity. He looked from Carlton to the ladder propped against the fence next to Jill's garage.

"What are you doing up there?" Barry called.

Carlton pleaded, "Can you climb up here and help me out?"

"I can call the fire department."

"Can't you just come up here?" Carlton begged.

Barry said, "I don't see what I could do."

I told Barry, "I've already called the fire department."

Five minutes later, the emergency response truck and a snorkel truck trundled up Water Street and turned into the alley. It took about ten minutes to get the stabilizer jacks set and the snorkel extended out over the garage.

The firemen went to work and shortly extracted Carlton from the hole in the roof and deposited him in the alley. By that time, Officer Durham was there pondering the question of the day.

"What were you doing up there?" he asked Carlton.

"I was just trying to help my ex-wife," Carlton said.

"Help her, how?"

"The branches were tearing up her shingles."

"Tearing up her shingles?"

"I was just trying to be helpful," Carlton grumbled.

"In the middle of the night?" Kaylin laughed.

"Middle of the night?" Durham repeated.

"Well, it was still dark out when I heard the crash," Kaylin said.

"It was a little bit early," Carlton objected, "but it wasn't dark."

"He waited until after Jill left for work before calling for help," Kaylin told me.

I still couldn't grasp what he was doing up there.

"Corrigan, you're the investigator here," Kaylin teased. "He was clearing a sight line from his upstairs window to Jill's bedroom window."

"You're kidding," I said.

"Nope," Kaylin said, again breaking up with laughter. "Just walk around to the other side, and you'll see."

We walked around the block to Carlton's house, and sure enough, the branches that Carlton was pruning out of the way were all that blocked his view of his ex-wife's bedroom window. I could only shake my head in wonder.

Barry said, "You know, last week I saw Carlton digging through Jill's mailbox. What's the deal with him?"

My theory remained that he was trying to drive Jill out of her house.

I speculated, "Maybe he thinks he can find something that'll change the divorce decree."

"Can that be done?" Kaylin asked.

"Not without going back to court," I said.

Barry said, "This is fun, but I have to get to work."

Kim was up, and my coffee was cold by the time I got back home. I got a fresh cup and told her the story of my morning adventure.

"You're just making that up," Kim said.

"No, it's all true," I insisted.

"There must be something toxic in the water supply down here, mercury or something like that, making people crazy."

"I suspect Carlton was a nutcase long before he moved down here."

We finished breakfast, and Kim headed off to work. I went out to search for the morning paper. By then, the fire trucks and police cars were gone. I wondered how Carlton was going to explain the hole in the roof to Jill.

Throughout the past six weeks, despite the snowstorm and flood, Martha and I remained busy with a variety of investigations, including the screening of the boat registrations. We slowly chewed through the long list—along with the remainder of Dennis Lawen's ten thousand dollar budget.

Lawen's money was long gone, but with Gates now paying me in cash, I was able to scrape by. Many of my other clients continued to pay by check, and each time I went to the bank to cash a check, I held my breath, fearing that the IRS might have decided to refresh their freeze on my accounts, something they could potentially do at any time.

My legal action against the IRS was still not on the court docket. Mattie Otis responded to my attorney's explanation for the lack of a bank statement dated in April of 2006, with a blunt statement that there was no excuse for my not having provided it at the time of the audit, which of course I had done. She refused to acknowledge that because April had ended on a weekend, the closing statement was dated in the following month.

It was clear to me that she knew perfectly well what had happened and was simply using the feigned confusion as a tool to justify the confiscation of thirty-three thousand dollars from my bank account. She had to know that the IRS would eventually have to give the money back to me, but she was determined to make the process as difficult as possible.

But since nothing I could do would change that, I tried to focus on things where I did have some measure of control. I picked up my phone and punched in the number.

"Have time for an update on my investigation?" I asked Walter Brooks, when he answered.

"I'm encouraged, just by the fact that you have something to report," Brooks answered.

"As I said before, the hard evidence from the crime scene suggests that Lawen had nothing to do with Tara Foster's death. We've felt from the beginning that our best chance of finding an alternate suspect would be through the carpet Foster's body was wrapped in."

"I understand."

"We believe that we've found the shop that cut and finished the carpet, and we have a 1996 invoice for the job," I said and then quickly added, "Unfortunately, it has only the customer's first name, and so far we've been unable to trace the thirteen-year-old phone number."

"But you're making progress! I'm pleasantly surprised."

"Here's where we are. We're screening a hundred forty-five thousand boat registrations in search of someone named John, who owned a large cruiser at the time Foster disappeared. We were unable to get anything but a paper printout, so we have to go through it line by line. It's very time consuming, and we're barely half done."

"But you're still working on it," Brooks said. It was more a question than a comment.

"We are as long as your client wants us to," I said. "The thing is, this is going to cost more than the ten grand Lawen has given us."

"How much more?"

"Probably another five to get through the registrations and cross-check with our list of riverfront properties. It'll be less if we spot someone named John with a cruiser that fits our carpet before we get clear through the list," I explained.

Brooks sighed. "I know what Lawen will say. He'll say 'Keep going.'"

"But can he pay? I'm all for finding the guilty party, but I still have to pay the bills."

"Oh yeah, he can pay," he assured me. "Keep on it unless I call to say otherwise. And thanks for the update."

Three days later a courier service delivered a package containing fifty crisp, new portraits of Ben Franklin, which I put away in my safe. The Tara Foster investigation went on. That meant more endless hours screening the boat registration printout.

17

Monday, March 4

Martha shouted, "We have a winner!"

It was midmorning on a rare beautiful March day. We were five months into our work for Dennis Lawen, and I didn't immediately grasp what Martha's exclamation meant.

"Who won what?" I asked.

"John Prescott registered a 1964 Chris Craft Constellation in 1995, *and* he lived in Charbonneau!" Martha said triumphantly.

"Are you serious?" I asked, knowing that she was.

I quickly Googled Chris Craft Constellation, and from photos on a yacht broker's website, I determined that it had a curved transom on the aft deck that just might match the shape of our carpet.

"He's our guy," Martha said happily.

Looking over her shoulder at the printout, I read the line she had just highlighted.

"Outstanding! Let's see what we can find out about John Prescott," I said. "Go through the usual websites. I'll go see if anyone at Bentley's remembers the name."

I grabbed the Bentley's invoice that Martha had found and rushed out the door.

"Remember this invoice?" I asked the guy behind the counter, whose shirt bore the name Jerry.

"Is that the one that lady found a few weeks ago?" he asked.

I nodded. "It is, but now we have some more information that might go with it. Were you ever able to identify who wrote up the invoice?"

He took the paper from my hand and contemplated for a moment. "That might be Todd's handwriting," he said. "He was vacationing in Mexico when the lady came in."

"Is Todd around?" I asked.

In answer, Jerry poked his head into the back room and called, "Hey, Todd, you got a moment?"

"What can I do for you?" asked the dark-haired man who emerged from the shop.

I handed him the invoice and asked what he remembered about it.

"I kinda remember it. It was just a small job," he said.

I explained, "We think the carpet was made for an old Chris Craft Constellation. That ring a bell?"

Todd scratched his head and said, "Customer didn't bring the boat in. He just brought us a paper pattern to work from, as I recall. But now that you say so, I think maybe it *was* for a Connie."

"How about the name Prescott?" I asked.

"Prescott," he repeated. "Naw, I don't think I ever got his last name."

"Would you recognize him if you saw his picture?" I asked.

"I don't know. Maybe, but that was a long time ago," Todd said. "You have a picture?"

"I don't have one here today," I said, "but I'm sure I can get one."

Back at the office, Martha said, "Okay, here's what I've found out so far. John Prescott is fifty-eight years old, worked for Mentor Graphics from 1994 to 2002. Now he lives in Tacoma. Looks like he may have taken the boat along when he moved because it hasn't been licensed in Oregon since then. I haven't found any criminal record for him, and he has a 710 credit score. I'm still looking."

I went to the filing cabinet and found my copy of the original missing-person file on Tara Foster. It was pretty thin, reflecting the fact that the investigators gave up on her pretty quickly. I scanned the names of people listed as friends and associates, hoping to find John Prescott. No luck.

I looked at Foster's address and compared it with Prescott's. Different streets. I entered the addresses in Google Maps, and the result made me smile.

"He's our guy," I told Martha. "They lived right around the corner from one another."

Martha said, "So you figure that they met, went for a boat ride, and Tara ended up in the river, rolled in carpet."

"It sure looks that way. Have you found a photo of him?" I asked.

"Oh sure, I have several," she said.

It was time to give Michael Wheeler a call.

"What do you have?" he asked, getting straight to the point.

"I think we've traced our carpet to a 1964 Chris Craft Constellation that belonged to one John Prescott, who lived in Charbonneau," I said.

"How'd you come up with that?"

I described how we'd found the invoice and tentatively matched it to Prescott's boat registration. "The guy at Bentley's says he might recognize him from a photo. I have some photos, but I think if anyone's going to do a lay-down for him, it ought to be you guys."

"Yeah. Thanks. If you email the photo, I'll get someone to put together a spread. Anything else?"

"Prescott and Foster were neighbors. They lived about 150 yards from one another."

"Was he interviewed when she disappeared?"

"Not that I can tell. It looks like nobody put any effort into finding out what happened to her. They decided early on that she was depressed and made herself disappear."

"Okay," Wheeler said. "We'll talk to the witness at Bentley's and see if he can identify the photo. If so, we may have an actual suspect."

18

Friday, March 15

Martha brought in the mail and dropped it on my desk "I see there's a moving van in front of Jill McDermitt's house," she said.

"Yeah, I think Carlton falling through the garage roof was the tipping point," I commented. "It's been my theory all along that he's been trying to drive her out, and if that's the case, it looks like he got his way."

"But if he didn't want to be around her, why'd he buy the house almost next door?"

"Jill thinks it was because he wants the house back. She told me that if she sells, Carlton has the first right to purchase—something that was written into the divorce decree," I explained.

The sound of gravel crunching under car tires drew my eyes to the window, where I watched a sheriff's office car roll to a stop. Only it wasn't Kim's marine unit Explorer. It was one of the new Dodge Chargers.

Sheriff Larry Jamieson climbed out of the car and walked up my front steps. I welcomed him in and offered him a cup of coffee, which he waved off.

"There may be trouble with the Blalock case," he said.

"What's happening?" I groaned, trying to stay calm.

"The DA wants more evidence. She's afraid that going to trial with what she has might end up with an acquittal."

I tabulated the evidence on my fingers. "You have the tape recordings from Devonshire's house. You have Blalock's credit-card receipts for Jessie's birth control pills and the clothes she was wearing when she died. You have Mickey Odell's testimony about how Sheriff Barrington covered for Blalock. You have the phone records tying him to Richard Elgin, and you have Elgin's testimony that he left the car for Blalock to drive home from the boat ramp after he dumped the car and the bodies into the river."

"You've already heard that the defense is going to challenge the authenticity of the tape recordings. And now Elgin seems to be backing down. He wants to cut a deal—he'll testify only if all charges against him are dropped."

"They can't make that deal! Elgin killed old man Devonshire. They have his prints on the weapon, his tire tracks in the dirt next to the car where Devonshire was killed, and they have the GPS tracking data that proves when he was there," I reminded him.

"And therein lies the problem. If the prosecutor uses the GPS data, the defense will claim that the data was illegally acquired and that the fingerprint is inconclusive, so the search warrant that resulted in the tire-track match was issued without probable cause."

"They can't possibly make a jury believe that!" I exclaimed.

"Hey, this isn't *my* idea," Jamieson protested. "I'm just telling you what's happening before you read it in the newspaper."

I took a deep breath. "So you're saying that Elgin might walk if he agrees to testify against Blalock."

"That's the way the DA sees it. Sometimes you have to let the little fish go in order to get the bigger fish."

"But Elgin is no little fish! Devonshire isn't the only person he's killed. What about those two deputies back in 1980? What about his two dead wives? He has no business being out on the streets!"

"By your own investigation, the two deputies were killed by Trey Bourne. Sure, he worked for Elgin, but Bourne's dead. He can't testify that Elgin ordered the killings. As far as the wives are concerned, maybe we can come up with something, maybe not."

"That's why he has to go down for the Devonshire thing," I insisted.

"Again, it's not my call. And no deal has been made. Not yet, anyway. I still have two detectives working with the DA's office on that case. Maybe they'll find some other way to strengthen the case against Blalock. Then the DA won't have to deal with Elgin."

After Jamieson left, I looked at Martha, who had sat silently through the whole conversation.

"If they cut Elgin loose, he'll come after you," she said.

"I don't doubt that," I agreed. "And without my testimony regarding the hard evidence against Blalock, the defense will claim that I fabricated all of it, and a soft-headed jury just might consider that reasonable doubt."

"This whole thing stinks. It has from the day Jessie Devonshire disappeared. How anybody could defend Alan Blalock is beyond my comprehension."

I agreed. "Blalock's propaganda machine has been doing everything possible to portray him as the saintly victim of phony charges based on fake evidence. That slimy editor at the *Chronicle* is trying to make people believe that the case against Blalock is just something concocted by right-wing extremists—the boogeyman behind everything he disagrees with."

"A year ago, I might have believed him," Martha admitted, "but trying to make *Blalock* look like a victim is just too much to swallow."

"A lot of people out there *will* swallow it because it's what they *want* to believe."

19

Saturday, March 16

Sitting at my desk gazing absently at my computer, I contemplated what I could do to push the Tara Foster investigation forward. I was impatiently waiting to hear from the sheriff's office about their interview with Todd at Bentley's Upholstery, but I felt a pressing need to get the investigation moving.

I'd been trying to locate people who had known Tara Foster but so far hadn't had much luck. I went back to the Wilsonville Police Department file on her disappearance and reviewed the basic facts of the investigation, hoping for some new insight.

On Tuesday, June 13, 2000, after Foster had failed to report to work or call in sick for two days, her supervisor phoned the emergency contact number she had on file. That turned out to be a sister in Portland, who said that she had no idea where Tara might be. They had talked on the phone the preceding Saturday, and Tara had given no indication that she might be sick or about to leave town.

The sister and supervisor decided it would be best to contact the police, who performed a welfare check at her condo and found no trace of Tara nor any clue where she might have gone. She was officially declared a missing person since it had been over forty-eight hours since her last contact.

Police talked with the sister, Tonia Hines, and learned that Tara had been divorced for about a year and a half. Her ex-husband, Thomas Foster, had moved to Texas after the divorce and had not spoken with Tara since. She did not own a computer, and her address book contained only about a dozen entries, mostly relatives. Nobody contacted could shed any light on Tara's disappearance.

It wasn't until mid-July that police got around to canvassing Tara's neighborhood. They found only two neighbors in the condominium complex who knew Foster, and neither had even been aware that she was missing.

That was about all there was to the investigation. A partial bottle of Prozac found in her bathroom led to a doctor who said that he had prescribed it a year earlier for clinical depression. That revelation, coupled with the lack of any other evidence, eventually evolved into the theory that Tara might have taken her own life. That was where the investigation was suspended.

I called Martha on her cell phone and asked if she wanted to work some overtime. I explained that a Saturday evening could be a pretty good time to find people at home, and I could use her help for a couple of hours.

I handed the short list of witnesses to Martha and asked her to track down current phone numbers. The first one she came up with was for Tonia Hines.

"Yes, this is Tonia," came the reply to my question.

"My name is Corrigan. I'm a private investigator in Oregon City, and I'm assisting in the investigation of your sister's death."

She grumbled, "It took you long enough to get around to calling."

"We've been focusing the investigation on the physical evidence," I said. "I am sorry nobody has contacted you."

"Yeah, okay," she said impatiently. "So what have you found out?"

"I can tell you only that we've made some progress," I hedged, "and we're trying to establish who Tara might have been in contact with around the time she disappeared."

I then read off four names. The first three were fictitious. The forth one was John Prescott.

Tonia said, "No, I don't recognize any of those. Wait, what was the second one? I think maybe there was something about a person named Jason something."

That was a strikeout. The name John Prescott meant nothing to Tara's sister. By the time I got off the phone with Tonia, Martha had produced another number for me to call. The best I could do with that call was leave a voice message. The third and fourth calls produced the same result as the first—no reaction to the name of John Prescott.

The fifth call was to Sophie Burns, who had lived in the same condo complex as Tara back at the time of the disappearance.

"Sure, I remember Tara," she told me. "When she disappeared, I hadn't been there very long, and she was about the only neighbor I knew."

"What do you remember about her disappearance?" I asked.

"Not much. I mean, she just wasn't there anymore. We weren't close friends, really—just casual acquaintances, you know? I noticed that she hadn't been around for a while, and then I found out that she was missing."

I read the same four names I'd given the other witnesses.

"John Prescott," Sophie said immediately. "I remember him. He lived right around the corner."

How did you know him?"

"He showed up at the swimming pool one day just as I was going in. He followed me through the gate. We talked a bit. That was all."

"Did Tara ever meet him?" I pressed.

"Oh sure. Here's the thing. John used to hang around the pool a lot," she explained. "I think the reason he went there was to meet women—a lot of us were recently divorced, and John was looking to score."

"Did he?"

"Score? Not with me!" she said defensively.

"How about with Tara?"

Sophie hesitated. "I don't know, but I suppose it's possible."

"Why do you say that?"

"Well, I heard him inviting her to go cruising on his boat. There was something in the way he said it that sounded, I don't know, kind of seductive, maybe."

"Did she go?"

"She might have, but that'd just be a guess."

"When was this—relative to the time she disappeared?"

"It wasn't too long. I don't know when she actually disappeared."

"You told the police that you didn't know of anyone she'd been dating," I pointed out.

She quickly said, "Well, they *weren't* dating, as far as I know. I don't even know if she went on his boat. I just heard them talking about it."

After I got off the phone with Sophie, Martha commented, "There it is—a connection between Prescott and Foster."

I said, "It's a connection, but it's pretty thin. A good interrogator might be able to use it to get Prescott to admit something, but it hardly breaks the case. But we're going the right direction. I think we need to keep working on people in the condo complex. Maybe we can find some others who saw him at the pool or with Tara."

"How will we go about that if their names aren't on the list of witnesses in the file?" Martha asked.

"Thank you for asking. On Monday, you'll contact the condo homeowners association and get the ownership history," I said. "Find the names of everyone who lived there in 2000, and we'll see how many of them we can find."

20

Tuesday, March 19

In answer to Walter Brooks's question, I said, "I've turned over everything to the sheriff's office. I think we've found a viable suspect, and they're going to check on him."

"Will they announce that Lawen is not a suspect?" he asked.

"Not a chance. But if they can build enough of a case to arrest this guy, that'll be just as good."

"What are the chances of that?"

"It's too soon to say. They have a name, a connection to the carpet, and a connection to the victim. It remains to be seen whether or not they can come up with enough to get an indictment."

"I'll pass that along to Lawen," Brooks said.

"While the sheriff's office works on that," I said, "I'm talking with people who were interviewed at the time Foster disappeared—to see if any of them know anything about this suspect."

After completing my conversation with Brooks, I offered Martha a beer and the afternoon off since it was an unusually warm early spring day.

"I'm going to go down and contemplate what I need to do to restore my beach," I said, "and I plan to do it from a seated position with an ice chest at my side."

The flood had left a thick layer of sandy silt over the entire beach, which previously had been carpeted in wild grass. I was hoping to see the grass growing up through the silt, but it hadn't come through yet. So far, the only restoration work I'd done was to scrape and wash the silt off the steps leading down from the railroad grade so that I could pack my beach furniture back down to the beach.

"Will it ever be the same?" Martha asked.

Where Daryl's beach cabin had been, only a row of pier blocks remained. The little shed I'd lost was of no consequence.

"It won't be the same, but I'll bet that by the end of the summer, it'll be nicer than ever," I said.

"Daryl's been down on the boat, taking the engines apart."

"Has he indicated when he's going to install the new ones?"

"No, but he has them on stands in Red Harper's garage, and he's been working on them."

"So pretty soon you might have to move."

"It looks that way," she answered. "Jill asked me about renting her house, but she warned me that Carlton might continue to make a nuisance of himself."

"After Jill's gone, he'll probably just let it go," I said without conviction.

While we were talking, the neighborhood new guy, Barry Walker, came down the steps onto his section of the beach. Okay, so he'd been living there for six months, but as far as the neighborhood was concerned, he was still the new guy. I'd held that title for *two years* before someone moved into the yellow house on the other side of my fence and took over the title. Now it was Barry's turn.

"What's happening?" I asked when he strolled over.

"I have some laborers coming down tomorrow to build a retaining wall over there," Barry said, indicating the steep embankment on the side of the railroad grade. "And I'm going to have 'em set forms for a concrete buttress to anchor a dock ramp too."

"So you're putting in a dock."

Back when Kaylin Beatty had first announced that the Dexters' house was for sale, I'd instructed her to make sure that she sold it to someone who could drive a ski boat. I was kidding, of course, but when Barry moved in, I was pleased to see the MasterCraft parked on his driveway.

"Yeah, I have one up at the houseboats. It got loose from somewhere up around Newberg during the flood. Captain Alan captured it and tied it up. The owners don't want it back. I guess their insurance is going to buy them a new dock, so I paid Alan a salvage fee, and the dock is mine. It saves me from having to build one," Barry explained.

"Sounds good. It'll be nice to have another skier on the river."

"Shoot. I have so many projects going, I don't know if I'll have any time for boating. And as if I didn't already have enough to do, I'm buying Jill McDermitt's place. That's going to keep me pretty busy for awhile."

Surprised, I asked, "Are you going to move into it?"

"No, it's purely an investment. I'm going to remodel it and resell it. I'd like it to be the first half-million-dollar property in Canemah."

"You'll probably have to put a new roof on the garage."

Barry laughed. "I don't know what Carlton's going to do for amusement with Jill gone."

"What's your plan for the place?"

"Have you ever been inside? It's the wildebeest of real estate. It's a mish-mash of different remodels and restorations. In some rooms they tried to restore it to original, and in other rooms it was 'modernized' in ways that are now badly dated. The kitchen looks like 1985, the bathroom like it came from the Dollar Store, and the bedrooms are all of the early nondescript period."

"So are you going to restore it to its original look?"

"No, it's too far gone for that. Besides, it'll be worth more if I can bring it up to modern standards. I think we'll strip it out to the studs and start over. I'd like to add some square footage somewhere, but Kaylin says that I'd have to get that approved by the neighborhood association, and I hear they can be pretty hard to deal with."

I nodded in agreement. "Some of those people have a set of pretty narrow ideas, and they stick with them."

"By 'some people,' I assume you mean Leonard Butts."

I just shrugged.

"I have an engineer coming over this week to look at the structural elements," he said. "What he tells me will determine what I'm going to do."

"In all the years Carlton worked on that place, he never did manage to get all four of the outside walls painted to match. The house has been three different colors ever since I moved down here," I said. "It'll be nice to see it finally done right."

"The first thing I'm going to do is have those big old trees taken down. That one out front completely blocks any river view you might have from the house," he told us.

Martha asked, "Don't you have to get a permit or something to cut down the trees?"

"That's a crusade that Oregon City hasn't joined. In other places—West Linn, for one—you need a permit from God," Barry said, gesturing across the river, "but not here."

21

Saturday, March 23

True to Barry's word, a crew arrived with chainsaws, ropes, a wood chipper, and a stump grinder. They worked all day taking down the massive basswood in the front yard, an even larger bay laurel in the back, and a couple of tall conifers in between. When they were finished, every trace of landscaping was destroyed and the ground stripped to bare dirt.

"It looks kind of naked," Daryl commented.

A few of us had gathered on the street to marvel at the defoliation project.

"For the first time ever, I have daylight coming in through the windows on that side of the house," Kaylin commented happily.

Kaylin's friend Kurt said, "This is going to test our relationship. About every four months for the past three years, Kaylin has had me clean the gutters. Now that won't be necessary, so who knows? I might be irrelevant."

"They've destroyed the whole neighborhood," Carlton complained. "That myrtle tree was a hundred fifty years old."

Kurt said, "The arborist told me it was a bay laurel, and it was fifty-four years old. He counted the rings."

Carlton wouldn't budge. "He's not much of an arborist if he doesn't recognize a myrtle tree. Those sections of the trunk are worth thousands of dollars, and they're just dumping them."

"If you think they're worth something," I suggested, "go over and ask for them. I'm sure Barry doesn't care where they go. He just wants them gone."

"I think I'll do that," Carlton said.

We watched him work his way around the worksite, over to where the remains of the laurel-myrtle tree were lying on the ground.

"Whatever kind of tree it was, it sure smelled good when they ran the branches through the chipper," Kaylin commented.

A voice from behind us said, "Whoever's behind this is in big trouble."

We all turned to see Leonard Butts busy shooting pictures with his flip phone.

"That big tree out front was planted by Jeremiah Applegate himself when he built this house in 1887," Butts said authoritatively.

Kurt said, "I don't think it was that old. The guy who counted the rings said that it was about seventy years old."

"There are photos of this place at the turn of the century, and that tree was there," Butts insisted. "Anyway, you can't just go cutting down trees without approval."

"Approval from whom?" Daryl challenged.

"Well, from the neighborhood association, for one, and the city requires a historical review before anything can be changed. You know, this is the only National Register historic district in all of Clackamas County!"

Kaylin said, "Leonard, the city's historical review applies to changes in the buildings. It says nothing about the trees."

Butts, who apparently was not accustomed to being challenged, said emphatically, "The rules apply to anything that changes the appearance of the neighborhood! Besides, those tree roots are needed to stabilize the ground here. Without the roots to hold it in place, this whole bench could slide into the river."

Daryl looked skeptical. "When did you become a geologist?"

"This whole flat area down here is the toe of an ancient landslide off the back hill. It's just loose soil, and that's why the people planted trees here—because they knew that the ground needed to be stabilized." The more Butts talked, the more agitated he got.

"There aren't any trees there," Kurt said, indicating the properties on either side, "and they haven't fallen into the river."

"The tree roots spread out that far in each direction. The removal of these trees will put all of the neighboring properties in jeopardy too!"

"Everything's a crisis with him," I whispered to Martha.

"I've already called Public Works, Code Enforcement, the planning department, and the city manager," Butts ranted.

Barry looked pained. "Can he do that?" he asked Kaylin.

"He does this kind of thing all the time," she said. "But don't worry too much about it. Everyone in the city knows that he's full of hot air."

"Yeah, he's full of *something*," Daryl said.

After Barry walked away, Daryl commented, "I just can't wait to see what Butts has to say when Barry starts working on the house."

Kaylin said, "Well, I think I talked Barry out of trying to add a new addition to the house. His idea was to bump out the west wall to make room for a new bathroom for a master suite on the main level. His new idea is to use the entire second story for the master suite and build two new bedrooms and a bathroom in the basement."

"That won't be much good," Daryl said. "The ceiling in the basement isn't even six feet high."

"Ah, well that's where Barry's getting creative," Kaylin explained. "He's going to tear out the slab and dig the basement three feet deeper."

"Wow. That won't be cheap. He'll have to jack up the house and pour a whole new foundation."

Kaylin shrugged. "I don't know how he's going to do it, but that's his plan."

Interest in Barry's project diminished quickly after the chainsaws went quiet, and everyone except Butts and Carlton drifted away to do other things. Carlton was still trying to wrangle a deal on some of the priceless myrtle wood, and Butts was blathering about his grandmother rolling over in her grave.

22

Monday, March 25

While Martha continued to search for possible witnesses in Tara Foster's condominium complex, I went in search of more witnesses who knew John Prescott. Based on the theory that his big boat would have attracted attention, I drove to the marina at Wilsonville. It is located on the site of the old Boone's Ferry, built by a grandson of Daniel Boone.

The boating season hadn't gotten started yet, so most of the boat slips on the rows of docks were vacant. It was a good time to talk with the marina manager because activity would be at a minimum.

"I was wondering if you had records on who rented space here back in 2000," I said to the elderly lady at the counter.

"Sure we do. What is it you want to know?" she asked.

"I'm trying to track down a 1964 Chris Craft Constellation, a big wooden cruiser. I think it may have been moored here between 1995 and 2002."

"There was a nice old Connie moored here about that time. I remember it because it's unusual to see a boat that big on the upper river."

"Would you have records to document that?"

"Probably, but they'd be in the bottom drawer of some old filing cabinet in the back room."

"It's really important. Could you try to find it for me?"

She shrugged and asked, "Important to whom?"

"I'm conducting an investigation on behalf of the Clackamas County Sheriff's Office," I told her. "I guess if you need it to be official, I could get a search warrant."

It was a hollow bluff, but it had the desired effect. She led me to a cluttered storeroom filled with cardboard filing boxes and mismatched steel filing cabinets.

"What year did you say?" she asked.

"It's the year 2000 I'm interested in," I said, "but the boat probably was here from 1996 to 2002. The owner's name was Prescott."

"So if he signed a multiyear lease, it could be in any file from, maybe 1995 to 2000," she complained.

"Do you get a lot of multiyear leases?" I wondered.

"Not a lot, but we get 'em."

"Then let's start at 2000 and work backward."

She made a noise that I interpreted to be grudging agreement. She pushed some boxes first one way and then the other, looking at the felt-tip markings on the boxes behind. Second from the bottom in a stack of boxes against the wall was a box marked 2000.

"You want to give me a hand with these?" she asked.

I lifted three boxes from the stack and got to the one we wanted. I carried it out into the front room where there was better light. It took about half an hour to find John Prescott's lease for a large slip in the eastern side of the marina. The boat listed was a 1964 Chris Craft Constellation. It was an annual renewal of a lease first written in 1996, shortly after the rebuilt marina had opened following the 1996 flood.

"Do you remember anything about the owner, John Prescott?" I asked.

"He paid his rent on time," she said.

"Did he use the boat very much?"

"He spent more time working on it than he did using it. Seems like he was always sanding or painting some part of the boat."

I knew exactly what she was talking about. Wooden boats require perpetual maintenance.

"He used to bring his lady friends down. Sometimes they'd go out on the river, and sometimes they'd just sit on the boat and listen to music. I had to tell him to turn it down a couple of times."

"Do you know who his lady friends were?"

"No. I never talked with them."

"Can you think of anyone who might have known Prescott or his friends down here?"

"I don't recall anyone in particular," she said. "It was a long time ago."

I asked for a copy of the lease to put in my file, but on the whole, I really hadn't learned much.

Later that day, Larry Jamieson called to let me know that a detective had been to Bentley's, and Todd had picked Prescott's photo out of a six-photo spread as the man who had ordered the custom mauve carpet.

He said, "I'm telling you this because I still don't have anyone to work on this case."

I said, "We've identified a solid suspect. That's a big step forward. And we know that he was acquainted with the victim. He's the guy."

"You're probably right, and we'll nail him," the sheriff insisted. "But it'll have to wait until we sew up the Blalock and Elgin investigations."

"I understand. But rather than just wait for that, I'd like to see if I can track down the boat. Its Oregon registration lapsed at the end of 2002. Prescott moved to Tacoma at about that time, so I figure he probably reregistered the boat in Washington. But I need some help getting registration records. The Department of Licensing in Washington won't even talk to me."

Jamieson sighed. "Give me what you know, and I'll put in the request."

"It's a 1964 Chris Craft Constellation that was registered in Oregon to John Prescott." I gave him the old Oregon registration number and the boat's HIN, hull identification number.

"If someone doesn't get you the information by the end of the week, give me a call back," he said.

A few days later, I received the ownership documents from Washington State. John Prescott had registered the Connie in 2003 and 2004 but sold the boat in July of that year. It was currently owned by Damien Hamilton of Olympia. It took about five minutes to find his cell phone number.

"This is Damien," came the voice on the phone.

"Damien Hamilton?"

"That's right. What can I do for you?"

"My name is Corrigan. I'm a private investigator in Oregon. I'm interested in a boat that I believe you own, a 1964 Chris Craft Constellation."

"What is your interest in my boat?" he asked cautiously.

"Nothing that involves you," I said quickly. "I'm looking into the previous owner, John Prescott. I believe you bought the boat from him?"

"I don't remember the name. I may have it on file someplace."

"Washington State licensing records indicate that you acquired the boat from Prescott in 2004."

"That's when I bought the boat. Why are you investigating this? The boat wasn't stolen, was it?"

"No. It's nothing like that. We're just trying to verify some history. Where is the boat now?"

"I have a slip at West Bay Marina."

"I'd like to take a look at it."

"What for?"

I hesitated and then said, "We believe that a crime may have taken place on the boat about thirteen years ago."

"Homicide? That's the only crime that doesn't have a statute of limitations."

"You're an attorney, right?"

"I am. So you're investigating a murder that may have taken place on my boat?"

"I'd like to bring a forensic expert to look at the rear deck area."

"If this is a murder investigation, why isn't it being done by law enforcement?" he asked.

"Outsourcing," I explained. "It's a cold case, and the authorities don't have the manpower right now to deal with it. I'm working on the case in cooperation with the Clackamas County sheriff."

"Does that mean that this is an official investigation?" he pressed.

"It does," I said, though I wasn't entirely sure that it really was.

"When do you want to do this? I want to be there."

"We'll do it at your convenience. Maybe this weekend."

"How long will it take?"

I didn't know, so I guessed. "Oh, no more than an hour."

"How about nine in the morning, Saturday?"

"I'll need to verify that with my forensic people, but let's plan on that time. I'll call you back if I find out that won't work. Otherwise, I'll see you there at nine on Saturday."

I phoned Intermountain Forensic Labs in Portland and explained what I needed. My call went to a forensic scientist named Catherine Williams.

"That's pretty short notice," she said.

"It is a potential homicide scene."

"Yes, but it's thirteen years old."

"I know it's a long shot, but I need to cover all of the bases."

When she told me what it would cost, I did some quick mental calculations. This was definitely going to use up the rest of Dennis Lawen's fifteen grand—and then some. I decided to lock it in. If Lawen decided not to reimburse me, I'd have to absorb the loss, but I figured it was worth the gamble.

23

Saturday, March 30

I met Catherine Williams and Damien Hamilton at West Bay Marina in Olympia. After introductions, Hamilton led us onto the dock and out to the slip where his boat was moored. The boat was nearly fifty years old but looked almost like new.

"Has any renovation work been done on the boat since you bought it?" I asked

"Of course," he said. "She's a wooden-hull boat. Renovation is a perpetual part of ownership."

"How about refinishing or redecorating inside?"

"Nothing major. It had been recently redone when I bought her."

Aboard the boat, I first measured the aft deck area and confirmed that its dimensions matched the piece of carpet Alan had fished out of the Willamette. There was no carpet on the deck nor any evidence of there ever having been any. But of course, the carpet wouldn't have been glued down. There were deck hatches that you'd still need access to.

"If anything happened, it probably happened right in this area," I said, recalling my theory that the murder most likely took place on the carpet that was used for disposal of the body. "While Ms. Williams gets started here, I'd like to take a look around the cabin, if that's all right."

Hamilton unlocked the cabin door and said, "Come on inside."

The interior was decorated in white, gray, and royal blue. There was no trace of mauve to be seen anywhere. I noted that the galley had been upgraded with built-in microwave, granite-looking countertops, and stainless-steel appliances. To me, the twenty-first-century décor seemed oddly out of place in the fifty-year-old yacht.

Looking around, I was particularly interested in the window coverings. There were two-tone drapes on all of the windows in the main salon, and behind the drapes were custom-fit miniblinds. The drapes were mounted on plain brass-colored rods without pull mechanisms. The drapes had to be opened or closed by hand, if they ever were moved at all, which was unlikely since they were backed up by the blinds.

Studying the blinds, I found pull cords on each side: the left-hand cords adjusted the tilt of the horizontal slats, and the right-hand cords raised and lowered the blinds. When I got to the blind on the rear window of the salon, I found it raised. I went to lower it but discovered that the cords were missing.

"What happened to the cords?" I asked Hamilton.

He shook his head. "Never had 'em. That's the way it was when we bought the boat. We never use that blind, so it didn't seem important."

I pushed the curtain aside and looked carefully at the end of the blind header. The short stubs of the pull cords still protruded from the slots.

"We may need to take this blind," I told Hamilton.

"Well, just because I said we don't use it doesn't mean I'm ready to give it away."

"I'm sure your insurance will cover it if it's taken as evidence in a homicide investigation." I was bluffing. Actually, I had no idea if insurance would apply.

Back out on the aft deck, Catherine Williams was opening each of the deck hatches and using a Sherlock Holmes-style magnifying glass to study the edges of both the hatches and the openings in the deck. In three different areas under the edges of the shore power connector and the battery selector switch, she carefully took scrapings of tiny spots that she thought might be blood, depositing the samples in glass vials.

After finishing her inspection of the deck hatches, she asked Hamilton to zip the flaps over the vinyl windows on the after deck canvas enclosure, shutting out much of the ambient light. After waving us back into the salon, she sprayed a Luminol solution over the deck area and switched on a portable ultraviolet light. Immediately a faint blue aura appeared over a large area in the portside corner of the aft deck, indicating that blood had once been present. She quickly photographed the area before the luminosity faded out.

"Could be that somebody cleaned fish there," she said. "But it might also be a crime scene. Analysis of the scrapings might help determine which."

After she cleaned up and put away all of her equipment, I called her attention to the venetian blind in the salon.

"We'd better take that along. We can see if the composition of the cord matches what you found on the victim," Catherine explained.

"So you really think someone was murdered here?" Hamilton asked.

"Given what I know about the crime, together with what I've seen here, I'd say it's very likely," Catherine told him.

"So what happens now?" he asked. "Are they going to hang yellow tape all over my boat?"

I said, "If the lab tests are positive for human blood and if the blind cords match, I'll report the results to the Clackamas County sheriff. After that, it's up to them, but the chances are they'll want to do a follow-up examination. For now, though, you are free to use the boat."

When the preliminary lab results came in the following week, they confirmed that the specks found on the boat were human blood. Catherine Williams asked if I wanted a DNA profile developed, and I gave her the go ahead, even though I had no guarantee that there would be anything to compare it with. My thinking was that with a nearly complete skeleton, there ought to be recoverable DNA available.

I wrote up a report on my visit to Damien Hamilton's boat and attached the preliminary blood report. I hand delivered it to the Homicide and Violent Crimes Unit headquarters at the sheriff's office, with a copy to Larry Jamieson. The substance of my report was that there would be a very strong case against John Prescott if the blood found on his boat could be matched by DNA to Tara Foster. That, together with his connection to Tara Foster and the purchase of the custom-fit carpet, ought to be enough for a successful prosecution.

Later in the day, I talked with Sheriff Jamieson on the phone, and he agreed that the samples taken by the pathologist who studied Tara Foster's remains should be sent to a lab for DNA analysis. The testing might take as long as six to eight weeks, and in the meantime, there was nothing more I could do on the investigation.

If the DNA came back a match, the sheriff's office and district attorney would take over the investigation. If they didn't match or were inconclusive, there might still be a case for prosecution, but it would have to be built entirely on circumstantial evidence. Either way, it seemed my job was done.

24

Saturday, April 6

The tall, thin man at my door said, "I'm Dave Blodgett. I'm doing some work on the old house up the street."

"So you're working for Barry Walker?" I asked.

"Right. I'm digging out the basement. I was wondering if you had a work light that I can borrow for a few minutes. The lady next door thought that you might have one."

"What kind of work light?"

"Something that I can lower down into a hole. I've been breaking-up the basement floor with a jackhammer, and I punched into an open space under the concrete."

Martha asked, "Like a bomb shelter? Or a hidden passage?"

"I don't know," he said. "I lost my jackhammer. I need to lower a light down the hole, so I can get it out of there."

I led Dave out to the garage where I found a drop-light on the end of a twenty-five-foot cord. I asked, "Is this what you're looking for?"

"That's perfect. Want to come along?"

It's hard to resist the prospect of discovering a hidden passage in a 125-year-old house, so I went with Dave back up the street to Jill's old house. Inside, I saw that all of the interior walls had been stripped out to the studs. In the back corner, a narrow stairway led down into the basement. As we approached the stairway, we heard footsteps coming up from below. Carlton McDermitt appeared, looking flustered.

"Just checking on the progress," he said with a nervous laugh. "Got to make sure you're doing it right."

Dave acknowledged Carlton's lame attempt at humor with a perfunctory chuckle. "We're going to check out a hole under the slab."

Looking suddenly interested, Carlton asked, "A hole? What kind of hole?"

"That's what we're going to find out," Dave said.

Carlton tagged along as Dave led the way down into the basement. I took note of the work that he'd already done. While most of the old basement floor was still intact, Dave had broken up the concrete all around the perimeter and was in the process of digging a trench three feet wide and three feet deep next to the foundation wall. I had to duck my head in order to clear the floor joists above.

"This was built for short people," I commented just before realizing that Carlton was able to stand up straight without difficulty.

"That's why I'm digging it out. We'll have an eight-foot ceiling when I'm done," Dave explained.

"So where's this hole?" Carlton asked.

Dave led us over to the corner beneath the kitchen. Right at the edge of the trench he'd been digging, there was a dark hole about a foot wide.

"There's water down there," Dave said. "I heard a splash when my jackhammer fell in."

"That doesn't sound like good news for the jackhammer," I observed.

Carlton nudged me aside to look down the hole. "I can't see anything," he said.

Dave took the drop-light and plugged it into an electrical outlet that hung from the floor joists above. He squeezed past Carlton and lowered the light into the dark hole. From where I was standing, I could see the neat stonework on the wall of what appeared to be an old well.

Excitedly, Carlton took the drop cord from Dave and poked his face into the hole. He lowered the light further in and said, "It looks like some kind of well. It goes down about fifteen feet. There's water in the bottom."

Dave and I took turns looking down the hole after Carlton finally moved aside. The well was about four feet in diameter and was completely lined with stone.

"I can see the jackhammer. It's in the water, but it looks pretty shallow. With the right kind of hook on the end of a rope, I think I can snag the handle and pull it up. Either of you have anything that'll work?"

Shaking my head, I said, "No. But we ought to be able to conjure something up."

Dave snapped his fingers. "The old kitchen cabinets are in the garage. There's a dishtowel rack that we ought to be able to bend into a hook."

I located the dishtowel rack and unscrewed it from the cabinet door. The towel bar was about a quarter-inch thick and appeared to be made of mild steel. We cut off the ends and hammered it into a kind of a giant fishhook. Carlton brought a small coil of nylon cord, which we tied to the hook.

After several attempts, Dave was able to snag the jackhammer and pull it up from the hole. While he and I inspected the jackhammer, Carlton peered down into the hole.

"I think it's an old water well."

"That would make sense," Dave said. "In 1887, there probably was no city water here, so they dug a well directly beneath the kitchen. There probably was a hand pump on the kitchen sink so that people didn't have to go outside to get water—quite the modern convenience."

"Seems strange that someone would pour the slab right over the well," I commented.

Dave shrugged. "They probably didn't want to go to the trouble of hauling a bunch of dirt down here to fill it, so they just laid down boards and concreted right over it."

He pointed to the surface of the concrete, where I could now see a faint outline where the patch had been poured over the hole. "I don't know when they brought city water down to this neighborhood, but once they did, they wouldn't need the well anymore."

"It'd be fun to go down and look for artifacts," I said. "Sometimes people would drop things down their wells."

Carlton scoffed, "Oh, there wouldn't be anything down there." He quickly added, "I mean, the well was probably always covered, even before they poured the slab over the top. I doubt that anyone could have dropped anything down the well."

"Just the same, I'm going to take a look after I break up the rest of the slab," Dave said.

"When are you going to do that?" Carlton asked.

"Not for a while," Dave told him. "For one thing, I'm going to have to dry out the jackhammer. I don't know how long that'll take, but I don't want to electrocute myself."

"It ought to be dry by tomorrow," Carlton suggested.

"No hurry. I'll just finish digging the trench. Then we'll set the forms and pour the new walls. After that's done, we'll dig pits for the shoring.

Once we have the house supported, then I'll be ready to take out the rest of the old concrete."

"When will that be?" Carlton persisted.

"At least a week. Probably two. It's hard to say how long it'll take to get the new footings and walls done."

When we'd all seen what there was to see in the old well, Dave pulled up the light and coiled the cord. We made our way back upstairs, and Dave started explaining Barry's plan. Carlton excused himself and went out the back door.

"We're going to put a big steel beam across the middle of the house. That'll let us take out all of the interior walls on this floor. The kitchen will stay where it always has been. There'll be a pantry and a half bath at the back, and the rest will be wide open."

"Great view of the river now that the trees are gone," I commented.

"Yeah, Barry's counting on that to sell the place," Dave said.

25

Friday, April 19

There was nothing for me to do on the Tara Foster investigation until the completion of the lab analysis on the samples from her remains. If the lab could get a DNA profile and match it to the blood found on Damien Hamilton's boat, the case against John Prescott would be pretty solid. But even though DNA processing was no longer the months-long process it used to be, it was still not something that could be done in a hurry.

I drove to Salem to meet with Dennis Lawen and Walter Brooks to give a progress report and explain why I had stopped working the case. Brooks was waiting for me in the visitor's area at the Oregon State Penitentiary. We were led to a private room reserved for inmates' consultation with their attorneys.

When Lawen extended his hand, I pretended to be studying something in the folder I carried. I extracted a sheet of paper from the folder and handed it to Brooks.

"That is the lab report on the blood that we found on the boat where we believe Tara Foster was killed," I explained. "The specks of blood were found under the edges of the shore power connector and battery-selector switch. It's really quite remarkable that they were still there after all this time."

Lawen interrupted, "So the blood proves that the broad was killed on this boat?"

"That can't be proved. What it *might* prove is that Tara Foster was injured and bleeding while onboard the boat."

"What the hell good does that do me?"

"If the lab can generate a DNA profile for Tara Foster that matches this profile, then we'll know it was her blood on the boat. We already know that the owner of the boat was Foster's neighbor, and we have a witness who heard him invite her to go cruising. We have made a solid connection between the boat owner and the carpet used to wrap the victim's body. Taken together, this makes a pretty strong case for prosecution," I patiently explained.

"So who is this guy? Why is the name blacked out?" he asked, pointing at the documents.

"I blacked them out because he hasn't been charged. The last thing we want to do is prematurely tip him off that he's under investigation."

"I want to know who he is!"

"I'm not authorized to release that information," I told him, looking to Brooks for some help.

Brooks said, "Dennis, I'm sure that this case will be prosecuted. When charges are filed, you'll be the first person I notify."

I nodded. "As things stand right now, I've given the sheriff's office everything I found. The next step is to get the DNA match. But with or without a match, the sheriff is going to turn the case over to the district attorney."

"Does that mean I'm off the hook?" Lawen asked Brooks.

"Like I told you before, you were never on the hook. Nobody outside the news media ever accused you of doing this," Brooks told him.

"So will that broad on the TV news bat her eyelashes and give us that oh-so-concerned look like she did when she said, 'This looks like the work of Dennis Lawen,' when she eats her words?"

"Come on, Dennis, you know she won't ever retract what she said," Brooks said. "But once this guy is charged, nobody will even remember you."

I doubted that was true but kept my mouth shut. My guess was that whenever the subject of a body wrapped in carpet came up, in this case or any other, Dennis Lawen's name would come up with it.

I said, "I've given Mr. Brooks a complete summary of my investigation, including a detailed accounting for my expenses. We went beyond the fifteen thousand dollars you gave me, but I'm not going to bill you for that since I went forward without your prior approval."

Lawen shrugged indifferently. "Whatever. Does this mean you're finished?"

"It does, at least for now," I said. "If something develops that requires additional investigation, I'll contact Mr. Brooks. But at this time, I believe I've done all I can for you."

"Do I get a copy of that?" he asked, indicating the investigation folder.

Brooks held up a manila envelope and said, "I have a complete report here. I'll give it to you when the sheriff's office gives me the green light."

I stood, and Brooks followed suit. He motioned to the guard watching through a window at the side of the room. Lawen stood and again offered his hand. This time, I reluctantly took it as he expressed his thanks for my work. He still gave me the creeps.

It was mid-afternoon when I got back to my office. Martha was busy with an on-line course on the laws and rules for private investigators in Oregon. A couple of months back, she'd told me that she wanted to get her own license, and I encouraged her to give it a shot.

"I'll do it on my own time, but I'll need to use the office computer," she had said.

"Why don't we just call it career development and you can do it on the clock? Maybe set aside half a day every week for it."

My reasoning was that it would be a benefit to me for her to have a license because it would enable her to do a broader range of work. Friday afternoons had become her study time. Not wishing to be a distraction, I went down to my beach to do some more flood restoration work.

The spring rains had done a fairly good job of washing the fine silt down through the layer of sand on the level part of the beach. I was raking the sand to facilitate that process and to collect the many small fragments of plastic foam that had been deposited with the sand when Barry Walker came down the steps.

"I'm going to have a slab poured on my beach," he commented as he watched me work. "Then next time it floods, all I'll have to do is hose the mud off."

"How will you get the concrete down to the beach?" I asked.

"There's a concrete pumping company that'll do it. They'll run a hose under the railroad tracks. If you want to pour a slab here, we could share the cost."

"I'll give it some thought. I've been pretty happy with the grass here, but it looks like it's not going to grow through the sand, at least not this year."

"You don't have to mow concrete," someone from behind said.

I turned to see that Bud had joined the conversation.

"No, but you can't play croquet on concrete," I said.

"I've never see you play croquet," Bud said as he helped himself to a beer from my cooler.

I conceded. "I don't own a croquet set. I was just thinking ahead to my old age."

Barry said, "I'm going to set up a half court for basketball. You can't do that on grass."

"I'll stick with volleyball."

"No reason you can't play volleyball on concrete," he argued.

"I'd rather play on grass—or sand, if that's how it works out," I answered.

Bud said, "Yeah, beach volleyball with hot babes in bikinis. That's my vote."

Changing the subject, I asked Barry, "How are things going with Jill's old house?"

Barry groaned. "Don't even ask. You know, we're digging the basement deeper so that we can have eight-foot ceilings down there. I'm going to put two bedrooms and a bathroom in the basement."

"So what's the problem?" I asked.

"My worker left in the middle of the day on Wednesday and hasn't come back," Barry said. "He was working on the excavation, and getting ready to pour the slab, and now I can't get hold of him—doesn't answer his phone or anything."

"You mean Dave?" I asked. "I met him a couple of weeks ago, and he seemed like a pretty hard worker."

"Yeah, I don't know what happened," he said.

"Maybe he saw a ghost," Bud suggested.

Barry looked at him with a blank expression.

Bud said, "That house is haunted. Chuck told me that he saw ghosts in there all the time."

I said, "I think Chuck was just pulling your chain."

Barry said, "Haunted or not, I have a new guy coming in next week to finish digging. The concrete is coming in next Friday whether we're ready for it or not."

"So you already have the new walls cast?" I asked, purely out of curiosity.

"Right. We left the existing foundation alone and formed up a new wall inside of it," Barry said.

"So did Dave get that old well uncovered?" I asked.

"Yeah," Barry said, "That's what he was doing on Wednesday. He got the well opened up and started filling it with chunks of the old concrete floor—a lot easier than hauling it outside. Then he just left. He was supposed to have the excavation all done by this weekend."

"He was hoping to find some kind of artifacts in the well," I commented.

Bud speculated. "Maybe he found a sack of double eagles and took off to Acapulco to spend the rest of his life on the beach drinking Jamaican rum."

"It must've been something like that," Barry said. "But I really expected him to show up today to pick up his paycheck. Normally he'd be bugging me for an advance so he could pay his rent or something."

"That doesn't sound good," I noted.

"Well, there's nothing I can do but get somebody else to finish the job."

"It's a pretty aggressive remodeling job."

"When I'm finished, it'll be a whole new house inside the old shell," Barry explained. "Once you go through the door, everything you see will be brand new—big master suite upstairs, wide-open great room on the main, and the two more bedrooms downstairs."

"How long will all of that take?"

"I want to get it on the market at least by the middle of summer," he said. "I'm going to put in a dock and fix up the beach too. Carlton and Jill never did anything with the beach."

I said, "Well, not until Carlton bought his houseboat."

Barry just shook his head. "The flood was the best thing that could have happened to that. Anyway, we're going to clear-off all of the brush so that we can see what's actually there."

Bud got back into the conversation, saying, "You know, Daryl used a goat to clear the brush off of this whole area. It ate everything, including all of the blackberry brambles."

"I'm going to use a small excavator," Barry said. "I don't have time for a goat."

"How are you going to get an excavator down there?" Bud asked.

"The guy says he can drive it across the tracks. He'll lay down some timbers between the rails to make it a smoother ride."

"What if a train comes along?" Bud asked. The same question had occurred to me.

"He says he can get across in two minutes," Barry said. "I'll send guys up and down the track to give us an all clear, and then we'll just drive it over."

I just shrugged, knowing that Union Pacific would never approve of Barry's plan. They'd want a bushel of paperwork and insist on having their own flagmen out on the right-of-way at a cost of several thousand dollars. Barry's approach was far more efficient and cost effective, but I shudder to think what kind of liabilities he would encounter if the excavator broke down or got stuck on the tracks. Barry had the ability to close such thoughts out of his mind.

26

Monday, April 22

After working the weekend on the river, Monday should have been Kim's day off, but she'd volunteered to fill in for one of the deputies on the Clackamas River patrol while he attended a family funeral. The spring steelhead run was underway, and there'd be a lot of boat traffic. We got up early so that she could be on the river by seven.

I took advantage of the extra time to study some of the material given me by Leo Gilchrist in preparation for my still unscheduled appearance in tax court. He was insistent that I needed to have all of my answers memorized before any questions were asked because the IRS attorneys would pounce on any flaw in my testimony.

A few minutes before eight, Martha came in and tossed the morning newspaper onto my desk.

"How was Seattle?" I asked her.

"Oh, you know how it is when I visit my mother," Martha said. "She just wants me to move up there and get a different job. She still hasn't gotten over the whole thing with Trey Bourne."

"I understand a mother's concern."

"When were you ever a mother?" she asked.

"All I'm saying is that I understand why a mother would worry if her daughter had nearly gone over Willamette Falls."

"Well that isn't going to happen again."

"No, I certainly hope not. Anyway, it looks like Daryl's going to be taking his boat back pretty soon."

"Yeah, I talked with Kaylin again about renting her little studio apartment."

"Is that going to work out?"

"I think so. The only hitch might be if she decides to marry Kurt."

"You think that's going to happen?"

"I wouldn't be surprised. He spends a lot of nights over there."

"So do you have a backup plan?"

"Barry has the apartment above his garage. He's offered to rent it to me, but he wants way more than I want to spend."

I picked up the newspaper, and an article in the lower corner of the front-page caught my eye.

Missing Gladstone Man's Car Found

A 1993 Honda Accord found Saturday in a vacant lot in southeast Portland has been identified as belonging to David Blodgett, a Gladstone man reported missing on Thursday. Thirty-eight-year-old Blodgett failed to report to work last Thursday and has not been seen since. He had been working at a construction site in Oregon City and was last seen Wednesday morning.

Blodgett's car was found near Johnson Creek Blvd. and 74th Ave. by Portland Police, who traced the vehicle ID to the missing man. The vehicle reportedly had been vandalized and stripped. Police transported it to an impound facility for further investigation.

Witnesses in the area stated that the car had been there "for a couple of days." A spokesman for the police bureau said that it was unclear how the vehicle might be connected with Blodgett's disappearance.

"Isn't that the guy who was working on McDermitt's old house?" Martha asked.

I nodded and said, "Barry told me last Friday that Dave hadn't shown up for work for two days, but I just figured he must have gotten a better job."

"He seems like a nice guy. I hope nothing's happened to him."

"The car was found in the heart of 'felony flats.' That can't be good."

"Do you think he might have been carjacked?"

"I doubt it. I can't imagine that a twenty-year-old Honda would be worth risking a kidnapping charge."

"He carried a lot of tools in his car."

"Yeah, but who kidnaps someone to steal his tools?"

"He might have had a breakdown and had to abandon the car."

"True, but where is he?" I wondered.

"I'm just trying to be optimistic. But you're right, it doesn't look good," Martha said.

Later in the week, I heard the sound of machinery and walked up Water Street to see what was happening. Barry Walker and several others stood on the railroad grade, looking down toward the beach in front of the Applegate House. A small excavator was tearing out the blackberry brambles and vine maples that covered most of the area between the railroad tracks and the river's edge.

"I'm a-thinkin' you'd be needin' a permit to go diggin' up the riverbank," Carlton McDermitt said in his fake brogue.

Barry said, "No. I checked first."

I was skeptical of that. When there was something he wanted to do, Barry seldom inconvenienced himself by seeking permission from various bureaucracies. His approach was to get the job done and then deal with any consequences. In most instances, that worked for him.

Carlton said, "That bein' in the greenway makes all the difference, laddie."

"Greenway rules don't apply inside the city limits," Barry countered.

I honestly didn't know who was right. At that moment, I spotted an Oregon City Police cruiser driving slowly up Water Street. It parked in front of the Applegate House, and Officer Durham got out.

"Ah, laddie, it looks like you've drawn the attention of the local constabulary," Carlton said smugly.

Durham waved for us to join him up on the street, and then he addressed us as a group. "I suppose you've heard by now that David Blodgett's car was found."

Carlton's smug expression faded away.

"I'd like to ask a few questions, if you have a moment," Durham continued.

"I don't know anything about it," Carlton said quickly.

"He was here at lunch time last Wednesday," Barry said, "but I haven't seen him since."

Durham asked, "Do you have any idea why he would have driven up to Johnson Creek Boulevard?"

"No idea at all. It appeared that he simply locked up the house and left. Some of his tools are still there, right where he was using them."

"What kind of work was he doing?"

"Manual labor. He was in the basement breaking up the old concrete floor."

"Could he have injured himself? Maybe had to go get some kind of medical help?"

"I suppose it's possible, but I didn't see anything to suggest that he'd been hurt."

"How about you?" Durham asked, looking at Carlton.

Accent gone, Carlton said, "I wasn't around here that day. I was at my car lot, detailing cars."

"Were you acquainted with Blodgett?" Durham asked.

"Not really. I mean I talked to him, casual like, you know."

He seemed kind of uneasy. I figured he was probably afraid that Durham would mention the still-unpaid city fines resulting from his houseboat fiasco.

Carlton was saved from further embarrassment by the approach of Señora Valensueva, who immediately launched a loud monologue in Spanish that none of us understood.

Durham waved for her to stop talking. "Do you speak any English?" he asked.

That started her off on another speech that might have gone on indefinitely but for the appearance of Señora Valensueva's daughter Rosita.

"She ees telling you that she doesn't want other people parking their cars in the alley," Rosita told us.

Looking perplexed, Durham said, "Tell her that I'll move my car in a few minutes as soon as I finish talking with these people."

"No, she does not mean you—eet was last week. Someone left a car in the alley all afternoon."

"What day was that?"

After consulting with her mother in Spanish, Rosita said, "She says eet was the day the truck brought the wood."

She pointed to a large stack of lumber in the front yard of the Applegate house.

Durham turned to Barry and asked what day the lumber was delivered.

"Uh, that was Wednesday, in the morning," Barry answered.

"The last day Dave was here," Durham noted.

He turned to Rosita and asked, "Can your mother tell us what kind of car it was?"

Following another conversation with the señora, Rosita said, "She doesn't know what brand it was. She says it was old and trashy—a piece of sheet—and eet was the color of grapes."

"Did she see who parked it or who took it away?"

"She deed not see no people. Just the car."

Durham made some notes and said, "It might have something to do with Dave's disappearance, but most likely, it was just someone with car trouble. If you see the car again, call us, okay?"

Rosita nodded and then translated for her mother.

Durham looked at me and asked, "Do you know anything about this?"

I shook my head. "Only what I've read in the paper."

"Were you acquainted with Blodgett?"

"I met him a couple of weeks ago when he came over to borrow a work light. I've talked to him a couple of times since then."

"Did you see him last Wednesday?"

"I don't think so. I spent the whole day in front of a computer in my office."

Durham then asked the three of us, "Have any of you noticed anything unusual around here?"

There was a pause, and then Barry said, "It's strange. The day after Dave was last here, I found a McDonald's bag in the house. There was an untouched Big Mac, an order of fries and a Coke."

"You figure that was Blodgett's lunch?" Durham asked.

"Sure. I don't know who else would've brought lunch in."

"Was there anything else?"

"Just a few fragments of old pottery and things," Barry said and then quickly explained about Dave's discovery of the old well under the slab.

Durham wanted to see it for himself, so Barry showed the way. I followed along, but Carlton excused himself and headed back toward his place. With the old stairway gone, we had to climb down a ladder into the basement. The trench around the perimeter now held the freshly cast foundation.

There were four stacks of timbers supporting a pair of temporary beams that had been put in place to allow the removal of the load-bearing posts from beneath the heavy beam that ran across the center of the house.

Where each of the posts had been, Dave had broken up the concrete and dug a deep pit. In the bottom of each pit was a new concrete footing for the new, longer posts yet to be installed.

We picked our way around this maze of obstacles to the corner where the old well was. As Barry had told me, the well was now almost completely filled with broken concrete, but the ring of rocks defining the shape and location of the well was still visible. On top of the new foundation next to the well, there was a small collection of broken pieces of pottery, a china teacup, and a small glass bottle labeled Bernard's Cocaine.

"I figure Dave found that stuff in the well before he started filling it in," Barry told Durham.

"Where was the Happy Meal?" Durham asked.

"It was upstairs, sitting on a stack of lumber, as if Dave was getting ready to sit down and have lunch."

"Whatever made him decide to leave must have come up pretty quickly," Durham said. "And unexpectedly—a guy doesn't go out and buy lunch and then just walk away from it."

"Maybe someone brought the lunch to him, and Dave was already gone when it got here," I suggested.

Durham asked Barry, "Was anyone else working here."

Barry said, "Sure. There've been at least a dozen different guys— the men who set the concrete forms, the carpenters who built all of the temporary supports, laborers who helped get the dirt out when Dave dug the trench—but none of them were here that day."

"Have you talked with any of them since Dave disappeared?"

"Of course. But none of them knows anything. The only person I've found who saw Dave that day is the real estate lady next door. She says she saw Dave drive away at about one thirty."

I accompanied Officer Durham over to the house next door, where we found Kaylin Beatty pulling weeds from a flower bed.

"I'm looking into the disappearance of Dave Blodgett," Durham told her. "Barry Walker says you might have seen him leave."

Kaylin stood up and brushed some of the dirt from her hands. "Like I told Barry, I saw him drive away at about one thirty that day. It caught my attention because he seemed to be in a big hurry."

"How so?"

"Well, what got my attention was the sound of a big fish or something splashing in the river. When I stood up and looked around, I saw Dave just getting into his car. He revved the engine, and then he took off down toward Miller Street. It's the only time I ever saw him drive like that— real fast. And then he was gone."

"What were you doing at the time?"

"Same thing I'm doing now, pulling weeds, right over there," Kaylin said, pointing to a rock garden at the corner of her yard.

"Did you see anyone else or anything unusual that day?" Durham asked.

"No, but I hadn't been here very long. I showed a home for sale in West Linn and then came home about ten minutes before Dave drove away."

That evening I sat with Kim on the beach, watching the sunset and enjoying a glass of Rex Hill pinot noir.

I said, "Durham came by today, canvassing the neighborhood for any information about Dave's disappearance. It's odd. He left a hamburger and fries untouched and took off spinning his tires."

"Someone call him with an emergency?"

"That's what Durham figures. He's requesting Dave's cell phone records."

"You know, HVCU is working on this too," Kim said.

"How'd they get involved?" I wondered.

"When Portland Police identified Dave's car, they called our crime scene techs. They know that I spend a lot of time down here, so they were hoping that I might know something. They won't come right out and say it, but it's pretty clear they think Dave is dead."

"Did they find something in the car?"

She shook her head. "A few fingerprints. But the thing is, they can't find any reason for Dave to be where the car was found. They think it was dumped there by the perps."

"But no signs of violence?"

"Nothing. But the car was pretty well stripped. Whatever evidence might have been in it was taken out, along with the stereo, the doors, the seats, the wheels, and all the rest."

"I assume they've processed the prints."

"Yeah. They were in the local database—a couple of gangbanger wannabees. They pulled them in and grilled them pretty hard. They admitted that they prowled the car, looking for something to steal, but they say it was already stripped before they found it."

"A dead end?"

"Looks that way."

"But they still think he's dead?"

"Here's what they're thinking—either he made himself disappear or he's dead."

"It wouldn't be the first time someone decided to abandon everything and start over with a new identity in a different city." It occurred to me that the very same thing had been said when Tara Foster disappeared.

"True enough, but Dave doesn't fit the profile. No financial problems, no history of depression, no problems in his marriage. By all accounts, he was stable and content."

"Bud thinks he found a pot of gold and took off to Acapulco."

"That's as good a theory as any," she said.

"So what's next?" I asked.

"Well, you know how busy the detectives are. They'll follow up on the leads they have, but if nothing pans out, they'll suspend the investigation until something new comes up."

27

Wednesday, May 1

I was working at my computer when I heard the sound of a car pulling-up out front. It was an old Dodge minivan driven by a petite, dark-haired lady with a toddler in the backseat.

"I'm hoping you can help me find my husband," said the lady, who introduced herself as Dave Blodgett's wife, Carrie.

"First things first," I said. "When did you last see him?"

"It was April 17, two weeks ago. He left for work, to come down here and work on that old house," Carrie answered, pointing in the direction of Barry's project.

"The guy who owns the house told me that Dave was working on Wednesday but didn't come back on Thursday."

"He never came home Wednesday night," she said, tears appearing in her eyes.

"I'm sorry I have to ask this," I said, "but were you having any difficulties in your marriage?"

"No!" she said quickly. "There was nothing wrong."

"No reason he might want to simply take some time away?" I pressed.

"He wouldn't just leave without telling me," Carrie insisted.

"Has he ever taken off before?"

"No, never!"

"I assume you've filed a missing person report."

"Certainly. I reported him missing right away. Then they found his car, and it had been abandoned and stripped, but they haven't found a trace of Dave."

"Did he ever say anything to you about his job here?"

She thought for a moment. "He said he was helping to renovate the old house, and he was digging the basement deeper," she said. "He told me that some people stopped by and said that they'd lived there as kids and that someone had committed suicide in the house a long time ago."

"Anything else?"

"He said there was an old well under the house and he was hoping to find historical artifacts—like bottles or something—when he finished uncovering it. That was a few days before he disappeared."

I explained my rates to her, and I could see from the look of disappointment that formed on her face that she couldn't afford to pay me. On the other hand, it seemed like I'd be setting a low standard if I were to let a case like this in my own neighborhood go unsolved.

"Mr. Corrigan, I know that Dave is probably dead. It's the only thing that would keep him from contacting me. I don't have any money to pay you with right now, but I promise I'll find some way if you'll just find out what happened to Dave," she pleaded.

"I'll poke around and see if I can come up with anything. Maybe there's a witness the police didn't talk to. And don't worry about paying me—I'll do this in my spare time."

As if I had any spare time.

Bud took a long swig from the can of beer I had just handed him and then released a loud belch to assure me of his appreciation.

"You always seem to know what's going on around the neighborhood," I said. "I was hoping maybe you'd seen something around the Applegate House that might help me figure out what happened to Dave Blodgett."

"Like what?" Bud asked.

"Like anything," I said. "Comings and goings, maybe something Dave said, anything at all."

"I talked with him some. He told me all about the project there. That's about it."

"Nothing strange or out of the ordinary?"

"Well, there were those people who said the house is haunted."

"You mean Chuck Hampton?"

"No. Dave said a couple of old ladies stopped in and said that they'd lived there as kids and that the house was haunted."

"Oh yeah, Dave's wife mentioned them. It's a sad story, but I don't think ghosts made Dave disappear."

"Well, then there's Carlton. Dave said that he was being a real pest, always snooping around and looking over his shoulder, like some kind of stalker."

Something in what Bud said or the way he said it struck a chord. Jill had called Carlton a stalker too. But why on earth would he be stalking Dave?

"What about the other workers? The guys who set the forms for the new basement walls? Was there anything questionable about them?"

Bud shrugged. "They were mostly Mexican, but that don't mean nothing. It seems like they're the only ones doing that kind of work anymore."

"You ever see them arguing with Dave, anything like that?"

"Naw. They did their jobs and that was that."

"Anyone else hanging around there?"

"Not that I saw." After a pause to take another swig of beer, he said, "but I did see lights sometimes."

"Lights?"

"Yeah, like someone with a flashlight in there at night."

"When was that?"

"Oh, I couldn't say exactly. Pedro got loose in the middle of the night, and I chased him all the way down to Miller Street. When I went past the Applegate House, I saw the light," Bud explained before draining the last of his beer.

Pedro was Bud's Chihuahua.

"Can you say how long ago that was?" I pressed.

"It was two or three weeks ago, I guess."

"Before or after Dave disappeared?"

"Before," he said after giving the question some thought. "It had to be before because they still hadn't delivered that big load of lumber."

I recalled that the lumber had been delivered on the morning before Dave disappeared. That had come out during Officer Durham's conversation with Rosita Valensueva.

"Did you see who was in the house that night?" I asked.

"Naw. I was too busy trying to catch Pedro. Got another beer?"

The responsible thing to do would have been to lie and say I was all out, but I took his empty and went and got him a reload.

"Did you see a car anywhere around the house?"

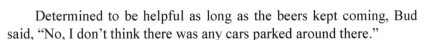

Determined to be helpful as long as the beers kept coming, Bud said, "No, I don't think there was any cars parked around there."

I had to wonder about Bud's observation skills. "Could there have been a car that you just didn't see?"

He looked mildly offended. "Hell no. If there'd been a car around, I'd have seen it."

"Maybe whoever was in there parked on Miller Street or Jerome Street," I suggested.

"I chased Pedro all the way down to Miller, and I didn't see any cars there," he said. "And you know there aren't any leftover parking spaces on Jerome Street."

The next time I saw Barry, it was early in the evening, and he was just walking up to Water Street from the beach. I asked him if he'd ever gone into the Applegate House in the middle of the night with a flashlight.

"No," Barry said. "Did you see someone in there at night?"

"I didn't, but Bud says he did," I answered.

"When was that?"

"Near as I can tell, it was shortly before Dave disappeared. Bud isn't sure of the exact day."

"There shouldn't have been *anyone* in there in the middle of the night," he insisted.

"Do you keep the house locked up?" I asked.

"Of course," he said. And then after a moment's thought, he added, "But we keep a key on the ledge over the front door. I suppose someone could have found it and let himself in."

"Any idea who would sneak in there in the middle of the night?" As soon as I asked the question, the word *stalker* flashed in my brain, and I immediately thought of Carlton.

"Dave maybe, if he left something behind, like his phone or something." I made a note to ask Carrie Blodgett if Dave had ever gone back to the Applegate House late at night. I also made a note to talk with Carlton McDermitt, who—according to Jill—had a key to the house.

28

Saturday, May 25

Bud said, "Something's really screwed up with the weather. Maybe there's something to that whole climate change thing after all."

I looked up at the perfectly clear blue sky and asked, "What're you complaining about? The weather is great."

"That's just it. It's Memorial weekend, and everybody knows it's supposed to rain. It *always* rains on Memorial weekend."

"We're way past due for this kind of weather," I countered. "It helps balance out things like blizzards and floods."

I'd spent most of the day on *Annabel Lee*, finishing the last of the wiring. It had been almost exactly a year since I first started working on the electrical systems, and I was anxious to move on to the next phase of the restoration—refinishing the interior woodwork.

But completion of the wiring project called for a celebration of some kind, and besides, it was too late in the afternoon to start a whole new project, so I went home to enjoy the rest of the day on the beach. Bud must have seen me carrying the cooler across the railroad tracks because he showed up moments after I sat down.

We heard the sound of an approaching boat, and at first I thought it sounded like Kim's patrol boat. Looking out across the water, I first realized that the approaching boat wasn't Kim's. Then as it swung into a wide loop off shore, I recognized it as one I'd seen a few times before.

It was one of those big, sleek jet boats that were popular in the 1970s, powered by a big block Oldsmobile V-8 attached to a Berkeley jet pump. They were long, low, and loud. They looked fast and sounded fast but, in reality, could be easily outrun by just about any tournament ski boat. I'm not sure what they're meant to do—you can't ski behind them, their cuddy cabin isn't tall enough to stand up in, they burn fuel at a fearsome rate, and they have seating for only four people. I've heard it said that such boat's primary purpose is to compensate for feelings of sexual inadequacy on the part of their owners. I wouldn't know.

This particular boat belonged to Chuck Hampton, who had an old dock on a little sliver of beach that he insisted had once been the end of Blanchard Street, which—according to Chuck—had never been vacated by the city and was thus open for public access, even though nobody could state with certainty that Blanchard Street had ever existed except on an old plat map. Chuck sometimes kept the old jet boat tied up there during the boating season, even though he lived somewhere on the other side of town.

The thing that caught my eye as I watched the boat rumble past was the pair of bikini-clad females on board. These were definitely eye-catching bikinis—minuscule patches of fabric tentatively held in place by frail strings and barely covering the essential features.

With their luxurious long hair blowing in the gentle breeze, these girls briefly made me admire Chuck, even though he was nowhere to be seen. The boat was in mid-river, about fifty yards off shore, circling at idle speed, and I couldn't tell if the ladies were simply showing off, in which case they were doing a pretty good job, or possibly waiting for Chuck to appear on shore for pickup.

Either way, they were interesting to watch—at first, anyway.

As they increased their turning radius, they cruised closer and closer to shore, and the nearer they got, the more it became apparent how mistaken I'd been in my initial impression. At a hundred feet, they started to look a bit worn. At seventy-five feet, they looked—as the cowboys say—like they'd been rode hard and put up wet. At fifty feet, they started looking more like longshoremen in drag than the babes I originally thought them to be. I made a mental note to see an optometrist.

"Pretty nice, huh?" Bud commented with a chuckle.

"Well, they looked good from a distance," I commented.

"The redhead is Sheila something-or-other. She kinda lives with Chuck. She got out of Coffee Creek a few months ago, and sometimes she works for him. I saw her swinging a sledge-hammer, busting up concrete, at the old house Chuck's fixing up on Hedges Street."

"Coffee Creek? She was in prison?"

"Oh yeah. She did about five years for hiring some guy to kill her boyfriend. The hit man botched the job, and the boyfriend lived. Somehow the hit man beat the rap, but Sheila wasn't so lucky."

"She tried to have her boyfriend murdered and Chuck lets her live with him?" I asked, incredulous.

"Go figure. Must be a damn good lay."

"Who's the blonde?"

"Oh, that's Sheila's girlfriend. I heard they were an item when they were in prison together. She lives with Chuck too. I guess they have some kind of a three-way thing going." Bud took a long gulp of beer. "Hey, speak of the devil, here comes Chuck now."

I turned to see him walking up Water Street with Kaylin Beatty, heading our way. Kaylin was carrying a folder full of papers, which probably meant that she was handling another of Chuck's many real estate transactions.

"Mind if I wave my boat in here?" Chuck asked.

"No, bring it on in," I said, even though the last thing I wanted was a better look at Sheila and her girlfriend. Fortunately, they didn't tie up. They just pulled in close enough for Chuck to step aboard. He took the controls, and with a ground shaking roar, they headed up river.

"Chuck buying another house?" I asked Kaylin.

She said, "No. This time he's selling one. Know anyone who wants a nice little cottage on Fourth Avenue?"

"You mean the sewage house?" Bud asked.

"It's all cleaned up and redecorated," Kaylin explained. "You'd never know that anything ever happened. It's one of Chuck's better jobs."

The "sewage house" was the victim of an unfortunate accident involving a piece of lumber that somehow found its way into the city sewer line and lodged just downstream from the house that was soon to earn its derogatory nickname. For two weeks, while the owners were on vacation, all of the sewage from a dozen or more homes uphill backed up and flowed into the recently finished basement master suite. The owners returned home to find a five-foot-deep pool of raw sewage simmering in the August heat.

They spent the next two years trying to collect compensation from the city, who turned it over to their insurance company, which refused to accept liability and blamed the whole thing on a contractor, despite there being no evidence to prove who was actually at fault. Eventually the property was decontaminated and put on the market, but it was so stigmatized that nobody would go near it. Chuck picked it up for next to nothing and put it back into livable condition. Now it remained to be seen if Kaylin could find a buyer for what may forever be known in the neighborhood as the sewage house.

"Hey," Bud said suddenly, "I have a great opening line for your newspaper ad!"

Even knowing what was coming, Kaylin had to ask, "What's that?"

"This is no shit!" Bud roared with laughter. "Indoor pool—cesspool, that is."

Kaylin looked to the sky. This kind of thing wasn't going to make the job any easier.

Wiping tears from his eyes, Bud said, "Two bedrooms upstairs and a turd bedroom downstairs."

"You're not helping," Kaylin complained.

"If any of the neighbors come around," Bud continued, "you just tell them that you're not going to take any more crap from them."

Kim's boat coming downriver saved me from any more of this. I excused myself and went up to the house to get some charcoal for the barbecue.

29

Thursday, June 6

My first phone call of the day was from Michael Wheeler. "John Prescott is coming in for an interview. I thought maybe you'd like to sit in."

"Sure, I'd like to hear what he has to say," I said. "He's coming in voluntarily? That surprises me."

"It's kind of strange," Wheeler agreed. "We told him we'd like to talk to him about Tara Foster, and right away he volunteered to drive down from Tacoma."

"Maybe he's one of those guys who think they can outsmart you in the interrogation room."

Two hours later, I sat in an interview room at the sheriff's Sunnybrook headquarters. John Prescott and Michael Wheeler sat facing one another across a small table. I was off to the side, not part of the interview.

After the preliminaries, Wheeler asked, "You were acquainted with Tara Foster, right?"

"That's right," Prescott answered.

"What was the nature of your relationship with her?"

"I wouldn't exactly say we had a relationship."

"Come on, John. Were you dating her? Were you intimate?" Wheeler pressed.

Prescott objected. "We were just neighbors. We talked a few times, but we never went out."

Wheeler abruptly changed direction. "You used to own a 1964 Chris Craft Constellation."

"That's right."

"Was Tara Foster ever onboard that boat?"

Prescott looked momentarily confused and then said, "Well, yes. She spent an afternoon on the boat once."

Wheeler leaned in and said, "You just told me that you'd never dated her."

Taken aback by Wheeler's aggressive tone, Prescott said defensively, "It wasn't a date! We just went for a boat ride."

"When was that?"

"I couldn't begin to guess the date. It was eleven or twelve years ago."

"Thirteen, at least," Wheeler corrected. "What time of year was it?"

"I suppose it was in June. It was Rose Festival."

"Rose Festival?"

"Yeah, they had the big carnival set up in Waterfront Park. I wanted to see the Navy ships tied up in Portland."

"So let me get this straight. You took Foster on a boat trip to Portland?"

"Yeah. She wanted to go through the locks at Willamette Falls, so we went on down to Portland, and the Rose Festival was going on."

"You spent all day on your boat with her? Did she get injured while on the boat?"

"Not that I recall."

"Maybe cut her finger or had a bloody nose?"

"No, nothing like that."

Wheeler persisted. "Like *what*, then?"

Prescott, showing some irritation, said, "Like *nothing*! She didn't get hurt."

"Then how is it that her blood was found on your boat?" Wheeler asked, knowing that he'd caught Prescott in a second lie.

"That's impossible."

Wheeler smiled grimly. "DNA doesn't lie, John. Tara Foster's blood was on your boat. How do you explain that?"

Prescott looked baffled. "Well, maybe she did cut herself, but I didn't see it."

"You were on the boat with her all day—just you and Tara Foster, and you don't know if she cut herself?"

"It wasn't just us. There were other people there," Prescott said, surprising both Wheeler and me.

"Who? Who else was along?" Wheeler demanded.

"I don't remember their names. They weren't people I knew," Prescott claimed.

"Hold it. Let me understand this," Wheeler said in a patronizing voice. "You invited people you didn't even know to spend the day on your boat with you and your girlfriend?"

"She wasn't my girlfriend," Prescott protested. "The other people were *her* friends, not mine. I never saw them before—or since."

Wheeler took a deep breath and paused long enough to make it uncomfortable. Finally he said, "Why don't you just tell me about that boat ride?"

Prescott looked at Wheeler then at me, as though looking for some kind of help.

"Look, I hardly knew Tara," he began. "I talked to her a couple of times at the pool at the condos where we lived. That was about it. I told her I was thinking about cruising down to Portland and invited her along, but she didn't say yes or no.

Next time I saw her, a day or two later, she asked, if I was still thinking about making the trip and if I would be taking the boat through the locks at Willamette Falls. I said yes, and she got kind of excited— you know, about going through the locks.

And then she said she had some friends who'd really like to go along because they always wanted to go through the locks and they were on some kind of historical committee that was trying to preserve the locks, or something like that. I said, 'Sure, bring them along.' I figured if that's what it took to get her to go on the cruise, it was okay with me."

Wheeler looked skeptical and asked, "You invited her to bring another couple along on your date?"

"I told you, it wasn't a date," Prescott insisted. "It was just a boat ride. Look, I wanted to get to know Tara better. If it took a day of entertaining her friends to do that, I was willing. It isn't like we were doing some kind of a Love Boat cruise."

"Okay, okay." Wheeler relented. "Who were these people? What were their names?"

"Hell, I don't remember! It was thirteen years ago. Who remembers names that far back?"

"Come on, John, help me out here."

Prescott shook his head. "I think the lady's name was Jamie—or something like that."

"Jamie," Wheeler repeated. "How about a last name?"

"I don't think they ever said their last name. His name was something unusual."

"Unusual how?"

Prescott shrugged. "Just something out of the ordinary. I don't know.

"Okay, can you describe these people?"

"She had red hair and freckles. I remember because she was worried about getting sunburned."

"Anything else?" Wheeler prodded.

"I think she was fairly tall, like five nine or five ten. Good looking, but not, you know, like a supermodel or anything."

"And the man?"

"He was about the same height. He had a bushy mustache, kind of sandy color, I think. His hair was thin, like he was going bald. And he had an earring, something that looked like a diamond."

"How old?"

"Maybe thirty. I suppose they were both about thirty."

Once again, Wheeler changed direction. "Okay, so tell me about the boat ride."

"Well, they met me at the marina in the middle of the morning. It was a Saturday, maybe a week or two before I heard that Tara was missing. The other couple was with her. We started off downriver, cruising at maybe ten or twelve knots—"

"Wait," Wheeler interrupted. "You remember how fast you were going, but you can't remember the names of people you spent all day with?"

"Hey, I'm telling you what I remember, okay?" Prescott protested.

"All right. Go ahead."

"We got to the locks at about noon, and it took forty-five minutes to lock through. I had a bucket of chicken from KFC and potato salad in the refrigerator, so I told Tara and her friends where the plates and things were, and they put together a lunch. We ate that while we cruised down to Portland.

"When we got there, we circled offshore, looking at the carnival rides in Waterfront Park. There were lots of other boats on the water, and I had to be careful of people running across my bow. The jet skis were swarming like a bunch of gnats. We cruised up and down the row of navy ships, about a dozen of them.

"We hung around awhile and then headed back upstream. I had to make sure that we got through the locks before they closed. So we got into the locks sometime around five o'clock, and everything was going fine. But when we were halfway through, something broke, and we were trapped in there.

"It took them *hours* to get the upstream gate to open so that we could start for home. By then, it was dark, and I didn't want to try to run up to Wilsonville by moonlight. There are some shallow areas in there, bedrock, and I didn't want to take a chance on running aground. So I pulled in at the public dock in West Linn.

"We scrounged up what we could find for food and then played cards for awhile. I was bushed. You know, it's kind of stressful keeping a boat that big under control for four hours in the locks, while they fill and drain and refill over and over. Anyway, I was beat and I'd had a few drinks, so I went below to sack out."

Wheeler said, "What about the others? You just left them there?"

"No, I showed them the bunks in the salon and second stateroom. They said they were going to stay up awhile, so I left 'em playing cards on deck. I went out like a light. In the morning, Tara was gone. The guy—I think his name might have been Calvin—said that Tara had called someone to give her a ride home.

It was raining when I got up in the morning. We got underway fairly early and got back to Wilsonville before nine. Calvin, or whoever he was, and his wife went up to their car. I never saw them again."

"What else happened that night?"

"Nothing special. We played cards, had a couple of drinks, and that was it."

"What happened to the carpet from the rear deck?"

"Oh, yeah." Prescott said. "First thing that morning, I noticed it was missing, and I asked Calvin about it. He said—I had this little glass kerosene lantern, just for atmosphere, you know—and Calvin said that he'd accidentally knocked it off the table while trying to light a joint and the kerosene spilled across the carpet. He said he had to throw it overboard to keep from setting the boat on fire."

"Hold it. Let me understand this. He knocked the lantern over and set the carpet on fire?" Wheeler repeated.

"Right. That's what he said, and he had to throw it overboard to put the fire out. He gave me three hundred dollars to replace the carpet, but I never did."

"Was there any damage from the fire?"

"None that I could find. I guess he got the carpet out of there before anything else got scorched."

"Was there anything else missing besides the carpet?"

"The little lantern was gone," Prescott said.

"Anything else?"

"Not that I recall."

"An anchor, maybe?" Wheeler coached.

Prescott said, "No, the anchors were still onboard."

Speaking for the first time, I asked, "Did you carry a dinghy on your boat?"

"I carried a little inflatable," he said, "like a Zodiac."

"And you had it along on that cruise?"

"Of course, but it was in its bag," Prescott said. "It was folded up and stored on the deck up forward."

"Did you carry an anchor for the Zodiac?" Wheeler asked.

"Well, sure," Prescott answered.

"What kind of anchor did you use?" I asked.

"Just a regular anchor," he said.

"What style? How big?" I asked.

"It was a cast-iron anchor. I think they call it a navy anchor, about ten or fifteen pounds," Prescott said.

"What happened to that anchor?" Wheeler asked.

"I have no idea," Prescott said. "Look, around boats, sometimes things get lost. One day I looked for the anchor and couldn't find it. No big deal, I just bought another one."

"I know where your anchor is," Wheeler said.

Prescott looked at him with a curious expression but said nothing.

"It's in the evidence room downstairs, along with the carpet off your boat," Wheeler said. "Funny thing, though, there aren't any burn marks in the carpet. You know what we found in the carpet?"

Prescott's eyes widened.

"We found Tara Foster all wrapped up in *your* carpet—with *your* missing anchor."

"You aren't serious…" Prescott began.

"What do you think this is all about, John?" Wheeler asked. "It's about how you killed Tara Foster, rolled her up in the carpet and threw her overboard. That's what it's about!"

"No! I didn't do *anything* to her! She was fine when I went to bed," Prescott insisted.

"And in the morning, she was gone, and you didn't know anything about it," Wheeler said in a mocking tone of voice.

"That's right. Just like I told you."

"You expect me to believe that?"

"It's the truth! You *have* to believe it!"

The interview went on for another hour, going back over and over the story, but nothing more came out of it. In the end, Wheeler had to turn Prescott loose. The story he'd told us, while implausible, was consistent with all of the known facts and evidence.

I won't say that I believed his story, but he really was fairly convincing. I hadn't seen any of the telltale signs of dishonesty—nervousness, sweating, evasiveness, lack of eye contact—during his entire interview.

I told Deputy Wheeler, "In my opinion, either Prescott was telling the truth or he's an unusually good liar."

Wheeler scoffed, "That's the thing about sociopaths—they're *always* good liars."

"Where do we go from here?"

"We'll check with the DA. If she thinks they can prosecute with what we have, then we'll make the arrest."

"What about this Calvin character?"

"I don't have time to look for him. Do you?"

"He's your 'alternate suspect' defense. If this thing goes to trial, you can bet that Prescott's attorney will make the most of it."

With a sigh, Wheeler said, "Yeah, I know. But I've already spent time on this case that I don't have. Jamieson will have my ass if I go looking for someone who probably doesn't exist and might—or might not—be named Calvin."

"If the DA doesn't take the case, I'll have to tell Dennis Lawen that it's still open. He'll insist that I go looking for Calvin."

Wheeler brightened. "That works out for both of us then, doesn't it? You get more of Lawen's money, and I can get back to what I'm supposed to be doing."

"Do me a favor, and run that past Jamieson first," I said. "I'm getting a little bit uneasy about being this far into your business."

"You got it," he said. "But first, let's see what the DA says."

I was disappointed when Wheeler called back the next day to say that the district attorney wouldn't touch the case as it stood. Still, I understood her position. She could do a ton of work and spend a ton of Clackamas County money, but the chances of getting a conviction were slim to none.

To Martha, I said, "Will you go through everything on Tara Foster and see if you can find anyone named Jamie or Calvin? Check neighbors, friends, relatives, coworkers, and anyone else you can think of. And look for organizations interested in preserving the Willamette Falls Locks."

"What are *you* going to do?" she asked.

"I'm going to contact Walter Brooks and see if Lawen wants me to reopen my investigation. But I already know what his answer will be. Let's find those people."

I was right. Lawen said, "Get to work. Find them—or prove that there is no Calvin or Jamie."

I really needed to clear my mind, so I packed up a few things and headed down to *Annabel Lee*, leaving Martha to suffer alone. I went to work stripping layers of varnish that had accumulated on the hardwood paneling during the last century and a half. Even the so-called fumeless stripping chemicals require the use of a respirator mask. I worked until my arms ached from scraping old varnish and my brain was numb from breathing fumes. I resolved to get a couple of big fans before resuming the job—anything to get some airflow through the cabin.

After I got home, I walked down Water Street, which was blocked by a concrete truck parked in front of Jill's house—the Applegate House. The alley was blocked by a pair of pickup trucks, and half a dozen workers were busy washing concrete-finishing tools and rinsing out the truck. Always curious about what's going on around the neighborhood, I picked my way through a gauntlet of construction debris to take a look.

Through the windowless opening in the foundation, I could see the freshly finished concrete floor in the basement glistening under temporary floodlights. The workers were all talking to each other in Spanish, so I turned to leave.

"Looking pretty good, isn't it?"

I looked back and saw Barry stepping over the stream of runoff from the concrete chute.

"Yeah, that's a big step forward. It actually looks like something other than a West Virginia coal mine, for a change," I kidded.

Changing the subject, Barry said, "Hey, you have a lot of friends in the sheriff's office. Have they come up with anything about Dave?"

"Not much. They've looked over his phone records, and the only calls on the day he disappeared were from his wife trying to contact him when he didn't come home after work. I think they're tracing the tower pings to see if they can figure out where Dave went that day. Beyond that, they don't have a thing.

"They checked at McDonalds to see who bought Big Mac meals that day. But of course, most people there pay in cash, and there's no way to track them down. Still, a few used credit or debit cards, so they have some names to track down. It's a long shot, but maybe they'll find someone who took lunch to Dave. All they know for sure right now is that if Dave bought it himself, he didn't use a credit card."

30

Monday, June 17

Martha had managed to come up with three different organizations that had actively campaigned for the preservation of the Willamette Falls Locks. Of those, only one was still operating, and I learned from the executive director, a very helpful lady named Sandy, that there wasn't an actual membership list—just an email list, which contained over a thousand names.

Named the Willamette Falls Heritage Foundation, they operated completely on a voluntary basis, and the staff was made up of the executive director and one or two office helpers. None of these individuals could recall any volunteers named Jamie or Calvin, but they were quick to point out that volunteers came and went. It was entirely possible that the couple had joined one of the organizations that melded to form the heritage foundation.

It was a disappointment, but hardly a surprise. A part of me really wanted to find the mystery couple and vindicate John Prescott because he had struck me as an okay guy. He didn't seem to be holding anything back, and everything he said conformed with the evidence we had. The fact that we hadn't been able to find Jamie and Calvin didn't mean that no such couple existed. The ongoing possibility that they *did* exist was the main reason the DA declined to prosecute Prescott.

I explained to Martha, "Over the weekend, I got to thinking that maybe Calvin was a last name instead of a first name. So I checked the white pages online and found about a hundred people in Oregon with the last name *Calvin*."

"I'm surprised there's that many," she said.

"I've eliminated about half of them because they're too young or too old. Prescott guessed the age of the couple on the boat to be about thirty. That would put them in their mid-forties now. I allowed a range of forty to fifty-five and ended up with forty-seven names."

Martha quickly scanned the list and said, "I don't see anyone named Jamie."

"Well, Mr. Calvin might not be married to Jamie anymore. Or maybe her name is Jane or something else similar to Jamie—Prescott wasn't sure. We'll just have to let that go for now and contact *all* of the Calvins of the right age."

"That's gonna take awhile," she lamented.

"It'll probably take you at least a couple of days to reach them all by phone."

I handed her a script that I'd prepared.

Hello, Mr. Calvin. I'm Martha with the Willamette Falls Locks Preservation Council in West Linn. I'm calling tonight because, as you may know, the Army Corps of Engineers is no longer providing funding for the maintenance of this nationally recognized historical landmark. We are working with other organizations to bring public attention to the situation and attempting to get state and federal agencies to work together to preserve the locks and keep them operating. The Willamette Falls Locks opened in 1873 and are the oldest operating multi-lift locks in the United States. Would you care to learn more about this?

John Prescott had said that the reason Tara Foster's friends were interested in joining them on the day cruise to Portland was that they were interested in preserving the Willamette Falls Locks. I figured that if they were interested then, they'd still be interested. Martha would not try to hit them up for any kind of donation, but she would ask for email addresses so she could send them a newsletter.

Our community service for the week would be to give any addresses we got to Sandy at the Willamette Falls Heritage Foundation, who would be happy to put our people on their newsletter list. And we would have a short list of candidates for our couple.

Martha did a great job of talking with the people. If she could get them to talk, she'd ask what part of the state they lived in—even though we already had that information from White Pages—and then she'd ask if they'd ever visited the Willamette Falls Locks, or had the opportunity to actually go through them on a boat.

After three days, she had talked with nearly everyone on our list. One hung up immediately, and another had recently passed away. She got seventeen email addresses for the newsletter, but only one person said that he'd seen the locks—from the Oregon City arch bridge, not from a boat.

It didn't mean absolutely that our couple's last name wasn't Calvin, but it was as far as we could take that screening. Maybe our couple moved out of state. More likely, Calvin was a first name, rather than a last. And there still was the possibility that the mystery couple was a complete fiction created by John Prescott.

Another angle we were working on was the possibility that Calvin and Jamie were people Tara Foster knew through her employment at The Museum of the Oregon Territory. Unfortunately, the difficult financial times in the past few years had resulted in a nearly complete turnover in personnel at the museum, and in fact, the museum had only recently re-opened after a three-year closure due to lack of funding. Nobody at the museum knew anything about prior employees.

I was able to look at records kept by the Clackamas County Historical Society, who owns and operates the museum, and confirmed that Tara Foster had been assistant to the director from 1992 until she disappeared in 2000. There was no record of any employee with a first or last name of Calvin.

But none of that precluded the possibility—in fact the likelihood— that Tara had met Jamie and Calvin as a result of her employment at the museum. After all, their common bond was an interest in history. It may have been as simple as one or the other visiting the museum and striking up a conversation with Tara Foster.

I scanned through the museum's current mailing list and failed to find anyone whose first name was Calvin. I found someone named Jamie, but she turned out to be too young to be the lady on Prescott's boat.

I dreaded the task, but my last resort would be to screen everyone whose first name was Calvin or Jamie. We'd start with Oregon City and West Linn because that seemed where we'd be most likely to find someone who had been interested in the locks in 2000. It would take Martha a couple of weeks to do that. But if we had to go statewide in our search, it could take months. I couldn't commit to that without talking to my client.

For all who think that the life of a private investigator is all glamour and action, the way it's portrayed on television, I offer you this glimpse of reality. Sometimes you sit around for hours, wracking your brain to find a way to scrape up the little piece of information that can solve a case—or might instead mean nothing.

Other times, you just say, "Hell with it. Let's go skiing."

It was a beautiful afternoon, and Kim had the day off. There were no boats in sight, the sun was out and the water was as smooth.

"You need to take a break," I said to Martha. "I'll bring the combos. This is going to be the day you learn to ski."

"Oh God, help me," she said. But she didn't run and hide.

We went a short distance upriver, where a ski club maintained a slalom course—not that either of us considered ourselves to be tournament skiers, but it was always fun and challenging to ski the buoys.

With Martha spotting, Kim went first, and she fairly cut the river to pieces at her standard speed of 32 mph. There is a true grace in the movement of a skilled slalom skier.

She shortened the tow rope by twenty-eight feet and cleared five of the six buoys—a very tough act to follow.

Setting out to show her up, I shortened the rope to thirty-two off and told her to give me 34 mph. I made some good practice turns on the open water, and when I felt I was warmed up, I pointed at the buoys.

Kim lined up and fine-tuned the throttle. I cut right and cleared the first buoy, already stretched out and leaning into my left turn. I accelerated across the wake, moving at twice the speed of the boat, before cutting hard into my right turn. I cleared the buoy but was too close. I tried to recover my rhythm as I shot back across the wake and leaned hard to my left.

Good sense would have told me to let go of the rope. The turn wasn't any good. I was too deep into it a split second too soon. But I tried to save it. The result was that my center of gravity moved forward a fraction of an inch too far, and I went cartwheeling over the tip of the ski. There is nothing graceful about a face-plant at fifty miles an hour. I was fortunate that both feet left the bindings at the same time when the ski dug in and stopped.

My pride was my worst injury, though a bloody nose did contribute to the overall effect. It really wasn't my best day on a ski.

After that spectacular exhibition, it wasn't easy to coax Martha into giving it a try.

"Don't worry," Kim assured her. "Unless you act like a jerk, things like that won't happen to you."

Sophisticated adult that I am, I chose to ignore that little jab and said, "Keep your arms straight and your knees bent. Start with your knees right up under your chin, and don't stand up until you're clear out of the water."

After she jumped in and put on the combos, I reset the rope to full length and tossed her the handle. Kim idled forward, slowly taking up the slack.

"Okay, keep the tips out of the water and the rope between them, knees bent," I coached.

She wobbled and got turned sideways. Kim pulled the throttle back to neutral, while Martha pulled herself back into position. Again, Kim eased back into gear and took up the slack.

"Hit it!" Martha said.

Kim pushed the throttle forward, and Martha popped up onto the surface. The boat quickly picked up speed, even as Kim eased off the throttle, and she settled in at 24 mph, which seemed to be a comfortable speed for Martha.

It took only a few minutes for her to get the feel for what she was doing, and then she steered herself out to the left side of the wake. She held her position there for a fairly long time, then eased back behind the boat, across the wake and out to the right.

Now I'm not going to tell you that she looked like a pro or anything close to it. She still hunched forward, as all beginning skiers do, and she still had trouble keeping the tow rope taut, but all in all, she had a great first day on water skis.

When afternoon turned toward evening, more boats started appearing on the river, many of them the bloated wake makers that are so popular these days. When the water got too choppy, we went back to the dock to cremate some chicken and sip some wine.

All of that vastly improved my outlook, but we still weren't any closer to finding Jamie and Calvin.

31

Thursday, June 20

Looking at the email I'd just received from Michael Wheeler, I said to Martha, "Well, that takes care of John Prescott."

"They nailed him?" Martha asked.

"Afraid not," I admitted. "He's not our guy. He voluntarily took a polygraph and passed with flying colors."

"Well, you said he struck you as an honest guy. I guess he is," she said sadly. "So what's next?"

"If Prescott was telling the truth—and the polygraph says he was—then there really *was* a couple named Jamie and Calvin on his boat the day Tara Foster disappeared."

"So that makes them our new number-one suspects."

"They have to be, but that's the problem. We've already tracked down everyone with the *last* name of Calvin and came up empty, and there's no search engine online that will do a search based only on the first name. We'll have to get our hands on old phone directories and plod through them line by line. Honestly, I doubt that Dennis Lawen can afford to pay for that."

"There *might* be another way," Martha said tentatively.

"I'm listening."

"Well, a couple of years ago, before my son went off to college, he and a friend were fooling around on my computer. When I asked what they were doing, they said that they were looking up a girl they'd met at the skateboard park."

"That's hardly a new concept," I observed.

"Yeah, but the thing is, all they had was her first name."

Now interested, I asked, "Are you telling me that they had a way to do that search?"

"I'm not sure how they did it, but they did find the girl's last name. Maybe they hacked into the cell-phone company's database. But what I know for sure is that all they had was her first name."

"Your son is a computer hacker?" I asked.

"No, but I think that might be an accurate description of his friend," Martha said. "He was a foreign kid—from India, I think. But he was really sharp with computers."

"And you think he might know of a way to find Calvin with just his first name?"

"It's worth a try, isn't it? I can call Jason and find out if the kid is still around."

After a long phone conversation with Jason, Martha hung up the phone and said, "He's going to text his old friend and find out if he knows how to do what we want. His friend will email us with the answer."

An hour later, we received an email that said:

hello mrs hoskins jason sez u need 2 find some body by 1st name i have program attachd hope it helps shahzad

For the thousandth time, I wondered about the future of communication. Don't kids know about capital letters and punctuation? Reluctantly, I clicked on the attachment, which turned out to be a self-extracting zip file. It didn't trigger any spyware or virus alarms, so I clicked on Setup and waited a few seconds for it to install.

When I opened the program, it looked like some primitive relic from the DOS age. There was a box where I could enter a first name, a box for a last name, and a box for a zip code. I entered *Calvin* in the first box, 97045 in the third box, and left the second box blank. When I pressed Enter, the screen went blank.

Then a name came up: Calvin Anderson. It was followed quickly by another name, and then a whole list of names cascaded down the screen until I had a list of everyone in Oregon City with the first name of Calvin. When I clicked on Calvin Anderson's name, the software returned a street address, home phone, and cell phone number. Shahzad, it appeared, had found a back door into one or more of the huge online databases and used his own search utility to do the first-name search. It was actually pretty cool.

The three-page list of Calvins presented a daunting task for screening, but it wasn't insurmountable. I sent a quick email thanking Shahzad for the software and asking what I owed him. The message I got back was one word: *whatever.* But he included a PayPal account, so I sent him twenty bucks. If he'd asked for two hundred, I'd have happily paid it, but I saw no reason to reward his indifferent attitude.

Martha went to work screening the list of Calvins, while I pondered the very real possibility that our guy wasn't on that list. He might have been from a neighboring community with a different zip code, and if we didn't find him in 97045, we'd have to start going through the long list of others. Using the same script as before, Martha went to work.

It was also quite possible that Calvin wasn't the actual name. Prescott hadn't been sure. And even if there had been a real person named Calvin in the area thirteen years ago, there was no guarantee that he was still around. But we simply had to play the cards dealt us. If it didn't pan out, well, that was the way it was in this business.

I focused on tracking down people through the historical society, looking for anybody who could remember anything about Tara Foster. I still believed that whoever Jamie and Calvin were, their connection to Tara was most likely the museum. One of the few people currently associated with the museum who had been there back in the 1990s was Marilyn Hamilton, current president of the historical society.

"I was there when the museum opened in 1990," Marilyn told me in answer to my question.

"Then you knew Tara Foster," I said.

"Sure. We're really a pretty small operation, more like a family than a business."

"What do you remember about her?"

"She was one of the first employees in the new museum. She went to school at the University of Oregon, and she worked for several years at the High Desert Museum in central Oregon. She moved here when her husband made a job change shortly after our museum opened.

"It turned out that she had a real talent for doing historical research, which was something we really needed. We had thousands of uncatalogued documents and photos—still have, for that matter. Tara knew how to set up a reference index so that at least we'd know what's in our vault. We gave her the title of Assistant Administrator."

"What was she like?"

"Hard worker. Quiet. Kept to herself mostly. She got a lot done."

"What do you remember about her disappearance?"

"She didn't show up for work one Monday morning. That was, I think, the first time she'd ever missed a day. It seemed out of character that she hadn't called in, but nobody was particularly concerned. Then she didn't come in on Tuesday, so we tried to call her on the phone but didn't get an answer. On Wednesday, we knew something was wrong and called the Wilsonville Police.

"They knocked on her door but left when they didn't get an answer. It wasn't until the following Monday that she was declared officially a missing person, and then they got a locksmith to open her door. They didn't find anything unusual in her condo. It was as if she'd walked out the door and ceased to exist."

I said, "We now know that she went on a boat ride on the Saturday before the day she failed to show up for work, and that is almost certainly when she was killed. She was accompanied on the boat by a couple named Jamie and Calvin—or something similar—who may have been working with Tara on a project related to preserving the Willamette Falls Locks. Do you know who they might have been?"

She thought about that for a few seconds before saying, "I wasn't involved in that kind of day-to-day activity, so I wouldn't know about her work on the locks."

"Do the names mean anything to you?"

"Jamie and Calvin? No, I can't think of anyone by those names."

"Was there anyone working with Tara at the time who might know more about what she was doing?

"Oh, gosh. You know, most of our volunteers are elderly. If they were around in the nineties, they're probably gone by now." After a moment, she added, "Debbie Corbett might know something. She was one volunteer who's still around. I know she helped Tara with some of her research."

"Debbie Corbett," I repeated. "How can I get in touch with her?"

"I don't have her phone number handy, but I think I can get it. I'll give her your number so she can call you," Marilyn suggested.

"I'd appreciate that," I said.

32

Tuesday, June 25

"Guess what?"

I just looked at Martha. I don't do guessing games.

"I got my license! I'm a licensed private investigator now," Martha proclaimed happily.

"Well, congratulations," I said. "This warrants a celebration. Let me take you to lunch."

In an old stone mansion on a high bluff overlooking the Willamette River, the Amadeus Restaurant is one of my favorite places to eat. Over lunch, Martha and I discussed our progress on the search for Calvin and Jamie.

"It's slow going," Martha said. "Every time I find someone who's interested in the locks, I end up in a long conversation about the history and the future of the locks."

I chuckled. "Well, I guess that's to be expected. But I still think that screening for interest in the locks is the best first step in identifying the Calvin we're looking for. The delicate part is when you ask if he's ever passed through the locks. The guy we're looking for killed Tara Foster right after coming up from Portland. If he's on guard, he might deny ever having made a trip through the locks. But if you can keep him at ease and give no hint that you're anything but a preservationist, there's a chance that he'll spill it."

"I get that. It's just that some of these people know a lot more than I do about the locks."

"That's okay. You're a volunteer. You don't *need* to know all of the history. In fact, it's actually better that you don't because that will help trigger the 'I know more than you' reflex. See, most people love to tell others how much they know. It's human nature. A good investigator is able to exploit that—and I *know* you're going to be a good investigator."

"Tell me, do you really analyze all of this stuff when you talk to people?"

"Not exactly. What's important is understanding human behavior—knowing what people are likely to do under any given set of circumstances. There's a lot of psychology in this work."

"Okay, well so far, I haven't found anybody named Calvin who says he's been through the locks. I hope I'm not scaring them off."

"I doubt that you are. The experience of going through the locks is a pretty rare thing. I'd be surprised if one person out of ten thousand in this area could honestly say yes to the question. Our guy is the proverbial needle in a haystack, and there's a lot of hay to sift through."

"Gee, thanks for the encouragement," Martha lamented.

"It beats getting shot at all the time, like the TV detectives," I said.

"What about the museum? Are they going to be any help?"

"They're completely willing to try. It's just a question of what they know. I still believe that Tara met the couple who went on Prescott's boat through her work at the museum. She told Prescott that Jamie and Calvin were interested in preserving the locks. That reflects an interest in history, and that points strongly to the museum as their common ground."

"Sure, but I can't imagine what there could possibly be about the locks that would motivate Calvin to murder Tara Foster."

"The locks are the reason they were on Prescott's boat, but that doesn't mean they had anything to do with the murder. It's far more likely that Calvin tried to make some kind of sexual advance, which Tara resisted. One hard push, Tara hits her head on the gunwale and goes down."

"Should we be looking for Calvin in the registry of sex offenders then? I mean, if there's a rapist named Calvin, he'd be worth checking out," Martha suggested.

"Good point! We'll ask Michael Wheeler to put in a request for an official search."

"Couldn't we just do it on one of the sex-offender websites?"

"We can try that, but those online sex offender lists aren't complete, and they aren't very well maintained. To get reliable results, we still need a law-enforcement data search. If our Calvin has a record as a sex offender, we'll find him."

"So are you going to call Michael Wheeler?"

"No, you are. You're a licensed investigator now."

"What are *you* going to do while I'm doing all the work?"

"Oh, I don't know. Maybe I'll take a minute and write payroll checks," I teased.

"I'm for that," she agreed.

"And I'm going to talk with Debbie Corbett," I said. "She was a museum volunteer who used to work with Tara Foster."

Debbie Corbett invited me into her house in the River Heights neighborhood of Oregon City. She was a tiny lady, about five feet tall, and probably no more than a hundred pounds. There may have been just a hint of blue in her silver hair, or maybe that was an illusion created by her strikingly bright blue eyes.

"As I said on the phone, Marilyn Hamilton said that you worked with Tara Foster back in the 1990s," I began.

"It's so sad about Tara. I always knew that something bad happened to her. She just wasn't the type to run away or commit suicide," Debbie said.

"So you knew her pretty well?"

"Well enough to know that she wasn't despondent or desperate. We spent a good many hours together researching things for museum patrons."

"Was Tara working with anyone in particular during the period before her death?"

"Oh gosh. People came in just about every day with some kind of a request—historical photos, legal documents, census records searches, and things like that," Debbie explained. "We didn't even try to keep records of that work."

"I'm actually thinking of some kind of long-term project," I qualified. "Maybe something having to do with the Willamette Falls Locks."

"Hmm. There wasn't much interest in the locks until seven or eight years ago, when the Corps of Engineers started talking about closing them. I don't remember any particular research we did—certainly nothing of any magnitude."

"What about other projects?

"There were people studying the paper mill. It was changing its name from Smurfit to Blue Heron, and I remember some interest in the history of the mill and the mill site. We dug up ownership records going all the way back to John McLoughlin."

"Do you remember the names of those people?"

"Not right off. But I think they were members of the city commission. If I had a list of the commissioners of that time, I probably could pick out their names."

"I can find that," I said. "Were there any other significant projects Tara was involved in?"

After some thought, Debbie offered, "Well, she did some research into the Wallowa County Massacre. It was a project that seemed to really interest her."

"The Whitman Massacre?" I asked, wondering if she was confused about the name. I'd never heard of anything called the Wallowa County Massacre.

"Oh no. The Whitmans were attacked by Cayuse and Umatilla Indians. The Wallowa County Massacre involved Chinese gold miners who were killed by a gang of horse thieves in the Snake River Canyon."

"I've never heard of that."

"It happened in the 1880s. A gang of rustlers from Wallowa County rode into the Chinese miner's camp on the bank of the Snake River and gunned down everyone there—two or three dozen, as I recall—and stole all of their gold. They threw the bodies into the river, and nobody knew anything about it until bodies started floating past Lewiston a couple of weeks later."

Surprised, I said, "That seems like a pretty big event to be left out of the history books."

"Yes. That's what Tara thought too. The story was that the rustlers came from families that had enough influence in Wallowa County to sweep the whole thing under the rug."

"How did Tara get involved in studying that?"

"As I recall, a young fellow came in and asked about an event he'd heard about. He didn't know much except that some Chinese gold miners had been killed in eastern Oregon. Tara did some research and confirmed that there was some truth to the story."

"When was that?"

"Oh, it was way back. Probably in the mid-nineties when he first came in. Then he'd come back every few weeks whenever he came up with a new question. But completely independent of that, other people started showing interest in the incident."

"You mean other people in the museum?"

"Sure, museum workers *and* members of the public. It was the kind of history that grabs people's imagination. Some people really got into it. One of them ended up writing a book about it—*Massacred for Gold*. But that was more recent, like in the last five years."

"But back in the nineties…" I coached.

"At first it was just that one fellow—I don't recall his name."

"Do you remember anything about the guy?"

"Not really. He might've been a hippy once from the way he looked. That's about all I recall."

"What makes you think he'd been a hippy?"

"Oh, you know, his hair was kind of long, he had a big mustache. Sometimes he wore a peace symbol on a chain, and he smelled like pot smoke. Ya know what I mean?"

That description sounded familiar. I asked, "Does the name Calvin ring a bell?"

Debbie contemplated for a minute before shaking her head. "No, I don't remember his name. He always worked with Tara."

"Would there be any records that would have his name on them?"

"Oh, I don't think so. We're pretty informal. If someone was looking for a document, he would scribble a note on a piece of scratch paper. If we found what he was after, we'd make a copy of it and throw away the original request. We'd have cash-register receipts for any copies we made, but we don't charge for doing the research."

"What was his interest in the massacre?"

"Well, at first it seemed like he was just interested in the history of it, but later it seemed like his interest was mainly in the gold that was stolen in the massacre."

"So he was a treasure hunter?"

"Tara thought so. Funny, the more she learned about the massacre, the more she wanted to do something about it."

"Like what?"

"Well, she recognized that it was historically significant, of course. And she thought that if anyone ever recovered the stolen gold, it should be given to the descendants of the victims. But that young fellow didn't agree. I think that's why he stopped coming in."

"Would anybody else know who he was?" I asked.

"No…well, maybe. There was a volunteer…a young lady. She helped Tara a lot and took a real interest in the massacre," Debbie said.

I could tell she was searching her memory banks, so I remained silent.

"It was so long ago. I can't remember her name right off. And I don't know if she ever worked directly with the hippy guy. But she took an interest in the massacre. She even went over to Wallowa County once to visit the site and research the museums there."

"Did she find anything?"

"She found some things about the aftermath—a box of old letters, as I recall. I think they had to do with the cover-up in Wallowa County, but there was some kind of connection with Oregon City. She showed copies of the letters to Tara and me. I don't remember what was there, but the local connection was interesting. There might be something about it in that book I told you about."

After leaving Debbie Corbett's place, I called around and found a copy of *Massacred for Gold* at a stationery store in Lake Oswego. I started reading it that evening and continued reading late into the night. It was a fascinating account that left no doubt about who perpetrated the crime, even though nobody was ever convicted.

33

Hells Canyon, May 25, 1887

Throughout the decade following the forceful eviction of the Nimipu tribe from their ancestral home in Oregon's Wallowa Valley, the inflow of settlers included a mix of ranchers, farmers, prospectors, and opportunists. The absence of a viable law-enforcement organization in the early days of Wallowa County gave failed ranchers and cowboys an alternative to honest work. By the spring of 1887, a gang of rustlers was raising havoc all over the western slopes of the Snake River Canyon.

They stole horses and cattle in Oregon, rebranded them, and sold them in Idaho. The leader of the gang was thirty-two-year-old Bruce "Blue" Evans, a black-bearded miscreant who lived on a homestead along Pine Creek, near Imnaha, Oregon. Though at least ten years younger than Evans, J. Titus Canfield was his closest and most trusted friend and accomplice.

Considered a black sheep in his family, Canfield sometimes attended classes in the one-room Imnaha schoolhouse, where he recruited gang members Frank Vaughan, fifteen-year-old Robert McMillan, and twenty-year-old Omar LaRue. LaRue had been raised by Benjamin Vaughan, Frank's uncle.

In their upper thirties, the oldest members of the gang were Hezekiah "Carl" Hughes, who was the brother of Blue Evans's wife, and Hiram Maynard, a neighboring rancher. The gang used a remote shack owned by Robert McMillan's family as their meeting place, referring to it as Mackie's Place.

For at least a year, the Evans gang had found easy pickings on the sparsely populated open range in the area around Imnaha, where ranchers raised horses and cattle to sell to the army at Fort Walla Walla. But in May 1887, the law was closing in.

Titus Canfield was arrested on May 10, and about the same time, word got to Evans that a warrant had been issued for his arrest as well, so he hid out at Mackie's Place. Canfield got out of jail when his mother posted bail, and he rode out to Mackie's Place to meet Evans. The two worked out a plan to get away from the law with their pockets full of gold.

Canfield went to Vaughan, McMillan, and LaRue and allegedly told them that they could do their neighbors and friends a favor by killing off a band of Chinese miners and maybe get some gold for their trouble. The idea must have appealed to them because they joined Evans and the others at an old cabin at Dug Bar on the Snake River. Also at the cabin was Tommy Harmon, an orphaned boy who had been staying with Evans's family.

At one time, the cabin had belonged to an outlaw named Thomas J. Douglas, for whom Dug Bar is named. Douglas was said to have stolen a strongbox containing three gold bars in a stagecoach robbery in Montana. Apparently, he had no means of melting and recasting the gold bars, which had official US government stampings that prevented him from selling them. Instead, when he needed money, he'd file off some "gold dust," which was easily traded.

The value of the three gold bars is said to have been $75,000, but there is good reason to suspect that an extra zero was added somewhere along the way. If it really had been $75,000 worth, it would have weighed about 250 pounds. It is difficult to imagine that a lone stagecoach robber could have transported a strongbox that heavy. It is also hard to imagine that the government would transport that much gold without a detachment of armed guards. It is far more likely that the Montana gold was worth $7,500, which still was an enormous amount of money—today it would be worth around $600,000.

Whatever the amount, Douglas kept it at his shack. It is generally accepted as fact that Blue Evans, possibly in partnership with Titus Canfield, killed Douglas for that gold. If so, they too were unable to liquidate it for the same reasons as Douglas. What became of the strongbox with the three gold bars is a subject of ongoing interest to treasure hunters.

On May 25, 1887, the Evans Gang carried out the plan that they figured would bankroll their escape from the rustling charges. They rode their horses three miles upriver to Deep Creek, where they ambushed a Chinese mining camp. From the surrounding hillsides, they opened fire on the unsuspecting miners. Among the men in the riverside camp, only one possessed a firearm—a six-shot revolver. When the revolver was empty, the miners were totally defenseless.

The horse thieves systematically shot down the miners. They fired until they ran out of ammunition and then used rocks to crush the skulls of any miners left alive. The outside world first learned of the massacre over two weeks later when bodies floating down the Snake River began to arrive at Lewiston. The total number of victims is believed to be thirty-four.

There are conflicting versions of which gang members actually committed in the massacre. By all accounts, Evans, Canfield, and LaRue were present and participated in the shooting. Vaughan and McMillan were also present, but in subsequent testimony, both denied having fired guns. Maynard and Hughes, by some accounts, were dispatched up and downriver as lookouts while the killing took place; but in court, both claimed to have stayed at the Dug Bar cabin.

Tommy Harmon, who may have been under ten years old, had no part in the massacre. In fact, upon hearing what the rustlers had done, Tommy ran away. Some say that Evans hunted him down and killed him to prevent him from talking.

It was estimated that the gang got away with $5,000 in gold. Valued at the time at $16.50 an ounce, it would have been about 300 ounces, worth about $450,000 at today's prices. After the massacre, the gang hid the gold somewhere at the cabin on Dug Bar, presumably to wait-out the investigation that was sure to follow.

Within a few days, Canfield left town, forfeiting the bail that his mother had posted on his rustling charge. When Blue Evans was arrested for rustling four days after the massacre, he must have known that the bodies of the miners were bound to start showing up downstream. With help from friends—probably other gang members—Evans escaped from jail in mid-June and hastily left town. LaRue also vanished and was never seen in Wallowa County again.

All of the gang members were subsequently identified, but only three of them—Carl Hughes, Hiram Maynard, and Robert McMillan—were prosecuted for the massacre, and they were acquitted on September 1, 1888, by a Wallowa County jury that apparently didn't feel that killing two or three dozen Chinamen was much of a crime.

The key witness at the trial was Frank Vaughan, who told the jury that the three defendants had not participated in the killing. According to Vaughan, all of the killing was done by Titus Canfield, Blue Evans, and Omar LaRue—coincidentally the same three who had already departed for parts unknown.

Blue Evans is believed to have lived out his life in Wyoming under an assumed name. Strangely, the name of B. E. Evans still appears on a plaque at the courthouse in Enterprise, Oregon, honoring Wallowa County's early settlers.

Omar LaRue was said to have been killed at a poker table in California. There is no evidence to suggest that he ever spent any of the Chinese miners' gold.

Frank Vaughan, who according to relatives, "was up to his eyebrows" in the massacre, was allowed to go free in exchange for his testimony— testimony that ironically resulted in both the indictment and the acquittal of the three who went to trial. Vaughan continued to live on the family ranch outside of Imnaha for years after the crime and never showed any indication that he had gotten a share of the stolen gold.

McMillan died of diphtheria within a year after his acquittal. Hughes is said to have also died shortly after the trial, but the cause of death is not known. There is no record of what became of Hiram Maynard.

Titus Canfield was arrested in Kansas for rustling mules and spent ten years in the state penitentiary. After his release, he showed up in Glenns Ferry, Idaho, and opened a blacksmith shop, where he worked for the rest of his life under the name of Charles Canfield.

It is speculated that Canfield bankrolled the blacksmith shop with some of the stolen gold. Whether that's true or not, nobody can say for certain, but historians have no better theory as to what became of the Deep Creek gold. To this day, treasure hunters scour the hillsides around Dug Bar in search of it.[1]

---

1. Even though *Deadly Gold* is a work of fiction this chapter is entirely true. Reference: R. Gregory Nokes, *Massacred for Gold* (Corvallis; Oregon State University Press, 2009).

34

Friday, June 28

"I don't *have* another ten thousand dollars!" I exclaimed.

Bill Cheshire said, "I'm pretty sure that won't change their minds."

I sighed.

"Look, somebody probably tipped off the state about the IRS audit," Cheshire explained.

"Gee, I wonder who," I said bitterly.

"The bottom line is that the Oregon Department of Revenue bases all of its tax claims on your federal taxes. If you owe the feds, you owe the state. That's how they see it."

"Even if the federal claim is fraudulent?" I asked, already knowing the answer.

"That hasn't been proven yet. Right now, all the state has to go on is the federal return."

"What are my options then?"

"Best call Gilchrist with that question," he said.

Five minutes later, Leo Gilchrist said, "Pay what they say you owe, or they'll slap a lien on any property you own."

"All this to defend a murderer, simply because he has the 'right' political credentials, and I'm labeled a political enemy," I griped.

"You're rather more than that, I think. Your testimony in court could put an end to the Blalock political machine. There are people who won't let that happen."

"And they think this will silence me?"

Gilchrist scoffed, "They don't want to silence you. They want to *destroy* you. And they *own* the government right now. You are their enemy, and that makes you an enemy of the state."

"There must be honest people *somewhere* in the IRS."

"Let's see, would that be Mattie Otis? Or maybe Lois Lerner? You simply can't trust anyone in an organization that allows itself to be corrupted the way the IRS has."

"But we *are* going to beat them in court, aren't we?"

"If we ever get the case to court, we'll win. But the IRS attorneys are experienced and extremely skilled at getting interminable postponements."

"Isn't there something more we can do?"

"Within the legal system, I'm doing everything possible. I've filed motions, petitioned the court, asked for a summary judgment—and I'll keep working on it."

"I can't help thinking about who appoints federal judges."

"That'll be a problem in the Ninth Circuit. They don't call it the Ninth Circus for nothing," Gilchrist agreed. "And don't quote me on that, or they'll slap a contempt citation on me."

I could only shake my head. "When will people wake up?"

"What people believe is only as good as what they're told. The mainstream news media have chosen sides, and your side isn't it. Your situation is hardly unique. There are thousands of other IRS abuses on record,[2] but you'd never know it from reading the *New York Times* or the *Washington Post*."

"You're making it sound pretty hopeless."

"About the future of our country? I'm not optimistic. The fact that things have gotten to this point leaves little room for optimism. But that doesn't mean we should just give up. I've been working cases like yours for ten years, and I haven't lost one yet."

I took a deep breath and shook my head. "They've already taken thirty thousand dollars that I don't owe. Now they are demanding another ten. Where does it stop?"

"I'm afraid they have you over a barrel. If you don't pay up, they'll simply take the money. If you don't have it, they'll seek a judgment against your future earnings. If you defy them, they'll prosecute you for tax evasion. And don't take that possibility lightly. It's what put Al Capone in prison."

---

2. While *Deadly Gold* is a work of fiction, all of the IRS actions against Corrigan are derived from actual cases where the U.S. Internal Revenue Service has abused private citizens.

"You're just a barrel of laughs today," I said.

"All I'm saying is that you really don't have much choice. Pay the ten grand and hope that we'll be able to get it back later."

Two hours later, I was back in my office after a trip to the bank to set up a home equity line of credit to finance payment of the taxes I didn't owe, thus violating a rule I'd always lived by: when you're in a hole, don't dig. I felt like I was one step away from being sent to the gulag.

I asked Martha, "How're you doing on the search for Calvin?"

"I've found a few people who are interested in preserving the locks, but so far, I haven't found anyone who's actually been through them," she said. "I'm about three-fourths of the way through the list of Oregon City Calvins."

"Well, stay on it. If we strike out in Oregon City, we'll start looking at surrounding areas. Meanwhile, I'll keep working on the museum angle. Debbie Corbett told me that Tara was working with someone who sounds a lot like our Calvin, but she doesn't recall the name."

"You'd think that would be in the investigation records from 2000."

"There was never any connection between her disappearance and the museum in the original investigation. Tara was last seen in the condo complex in Wilsonville. All of the police interviews were with people around there."

"Still, someone's going to feel pretty stupid if we find the solution to this at the museum, where they never even looked."

"It's all a question of where Tara met Jamie and Calvin. Their interest in the locks suggested that they were history buffs, and the museum would seem to be the common denominator. But making that connection is proving difficult."

We were interrupted by the ringing of my cell phone.

"Corrigan," I answered a bit more harshly than I'd intended.

"This is Debbie Corbett. We spoke a few days ago about Tara Foster."

"Yes, of course," I said. "Funny, we were just talking about you."

"Something good, I hope." She continued, "The reason for the call is that I remembered the name of the volunteer who was helping Tara. Her name was Janet Monroe."

"Do you have any idea how to get in touch with her?"

"Goodness no. That was nearly fifteen years ago," she reminded me.

"I know. But I had to ask, just in case," I said.

After I got off the phone, I said to Martha, "Now we have to find someone named Janet Monroe."

"I hope you don't need me to work this weekend."

"Got something going?"

"Yeah, I'm moving off the boat and into Kaylin's apartment."

"Need any help?"

"Bud's going to give me a hand. There isn't that much to move. The main thing is that I'm going to have to go shopping. I gave away all of my kitchen stuff when I moved onto the boat."

"I guess that means Daryl is finally going to install the engines," I speculated.

"Yeah, he wants to have the boat running by the Fourth of July weekend."

"He's going to have to work fast."

35

Tuesday, July 2

The Trail's End Saloon sits near the north end of Main Street in Oregon City. It is a rustic place with a false front just like the saloons in old Western movies. The interior is decorated with an oddball collection of artifacts and memorabilia. A row of ceiling fans all linked together and driven by a long, serpentine leather belt is powered by a single electric motor that might date back to 1889, when electricity was first generated at Willamette Falls.

A horse-drawn carriage hangs above the bar, and the walls are covered with odds and ends that have accumulated over the decades. There are signs advertising half a dozen beer companies that are no longer in business, and there are curling photos of the saloon taken in years past.

Hanging on a nail behind the bar is a tarnished 1873 silver dollar with a bullet hole through the middle, testimony to the saloon's Wild West heritage. Scratched next to the face of Lady Liberty is the inscription B.E. NOV 7 87. The bartender claims that a gunslinger shot the dollar out of the air inside the saloon in a demonstration of his skill with a Colt .45. Then she'll point to a hole in the ceiling where she says the slug is lodged.

"Could I have some more hot sauce, please?" I asked the waitress.

It was Tuesday evening—Taco Tuesday at the Trail's End Saloon. I'd already used up the little paper cup of salsa that came with my three tacos, and I still had two tacos left.

"That stuff's going to burn a hole through your stomach," Kim said.

"Nonsense. Capsaicin is good for you," I countered.

"When did you become a dietary expert?"

"I'm no dietary expert," I began.

"But I know what I like," we said in unison.

"You shouldn't go around hijacking other people's thoughts," I complained.

"Your thoughts shouldn't be so transparent."

After the waitress returned with more hot sauce—the bottle this time, rather than the little paper cups—I resumed eating my tacos.

"I finished reading that book about the Chinese massacre. It's a fascinating story," Kim commented after we'd finished our tacos.

"Yeah," I agreed, "but I don't see any connection with Tara Foster's murder."

"There's over a million dollars worth of gold left unaccounted for— $600,000 from Thomas Douglas's stage coach robbery and $450,000 from the Chinese miners," she said. "That much money could provide a motive for just about any crime. It cost the thirty-four miners their lives. Is it unreasonable to wonder if it had also cost Tara Foster hers?"

"It's an intriguing thought, but one without a shred of evidence to support it. But for that matter, Martha and I haven't found evidence to support any *other* motive, either. Given the circumstances relating to the crime scene, though, it seems almost certain that the killing wasn't something planned in advance."

"Motive is at the heart of any murder, right?" Kim asked in her lecture voice.

"Sure. Even if the motive is something as irrational as Helter Skelter, there is *some* reason behind the taking of someone else's life."

"So why is Tara Foster dead?"

Playing along for the moment, I said, "Here's how I see it. The killer could not possibly have predicted that John Prescott would tie up his boat at West Linn that night, and even if he had intended to murder Tara on board, he wouldn't have planned it so as to leave the trail of evidence that led us to Prescott thirteen years after the crime. That means that something unplanned happened on board that boat."

"If it was spontaneous, the crime would be manslaughter rather than murder, and it probably will be impossible to track down the killer based on motive," Kim pointed out.

"Exactly. That's why we're trying to find Calvin. If we find him, we can fill in the motive later."

"Maybe it was a sex crime. That would explain the spontaneity of the crime and provide a motive too."

"And if it were a sex crime, we might assume it to be part of a pattern of behavior rather than an isolated event. We checked on that. Nobody the right age named Calvin showed up in the state's sex-offender database."

"Then again, it could be something as trivial an argument over a card game."

"And if this was something as spontaneous as that, we'll *have to* track down Calvin and Jamie some other way. But it's a slow and tedious process."

"What about Lawen? Is he going to keep paying you to do this?"

I shrugged. "It doesn't make much sense, but I sure hope he does, now that I've had to borrow money to pay the taxes I don't owe."

"I'm sure your attorney—"

"Gilchrist," I filled in.

"Will get your money back," Kim finished.

"I'm glad *you* are because Gilchrist isn't," I said seriously.

"But he *knows* you're in the right," she protested.

"Yes, but he also knows that the entire IRS right now *belongs* to people who have no compunction about on using it as a weapon against people they don't like."

"You're talking about that whole Tea Party thing. But that's over, isn't it? Once it all became public, they canned Lois Lerner, and it's done."

"Not really. The whole point of Lois Lerner targeting the Tea Party groups' tax-exempt status was to prevent them from raising campaign money to oppose the president's reelection. The election is over, and the administration won. They fired Lerner to demonstrate their good intentions, but the damage can't be undone."

"But aren't they offering the targeted groups a fast track to getting their tax-exempt status approved?"

"Oh, sure they'll get expedited approval, but only if the groups agree to spend the majority of their time and money on things *other* than politics—which kind of defeats the purpose of their existence. It's a typical political lie. The administration can proclaim that they've fixed the problem and even offered the Tea Party groups a special deal. That's all the public will hear."

"Yeah, but the Tea Party thing isn't quite the same as Blalock calling the IRS to audit you."

"Not in terms of the way the attacks took place. Obviously, they're two completely different tactics, for two completely different purposes. But the point is that *all* of these people, from the president, the senators and congressmen, down to the local party hacks are in control of the IRS, and they have no qualms about using it as a weapon. And the IRS is a *powerful* weapon."

"I might have to take away your beer. You're turning into a mean drunk," Kim teased.

"It'll take more than one beer to get me drunk, but I'll admit that I am feeling kind of mean—and it isn't just the IRS. I might as well tell you the rest of the good news. I got a letter from the Department of Public Safety Standards and Training this afternoon. My license is officially suspended."

"Oh no," Kim said, all kidding gone. "On what grounds?"

"It is mostly based on the charges that Roger Millican filed against me last October when they were trying to suppress the evidence in the Mendelson-Devonshire case."

"But the charges were dropped," she objected.

"Sure, but if Blalock somehow gets acquitted, you can bet the charges will be reinstated—and the charges against Millican and Bill Kerby will be dropped."

"But that can't possibly happen!"

"I certainly hope not, but it seems that even in jail, Blalock has a lot of influence," I said. "There is no doubt that he's responsible for this suspension. And now the DPSST is onboard with Blalock's attorneys and Roger Millican in charging that I planted the tapes, which they claim were made in some invisible high-tech audio lab."

"But that's—"

"Completely preposterous," I finished. "Sure it is. And that isn't the half of it. They also have the IRS audit. If I can't be trusted to pay my taxes, I can't be trusted to be an investigator."

"But you *paid* the taxes they said you owed. Doesn't that get you off the hook?"

"Apparently not. They say I demonstrated bad character in trying to cheat on my taxes. I think I'll have to win my suit against the IRS to make that go away. And the IRS is dragging their feet because they know they will lose."

"If they know that, why don't they just settle?"

"They don't care if they lose. All they care about is how much damage they can do to me in the meantime—because damaging me helps Blalock."

"You think the IRS will back off once Blalock is convicted?"

I shook my head. "I really don't know. But you can bet that if Blalock walks, I'll *never* see my license again."

"Any word on a trial date?"

"Not since the last postponement. Right now, it looks like September or October."

"So what are you going to do in the meantime? I mean without your license."

"I'm going to go to work for Martha. Officially, she's the investigator now, and I'm her assistant. I'm just glad she got her license when she did. Otherwise, I'd be out of business."

Kim sighed. "Where does all this end?"

"When Blalock is convicted, publicly recognized for the sleaze-ball that he is, and sentenced to life in prison."

36

Wednesday, July 3

My first order of business was to find Janet Monroe, the museum volunteer. The easiest place to start looking was on the computer, using the various people-search websites. From my conversation with Debbie Corbett, I knew that the lady who had worked with Tara Foster at the museum was "probably about thirty years old" at the time. That would make her current age about forty to forty-five. I did find a few people named Janet Monroe in Oregon, but they were well outside the age range for the person I sought. So much for easy.

My next stop was the county clerk's office. It is astounding how much information about people is attainable through a public records search. I can find out if you own property, pay your property taxes, have been married or divorced, own a vehicle, have a driver's license, have an arrest record, have mental health issues, have applied for a building permit, have participated in public hearings, have children in school, own a dog, are registered to vote, receive veteran's benefits, or any number of other details of your life that have been defined as "relating to the conduct of the public's business."

Much of this information is available without charge, but for an in-depth records search, the public employees who retrieve the information are authorized to charge a fee for the time they spend processing your request. From past experience, I knew that a full, in-depth search could cost several thousand dollars, so I decided to limit my public records request to the things that are most easily accessed and most likely to produce results.

It's always tricky to track down women because they usually change their names when they get married, and Janet Monroe had been in an age group where that often happens. The starting point had to be DMV records circa 1999 and 2000. When a search of vehicle titles came up dry, I went to work on drivers' licenses. I found two. One was an elderly lady in Hood River, but the other was the right age. Janet Lea Monroe was twenty-four when she got her Oregon driver's license in 1996. Her address was on East Dartmouth Street in Gladstone—about three miles from the museum.

A quick check of property tax records showed that the house at that address had been owned by the same person since the late 1980s, and it wasn't Janet Monroe. That meant the house was probably a rental. I made a note of the owners' names, in hopes that they might have some idea where I could find Monroe.

I tried the post office, but if there had ever been a forwarding address, it was no longer on file. I searched Clackamas County records for marriage licenses, divorce decrees, and death certificates without success—but then any of those events could easily have taken place in other counties. After leaving the county clerk's office, I drove to the Oak Grove home of the owners of the rental house on East Dartmouth.

After introducing myself to the elderly lady who answered the door, I explained, "I'm trying to locate a young lady who may have rented a house from you in Gladstone a few years ago. Her name is Janet Monroe."

"Oh, that *was* a long time ago," the lady said.

"But you do remember her?"

"She was a very nice girl. Always paid her rent on time. But then some man moved in with her—they said they were married, but I don't know if that was really true. Her rent checks still said Janet Monroe."

"How long did she—they—live there?"

"Janet moved in sometime around '93 or '94, the man maybe three years later. They moved out a couple of years after that."

"Do you have any idea how I could find her now?"

"Goodness no, I never heard from her after she moved out. That was over ten years ago."

"Did she fill out an application form before you rented the house to her?"

"Well, yes," she said. "I'll bet that's still around. Let me take a look."

She led me to a bedroom that was set up as a home office of sorts. There were three or four filing cabinets and two desks, one of which held an old IBM Selectric typewriter. I hadn't seen one of those in years—at least not one still in use. There wasn't a computer anywhere to be seen. Each filing cabinet drawer had a neatly typed card in the little holder, and she found the one with the address of the house Janet Monroe had rented.

Thumbing through the files, she eventually located a folder for tenant applications. She carried it to the desk, sat down, and switched on a lamp. It took several minutes for her to find what she was looking for. Either she was a very slow reader or she was taking the time for a trip down memory lane.

When she finally handed me Janet Monroe's application, I found the names of several people she had listed as references. A checkmark next to each name indicated that they had all been contacted. Not seeing a photo-copier anywhere in the office, I wrote the names on a sheet of used paper that she pulled from the wastebasket for me.

Back in my own office, I started calling the people Janet had listed on her application. The first two numbers returned a computerized voice telling me that the numbers were no longer in service. The third call rang through.

"Of course, I remember Janet Monroe," the lady on the phone said in answer to my question. "She's my husband's sister."

I was so well prepared for another disappointment that I had to take a moment to remember the story I'd concocted from employment information I'd seen on the rental application.

"I'm representing a law firm that is engaged in litigation involving a former employer of Janet Monroe, and it appears that she might be entitled to some compensation if the plaintiff prevails in court. Can you tell me how I can get in touch with her?"

"I always knew someone would sue that old bastard," Janet's sister-in-law said. "He was as crooked as a goat path up a mountainside."

"Well, uh, yes. I guess so," I agreed.

"How he ever got elected is a mystery to me."

"Who's that?"

"Well, Eugene Horton, of course!"

"The congressman?"

"Well, who else would I be talking about? I told Janet before she ever went to work for him that there'd be trouble. I didn't hear that he was getting sued, though. Who's suing him?"

"Uh, nobody is suing Congressman Horton, as far as I know. The defendant in this case is a drugstore chain."

Sounding disappointed, she said, "Oh. The drugstore, huh? Well, I don't know anything about that, but Horton's the one who *ought* to be sued."

"Do you have that contact information for Janet?" I asked, trying to regain control of the conversation.

"Well, she's gone, you know."

"Gone?" I asked with a sinking heart.

"Gone. Out of town. Out of state. She lives in Reno. Or maybe it's Carson City."

I caught my breath. "Do you have an address? Or a phone number?"

With a deep sigh, drawn out to impress on me how I was imposing on her valuable time, she put down the phone, and I could hear her rummaging through a pile of loose papers.

"Okay, let's see," she said when she returned to the phone. "Here it is. Janet Monroe."

She read the address and phone number, which I copied into a small spiral notebook.

"Is she going to get a lot of money?"

"It all depends what happens in court," I said. "Sometimes, nothing happens at all."

"What the hell's the point then?" she demanded. "Why don't they sue Old Man Horton? He's the one they ought to get!"

As I hung up the phone, I shook my head. The words of Sir Walter Scott came to mind: *"Oh what a tangled web we weave, when first we practice to deceive!"*

"Is this Janet Monroe," I asked the lady who answered the phone. "Who's calling?" she asked in return.

"My name is Corrigan. I'm an investigator in Oregon City. I'm looking for a Janet Monroe who used to work at the Museum of the Oregon Territory."

The pause was too long. "What's this about?"

"I'm investigating the death of Tara Foster," I said.

"Death? I thought she just disappeared."

"Her remains were found a few months ago. I understand that you worked with her at the museum."

Another pause. "I helped her sometimes. I didn't work there—I mean, not as a job. I was a volunteer."

"Do you remember Debbie Corbett?" Without waiting for a response, I continued, "She said you worked quite a bit with Tara."

I waited. It reminded me of watching United Nations proceedings on C-SPAN, where everything had to be translated before there could be a response.

"I worked with her sometimes."

I already knew that. "I was wondering if Tara Foster was working on anything unusual in the weeks or months before she disappeared."

Pause.

"Like what?" she said finally.

It's bad practice to lead a witness. "Anything that you spent a lot of time on."

"I don't remember anything in particular." She wasn't going to make this easy.

"Do you remember any particular museum visitor or patron whom Tara Foster did research for?"

She again hesitated, and I detected a nearly inaudible stammer. "There were several."

"Ms. Monroe, is there some reason you don't want to talk about this?"

She sighed, "It was a long time ago."

"How long did you continue working at the museum after Foster disappeared?

She took her time answering, and I started to worry that she'd end the call right there. "I don't know, maybe a few weeks."

"Why did you stop volunteering?"

"There wasn't anything to do." No hesitation.

"What do you mean?"

"Tara was the one who was in charge of all the research. When she was gone, there was nothing to do."

Now that she was talking, I wanted to keep her talking.

"I've looked in the museum vault. It must have been fascinating to work in there and see all of the things that weren't available to the public."

"I've always been interested in history. Sometimes we'd find the most amazing things."

"What kind of things?"

"Well, did you know that the original plat map for San Francisco is in there?"

Only the ubiquitous Geico commercials on TV kept me from saying, "Everybody knows that."

Instead, I said, "Really?"

"There's a lot of stuff like that."

The phone interview had been a bad idea. I put my phone down just long enough to type a Google search for the best restaurant in Reno. I scrolled quickly down the restaurants listed and picked one.

"You're in the Reno area, aren't you?" I asked.

"That's right."

"Well, I'm actually going to be in Reno next week on an unrelated matter, but I'd like to meet you. I have something I'd like to show you."

"I'm pretty busy."

"I won't take much of your time. I'll tell you what. I'll buy you lunch at LuLou's, if you want to talk over lunch."

I think I heard her sigh.

"LuLou's, huh? What day are you going to be here?"

"All week, actually," I said, hedging my bets. "Take your pick."

"Well, I guess I could meet you there on Wednesday."

"That'll be perfect. Shall we make it one thirty?"

"Okay. That's on Virginia Street, right?"

"It is. I look forward to meeting you," I said.

After hanging up, I got onto Southwest Airline's website and booked a seat on an early Wednesday red-eye flight to Reno. I hoped that Janet Monroe would be easier to talk with in person than she had been on the phone.

37

Friday, July 5

"A nything new in the search for Dave Blodgett?" Kaylin Beatty asked. I was walking around the block to give myself a short break from work I'd been doing on the computer. I found Kaylin crouched down pulling weeds from a flower bed next to the curb.

"It's as though he vaporized," I said. "Nobody's using his credit cards or trying to get into his bank accounts. Either he was very well prepared to jump into a new identity or he's dead. At least, that's the way I see it. And I don't think he had the wherewithal to create a new identity."

"So what happened to him?" she asked, gesturing in the direction of the Applegate House.

"There was no sign of a struggle. Whatever happened, it was quick and unexpected. You don't drive halfway across town to buy lunch and then just leave it on the table untouched."

"That's just strange. Why would he just take off?"

"I don't think he intended to disappear. Somebody did something that made him leave—and you saw him leave in a real hurry. Most likely, something urgent lured him away."

"A phone call?"

"Not on his phone. We checked. He didn't receive any calls that day."

"Maybe he had another phone, or a pager."

"It's not impossible, but there's no evidence of that. My best guess is that someone stopped by right about the time Dave returned with his lunch. Or maybe someone left a note in the house while he was gone. When he got back, he found the note and left in such a hurry he forgot about his Big Mac. But there's no note, and I haven't found anybody who saw anyone going in or out of the house."

A familiar nudge at the back of my leg told me that my prodigal cat had returned from wherever he'd been hanging out.

"Well, DC, where have you been all morning?" I asked him.

"Out," he replied with his customary brevity.

The sudden roar of an engine drew my eyes down to Daryl's dock, where he and Bud were working on the boat. They gave each other high fives just before the engine sputtered, coughed and died. On my way back home, I detoured down to the beach to take a closer look at their project.

"It sounded like it ran out of fuel," Bud was saying.

"Can't be," Daryl said. "I just poured twenty gallons into the tank."

"Maybe there was water in the tank," I speculated. "It's been sitting a long time. Condensation can build up."

"I didn't check that," Daryl admitted.

"Why don't we hook up a portable tank and see if the engines run," Bud suggested. "If they do, we'll know where the problem is."

"I hope I didn't waste twenty gallons of gas," Daryl lamented. "It was almost five dollars a gallon."

I looked up at the sound of a car turning onto Water Street and recognized it as Sheriff Jamieson's unmarked cruiser. I excused myself from my conversation and hurried back up to my office, with DC following close behind.

"They made the deal," Jamieson told me. "They're dropping the murder charge against Richard Elgin in exchange for his testimony for the prosecution when Alan Blalock goes to trial."

"How can they *do* that? Elgin's a dangerous man, and they have him dead to rights on the Devonshire murder," I groaned. "They have matched his car to the tracks in the dirt next to Devonshire's car, and they have his fingerprint on the weapon."

"His attorney convinced the DA that there was no proof that Elgin was the one who drove the car or fired the gun."

"But the fingerprint—"

"It was not on the trigger, the grip, or the slide. Elgin admits the gun is his, so it wouldn't be surprising to find his print on it. He says the gun was in the Subaru, which he claims was taken out of his company garage by some unknown person. He says he has a printout from his security system showing that there were two unauthorized entries into his garage, once to take the car and once to return it."

"That's ridiculous," I complained, even as I realized that a part of Elgin's story might be true. If he actually had a printout, it would indeed show that someone had broken into his garage. And I could hardly challenge him on it since I was the one who'd broken in.

"Look, this isn't the way we wanted it to go down, but his testimony will nail down the Blalock case. He's going to tell all about how he drove Blalock to Devonshire's house for his afternoon with Jessie and how he participated in the cover-up of the murders. No way Blalock can weasel out of that."

"Still, Elgin is—"

Jamieson held up his hands. "I know, I know. He needs to be locked up. We're still working on the thing with his wife up on the Clackamas River. We're finding witnesses. I think we can get him."

"And in the meantime, he's on the loose to do…whatever," I said.

"He'll be under full-time surveillance. If he so much as jaywalks, we'll take him down."

Martha, who'd quietly listened to the whole conversation, finally spoke up. "Do you think he still wants to kill us?"

"Impossible to say," Jamieson conceded.

"So when's he going to be out?" I asked.

"Tomorrow morning. Ten o'clock. Take whatever precautions you feel are appropriate."

In the news media, the release of Richard Elgin was treated with indifference. It was as though the death of a state Supreme Court justice had been of no consequence. But I, for one, would not sleep well as long as Elgin was on the street.

38

Saturday, July 6

On what would probably turn out to be the busiest day of the year on the river, Kim and I got up early and took my boat out to do some early-morning skiing before she had to go to work. We talked Martha into coming along to give it another shot, and she got up on her first try.

We all took turns on the rope, but when other boats started to appear, we headed back home. Kim changed into her uniform and I shuttled her across the river to her patrol boat, where Sammy Cushman already had the engine warming up. I got back to my dock just as Daryl and Bud came down the steps, each carrying a six-gallon auxiliary fuel tank.

"Did you find out what the problem was?" I asked.

"There's some kind of gunk in the fuel lines. We had to clean the strainers and replace the filters. I think the engines will run now," Daryl said, "but I don't know what it's going to take to clean the lines."

"We're going to hook these up to get the engines running, then we'll figure out what to do with the main tank," Bud added.

"Good luck," I said as I turned to walk up to my place.

"Luck won't do it," Daryl answered. "I already invited a bunch of people to go out for an evening cruise, so we *have* to get it done."

Sometime around noon, while I was busy with an online-fraud investigation for an insurance company, I heard the boat engines start. Over the next hour, they repeatedly started and stopped, revved up, and idled down as Daryl tuned the timing and carburetors.

Honestly, what Daryl and Bud were doing was a lot more interesting than what I was doing, and I'd probably have been out there with them if I didn't have to pay the bills. Sometime in the middle of the afternoon, I looked out and saw the big Sea Ray pull away from the dock under its own power for the first time in a year and a half.

I could tell from the sound that there were still some issues to be resolved. The engines seemed to run okay at idle speed but faltered intermittently whenever Daryl tried to accelerate up to cruising speed. The occasional backfiring that I heard suggested to me that the ignition timing was still not right. I admonished myself for not concentrating on my work and pulled the blinds shut.

Late in the afternoon, when Kim phoned to say that she'd be at the sheriff's dock in fifteen minutes, I ventured outside for the first time since morning. As I walked down toward my dock, I noticed that Daryl's boat was absent. Bud was lying on a reclined beach chair, apparently asleep; a beer can balanced on his belly rising up and down with his breathing. Cosmic harmony.

Having been out on the river all day, Kim had no interest in going boating, so we spent the evening on the beach barbecuing steaks and watching the river.

"I guess you noticed that Daryl finally got his boat running," I commented.

"Yeah, I saw him up at Forest Cove when I was coming in. We noticed that his tags are two years out of date, but since he had a whole crowd on board, we decided not to stop him. If you see him before I do, tell him that was his free one. Next time, I'll have to write it up."

"Was the boat running okay? Last time I saw it, they were having some real issues."

"Far as I could tell, it was running fine."

We were awakened by the emergency tone from Kim's pager. She jumped out of bed and read the text message and then quickly picked up her VHF radio.

"Dispatch, this is Marine One."

"Go ahead, One," came the reply.

"I just received notification of an emergency on the river. Is anybody responding to that?"

"That just came in. Can you respond?"

"Give me the details," Kim said.

"A citizen in West Linn reports seeing an explosion on a boat in the vicinity of the old Oregon City Marina."

"Okay, I can be on my boat in five minutes. Can you get someone to assist?"

"We'll put in the call. Stand by."

I was already pulling on my t-shirt and shorts. I put on my sandals, grabbed my keys, and hurried out the door.

"I'll get the engine running and the boat untied," I called back to Kim, who was quickly getting dressed.

When I got down to my boat, I could hear sirens as emergency vehicles headed down Highway 99. As soon as Kim came aboard, I pulled away from the dock and raced across the river. Upstream we could see a large boat fully engulfed in flames.

At the sheriff's dock, Kim ran over and started the engine on her Jetcraft while I tied up. She was on the radio with the dispatcher.

"Fifteen minutes is too long. I have to go now. I'm taking a civilian along—name's Corrigan."

I untied her boat and hopped aboard as Kim pulled away from the dock.

She pointed at the life preservers hanging on the railing.

"Take your pick."

We raced upriver with the spotlights on and the red and blue strobes flashing. Even before we got there, I identified the boat as Daryl's Sea Ray. Spotting a cluster of swimmers in the water about fifty feet from the burning boat, Kim pulled back the throttle and turned sharply toward them.

"Board the boat at the rear," she said over the loudspeaker. "Please assist anyone who is injured."

She carefully drew up alongside the swimmers and cut the engine. We both climbed onto the swim platform and started helping people out of the water. Nobody wore a life jacket, and several of the people had minor burns. Among the last to board were Daryl and Joanie.

"Is everybody accounted for?" Kim asked.

Several people answered together that everyone was onboard. I heard a familiar rumble and turned to see *Misty Rose* approaching from upstream.

"Do you need assistance?" Captain Alan called.

"Stand by," Kim said on the loudspeaker.

On the VHF, she said, "I have injured people aboard. Where are the emergency responders?"

The dispatcher answered, "There is a fire department rescue unit and an ambulance on Highway 99 adjacent to your position."

"Okay, I have them in sight. Inform them that I cannot land at the marina. The dock there is not maintained, and I believe it is unsafe. The nearest good landing is the houseboat moorage. We will meet them there."

On the speaker, Kim said, "*Misty Rose*, please stay back. We are informed that there is a large amount of gasoline aboard."

We tied up at the houseboats and helped everyone onto the dock where they were met by EMTs and firemen, who led them up to the parking area at Paquet Street. It didn't appear that there were any serious injuries, but just about everyone had minor burns.

"Let's go," Kim said.

We pushed off and hurried back toward the burning boat. There was an explosion that sent a huge fireball rising toward the sky.

"Probably the main fuel tank," Kim speculated.

The force of the explosion sent the derelict boat moving toward the old marina. Although it hadn't been used in decades, the building was a landmark. Built on tar-soaked wooden pilings, the marina building stood out over the river, about twenty-five feet above the water. In front of it was a floating dock with a Chevron gas pump on it.

Beneath the marina building there was a three-thousand-gallon fuel tank, and even though the gas dock had been closed for many years, the probability that there was still some fuel in the tank made the prospect of an explosion terrifying.

Daryl's boat was engulfed in flames from stem to stern, and it was within ten feet of the gas dock. We made one attempt to get close enough to grab it with a pike pole, but the heat was too intense, and we had to pull away. Kim got on the radio warning about the possible explosion and recommending that the highway be closed down and the area evacuated.

My attention was drawn by the rumble of Captain Alan's old Chrysler Hemi, and I looked over to see *Misty Rose* edging toward the burning wreck. With his bow against the corner of the gas dock, Alan pushed the accelerator forward. The thirty-six-inch propeller created a huge mound of water behind the old tug-boat, and the wave crashed against the side of the Sea Ray.

The current created by that action pushed the burning boat away from the gas dock, out toward the middle of the river. Kim backed in toward the boat and attempted to douse the fire with her jet pump, but the effort was futile. The boat burned down to the waterline and eventually sank, leaving only a few smoldering scraps of wood floating on the water.

"Thanks for your help," Kim told Alan. "I hope you won't do anything that stupid again!"

"I think I'll call it a day," Alan shouted back.

Over the next two days, we learned the details of the accident. Daryl had not gotten the fuel lines from the main tank cleaned out, so he put the two auxiliary tanks down in the engine compartment so that he could entertain his guests. That alone was a hugely dangerous thing to do because that kind of tank is vented. Gasoline fumes in the engine compartment are an invitation to disaster.

Making matters worse, the halon fire-suppression system in the engine compartment had been removed during the engine replacement to keep it from getting damaged. It hadn't been reinstalled. All evening, Daryl had experienced engine trouble. One engine had quit running altogether, and the other was running very rough.

When Kim passed them at Forest Cove, they had been going up river, intending to go all the way to Wilsonville. But with the engine trouble, they turned and headed back toward West Linn. While in the narrow passage between the Rocky Islands, the engine quit. Daryl and one of his friends opened the engine compartment hatch and went to work on the engine, while everyone else partied on.

Joanie told me, "Daryl got the engine running a couple of times, but it would run for only a minute or two at a time. He cranked it and cranked it. It would sputter but wouldn't quite start. He thought the engine was flooded, so he took that thing off the top of the engine."

"The flame arrester?" I asked.

"Whatever that thing is. It was shaped like a little round cake pan."

"Yikes."

"Next time he cranked the engine, it backfired, and there was a huge explosion that blew everyone on the back of the boat into the water. Immediately, there was fire all over the back of the boat. Someone who was out on the front of the boat called 911 on his cell phone before jumping overboard. Once we were all in the water, we all gathered together and started swimming toward shore."

"I trust that it was insured," I commented.

"No. It wasn't. It was all paid for, so insurance wasn't *required*, and Daryl decided to take the risk and save the cost of insurance."

One of several bad choices, I thought to myself.

39

Wednesday, July 10

Long before sunrise, I drove to the airport to catch my flight to Reno. Most of the plane had been booked by a boisterous group heading out on a gambling junket. Their plane fares were paid by a casino in exchange for the advanced purchase of a substantial number of chips. They'd be given free cocktails during the flight to ensure that they'd arrive at the casino with minimal inhibitions about losing money.

I was in no hurry, so I found McDonald's on the concourse and got a couple of Egg McMuffins and a cup of coffee. I managed to fritter away an hour reading the Reno newspaper before heading out to rent a Kia sedan from Enterprise. My iPhone provided driving instruction to Virginia Street, where I found LuLou's Restaurant with half an hour to spare.

Inside, they told me that it'd be a forty-five-minute wait since I didn't have reservations. I took a seat in the lobby, where I could watch people coming through the door. At precisely one thirty, a tall blonde wearing stonewashed Levi jacket and jeans came in by herself and looked around.

"Janet Monroe?" I asked.

She nodded, so I said, "I'm Corrigan."

We stood together talking awkwardly while we waited for my name to be called. I didn't want to get into the discussion of Tara Foster's death while in the lobby, so we talked about the weather and the imaginary case that had brought me to Reno.

I looked her over while we talked. She appeared to be in her mid-thirties, although I knew her age to be closer to forty-five than thirty. She wore no rings, which was mildly surprising, given her general good looks. Her hair had subtle streaks of auburn mixed with the peroxide blond, and the freckles on her forearms implied that she might be a redhead. Her pale blue eyes took careful inventory of me, and something in her manner told me that she was not going to be a pushover.

"How long did you work as a volunteer at the museum?" I asked after we'd been seated.

"On and off, for about six years, I guess," she said.

"I think you said on the phone that you are a history buff."

"I like things connected with the old West," she said with an air of indifference.

"Was that what drew you to volunteer at the museum?"

"Well, sure. I mean they have a lot of stuff on display, but the *real* history is in the document vault, and that isn't open to the public."

"How well did you know Tara Foster?"

"I considered her a friend, but not on a social level. We worked together. That was about it."

"Did you know anything about her private life?"

"Like what?"

"Anything. Did she ever talk about what she did outside the museum? Who her friends were—things like that?"

"She went through a long period of...I don't want to call it depression, but just unhappiness. Her husband was losing interest in her, and she didn't know what to do. We talked about that sometimes."

"My records indicate that they were divorced about a year before she went missing."

"Yeah, he—uh, Tom—moved somewhere out of state. I heard that he was already involved with someone else."

"Any idea where he went?"

"I think Texas or maybe New Mexico."

"Did Tara start seeing anyone after the divorce?"

"Not that I know of. I mean, she kept hoping that something would happen and her ex would come back to her, but of course, he never did."

"What about people at the museum? Was there anyone in particular that she spent a lot of time with?"

"Not that I remember."

"Debbie Corbett mentioned something about a man," I began.

Janet quickly corrected herself. "Well, there was one man—kind of a strange guy—who used to come in from time to time. He always asked for Tara."

"What was strange about him?"

"I don't know. He was one of those guys who seem to be permanently stuck in adolescence. He always thought he was such a comedian, making lame jokes and the like."

"So was he pursuing Tara—you know, trying to strike up a relationship of some kind?"

"No, it was nothing like that. In fact, I think he might have been related to Tom—Tara's ex. I'm not sure about that, but it seems that Tara said something along those lines."

"Related in what way?"

She shrugged. "I have no idea. It was just some offhand comment she made."

Changing the subject, she said, "You said on the phone that you had something to show me."

I opened my small briefcase and pulled out my book about the Wallowa County Massacre. "Have you ever read this?"

I thought I saw a momentary look of surprise on her face.

"No, I didn't know there was a book about that," she said after a pause that was a bit too long.

I said, "I'd never heard of the massacre until a couple of weeks ago when someone at the museum told me about it. She said that Tara Foster was researching documents related to it."

The waitress chose this moment to deliver our lunches, interrupting our conversation, which was suspended while we gave our full attention to LuLou's famous lunch. When at last I was grazing on the last few sweet-potato fries on by plate, I finally picked up the book.

"I just finished reading this, and since Tara Foster was doing research on the massacre, I was hoping you might be able to tell me some more about it."

Janet thought about it just a few seconds too long. I had a strong feeling that she was deciding how much to tell me—or what she wasn't going to tell me.

"There seemed to be a growing public interest in it," she finally said.

"Did the museum have any kind of exhibit on the massacre?"

"Not while I was there."

"Then what triggered the public interest?"

"Who knows? I think there might have been a newspaper article or something."

"Do you remember Debbie Corbett?"

"I know who she was. I never worked directly with her."

"She's the one who first told me about the massacre, and she also said that you made a trip to Wallowa County in search of documents," I said.

I saw a flash of surprise in her eyes, and she hesitated before speaking.

"It wasn't exactly that way. We were on vacation in the area, and—"

"We?" I interrupted.

"My husband—ex-husband. He was an asshole. I don't know what I ever saw in him."

"Sorry," I said. "Go ahead."

"We were in Joseph, and I had some spare time, so I went to the museum. I mentioned to the lady there that I worked in the museum in Oregon City, and she asked me about my job. I guess I said something about the massacre, and she said they had quite a bit of stuff related to it. Naturally, I wanted to see it. In a back room they had three or four cardboard boxes just filled with papers and documents about the event. Most of it had to do with the trial."

"Debbie Corbett said something about some letters," I prodded.

"Oh well, there were lots of letters in there," she said dismissively. "I didn't have time to read them."

"She said you found some letters that had to do with what happened after the massacre."

This time, I saw a flash of annoyance. "Everything there had to do with what happened afterward. Like I said, most of it had to do with the trial."

"She specifically mentioned a bundle of letters," I persisted.

Janet put on a show of deep thought, as though she was accessing an obscure database in the recesses of her memory.

"She might be thinking of the Benjamin Vaughan letters," she ventured.

"Benjamin Vaughn? You mean Frank Vaughan's uncle?" I asked.

"That's right. Anyway, as I recall, the letters were donated to the museum in the '20s or '30s."

"What did they have to say about the massacre?"

"Nothing. They were between Benjamin Vaughan's wife and the sister of...one of the gang members. I don't remember which one."

"According to this book, Omar LaRue was raised by Benjamin Vaughan."

"Okay, then it was probably his sister. I don't remember, really."

"Debbie said there was an Oregon City connection."

She closed her eyes. "Oh, that's right. I think some of the letters were from Oregon City."

"The sister's letters?"

"I guess so, yeah."

"What did you do with the letters?"

She shrugged. "Nothing. I just left them there—at the museum in Joseph."

On the flight back to Portland that evening, I had time to put the new information into the big picture. The revelation that Omar LaRue had a sister in Oregon City strengthened the theory that the Wallowa County Massacre might have had something to do with Tara Foster's death. But I still couldn't make the connection.

I went back through Greg Nokes's book about the massacre and reread the part about Omar LaRue having been raised by Frank Vaughan's uncle, but there was no mention of him having a sister in Oregon City or anyplace else. I needed to find out more about this sister.

40

Thursday, July 10

"Well, that was easy," I said out loud.

"What's that?" Martha asked.

I was two minutes into my search for Omar LaRue's sister. I had gone to Ancestry.com and entered *Omar LaRue, Oregon,* and *1865* for his approximate birth year. The first name that came up was Mary E. LaRue, born in 1860 and died in 1910 in Linn County, Oregon. Could she have been Omar's sister?

But what really got my attention was the second name: Charles Omar LaRue, born in 1864 and died in 1940 in Ukiah, California. After leaving Wallowa County following the massacre, LaRue had vanished. It was rumored that he'd been killed somewhere in California.

The Ancestry.com entry was from the US Find a Grave Index, and the only information was what was carved on the tombstone. Was it possible that Omar LaRue from Wallowa County was actually Charles Omar LaRue? I did a Google search of the name and location and came up with a long list of people around Ukiah named LaRue.

That didn't fit well with my understanding that Omar LaRue had been an orphan in Wallowa County. Still hoping to find a connection, I persisted with my search until I found a family tree for Charles Omar LaRue, which went back at least five generations and had no apparent connection with anybody in Oregon. It was a false lead. Disappointed, I went back to the accepted theory that Omar had died in a gunfight over a poker hand.

But what about Mary LaRue? The Ancestry.com entry had been pulled from the 1910 US Census. She would have been about five to eight years older than Omar. I went to Google but was unable to find anything relevant in the avalanche of data. So much for easy.

If I was going to track down the sister, I'd need to see the letters that Debbie Corbett said Janet Monroe had shown to her and Tara Foster. Two things about that raised questions. If the letters were of no consequence, as Janet had told me in Reno, then why had she made copies of them and shown them to Tara? And since she *had* made copies, where were they now?

"Oh, yes, she definitely had photocopies of the letters," Debbie Corbett said when I telephoned her and tried to clarify the matter.

"Any idea what became of them?" I asked.

"In a perfect world, where all of our documents are catalogued and stored in an organized way, the copies would be in a file with everything else related to the massacre. Unfortunately, no such file exists, and our inventory of documents is only about 10 or 15 percent complete."

"Can you check and see if the letters are in that 10 or 15 percent?"

"I can't, but anyone at the museum today can. And if they aren't listed in the inventory index, you might be able to get someone to help you look through the physical records."

I walked up the hill to the museum and spoke to the lady at the desk in the museum's library. She opened a computer file and entered several different queries in search of documents relating to the Wallowa County massacre. Not surprisingly, nothing came up.

When I asked about looking through the documents in the vault, she shook her head.

"I don't have anyone here today who can help you, and I can't let you go into the vault unaccompanied—we just don't do that. However, if you fill out a request form, I'll have somebody search for your documents when there's time. Unfortunately, we're very short-staffed, and it may take weeks or months to get to it."

I didn't want to wait for weeks or months, but I filled out the form anyway, thinking all the while what my next move would be. Back in my office, I phoned the Wallowa County Museum and asked about a box of letters relating to the massacre.

"The letters I'm looking for were written to relatives of Frank Vaughan—his uncle Benjamin Vaughan and his wife. As I understand it, the letters were donated to the museum around 1930. They were seen about fifteen years ago by a volunteer from the Museum of the Oregon Territory."

"Mr. Corrigan, we have lots of correspondence in our archives. Finding one letter out of the thousands we have could be impossible."

"The volunteer did it," I offered.

"Well, if you know someone who knows where these letters are, perhaps you could bring that person in here to show you."

I thought about my talk with Janet Monroe. "I don't think that's possible."

"Well then, I guess you'd be on your own."

I was beginning to feel some of the resistance that Greg Nokes had experienced during his research while writing *Massacred for Gold*. Even after 125 years, people in Wallowa County were still very reluctant to let outsiders see their dirty laundry.

The museum clerk explained, "There are tons of un-catalogued documents in the back rooms. The only way to find what you want is to come here and look through the boxes. Maybe you'll find something, maybe not."

It didn't sound promising, but Janet Monroe had succeeded. Maybe I could too. Besides, what alternative did I have?

"Lost him! How in hell could they have lost him?" I shouted into the phone.

Larry Jamieson said, "They followed Elgin into Town Center, and he browsed the mall. They couldn't follow him in and out of every store without blowing the surveillance, so they had to wait around for him to come out. Somehow, he managed to get out through a service entrance."

"But you can still track his car, can't you?"

"No good. He left his car in the mall parking lot. He definitely had this planned out in advance."

"You had his phone tapped, I assume. Who did he talk to? Somebody must have helped him get away."

"He could have—probably did have—a phone that we didn't know about. But he could have just as easily used public transportation."

"Then what? The airport?"

"We alerted Homeland Security as soon as we realized he'd given us the slip. They're watching the airport and train station."

"Elgin never should have been let out. You *knew* he'd do this."

"We're checking all of the security video from the mall. There's a very good chance we'll be able to see how he got away. If he used the

MAX train, there'll be video, and we'll know where he got off. What I'm saying is we're not giving up. We're confident that we can find him."

"Save that speech for the reporters. They might buy it, but I don't."

"Damn it, Corrigan, it wasn't my idea to let him out! You know that."

I backed off. "Yeah, I know. So are you going to put a car down here or what?"

"If you think it'll help, we'll assign someone to keep an eye on your place. But you know the difficulty with that as well as I do. There's no place for a surveillance team to hide. Even an unmarked car will stand out like a neon sign."

"Okay, hide 'em in my garage! They can peek out through the windows. Even if they don't spot Elgin, they'll at least come away with a list of cars stopping to buy Red Harper's 'medical' pot," I suggested.

"I'll talk it over with my team," Jamieson promised. "If they think there's a chance we'll get Elgin that way, we'll do it. Just bear in mind that we don't have unlimited resources."

"Fine. And you can bear in mind that I'll be carrying my .45 automatic wherever I go," I retorted.

"I took that for granted," he said.

The worst part about Richard Elgin's vanishing act was that he'd be unavailable to testify in Alan Blalock's trial, which defeated the whole purpose of letting him out of jail in the first place. Greater than my fear of what Elgin *might* do was the certainty of what Blalock *would* do if acquitted. With the reassertion of his power over the law, he would feel free to act without constraint to destroy all of his adversaries, political and otherwise. And I was among the "otherwise."

41

Friday, July 11

The drive to Joseph, Oregon, in Wallowa County normally might take six hours. I left early, drove hard, and made it in less than five. At 10:00 a.m. I parked in front of the museum.

"I spoke with someone on the phone yesterday about some letters related to the Chinese miners killed in Hells Canyon," I said to the elderly lady at the desk.

Her badge identified her as Greta, and her expression conveyed a mixture of surprise and defiance. "So you actually want to waste your time looking?"

"I'm working on a criminal investigation, and these letters may have something to do with motive," I said, hoping to bluff her into a more cooperative mood.

"What criminal investigation?" she asked suspiciously.

"Homicide. An employee at the Museum of the Oregon Territory in Oregon City was murdered while doing research on the massacre in Hells Canyon."

"I never heard anything about any murder."

"It happened thirteen years ago, but the body wasn't found until a few months ago."

"I don't see what that has to do with us."

"It probably doesn't have anything at all to do with you—or anyone else in Wallowa County. But a lady who worked with the victim was here shortly before the murder and found a packet of letters that allegedly connected people in Oregon City with the massacre. You can see how that might be a motive for murder."

I was trying to calm her defensive attitude. I wasn't looking for dirt on anyone in Wallowa County. I intentionally implied that maybe someone in Oregon City had been responsible for the massacre. Her continued scowl indicated that she wasn't buying it.

"I don't *have* to let you in there, you know," she said sourly.

"Are you going to force me to get a search warrant?" I bluffed.

She sighed. "If you want to waste your time, I won't stop you."

Greta led me to the back rooms, where rows of shelves were stacked full of dusty, old cardboard and wooden boxes.

"Have a good time," she challenged.

I could see that I wasn't going to get any help, so I nodded and picked a starting point in the corner to my left. Small typewritten labels were glued to many of the boxes. Some of the labels were dated, and others had the names of people or places. The arrangement of the boxes on the shelves appeared to follow no pattern. And yet, I reminded myself, Janet Monroe had found the Vaughan letters.

As I walked up and down the rows of shelves, looking from box to box, I noted that the dust on most of the boxes appeared undisturbed— perhaps for decades. But a few of the boxes showed clear signs of having been handled. The question was whether a box that was handled thirteen years before would be among those "recently handled" boxes.

Still, I had to start somewhere, so I accepted that premise and started looking in the boxes that had been dusted off or had handprints in the dust. What I found inside the boxes ranged from old pieces of pottery to Indian artifacts to military insignia to unlabeled photographs, and of course, letters—lots and lots of letters. By midafternoon, my legs ached from climbing up and down the step ladder, and my back ached from lifting heavy boxes off the shelves and back. I finished the first room without finding a single thing related to the massacre in Hells Canyon.

The scowling old lady unlocked the second room and waved me in with an unnecessary admonition to be careful handling the old documents. I resumed my search, again focusing only on the boxes that looked like they'd been opened sometime during the past two or three decades.

In the second row, I almost passed up a carton on the bottom shelf that was conspicuously newer than all of the boxes around it. Then I thought perhaps an old carton had fallen apart and had to be replaced. The new box had no markings, but I slid it off the shelf onto the floor.

Inside I found a folded tapestry of some kind, an old lace tablecloth, and a wooden case containing an incomplete set of silverware. I looked at the underside of a fork and read, 1881®ROGERS®A1. It was silver plate and of no particular value, but as I closed the box, I noticed small letters neatly carved into the lid:

VAUGHAN

I considered asking Greta about the box but rejected the idea. She'd made it abundantly clear that she wasn't interested in helping. I ran my fingers over the carved letters, wondering. Wondering if this might have belonged to the family of Benjamin Vaughan. Wondering if this was where Janet Monroe had found the bundle of letters. I carefully unfolded the tapestry and tablecloth, but found nothing concealed in them.

I looked at the boxes adjacent to the one I'd removed from the shelf. There were handprints on them, so I pulled them out and opened them. The first contained a stack of picture frames containing mounted displays of arrow points made of flint and obsidian. The second box was filled with maritime documents apparently belonging to a merchant sailor—an odd thing to find four hundred miles from the ocean.

Just before sliding the boxes back onto the shelf, I caught a glimpse of a piece of faded red ribbon sticking up at the back edge of the shelf. When I tugged on the ribbon, I could feel the weight of something attached to it out of sight beneath the bottom shelf.

Lying on my stomach, I got both hands back to where the ribbon was. The gap was barely an inch wide, and I could get only the tips of my fingers down behind the shelf. Tugging gently on the ribbon with one hand, I poked a finger down where I could feel what was attached. I got out my pocket knife and used the blade to manipulate the bundle attached to the ribbon.

The corner of a tied bundle of yellowed envelopes appeared from the gap. I carefully pulled the ribbon upward and extracted the bundle. I rarely get overly excited about things that might have nothing to do with my investigation, but my heart was beating hard as I looked at the packet of letters in my hand. The top letter was addressed to Dr. Benj. Vaughan.

I heard footsteps approaching, so I hastily slid the three boxes back onto the shelf, tucking the letters in between the first two. The old lady found me studying the labels on a row of boxes at eye level on a shelf opposite where I'd found the letters.

"We close at four. You need to finish up."

I looked at my watch. It was three fifteen.

"Okay," I said. "I'll be just a few minutes."

She snorted. "I can't stay overtime for you."

"I'll wrap it up here in a few minutes."

When Greta left me alone again, I untied the bundle of letters. One by one, I removed the contents of the envelopes and arranged them on the floor. With my iPhone I quickly shot a photo of each letter—thirty-seven photos in all. I put the letters back into their envelopes and retied the ribbon around them. I slipped them into the box containing the silverware, tapestry, and table cloth, where I guessed they had originated.

No Vacancy signs greeted me at the two motels in Joseph, so I drove eight miles back to Enterprise, where I found a room at the Ponderosa Motel. Once I got settled into my room, I got out my iPhone and started going through my photos. The hastily shot pictures weren't as good as I'd hoped. There were issues with exposure and focus, on top of the faded ink and arcane penmanship. I struggled to read each word.

Disappointment followed disappointment as I went through the photos. Some of the letters were addressed to Dr. and Mrs. Benj. Vaughan, but most were addressed to Pearl Vaughan, whom I identified through context as the wife of Benjamin Vaughan. Few of the envelopes had return addresses, and someone had cut off the postage stamps, taking with them the postmarks that might have revealed the origins of the letters, leaving me with no quick way to determine if any of them had been sent from Oregon City.

The tedious reading of the letters gradually helped me identify some of the writers as relatives in Wisconsin and Nebraska. I could skip reading letters from those people, as well as those that were local. But I was beginning to wonder if this really was the packet of letters than Janet Monroe had found, and I finally yielded to a combination of eyestrain, headache, and hunger.

I suspended my study of the letters and went out in search of something to eat. I found a restaurant that was like a cross between Denny's and the Long Branch Saloon and selected a booth as far away as I could get from a noisy family that featured two kids who were unable to stay in their seats and an infant that wouldn't stop crying.

After ordering a steak dinner and a beer, I switched on my phone and returned to the letters. For the first time, I recognized the need for an iPad—how much easier this job would be on a ten-inch screen! Hunching over my little iPhone, I scrolled past the letters I'd already screened and resumed reading while poking at my salad.

A letter that opened with "We heard about the recent trouble involving your nephew" turned out to be from an acquaintance in Pendleton, but it was the first time I'd found a direct reference to the massacre. It offered no insight into the event, so I opened the next file. And there it was.

July 13, 1887
My Dear Pearl,

I trust that all is well with you and your family. It has been some time since I have heard from you, owing I am sure to our vagabond way of life, tho all of that is near an end. This town has much opportunity for a skilled watchmaker, and J's new store is in high demand. He has rented a shop downtown and we found a room in a nearby boarding house.

It is still our plan to buy a real house but it is proving difficult to find the kind of place we want. Just this week past, J. secured title on a nice piece of land in trade for some old jewelry he acquired from an estate liquidation back in Arlington. It is close upstream of the great falls of the Wallamet and lies next to the rail line so we may not need to keep a horse and carriage to get to town which is only a short distance away.

Oh my, what a dry summer we are having! Except for a single day of rain in June there has been no rain since April. From all that we heard before coming here we expected to see much more rain than that. I hope that things in your area are more favorable for the farmers and ranchers.

I sent a card to the post office in Arlington so any letters sent to us there will soon be delivered to us here. Until we have our own place, you can send mail to J's shop at 616 Main St, Oregon City, Ore.

I miss hearing from all of you. It is the hardest part of pulling up stakes and coming here. I look forward to having a place where we can finally settle down.

Always in your debt,
Rebecca

My dinner arrived as I finished reading the letter, but I was so excited by what was revealed that I took the time to reread it, not once but twice, attempting to digest all that was there. While there was no mention of the massacre, it clearly established that the Vaughans corresponded with someone in Oregon City, validating what Debbie Corbett had told me.

While eating my steak I pondered what I was missing. I couldn't see anything in the letter that Janet Monroe should feel compelled to hide. And yet she had been very elusive when I spoke to her, and someone—probably Janet—had tried to conceal the letters in the museum. There had to be another letter, one that revealed a secret worth protecting.

Back in my room, I scanned through the remaining photos with renewed energy, finding three more letters from Rebecca. And in them I found the clue I was looking for.

August 1, 1887
My Dear Pearl,

What a surprise we had when Omar appeared at our rooming house a few days ago! Last we heard he was still running horses with Frank and Tighty out on Fred Nodine's place. I guess that didn't pan out, because here he is.

Omar's unexpected arrival has turned out to be a real boon to us, because we have started building our house on the Falls City property. Omar has been a big help and we are making good progress. Not wishing to stay at the rooming house, he built a tent house next to our place and he has worked tirelessly digging our cellar and constructing forms for the foundation walls.

With Omar's help I think we can get ourselves under a roof before the rainy season arrives for real, and how I look forward to being in our own place. Marla and Howard are wonderful folks, but the rooming house life is not for me.

I received the letters that you sent in April and May, which had been held at the post office in Arlington. It is always so nice to hear from you and Dr. Vaughan. Give him my best.

You are always in my heart,
Rebecca

Here was proof that Omar LaRue had left Wallowa County after the massacre and shown up at his sister's place in Oregon City. For the past 125 years, people have been unable to trace LaRue's movements following the crime other than a vague reference to his being shot to death in a California saloon.

The fact that LaRue had stayed around to help build a house for his sister does not paint a picture of a desperado on the run. Some historians, as well as members of his own family, believe that Frank Vaughn was among the primary participants in the massacre and lied in his testimony in order to pin the whole thing on the three who weren't around to defend themselves—Evans, Canfield and LaRue.

Now LaRue's apparent complacency in taking up residence with his sister seemed to imply that he wasn't worried about getting caught. Had his involvement in the massacre been incidental? Had Frank Vaughan reversed roles with LaRue when he testified in the trial of three other gang members? It sure looked that way.

October 29, 1887
My Dear Pearl,

I received your letter of September 12 and you can only imagine my distress upon learning of the raid on the Chinamen's camp, and more particularly of your nephew's association with those who did it.

You know that Frank has always been like a brother to Omar and me, and it is painful indeed to find that he was in company with those who would kill people, even Chinamen, to take their gold. Here in Ore. City last February about forty Chinamen were chased out of town by an angry mob. No harm was done to them, but the tide is clearly against them.

Still and all, I am glad to hear that Frank decided to come forward and identify the guilty parties. I shall be most interested to hear the whole story and learn who the guilty ones are.

It is raining hard today and I am so pleased to have a dry roof over my head. Building this house has been a difficult task, but will be worth it in the end. Omar is installing a pump in the well today so that we will have water right in the kitchen sink. We should be ready to move in soon.

I hope and trust that all is well with you.

With all my love,
Rebecca

It was interesting that in October, people in Oregon City still hadn't heard about the Wallowa County Massacre. Granted, it had taken weeks for the victims' bodies to float downstream to Lewiston, where the crime was first discovered, but by August, a full investigation was underway, and the news could have been sent by telegraph to newspapers in Portland or Oregon City. Apparently, the deaths of three dozen "Chinamen" was not deemed newsworthy in 1887.

But I still couldn't see why Janet Monroe would want to hide this information—until I found the final letter.

November 9, 1887
My Dear Pearl,

A week ago I had a most troubling encounter with Mr. B. Evans, with whom you are acquainted. Giving no advance notification he appeared at our door demanding to see Omar, who at the time was not here, having left earlier in the day to obtain some needed hardware from Portland. Mr. Evans was quite agitated and left immediately to find Omar, tho I know not his purpose.

Then when Omar failed to return that day my heart became burdened that Mr. Evans had found him and done him some harm. I cannot perceive why Mr. Evans should harbor this malice. Such has been my state of mind that I have been unable to sleep.

Today I received word from an acquaintance that he had talked with Omar while crossing the Wallamet on Jesse Boone's ferry boat on the very day that he departed from here. Omar told this acquaintance that he was hurrying to see a sick relative in Corvallis.

Of course you know that we have no relatives in Corvallis, so I can only surmise that Omar found out that Mr. Evans was in his pursuit and took the occasion to avoid a confrontation.

I will write immediately if I hear anything more, and I hope that you will do the same.

Yours Always,
Rebecca

I had to read and reread all of the letters in order to see the probable sequence of events and understand what Janet Monroe had seen and why she might want to conceal it.

The Wallowa County Massacre had taken place late in May. Janet probably knew that by mid-June, Titus Canfield had left town and Blue Evans was in jail on rustling charges. LaRue appeared in Oregon City sometime in July, possibly knowing that the locals had no love for Chinese people and might thus be inclined to overlook his role in the massacre, whatever it had been.

If both Canfield and LaRue left town while Evans was in jail, it was possible that they had decided to split the loot and go their separate ways.

In that case, LaRue might have been carrying about eight pounds of gold when he showed up at his sister's place.

When Rebecca wrote to Pearl and mentioned that Omar was in Oregon City, she inadvertently tipped off Evans, who had broken out of jail in mid-June. Pearl probably shared the news about Omar with her family, including Frank Vaughn, who had helped spring Evans out of jail and certainly would have passed along the news to him.

Presumably, Evans and Vaughan had realized by that time that they had been double-crossed, so upon learning where LaRue was, Evans made a mad dash to Oregon City to recover the gold. Rebecca was probably right in her guess that Omar found out that Evans was on his trail and made a run for it. Because there is no record of Evans ever spending or having a large sum of money, it is unlikely that he ever got the gold from LaRue. So what happened to it?

There seemed to be only two possibilities. Either LaRue took it with him and somehow evaded Evans and perhaps even staged a fake death in California to end any search for him or he never had it in the first place. And then a third possibility occurred to me. Maybe Omar hid the gold in Oregon City before going on the run.

I had no idea who Rebecca was, beyond the fact that she was Omar LaRue's sister. I'd already been unsuccessful at tracing a family tree, and I had no idea what her married name might be. But suppose Janet Monroe knew. She might therefore also know where Rebecca had lived and thus where the gold might be hidden. That would most certainly explain why she would conceal the letters and be reticent to talk about them. She wanted the gold.

42

Monday, July 14

First thing Monday morning, I went to the museum and cancelled my request for the Vaughan letters. Then I filled out a request for photographs of downtown Oregon City showing main street between sixth and seventh. I was particularly interested in 616 Main Street.

My next stop was the county tax assessor's office, where I searched the ownership history of 616 Main Street. It was a long shot, admittedly, since Rebecca's letter had indicated that her husband had rented the shop space in 1887. But if someone with the first initial J had purchased the building at some later date, it might reveal the missing surname.

That exercise was a bust. On my way home, I had the radio on but wasn't really listening, when something caught my attention. I turned up the volume.

"We have breaking news today from Clackamas County," Lars Larson said on the radio. "As all of you know, Alan Blalock is being held in the Clackamas County jail awaiting trial for the 1980 murders of Jessie Devonshire and Randy Mendelson. Just minutes ago, the presiding judge for the case denied a defense motion for a change of venue.

"Blalock's attorneys petitioned the court to move the trial from Clackamas County to neighboring Multnomah County, because of what they called 'pervasive and prejudicial' news coverage in the county where the crimes took place—Clackamas County. In my opinion, this Clackamas County judge made the proper decision in denying the petition. I'd like to hear what you think about it.

"We have James in Beaverton on our naysayer's line, with something to say about the decision not to move the trial. James, welcome to the program."

"Thank you for taking my call," came the voice over the phone.

"We always put naysayers at the front of the line," Lars said.

"Well, Lars, I just want to say that I don't think there's any way Senator Blalock can get a fair trial in Clackamas County."

"Tell me why you don't think Blalock can get a fair trial in the county where the crime was committed."

"Lars, there's been so much negative publicity it'll be impossible to find an impartial jury. I mean it's been all over the news for two years."

"Now, James, that simply isn't true," Lars began.

James interrupted, "Of course, it's true! It's about all you talk about."

"No, James, it is *not* true. The victims' bodies hadn't even been found two years ago."

"Uh, whatever. All I've heard since then is all the evidence against Senator Blalock. That's all that's been in the news."

"I listen to the news all the time, James, and I don't agree that the news coverage has been prejudicial. In fact, I'd say that most of the media have been deferential to a fault in their treatment of Senator Blalock."

"That's *your* opinion."

"Well, let me ask you this. You say that Blalock can't get a fair trial because of the media coverage in Clackamas County. Where does that news coverage come from?"

"It's *everywhere*, Lars! Television, radio, newspapers—everywhere!"

"And where do the newspapers and broadcasts originate?"

"Huh? It's everywhere."

"James, where does it *originate*?" Lars persisted.

"Originate? Well, from radio and TV."

"And where are the radio and TV stations located?"

"I don't know, but—"

"They're located in Multnomah County."

"Okay, so?"

"Blalock's attorneys wanted to move the trial to Multnomah County—the *source* of the media coverage they say is prejudicial. What does that tell you?"

"It tells me that...you don't—" James sputtered.

"It tells you that the defendant's choice of Multnomah County for a change of venue had *nothing whatsoever* to do with prejudicial publicity because whatever publicity existed in Clackamas County *came from Multnomah County*."

Obviously confused, James said, "Well, I don't see what that has to do with—"

Lars spoke slowly. "If the jury pool in Clackamas County is contaminated by publicity, so is the pool in Multnomah County. We all read the same newspapers, listen to the same radio stations, and watch the same TV channels. Blalock's attorneys wanted the trial to be in Portland so that they could pick jurors from a pool of registered voters where Democrats outnumber Republicans by a 2 to 1 margin. They wanted the verdict assured before the trial even started."

"Come on, Lars, that's ridiculous," James insisted.

"No, James, what's ridiculous is the idea that publicity in Clackamas County is somehow more prejudicial than publicity in Multnomah County, where all of the publicity comes from."

The rejection of the defense motion for a change of venue was the first *good* news I'd heard in months with regards to the Blalock prosecution, which was now scheduled to go to trial in the first week of August.

There was still no sign of Richard Elgin, and it was extremely unlikely that his videotaped deposition would be allowed into evidence. That, I figured, was one reason the defense had stopped seeking postponements—to get the case tried before Elgin could be found.

For his defense, Blalock had brought in a team of prominent attorneys headed by Jason Hardman, who was best known for his successful defense of the Garcia twins for the murder of their parents despite their repeated confessions and overwhelming physical evidence. Following the tactics used by O. J. Simpson's dream team, Hardman and his team of jury consultants managed to seat jurors whose antipathy for the police made it impossible for them to evaluate the evidence against the Garcias.

As with the Simpson trial, the verdict had been guaranteed before the opening statements. Now Blalock, with virtually unlimited financial support, had the best defense money could buy, and he'd surely get the best jury money could buy.

Leading the prosecution team was Denise Andrews. Although this would be her first capital case, she was known for her dominating presence in the courtroom, and she had a proven track record in winning the tough cases.

From time to time she would call me to discuss the evidence I had found and what my role would be in the trial. She assured me that she would not repeat the kind of mistake made by the prosecution in the O. J. Simpson trial, where the defense managed to put the prosecution witnesses on trial instead of the defendant.

"I don't want you to become the focus of this trial," Denise told me. "The defense will try to discredit you in order to cast doubt on the key evidence—mainly the Devonshire audio-tapes. I plan to establish the authenticity of the recordings using testimony by technical experts in voiceprint analysis, so that the provenance of tapes—that is, your involvement in their discovery—becomes irrelevant."

"Is the science of voiceprint analysis good enough to do that?" I asked.

"We've had three independent audio laboratories analyze the tapes, and they all say that there is no indication that they are fabricated or that they have been doctored in any way."

"Won't they have experts who will say the opposite?"

"They probably will. You've undoubtedly read the editorials, which I believe were written in collusion with the defense team. They are trying to cast doubt on the authenticity of the recordings by referring to the audio analysis as voodoo science. That will be the mantra from all of Blalock's supporters in the news media. But believe me, this is a highly refined and thoroughly documented process."

"DNA analysis was pretty well refined and documented before OJ's trial," I reminded her.

"Yes, and I'm afraid the prosecution took that for granted. They were completely unprepared to deal with the nonsensical arguments made by Simpson's lawyers. We won't make that mistake."

"A lot of people felt that the DNA arguments were rooted in science that the less-educated members of the jury simply didn't understand. And what they didn't understand, they rejected."

"We're prepared to present some basic education in voiceprint analysis before we bring in our experts to testify. We won't allow our jurors to be ignorant."

"Okay," I conceded without conviction. "What about Richard Elgin's interrogation video? Is there any chance that the court will allow it if Elgin can't be found?"

"Elgin's testimony is important. He's going to tell how he chauffeured Blalock to various rendezvous with Jessie Devonshire, including the one on the day she died. And he's going to testify to having parked the mayor's car near the boat ramp for Blalock to use after dumping Mendelson's El Camino into the river. But even without Elgin, we have strong circumstantial evidence to support these points."

"But his interrogation—"

"If Elgin isn't found, we'll try to present the interrogation video. But remember, courts are very reluctant to allow such evidence because it denies the opportunity for cross-examination."

"Isn't there precedence for allowing interrogation video in trial in a case like this?"

"It's pretty limited. I wouldn't count on it."

So there it was. Elgin, who never stopped working for Blalock, negotiated his own release in exchange for testimony against his employer and then made himself disappear, leaving a big hole in the prosecution's case. Exactly what I'd feared.

43

Tuesday, July 15

"We've found some good photos of Main Street," said the cheerful voice on the phone. "We are still looking, but I thought you might want to take a look at these and see if there's anything useful."

I took a 64-gigabyte flash drive to the museum in case any of the photos showed the building at 616 Main Street. I knew that it was common for tradesmen to have their names painted on the front windows of their shops. If Rebecca's husband had done that, I might be able to read it in a good photograph.

There were five photos, of which three were 1888 shots of the newly constructed suspension bridge over the Willamette River. The bridge was on Seventh Street and whatever buildings showed in the photos were on the wrong side of Main Street.

The other two photos were taken in the 1890s, when an electric trolley line began operations on Main Street. One shot showed the new trolley car in the 600 block, but the building at 616 was directly behind the vehicle. The other was looking straight down the tracks from Seventh Street, looking south.

On the left side of the photo, I could see the storefronts and read some of the signs. There were no address numbers visible, but I was able to see lettering on some of the windows. With high hopes I asked for a high-resolution scan of the photo, which was copied onto my flash drive.

Back on my computer, I opened the scan in Photoshop and zoomed in on the store-fronts on the east side of Main Street. The lettering was visible and tantalizingly close to readable but not quite. I cropped away all but the part of the photo showing 616 Main. I stretched the right-hand side of the photo until the windows appeared square. Then I stretched

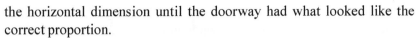

the horizontal dimension until the doorway had what looked like the correct proportion.

This gave me a kind of synthesized straight-on view of the store fronts with 616 Main Street right in the center. But the focus was very soft. I could plainly see that there was Roman lettering on the window, but I couldn't quite make out the letters.

I spent about two hours manipulating the image in hopes of coaxing it into clearer focus. At that point, I was able to count the letters and even identify a few of them. There were two lines of type, resembling a *Wheel of Fortune* game:

J▮▮▮▮▮▮▮ ▮▮▮L▮▮▮T▮

▮▮T▮▮▮▮▮▮▮ J▮▮▮▮L▮▮

With that, I knew I was on the right track. The bottom line would read WATCHMAKER & JEWELER. What's more, the first name started with J, corresponding with the abbreviation Rebecca used in her letters. I wished I could buy a vowel: "Give me an *E*, Vanna." I continued for another hour, changing contrast, resolution, and sharpness.

J▮▮▮▮▮A▮ ▮▮▮L▮▮▮TE

WATCHMAKER & JEWELER

By then it was late in the afternoon and I was losing the ability to concentrate. I leaned back in my chair and stretched.

"Well, that's it," Martha announced. "I've gone through the entire list of Calvins in Oregon City and West Linn. Not one of them has been through the locks."

I sighed. That part of our investigation was going nowhere. "I guess we'll have to start looking in surrounding zip codes."

"What'll it be? Canby? Gladstone? Clackamas?" she asked.

"Flip a coin. I don't think the odds change one way or the other."

"I'll go with Gladstone. It's closer."

"Fine," I said, rubbing my eyes. "Sorry if it sounds like I'm not interested. It's just that I'm kind of burned out."

"Making any progress at all?" she asked

"Take a look," I invited. "Maybe you can see something that I can't."

She walked over and stood looking at the image on my screen. I pointed to the notepad where I'd written in what I'd figured out. Picking up the paper and holding it next to the monitor, Martha squinted and moved her head slightly from side to side. She was moving her lips silently, and I recognized that she was running through the alphabet.

"*Jeremiah*," she finally said. "That has to be it."

I stared at the screen and imagined that I could read *JEREMIAH*. I squinted and moved back and forth as Martha had done. But I still saw only a *J* and an *A*.

"I don't actually see it," Martha explained. "But it's an eight-letter name starting with *J*. The second letter has to be a vowel. It isn't an *A*. It doesn't have the point at the top that we see in the other letters that you've identified as *A*. And it's too wide to be an *I*. That leaves *E*, *O*, and *U*.

Eight letters means *Jeremiah* or *Jonathan*. The fourth letter doesn't look like an *A*, for the same reason as the second letter. So that rules out *Jonathan. Jeremiah* is the only name I can think of that fits."

"Wow. I'm impressed," I said. She'd figured out in three minutes what I'd been unable to see in three hours. Still, we both knew that it was the *last* name that we really needed. Who were Rebecca and Jeremiah? I felt a vague familiarity with those two names in combination, but I couldn't quite put my finger on it.

"It's pretty hard to read these things," Kim said.

She was looking at laser prints I'd made of the four letters from Rebecca to Pearl Vaughan. They were spread out on our table at the Trail's End Saloon, and we were waiting for our tacos. I'd already told her what the letters said, but she said that hearing it and seeing it were two different things.

"Right after the massacre, the gang started falling apart," I said. "First, the Harmon kid ran off—"

"Or was killed by Evans," Kim interrupted.

"Right. Then Evans got arrested on the rustling charge. Everyone in the gang had to know it was just a matter of time until the massacre was discovered. They knew that the law was after them for rustling, and with Evans already in jail, they had every reason to believe their own arrests were imminent.

"If the bodies turned up while they were in jail for rustling, they might have no chance to get away. Canfield had been arrested *before* the massacre for rustling, and was out on bail. So when Evans got arrested, Canfield decided to skip bail and leave town rather than stick around and risk getting nailed for the murders. LaRue left about the same time."

"So you think LaRue and Canfield took the gold when they left town?"

"A lot of historians believe that Canfield got away with at least some of the gold. Except for these letters, next to nothing is known about LaRue."

"Then why do you think he got away with some of the gold?"

"It's because of Janet Monroe. She knows something. And I think Tara Foster knew it too."

"But what did they know?"

"They somehow knew that LaRue got away with the gold—or at least some of it," I speculated.

"But if Janet Monroe already knew that, what was she looking for when she went to the museum in Wallowa County?"

"I'd guess that she was looking for correspondence from Omar LaRue—something that would say where he went. She got the next best thing. Rebecca provided the information. Unfortunately, Rebecca also tipped off Evans, who came looking for LaRue."

The waitress delivered our tacos, so we stopped talking and went to work on them. When I first found out about Taco Tuesday, the deal was three tacos for a dollar. Now it was $2.50, but still a good deal—except that they never gave me enough hot sauce.

Rather than wait for our server, I went up to the bar. The bartender wasn't there, but I could see half a dozen bottles of Salsa Brava on a shelf behind the bar. I stepped around the end of the bar and reached for the hot sauce. At that moment, the silver dollar with its bullet hole caught my eye. I'd never paid much attention to it. Hot sauce was my priority at the moment, and I wasn't focused on the dollar—and yet it held my eyes for a split second.

I looked again and caught my breath. It was the scratched inscription—B.E. NOV 7 87.

Bruce Evans!

In my imagination, I saw him coming into the Trail's End Saloon on his way to find Omar LaRue. Something provoked him into making a demonstration of his marksmanship. I shivered at the thought of that kind of marksmanship leveled at defenseless Chinese miners.

"It was Evans!" I said excitedly to Kim. "He's the one who shot the silver dollar!"

"Huh?" Kim said as she bit into her taco.

"Bruce Evans. He was *here*. Those are his initials scratched into the dollar!"

Kim answered with her eyes while she tied to swallow.

"November 7, 1887. That was two days before Rebecca wrote her letter saying that Evans had come looking for Omar. It means that LaRue got away."

"How does it mean that?"

"Rebecca said that Evans visited her 'a week ago.' That would be around the second of November. Even if you allow two or three days, it still only gets to the fifth. If Evans was still around on the seventh, it means that he hadn't yet found out where Omar went. And that means that Omar had a three to nine day head start on Evans."

"So maybe Omar got away with the gold," Kim speculated.

"Probably. But maybe he hid it someplace around here before he left," I said. "I wonder if Tara Foster figured out where it was."

"Possible, but that doesn't fit very well with the way she was killed."

"Why not? Maybe she was sitting around playing cards with Calvin and Jamie and let it slip that she knew where there might be half a million dollars in gold. Maybe Calvin was a greedy guy, so he tried to beat the information out of her. He got carried away, and she died."

I had to admit that it was plausible. Unfortunately, that brought us right back to our fruitless search for Calvin.

44

Wednesday, July 16

The librarian at the museum called to tell me that she hadn't found any additional photos showing the buildings in the 600 block of Main Street, so I spent most of the morning trying every trick I knew to bring up more detail from the store front photo.

As she was shutting down her computer for the day, Martha asked, "Have you looked on the Oregon City website?

I was at the point of giving up on the photo. There are experts at extracting hidden information from photographs, and they had much better software and skill than I had. But it would be expensive, and as long as there was a chance that I might be able to solve it myself, I had to keep trying.

"Look for what?" I asked.

"You can look at the historic-building inventory forms. They have a lot of information about the buildings, including ownership history," Martha explained.

"Of course, but our guy was just renting the office."

"Sure, but all we need is a name. If he did anything notable while renting the shop, it might be mentioned in the history. Besides, buildings are commonly known by the names of the occupants," Martha argued.

She excused herself, leaving me in thought. Martha was right. It made me start to wonder if all of the stress about my finances, my license, my fight with the IRS, the prosecution of Alan Blalock, and the release of Richard Elgin was interfering with my ability to think clearly. That was troubling.

I went to the city website, and after some poking around, I located the historic-building inventory forms. There was none for 616 Main St. I looked at the form for 610 Main St. on the possibility that the same building held both addresses. No luck. It appeared that the current buildings were built in the 1930s or 1940s. They looked nothing like the storefronts on the 1890 photo. There was no inventory of structures that no longer existed.

Forcing my imagination to get back to work, I focused on the things that I knew. Our guy, Jeremiah or Jonathan—I still wasn't convinced that the second letter couldn't be an O—was a watchmaker. He was a retailer.

He would have advertised his shop.

A quick Google search led me to a University of Oregon library website featuring historic Oregon newspapers, where I found photocopies of five issues of the *Oregon City Enterprise* from the second half of 1887. Ignoring the news content required that I suppress my natural interest in history, but I focused my attention on the advertising.

I found an ad for Hunt's Remedy: "The Best Kidney and Liver Medicine." Another ad offered cheap Florida Land—I guess some things never change. A "self-heating" bathtub was interesting. The biggest ad on the page was for Golden Medical Discovery, a product that would cure liver, blood, and lung diseases, including cirrhosis and consumption.

Local retailers advertising in the paper included the Charman & Son Pioneer Store; Pope & Co., dealers in stoves, tin plate, and iron pipe; The Great Eastern Store—Leader in Low Prices; and William Barlow & Co., selling Studebaker wagons, "The Best and the Cheapest." I must admit that I was distracted by the entertainment value of the ads, and I had to force myself to stop reading things that didn't contribute to the investigation.

I nearly overlooked the tiny single-column, one-inch ad that read,

J. E. APPLEGATE, Watchmaker & Jeweler. Having located in Oregon City, is prepared to do any work in this line. All work warranted and satisfaction given or money refunded. New shop on Main Street.

"I've found him!" I declared in triumph.

DC looked at me and yawned.

J. E. Applegate—whether Jeremiah or Jonathan, he was Rebecca's husband. The significance of the name didn't register immediately. What *did* register was that vague sense of familiarity. It wasn't just that Applegate is a common name all over Oregon. There was something else.

I did a Google search for "J. E. Applegate Oregon City" and sat staring in stunned silence at the search result: "Jeremiah Applegate Residence 1887 - City of Oregon City."

And then I recalled a conversation I'd had with Jill McDermitt way back in January.

She'd said, "Jeremiah and Rebecca Applegate were Carlton's great-great-grandparents."

I whispered, "Well I'll be damned!"

I heard the familiar rumble of Kim's patrol boat coming down river, so I grabbed my boat keys and hurried out the door.

"I knew it!" Kim exclaimed over dinner that evening. "Half a million dollars in lost gold is a hell of a motive for murder."

I'd thought about it for the past two hours. A lot of seemingly disconnected facts fell into place and created a plausible scenario.

"Jill told me a long time ago that Carlton was obsessed with the house. She said that he 'flipped out' when the divorce court awarded it to her, and she also said that the entire time they lived together in that house, Carlton was remodeling one part of the house or another—tearing open walls, floors, and ceilings, ostensibly to fix bad wiring, plumbing, or whatever."

"But now we know that he was hunting for the gold. For some reason, he believed that the gold was hidden somewhere in that house!"

"Now I don't know exactly how this connects to Tara Foster's death, but I have a pretty good idea what became of Dave Blodgett," I said.

"Yeah, that's the first thing I thought of too," Kim said. "Funny though, I've never pictured Carlton as a killer."

"Neither have I. But the conclusion is inescapable. Dave found that old well under the basement floor. I was there when he first looked down into it, and so was Carlton. I remember how strangely he was acting—he pushed Dave and me aside to get the first look into the hole. He knew something that we didn't."

"So all of his harassment of Jill was actually just aimed at keeping track of whether or not she found the gold in the house."

"And on the day when Dave finally opened access to the old well, he vanished from the face of the earth. I'll bet Carlton went down into the well when Dave went out for lunch and was still in the house when he returned with his Big Mac."

"Dave caught him in the house, maybe with the gold, so Carlton killed him. That means—"

"That means that Dave is in the bottom of that old well," I finished for her.

"Can you make a case for digging it up?" Kim asked.

"I doubt that any judge would grant a search warrant based on what we know today."

"Do you think Barry would let you do the excavation?"

"And demolish the house that he's just spent two hundred-fifty grand remodeling? I sincerely doubt it."

"So what's your plan?"

"I've been thinking about that. I need to build the case, from top to bottom, so that Carlton can be arrested and search warrants issued."

"Can you do that without a body?"

"It's the same old dilemma. We can't get a warrant without the evidence, and we can't get the evidence without the warrant," I said.

45

Thursday, July 17

When Martha came in prepared to resume her seemingly endless search for Calvin, I told her that I had a new theory about Calvin and Jamie.

"Go back and reread what John Prescott said about the couple who accompanied him on Tara Foster's last boat ride. He said the woman was attractive, had red hair and freckles, and was about five-nine or five-ten. The man was about the same height. He had a bushy mustache, kind of sandy color, I think. And he wore an earring."

Confused, Martha said, "I remember all of that, so what's your point?"

"Suppose their names were Carlton and Jill, instead of Calvin and Jamie?"

She laughed. "Where on earth did you come up with that?"

"Just think about it. Do the descriptions fit?"

She thought it over before answering. "Well, yes, but didn't Prescott also say that they were about thirty? That's at least ten years younger than Carlton and Jill."

"True, but estimating people's ages is pretty tough. Everyone's perception of age is different."

"Okay then. So Carlton and Jill *might* fit Prescott's description of the people on the boat. But what makes you think that it could possibly have actually been them?"

"After you suggested looking at the city's historic buildings inventory forms yesterday, I gave it a try, but there was nothing for the building at 616 Main Street. Then I got to thinking about why our guy was there— on Main Street. It was because he was a watchmaker. I figured a watchmaker would advertise his business."

"In the newspaper!" Martha exclaimed.

"Right. So I got online and found copies of the *Oregon City Enterprise* from 1887, and sure enough, there was an ad for J. E. Applegate."

Martha's blank expression said that she needed further explanation.

"You remember when Jill came in here—right after the houseboat fire?"

Martha nodded. "She was complaining about Carlton."

"She was telling us all about how he was making such a nuisance of himself, and she said that he was obsessed with the house. She said that Carlton's great-great-grandparents were *Jeremiah and Rebecca Applegate* and that he went nuts when he didn't get the house in the divorce."

"The Jeremiah Applegate House! I never even thought about that!" Martha said.

"Nor did I. But as I remember it, Jill said something to the effect that the death of a distant relative over in Central Oregon sparked Carlton's sudden interest in his family history. Exactly what that 'something' was we don't know, but it's going to become the central issue in this investigation."

"I don't get it."

"Jill told us that Carlton contacted the historical society way back in the 1990s—that's where he first learned about his connection with the Applegate House. And after that, he was determined to buy the house. Knowing what we know now, we can guess why."

"The Hells Canyon gold!" Martha said. "And if he went to the Clackamas County Historical Society, he probably dealt with Tara Foster!"

"You got it. And that might well be what got her interested in the Wallowa County Massacre."

"Oh my god. *Oh my god!* If he killed Tara, then—"

"It was because he believed the gold was in that house, and she must have reached the same conclusion."

"And she told him so when they were on Prescott's boat!" Martha exclaimed. "It *wasn't* planned in advance, but the gold was the motive. Every bit of it makes perfect sense."

"Then after Jill sold the house to Barry and he started remodeling it, Carlton *really* started to panic. He watched everything that went on in there—right up to the day Dave Blodgett disappeared."

"So you think—"

"That was the day that Dave opened up the old well under the cellar floor. My guess is that Carlton went into the house when he saw Dave leave for lunch. He went down the well and found the gold, but Dave returned before he got out of the house. You can guess what happened next."

"Do you think it's really possible that Carlton has a half million dollars in gold?"

"You got me there," I had to admit. "If he has any kind of wealth, he's hiding it pretty well."

"Maybe he's just lying low, as they say, until things cool down."

"It would certainly be the smart thing to do, but Carlton's never struck me as possessing that kind of patience."

"So maybe he *didn't* find it," Martha speculated.

"But if he didn't find it, there wouldn't have been any reason to kill Dave," I pointed out. "He could have simply explained away his presence in the house as idle curiosity."

"Wow. So what's next?"

"We'll have to be pretty careful what we say outside this office," I advised. "If Carlton gets word that we're looking at him, he'll take the gold and vanish. But the first thing we need is a photo of Carlton and Jill, preferably circa 2000, to show to John Prescott."

"How are we going to get that? We can't walk up to him and ask for it," Martha said.

"I wonder if anyone in the neighborhood has snapshots or video from neighborhood functions—beach picnics, that sort of thing."

"I could ask around, saying something like I'm putting together a neighborhood photo album," Martha suggested.

"I like that. We can also search the web and newspaper archives. When we come up with photos, I'll see about getting the sheriff's office to do a lay-down for Prescott."

"Will that be enough?"

"Not by itself. We'll have to establish the connection between Tara Foster and Carlton. Janet Monroe said that Tara's ex was a relative of Carlton's. Whether or not that's true, she can testify that Carlton spent a lot of time with Tara at the museum."

"What *about* Janet Monroe? Do you really think she'd cooperate with us?"

"Good question. The whole time I was talking with her, I had the feeling that she was hiding something. In view of what we've learned, I think that she may have had her eyes on the gold too."

"You think she knew about the Applegate House?"

"She knew that Omar LaRue had a sister named Rebecca. Whether or not she was able to figure out that she was married to Jeremiah Applegate is an open question. But I'm inclined to think not. I mean, if she thought the gold was in the Applegate house, wouldn't she have done something about it?"

"So at this point, she'd really have nothing to gain by refusing to cooperate."

"I'd like to believe that, but you never know what people will do when half a million dollars in gold is at stake."

"What's next then?" Martha asked.

"We'll need to firm up that motive—prove that the Hells Canyon gold is behind Tara's murder. We can document the link between the horse thieves and the Applegate House. But we'll still have to be able to prove that Carlton knew about it. The circumstantial evidence just might make this case—it'll give a jury the reason why Carlton was on that boat, and John Prescott's testimony will close the deal."

"There's just one thing."

"What's that?"

"Jill. I mean, she just doesn't strike me as a person who could possibly be involved in something like this. Carlton—I *might* believe it. But Jill? No way."

"I have the same feeling," I admitted. "I don't see how she could have been on the boat that night and not witnessed what happened, but it isn't impossible. John Prescott was there, and he didn't know anything about it until we told him."

Martha's face brightened. "Maybe Jill was down in the stateroom with Prescott. That'd explain why they didn't see or hear anything."

I looked at her skeptically.

"Well, it *could* have happened," she said lamely.

"If Jill really had been in Prescott's stateroom, why wouldn't he have said so? It seems like that would have bolstered his claim to having no knowledge of the murder."

"People don't like to talk about their illicit affairs. Or maybe she simply went below by herself, leaving Carlton on deck with Tara."

"Regardless how events onboard the boat had played out, we need to establish that Carlton and Jill were there. Martha, do you think Jill would recognize your voice in a phone conversation?"

"Probably not. I've never talked with her beyond just saying hi."

"Okay then, it's time to try your 'locks preservation' speech on her. If she acknowledges having made a run through the locks, try to get her to talk about the passage. Pump her. Ask what it was like. Tell her that you wish you'd been able to go through before they were shut down. Get her to tell you why she was there and who she was with."

"Do you really think she'll admit having been on Prescott's boat?"

"Not if she's aware that the murder took place on the boat. But that information hasn't been made public, so unless she was involved, she would have no reason to deny it."

"If she was innocently aboard the boat and knew nothing about the murder, wouldn't she have come forward when news of Tara Foster's disappearance came out back in 2000?"

"Maybe she never saw the news," I speculated unconvincingly. "The thing is, if she'd known that Carlton had killed Foster, she probably wouldn't have told me about the way he became obsessed with the house or about the way he systematically opened up the walls and floors, since it's all connected."

"Okay," Martha said, "I'll give it a try."

46

Friday, July 18

Martha's call to Jill McDermitt proved to be another dead end. Jill said that she'd never made a trip through the Willamette Falls Locks. If true, that might mean that she and Carlton had not been the couple onboard John Prescott's boat the day Tara Foster was killed. It was conceivable that Carlton had been there with some unknown other woman who coincidentally resembled Jill, but the chances of that seemed pretty remote.

The better interpretation of Jill's denial was that she knew, or at least suspected, what had happened on the boat and was canny enough to avoid saying anything that might force her to admit that she'd been aboard. But if this were the case, wouldn't she have also known better than to tell me about Carlton's obsession with the Applegate house and his relationship to Jeremiah and Rebecca Applegate?

"What about Tom Foster, Tara's ex?" I asked Martha.

"Didn't they determine during the original investigation that he was out of the state when Tara disappeared?"

"They did, but there's something else. Janet Monroe said she thought Carlton and Tom Foster were related somehow. I'd like to know if that's true and, if so, how it bears on the case. Let's see if we can find him."

"Okay. But there must be a lot of people named Tom or Thomas Foster. A middle name would narrow it down a lot."

"Tara was working at the museum when she and Tom got divorced. Odds are good that the divorce was recorded in Clackamas County. If you can find that, you'll almost certainly get a middle name. And with some luck, you might find some hint as to where we can find him."

While I was talking, Martha turned to her computer screen and started typing. After a few keystrokes, she paused and typed some more.

I could see that she was doing some kind of search, so I asked, "You have an idea?"

She didn't answer right away. Instead, she typed a few more keystrokes.

"Okay," she mumbled, typing again. "One more…"

She was clearly talking to herself, not to me.

"Eureka! His name is Thomas Robert Foster, and he is…let's see…wow! He's Carlton's fourth cousin."

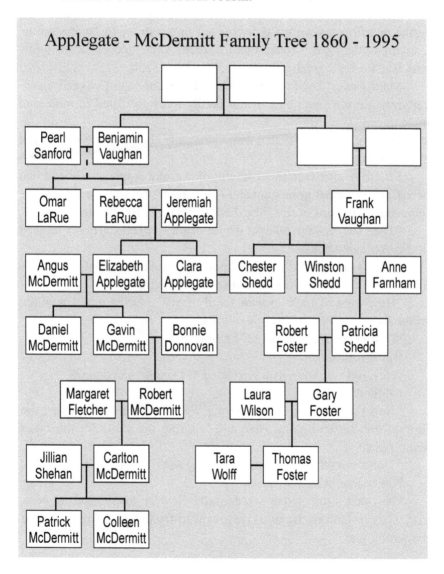

Applegate - McDermitt Family Tree 1860 - 1995

"How on earth did you come up with that?" I asked.

"Ancestry.com," she said. "I'm looking at Carlton's family tree."

I went and looked over her shoulder. The portion of the family tree that she was looking at covered six generations, dating back to the 1870s. I followed Carlton's lineage back and found that his great-grandmother was Elizabeth Applegate, daughter of Jeremiah and Rebecca Applegate, confirming his connection with the Jeremiah Applegate house.

Joshua and Matilda LaRue were the parents of Omar LaRue and Rebecca LaRue Applegate. Omar's family tree ended with his name. This further confirmed what we'd discovered since talking to Janet Monroe. Looking to the right, I found that Elizabeth Applegate's brother-in-law was Tom Foster's great-grandfather, Winston Shedd.

Martha said, "You probably couldn't have found this five years ago—certainly not ten years ago. These family trees get filled in more and more as time goes by."

"I'm amazed," I admitted while internally chastising myself for not having thought of it.

I tried to save face by observing that Clara Applegate-Shedd had been Carlton's great-great-aunt and Tom Foster's first cousin three times removed. "And look at this. She died in 1994—in Redmond, Oregon."

"Then she was the relative whose death sparked Carlton's interest in the Applegate house."

"I don't know if I'd have ever put that together without that family tree," I said as a grudging compliment to Martha.

"Hey, want to look up *your* family tree?" Martha asked brightly, while the printer spit out a copy of Carlton's.

"Don't even *think* about it," I grumbled.

But it was too late.

"Hey, did you know you're related to Douglas Corrigan?"

I sighed.

"He's the one they called Wrong Way Corrigan for carrying the football to the wrong end zone and winning the game for the other team, right?"

"That's not why he was called Wrong Way."

"Of course, it is. Why else—"

"No, that's not it. He accidentally flew an airplane from New York City to Dublin, Ireland. He meant to fly to California but went the wrong way."

"Oh, come on! How could that happen?" Martha asked.

I cleared my throat and said, "Now that we know *who* Tom Foster is, we need to find out *where* he is. Janet Monroe thought he moved to Texas or New Mexico."

Martha scowled at me.

The ringing of my phone concluded that conversation.

"They've set a trial date," Sheriff Jamieson said. "Jury selection will begin August 6."

"This year?" I asked, astonished.

"Yep. And they're staying in Clackamas County."

My momentary excitement faded quickly when I remembered that we'd lost a key witness when Richard Elgin disappeared.

"So they delay, delay, delay, until Elgin's gone, and now they're in a mad rush," I said cynically.

"That's about it," Jamieson confirmed.

"What's the DA think about that?"

"She has no choice. The whole time Blalock's attorneys were demanding postponements, she was insisting that there was no sound reason for the delay. Now she's stuck."

"Can she win it?"

"I guess we'll find out."

I did a quick mental inventory. We still had the physical evidence—mainly the audiotapes and the receipts that we found inside the bronze eagle from Wilson Devonshire's study. We had Barbara Devonshire's testimony about how Alan Blalock had recruited her daughter into his "internship" program. We had Mickey Odell's testimony about how former Sheriff Barrington and his successor, Bill Kerby, had employed him to help cover up the murders of Jessie Devonshire and Randy Mendelson.

"It was Elgin who could place Blalock at the crime scene," I pointed out.

"So do the audiotapes. Watch your ass, Corrigan," Jamieson advised before hanging up.

If the case was going to hinge on the audiotapes, then it would all depend on the prosecution's ability to prove the tapes were authentic. Provenance would be critical. District Attorney Denise Andrews would have to be able to prove to the jury that the tapes had been put inside the bronze eagle by Wilson Devonshire and had remained there until I pulled them out in front of witnesses last October.

With Blalock's hit man, Richard Elgin, on the loose, the lives of everybody who could testify to the authenticity of the audiotapes were in jeopardy. That included everyone present when I opened the eagle and found what was inside—Barbara Devonshire, Kim, Martha, William Gates, and me.

47

Thursday, July 24

Martha showed me a handful of photos that she'd collected from around the neighborhood showing Carlton and Jill. At the time of the 1996 flood, Joanie Tiernan had shot a bunch of pictures, including several that included neighbors looking out on the high water. The day the flood reached its crest was warm and sunny, so the photos were very clear. Joanie let Martha borrow the negatives, which we sent to a good photo lab. They zoomed in on the faces of Jill and Carlton and made high-resolution scans.

"Here are some photos that we think might show the people who were on the boat with John Prescott the day Tara Foster was killed," I told Michael Wheeler as I handed him the envelope.

"Calvin and Jamie?" he asked.

"Close enough," I said. "Actually, they're named Carlton and Jill."

Looking at the photos, Wheeler asked, "Who are these people, and why do you think they were the ones on Prescott's boat?"

"Their name is McDermitt. In talking with Foster's associates and coworkers at the museum, I learned that she had been spending a lot of time looking for documents relating to the Wallowa County massacre."

"What massacre?"

"In 1887, a gang of rustlers gunned down three dozen Chinese gold miners on the banks of the Snake River. Three different people told me that Foster was working with a guy who claimed he was writing a book on the subject, and their descriptions of the guy sounded a lot like Prescott's description of the man on his boat."

"There'd better be more than that," Wheeler said impatiently.

"I found out that one of the rustlers, Omar LaRue, took off right after the massacre and came to live with his sister in Oregon City. The sister turns out to be Carlton McDermitt's great-great-grandmother. I'm pretty sure that McDermitt believes that the Chinese miners' gold—maybe half a million dollars worth—was brought here by LaRue."

"Okay," Wheeler said slowly, "so you figure McDermitt was looking for the gold."

"Right. And I think Foster figured it out and said so during Prescott's boat cruise."

"And that's why they killed her? It's a nice theory, but I'll need more than that—"

"If Prescott can ID the McDermitts as the couple on his boat, then we'll know that we're on the right track. I'm still trying to firm up the connection with the gold."

"Fair enough. It'll probably take a week or more to put together a spread and get Prescott in to look at it," Wheeler said. "I'll let you know how it comes out."

"Thomas Robert Foster?" I asked the person on the phone.

"I don't need Viagra, and I don't buy drugs over the phone," he said impatiently.

"I'm not a telemarketer," I quickly explained. "I'm a private investigator in Oregon. I'm investigating what happened to Tara Foster. Were you her husband?"

"I was, but we were divorced long before she disappeared."

"Maybe you heard that her remains were found last fall?"

"A friend sent me a newspaper clipping. It's sad, but I don't see how I can help."

"I'm looking at people she was working with at the museum," I began.

"I don't think the old ladies at the museum wrapped her up and threw her into the river." He laughed.

"No, I don't mean coworkers. I'm looking at patrons—people she was doing research for."

"Okay," he said slowly. "I don't see how I can help you with that. We were divorced a long time before that, and I was living in El Paso."

"Well, a couple of the 'old ladies' told me that Tara worked for several years tracking down material relating to the killing of three dozen Chinese gold miners in Hells Canyon back in 1887. Do you know anything about that?"

"Oh. Yeah, she talked about that a few times when she'd find something interesting."

"What kind of things?"

"I don't remember specifically, just things that added detail to the history."

"Did she ever mention who she was working with?"

"Not that I recall."

"Wasn't she working with your cousin?"

"Huh? What are you talking about?" He sounded genuinely confused.

"Carlton McDermitt," I said. "He's your cousin, isn't he?

"Oh. Carlton. I forgot about him. He isn't really a relative. I mean, not a blood relative. He was…"

He paused a moment to think it through.

"Okay. A brother of my great-grandfather was married to a sister of Carlton's great-grandmother."

"Clara Shedd," I said, looking at the family tree Martha had printed.

"Aunt Clara—that's what I called her—moved in with my grandparents after her husband died. She was actually closer to his family than to her own. Anyway, when my grandparents died, they left their house in Redmond to Aunt Clara, and she lived there the rest of her life. Tara and I used to visit her regularly back when we lived in Bend."

"When was that?"

"We moved to Oregon City in 1991. I always felt kind of guilty about leaving Aunt Clara alone. We still went to visit her, but not as often as when we lived nearby."

"So what about Carlton?"

"Heck, I never even knew he existed until after Aunt Clara died in 1994. That's when Carlton showed up, claiming her estate. I don't know if he'd ever even met her. Apparently, probate court notified him."

"Not to be too personal, but did she have a big estate?"

"Naw," he scoffed. "She had almost nothing. Her only source of income was a reverse mortgage that she'd taken out on the old house. She didn't even have social security. I suppose that's why she never wrote a will. She didn't have anything to pass on."

"So what was Carlton's involvement?"

"About two weeks after she died, he called me and introduced himself as Aunt Clara's 'rightful heir,' as he put it. By then, the probate judge had told me of his existence, but it was still a surprise when he came out of the woodpile to claim the estate."

"What did you do?"

"Tara and I met Carlton and his wife—Jill, I think—and I explained that we needed to go over to Redmond to clear out her house because it belonged to the bank on account of the reverse mortgage, and it was only a few days before they were going to take possession. Carlton went with me, and we spent an afternoon going through her things."

"Did you find anything?"

"She didn't have anything of value. Except for a few antiques, we donated everything to Goodwill."

"What kind of antiques?"

"Some glassware and china, an old pedal organ, a table-and-chair set, a few books."

"And it all went to Carlton?"

"No, all he wanted was an old family bible. It went back about six generations. He gave the rest to me, which was fine, because he didn't deserve anything anyway."

"So that's how Tara met Carlton—because of your aunt's death?"

"That's right, why?"

"Well, people at the museum have told me that Tara was doing some historical research for him."

That wasn't exactly the truth. They had told me that Tara was working with *someone*, and I suspected it was Carlton. I was hoping Tom Foster would confirm it. He did.

"Yeah, once he found out that she worked at the museum, he developed an interest in learning his family background. She helped him figure out exactly how he was related to Aunt Clara. The funny thing was that once he tracked it back, he discovered that Aunt Clara and her sister Elizabeth had been born in Oregon City—and the house where they were born was still standing. Carlton ended up buying it."

"Funny how things work out," I mused. "But my understanding is that Tara continued doing research for Carlton, right up until she disappeared."

"Well, I wouldn't know about that. I mean, sure, Tara mentioned him from time to time, but I don't know any of the details."

I thanked Tom Foster for his time and disconnected.

"Well, now we have solid confirmation that Tara Foster was working with Carlton," I told Martha after I put the phone down.

"So how did that turn into a search for the Chinese gold?" she asked.

"I think it's the other way around. It was the gold that got him interested in the history. My guess is that he found something in Aunt Clara's house that tipped him off. Tom Foster says that the only thing Carlton kept was the family Bible. That would be the first place I'd look."

"In the Bible? You're thinking that something in the Bible mentioned the gold."

"Foster said the Bible went back about six generations," I said, looking at the family tree from Ancestry.com. "That would go back to Jeremiah and Rebecca Applegate."

"Aha, so maybe Rebecca left a note about the gold!" Martha said excitedly. "With a search warrant, we could get that Bible—it could seal the case!"

"And if John Prescott identifies Carlton and Jill, we'll get that warrant," I concluded.

48

Wednesday, July 30

"We showed the photos to John Prescott," said Michael Wheeler.

"You don't sound excited," I observed.

"The results weren't much good. He didn't identify any of the women in the lay-down as the one who was with Tara Foster on his boat. But he *did* pick out your guy and then promptly said he couldn't be sure, but he thought that it *might* be the one on his boat."

"Well, that's *something*, isn't it?"

"We'll need a more solid ID than that. Can you get other photos?"

"We have some others, but they're more recent."

"Send them over. It's worth a try—you know how people, especially women, can look different from one photo to the next."

"Yeah, that's true. Now that I think about it, Jill wasn't wearing any makeup at the time the flood photos were taken. *With* makeup, she can look like a different person."

"Get me the best pictures you can that show how they both might have looked on the kind of outing Prescott described. You do that, and I'll put together another photo spread."

"There's more. Remember I told you that Tara Foster's coworkers described a man she was doing research for—a man whose description sounded a lot like Carlton McDermitt? Well, I've found a witness who confirms that it *was* McDermitt."

"A reliable witness?"

"Tara Foster's ex. Turns out that he's a shoestring cousin to McDermitt. I tracked him down, and he confirmed that Tara was doing research for Carlton."

"That still doesn't prove he killed her."

"How about if we can prove that he knew where the Hells Canyon gold was hidden or at least thought he knew?"

"Where're you going to find that?" he asked and then added, "It'd be a good motive but still not proof."

"McDermitt's interest in the gold seems to have started when his great-great aunt died. I think he found something while cleaning out her house—some kind of note that tells where the gold is. I'm pretty sure that McDermitt believes that the Hells Canyon gold was hidden in his house—the Jeremiah Applegate house down here in Canemah—and that note will prove it," I explained.

"But you don't know that for sure."

"I'd sure like to search McDermitt's house."

"Without Prescott's ID on the photos, I have no probable cause for a search warrant."

"Well, think about this. The Applegate house is where Dave Blodgett was working when he disappeared. That can't *possibly* be a coincidence."

"Jesus! Does Jamieson know that?"

"Not yet. Without firming up the Foster case and getting our hands on that note, there's nothing to tell him. I was hoping that Prescott's identification of the McDermitts would take care of that."

"The timing on this really sucks," Wheeler commented, "especially with the Blalock trial now on the fast track. That's still my priority."

"I understand that," I said. "And I know that Blodgett isn't your case. I just thought that you needed to see the big picture."

Does the sheriff's office have a cadaver dog?" I asked Kim. "Not in Clackamas County," she said. "Yamhill County has dogs, and they make them available through the Oregon State Sheriff's Association. What do you have in mind?"

"Dave Blodgett. If Carlton killed him and dumped the body down the old well in the Applegate house, would a dog be able to pick up the scent?"

"Good question. How deep is the well?"

"When I looked down it, it seemed to be about twelve to fifteen feet deep. That depth was from the original cellar floor. The new floor is about three feet lower, so the depth would be nine to twelve feet. But they laid down a solid vapor barrier before they poured the slab, so I don't know if any scent would come through."

"I've seen dogs do some amazing things, but I don't know about this."

"Do you know someone who might be able to take a guess?"

"No, but maybe I can find out who works with Yamhill County's dogs."

She flashed me one of her suggestive expressions and added, "What's the information worth to you?"

I pretended to ponder the question before saying, "How about dinner at the Fernwood?"

"Is that all?" she asked with a sly smile.

"With fine wine."

"And…"

"That too," I promised.

She called one of the search-and-rescue divers, because they sometimes work alongside dog handlers when searching for missing persons. From him, she got the name and number of the officer who worked with the dogs on the Yamhill County Sheriff's Search and Rescue Team.

"Deputy McCredie?" Kim asked.

"This is McCredie. What can I do for you?"

Kim's phone was loud enough that I could hear both ends of the conversation.

"This is Deputy Kim Stayton, Clackamas County Marine Unit. I need your opinion regarding the capabilities of your cadaver dogs."

"What exactly do you need?"

"We think there may be human remains in the bottom of an old well that has been filled in and covered with concrete."

"How deep is the well and how long ago did this happen?"

"The victim went missing three and a half months ago. The well is nine to twelve feet deep, with about a foot of water in the bottom. It was filled with chunks of broken concrete. A thick plastic vapor barrier was laid down, and then a concrete slab was poured over the top. It's in the basement of a house."

"Someone went to a lot of trouble to hide the body," McCredie commented.

"It was a crime of opportunity," Kim explained. "The house was midway through an extensive remodeling project. The vic was a laborer.

The old well was scheduled to be filled in and covered at the time he disappeared."

"Okay. The depth of the well isn't too big a problem, especially since it was filled with chunks of concrete. If it had been filled with clay or even tightly compacted dirt, it might be tougher for odors to penetrate, but concrete chunks—that wouldn't hold it down. The vapor barrier over the top could be a problem. It's designed to prevent any circulation of air. If it's done right, the dogs might not be able to pick up anything."

"There's also Marmoleum flooring on top of the slab," Kim added.

"In that case, I wouldn't waste the time. Not much chance of success," McCredie said.

"How about off to the side? It was an old stone-lined well from the 1800s. Could the odor get through the surrounding soil and reach the surface outside the house?"

"Depends how far under the house the well is and what the soil in the area is like."

"The well was in the corner of the original cellar, so it isn't very far under the house. As for the soil, it's pretty solid—probably undisturbed."

"You say the well was in the cellar. How deep was the cellar—that is, how deep is the bottom of the well below the outside ground level?"

Kim looked at me as I did some quick arithmetic. I scribbled on a scrap of paper and handed it to her.

"Eighteen to twenty feet," she said.

"That's going to be tough. Do you have a warrant?"

"No, but we might be able to get the property owner's permission."

"It's a long shot," McCredie said.

"Just one thing," I said loud enough for him to hear. "A huge tree was taken out just a few feet from the house. The stump grinder had to go pretty far into the ground."

"Who am I talking to?" McCredie asked.

"Corrigan. Private investigator," I said.

"I've heard of you. What's your part in this?"

"I'm working for Sheriff Jamieson on a cold case that appears to be connected with the laborer's disappearance."

"Don't hand me that." I could hear the contempt in his voice. "The sheriff's office doesn't hire privates."

I hastily corrected myself. "No, I'm working on the case for a private party, but I'm sharing information with Jamieson. His people don't have time to work the cold case."

"A three-month-old body in the bottom of the well isn't exactly a cold case."

"Of course not. But like Stayton said, it was the cold case that led me to suspect that the recent disappearance might be related. I'm not asking you to do anything. I'm just trying to determine the feasibility before I take it to Jamieson. If he thinks there's something to find, he'll make the request."

"Fair enough," McCredie conceded. "Tell him that there's maybe a 5 to 10 percent chance that the dogs will be able to pick something up. That means that there's a 90 percent chance that they'd miss it even if the guy's down there."

Over dinner at the Fernwood Inn, I asked Kim, "Do you think Jamieson would request the dogs if we explained the whole thing to him?"

She shrugged. "He might, if you could get him to hear the full explanation. The problem is, I don't think he can give you enough time to do that. This case of yours is a convoluted mess."

"Tell me about it."

"Is there anything you can do to beef up the case against McDermitt?"

"Wheeler is going to give Prescott another photo spread."

"Yeah I know about that. Anything else?"

"I'm thinking about making another run at Janet Monroe. She was evasive when I talked with her in Reno, and I think that she deliberately tried to conceal the letters that I found at the museum in Joseph. I want to know why."

"What's your plan?"

"I don't have a plan yet—just an idea."

She persisted. "Okay. So what is your *idea*?"

"Another trip to Reno. I'm still working on how to get her to spill her guts. Why don't you take a couple of days off and come along," I suggested.

She eyed me suspiciously. "Do you have something else in mind?"

"Like what?"

"You know what!"

I continued my blank stare until she broke.

"You'll want to get married while we're there," she blurted.

"Hey, that's a great idea," I said. "I thought you'd never ask."

"I didn't," she said with a scowl.

I refilled her wine glass.

"Still, it's worth considering," I said.

49

Friday, August 1

Not many years ago, everybody in Canemah (and most other communities) had a burn pile in the corner of their yard. When you had scrap lumber, you'd throw it on the burn pile. When you had empty cardboard boxes, you'd throw 'em on the burn pile. When you had hedge trimmings, you'd throw 'em on the burn pile. Then about once a month, you'd put a match to it, and if the pile was unusually large, you might stand by with a garden hose.

So a column of smoke rising up from among the houses in most neighborhoods was a fairly common occurrence and generally not cause for concern. Then after most open burning was banned, there were the years of transition—when you might see smoke but merely assume that some scofflaw was bending the rules for personal convenience. But smoke rising out of the neighborhood today nearly always demands a phone call, either to city Code Enforcement or to 911.

I don't know who first spotted the smoke rising out of Canemah. I heard someone shouting and looked up from my beach chair to see a dark cloud of smoke that looked at first like maybe someone had just started an old diesel truck engine. But the cloud quickly grew, and the commotion up on Water Street told me that something was up.

In the minute or so that it took to come to that realization and dash up the steps, across the railroad tracks, and down Water Street, the smoke cloud billowing into the evening sky doubled in size and doubled again. I could hear the crackle of burning wood as I rounded the corner in front of Kaylin Beatty's house. Fire was visible through the fence on the far side of Kaylin's yard, and I could see that the flames were coming from Carlton McDermitt's garage.

Incongruous images registered simultaneously. Angry dark-orange flames curled out from under the eaves on both sides of the old garage. A Ford Explorer with a picture of a salmon painted on the door was parked crazily on the sidewalk along Highway 99, and a large bald man was waving frantically with one hand while holding a phone to his ear with the other. In front of the garage sat Carlton's red pickup. Radiant heat from the fire was already starting to warp the plastic windows on the canopy.

The distant sound of a siren from the direction of the fire station a mile away told me that someone had already made the emergency call. Cautiously, I approached the side window of the garage, holding up my hand to shield my face from the heat. But as I was edging my way past the front corner of the garage, there was a sound that I felt more than heard. The glass shattered out of the window I was just about to peek through, and the carriage doors on the front of the garage flew open. Clouds of sparks belched out of both openings, raining embers on me and the ground around the garage.

As I backed away, I got a glimpse inside the garage. On the floor just beyond the open doors, I saw the soles of two work boots and, beyond them, the still form of the person wearing them. The first fire engine was still perhaps two minutes away, and that was way too long for the victim to have any hope of survival. The old wood of the 1920s–era garage was like tinder, and the building was already fully involved.

I spotted an old quilt or moving blanket in the bed of Carlton's pickup, so I grabbed it and threw it over my head and shoulders. Dropping to the ground, I belly crawled toward the fire, attempting to keep myself beneath the heat as much as possible. A heavy chunk of burning wood fell from somewhere above and landed two feet to my right. Beyond that, I could make out the lawn mower with its burst fuel tank, probably the source of the explosion that had blown the doors open.

Smoke was rising from the victim's blue jeans, which appeared to be on the verge of flashing into flames. I was pretty sure that it was already too late, but I pushed myself forward until I was close enough to grab the cuff on one leg of the jeans with my left hand. I felt a cooling breeze passing over as the fire sucked in surrounding air to feed the combustion. The breeze was the only thing preventing me from broiling.

Off to the side of the victim, I caught a glimpse of a bright blue flame, which I immediately recognized as coming from a welder's torch.

With that came the terrifying realization that there was an oxyacetylene rig somewhere in the burning garage. When the tanks ruptured, the resulting explosion could wipe out everything within a hundred-foot radius. The best I could hope for would be that relief valves might provide a less-than-explosive release of pressure, but even a gentle release of acetylene and pure oxygen would increase the intensity of the fire by factors I did not want to contemplate.

The hair on the top of my arm and the back of my hand curled and smoked, and I fought the instinct to pull back and get the hell out of there. I tugged as hard as I could. The body moved only a couple of inches before I lost the little bit of leverage I had. I pushed my body backward to regain the leverage and gave another tug. The body moved a few more inches. I felt hands grab my ankles, so I grabbed the victim's boot with both hands and held on while somebody pulled me out from under the fire. The gravel on the ground scraped my entire body, but I focused all of my attention on maintaining my grip on that smoldering boot.

Water sprayed on my back and arms, and suddenly the air around me felt deliciously cool. I opened my eyes and saw that I was in the street, partially shielded from the heat by Carlton's pickup. Someone touched my hands, and I let go of the boot. The quilt was lifted off, and cool water was sprayed on my head and shoulders. I looked up to see Kaylin Beatty with a garden hose. Her expression was frightening to see because she was looking straight at me.

I pushed myself up onto my hands and knees and scrambled crab-like back from the fire. "Get back! Get back!" I tried to shout. "Welding torch. It's going to explode!"

Even as I croaked out the words, there was a hissing noise that turned into a roar that sounded like a jet-airplane engine spooling up for takeoff. The pavement around me was suddenly illuminated by white light, and I knew that the oxygen tank had just ruptured, turning the burning wood of the old garage into a blowtorch. I scrambled to my feet and lurched over toward Kaylin's yard, where I sat heavily on her lawn.

"What can I do?" she asked urgently.

"Get me some ice. Lots of it," I said.

Applying ice to a minor burn can take away a lot of the heat before it penetrates deeper into the tissue beneath the skin, thus greatly reducing the trauma. Kaylin brought the entire ice-maker tub from her refrigerator, and I plunged my hands into it, feeling the sting and hoping for the best. She filled Ziploc bags with ice and held them gently against my forearms.

I looked up in time to see the first fire engine arrive just as the garage collapsed. Other emergency vehicles arrived in quick succession, including two rescue units, an ambulance, another fire engine, and several Oregon City Police cruisers. I found myself surrounded by paramedics checking out my hands and arms.

"I'm okay," I insisted. "Take care of the other guy!"

"He's being taken care of," somebody said. "Don't worry about him."

"Who pulled us out?" I asked.

The paramedic looked puzzled, but Kaylin said, "It was some big guy—I guess he was just passing by. He got to you just in time."

There was suddenly a huge sizzling sound as the first fire hose was directed at the heap of burning rubble that had been Carlton's garage just five minutes before. The flames were replaced by a massive cloud of steam. I started to take inventory of my injuries as the firefighters hosed down the coals.

My chest and belly were scraped raw in parallel vertical lines, where I'd been dragged across the gravel. The lower part of my back felt sunburned where my shirt had ridden up. And of course, the tops of my arms and the backs of my hands were stinging from burns, though I was pleased to see that no blisters had formed.

Someone handed me a can of beer, and I looked up to see Bud.

"You need to cool down on the inside too," he said. "What the hell happened?"

"Was that Carlton in there?"

"Probably," Bud said. "But I'm not sure. They hauled him away in an ambulance."

"You really ought to go to the hospital," the paramedic told me. "And you really shouldn't be drinking that. The alcohol and that ice might put your body into shock."

"Thanks. For everything. I appreciate your advice," I said, "and I know that you know a lot more about this stuff than I do. But I can't think of a single thing they could do for me at the hospital that I'm not already doing here."

I spotted Officer Durham and waved him over.

"You okay?" he asked.

"I think so," I said. "Was that Carlton?"

"I couldn't tell," he said, "but I think 'was' is the right word."

"Dead?"

"Looked that way. You know anything about the fire?"

"I saw a cutting torch burning in there. That's probably what started the fire."

Durham glanced over at the smoldering pile of rubble where the garage used to be. The two steel tanks were lying on their sides amid the debris.

He nodded. "You saw the torch burning?"

"That's right. It was on the floor right next to Car—next to the victim."

At that point, we were interrupted by the bald man I'd seen by the highway just before approaching the burning garage.

"Excuse me, Officer. I really need to get going," he said impatiently.

I said to Durham, "Go ahead. We can talk anytime."

He turned and asked the man's name.

"Guido Barcelli," the bald man answered. "I was coming down the highway minding my own business when some guy ran right out in front of me. I had to swerve to miss him, and I ended up there—on the sidewalk."

He gestured toward the Explorer with the salmon on the door, while Durham took notes.

"Were you by yourself? Was anybody injured?" Durham asked.

Guido said, "I'm okay, but I sideswiped that telephone pole."

"The person who ran out in front of you—did he come from Jerome Street?

"Yeah, he ran right out in front of me. I almost flattened him!"

"What can you tell me about him?"

"I think he was a black kid, you know, like a break-dancer."

"Why do you say that?"

"He was wearing one of those sweatshirts like they all wear—you know, the ones with a hood."

"You mean a hoodie?"

"Yeah, that's what I'm telling you. He probably couldn't see where he was going because his face was half-covered by his hood," Guido answered.

"Did you see where he went?" Durham asked.

"No, he was in front of me one second, and then I was on the sidewalk. I didn't see him after that."

"Anything else you can tell me?"

"Old Navy. The sweatshirt said 'Old Navy.' And he was carrying something."

"What was he carrying?"

"It was a kid's baseball bat—one of those metal ones."

"What the hell happened here?"

I turned to see Kim walking up from Water Street. She was still in uniform, fresh in from working the late shift on river patrol.

"Carlton's garage burned down," I said.

"I can see that. What happened to you?" she asked.

"I was trying to pull him out. The fire was too intense. Someone grabbed me and dragged us both out," I rambled.

"It was this man," Officer Durham said, gesturing toward Guido.

"Then I owe you," I said to Guido. "I was just about to give up."

Guido shrugged. "It was no big thing."

"It was pretty big to me. Thanks."

"How bad is it?" Kim asked, pointing at my forearms.

"Not too bad," I said. "About like a bad sunburn."

I drained my beer can, and Bud promptly handed me a fresh one. I took it with gratitude.

50

Saturday, August 2

There were some small blisters on the backs of my hands and a persistent stinging from the reddened skin on my arms, which I treated with a spray can of Solarcaine given to me by Kim. She always carries it on her patrol boat for people who get too much sun out on the river. The morning paper confirmed the two things that I had suspected. The victim was Carlton McDermitt, and he was dead on arrival at the hospital.

That left me with a hollow feeling. I hadn't liked Carlton much, and he had become my number one suspect in two murders. But that didn't mean I wanted him dead. On the contrary, there were many questions that I'd wanted to ask him that would now go unanswered forever. I had to completely reevaluate my investigation.

The easiest thing to do, of course, would be to simply declare Carlton guilty and close both cases; and in reality, that probably was the right thing to do. It made little sense to spend any more time gathering evidence against Carlton since there'd never be a trial. I knew he was guilty, and that was that. But there was still the unanswered question about Jill McDermitt's involvement in the Foster murder.

If she had been a part of it, she should be prosecuted. We might learn something about her involvement if Michael Wheeler followed through with the new photo lay-down for Prescott, but with Carlton dead, he might decide to drop the whole thing. And did it really matter? I was already leaning toward believing that Jill had no knowledge of the murder, even if she was on Prescott's boat.

I went to work writing up a case summary for Michael Wheeler and yet another for Dennis Lawen.

A third note was intended for Sheriff Jamieson, outlining my suspicions regarding Dave Blodgett's disappearance and my belief that his body could be found at the bottom of the old well under the basement floor in the Applegate house. I passed along Barry Walker's name and number so that they could discuss the options for determining if I was right about Dave.

I stalled on the fourth note. Carrie Blodgett deserved to know what had happened to her husband, but I simply couldn't force myself to write the words—at least not until I was sure. That is, not until his body was found.

The day was overcast, but even with the cloud cover, the sun caused my arms to sting when I went outdoors. I went back inside and found a Seattle Seahawks sweatshirt that I put on to cover my burns. There was a Clackamas Fire District pickup parked next to Carlton's house, and two men in Tyvek suits were poking at the remains of the garage.

I introduced myself and explained how I'd seen the welding torch burning when I crawled into the garage.

"Was the victim a welder?" asked one of the fire investigators.

"Hardly." I laughed. "He was a used car salesman. I never even knew he owned a welding torch."

"Maybe he didn't," the investigator said, pointing at the oxygen tank.

Even after the fire, the stenciled lettering still showed in the fully oxidized paint: **MAVERICK WELDERS SUPPLY**.

"So maybe he didn't know how to use it," I speculated.

"That's what we're thinking," the investigator said.

"Any idea what he was doing with it?"

"Don't know for sure. What we've found doesn't exactly add up."

"Well, he wouldn't go to the trouble of renting a torch unless he had a pretty good project in mind."

The investigator shrugged. "You knew this guy. Was he a scuba diver?"

"A scuba diver? Not a chance. Why?"

He pointed to some things I hadn't noticed. Lying on its side amid the rubble was a small stainless steel saucepan, and next to it was a block of ceramic material with a row of parallel rectangular slots, each measuring about 2 ½ inches long and ¾ inch wide.

"That's a mold for casting lead bars to go into the pockets on a scuba diver's weight belt. And take a look at this," he said.

He opened a steel fishing-tackle box to reveal that it was nearly full of lead, melted by the heat of the garage fire into a single large brick. A few crimped steel fasteners protruded from the lead, revealing that the tackle box had been filled with used wheel-balancing weights.

"Maybe he was going to use them for fishing weights," I suggested. "I've seen him fishing a few times."

The investigator nodded and said, "Could be. But you don't need a cutting torch to melt lead. You can do it on the kitchen stove."

"Has anybody talked with his wife—ex-wife, that is? She might have some idea. Or more likely, her son might have some idea what he was doing."

"I'm sure the police department will be talking with her. Anyway, thanks for the suggestion."

The investigators went back to work, and I headed back home. The sun was starting to break through, and even with the sweatshirt, it made my burns sting. Martha spotted me as I was walking up Water Street, and she hurried to catch up.

"Bud told me about the fire last night," she said. "I can't believe I slept through the whole thing."

"It didn't last long. Start to finish, it didn't take twenty minutes," I said.

I could see her looking at my reddened hands, so I added, "I'll be okay. It's not much worse than a sunburn."

Actually, it was.

"Did they determine who it was…in the garage?"

"It was Carlton. He didn't make it. I didn't have much hope about that. The fire was awfully intense."

She shook her head. "How did it happen?"

"Looks like he was trying to melt some lead with a cutting torch. He was wearing dark goggles and probably didn't notice when the garage caught fire. Then it spread so fast he couldn't get out."

"Why was he melting lead?"

I shook my head. "Who knows? It looked like maybe he was making fishing weights."

"Why wouldn't he just buy them?"

"These were bigger than what they sell. Fishermen use the big, heavy weights when they fish for sturgeon down below the falls because the water's so deep and swift."

"Oh. Bud just uses old railroad spikes that he picks up along the tracks."

"Yeah, I know. I guess Carlton never thought of that."

"What are we going to do about Tara Foster?" Martha finally asked.

"That's up to the sheriff's office. There isn't much else we can do. I just hope I can convince Dennis Lawen to drop it because I don't intend to make this my life's work."

"It's been good money, though."

51

Monday, August 4

"Jamieson wants us to get the cadaver dogs out there to see if you're right about Dave Blodgett," Michael Wheeler said on the phone.

"Any idea when that's going to happen?" I asked.

"Nothing's been scheduled yet. They still need to get the owner's permission. I'm meeting him for lunch at the Caufield House. The tough part will be telling him that if the dogs find something, we're going to have to tear up the floor and dig out the well. That won't make him happy. In fact, even if the dogs *don't* find anything, we'll probably have to dig up the floor."

"I've been thinking about alternatives. The lady next door to the Applegate house has a couple of sons who run excavating equipment. I talked to one of them, and he thinks he can do the excavation from outside the house. You know, dig a pit next to the foundation and then tunnel over to the well."

"That would probably sit better with Barry Walker. Who is this equipment operator?"

"Name is Beatty. Justin Beatty. His mother is Kaylin Beatty, the witness who saw Blodgett's car speed away from the house the day Dave disappeared. You'll find her number in your witness log."

"Good. That might make this easier. Now as far as the Foster thing is concerned, Jamieson isn't convinced that we have enough to pin it on McDermitt. I'm driving up to Tacoma this afternoon to show your latest photos to John Prescott. If he can ID McDermitt, then we'll probably call it good."

After I wrapped up the phone call, I handed the Foster case file to Martha.

"I'd like you to start working up the final billing on this. Let's see if we can get the county to reimburse us for the forensics—the DNA lab work and the crime scene investigation that we paid for. Add up all of our hours and mileage, and see how it balances out against what Dennis Lawen has paid us."

We heard footsteps on the front porch, and I looked up to see Jill McDermitt. She had an old-fashioned leather briefcase, and from the way she was carrying it, it appeared to be heavy.

"Come in," I said, trying my best to conceal my surprise.

"Thanks," she said. "I heard what you did."

I waved it off.

"I feel terrible about this whole thing. I mean, after all of the conflict and frustration, Carlton's gone, and I just can't make myself feel right about it."

"It's not because of anything you did," I consoled.

"No, but I think there might be more to it," she said. "I'm probably just letting my imagination run wild, but I think there's a chance that Carlton may have had something to do with that worker's disappearance."

"Dave Blodgett? What makes you think that?"

"Well, I don't actually *know anything* about it."

I said nothing, waiting for her to elaborate. The silence reached the point of being uncomfortable.

"I've been over at Carlton's house, going through his things. He never wrote a will, so everything will go to Patrick and Colleen," she finally said.

"What's the hurry?" I asked, surprised that Jill was going through Carlton's possessions just two days after his death.

"The bank wants to take possession of the house by the tenth. He was in default and had received his final foreclosure notice. We need to get everything out by Friday."

I nodded and let her continue.

"Well, I found something in the house that might explain a lot of the peculiar things he's been doing—things like digging in my trash, snooping in my house—even things that went on for years before we got divorced."

"Such as…"

"Everything—buying the old Applegate house, all of the remodeling he did inside, cutting holes in the floors and walls—all the things that used to aggravate me and make me think he was crazy."

"So have you found something to change that opinion?" I asked.

"God," Jill said. "Okay, this goes way back. Years ago, we were living in Gladstone when Carlton's great-aunt died. He didn't even know her, but he and a cousin ended up going through her things. It was shortly after that that Carlton developed a big interest in his family history, and that led to his obsession with the Applegate house."

"Didn't you once tell me that the house had been in Carlton's family before?"

I knew all of this, but I wanted to hear her tell the story.

"That's right. Jeremiah and Rebecca Applegate were his great-great-grandparents. They're the ones who built the house. Anyway, I was over at Carlton's place yesterday with the kids, trying to figure out what to keep and what to get rid of, and I found this."

From the briefcase, she extracted a thick leather-bound book that appeared to be very old. When she laid it on my desk, I could see the embossing on the cover—Holy Bible.

"Carlton brought this home back in 1994, when he cleaned out Aunt Clara's house. He said it was an heirloom. He put it away and never let anybody handle it. I never saw it again until yesterday. I thought it would mean something to the kids, maybe not now but later in their lives, so I took it home and looked through it last night."

"It looks like it might be valuable," I observed.

"The thing is, it was this Bible that sparked Carlton's interest in his family history. He was very excited to learn that it had belonged to his great-great-grandmother, Rebecca Applegate. That's when he learned about the Jeremiah Applegate house. Now I know why he wanted to buy the place."

I noticed that her hands were shaking a little bit as she leafed through the pages. She stopped when she found the place she was looking for. At the end of the book of Proverbs and in front of the first page of Ecclesiastes, there was a sheet of badly faded paper. It seemed to be stuck in place and too fragile to handle.

Jill turned the open bible so that I could read the crude writing on the old parchment. It had been written in ink that had faded to a brownish color that was only a shade darker than the sepia paper. I pulled my desk lamp over the page and was able to make out the words. I held my breath as I read.

Dear Rebecca,

I am leaving this note for you to find in case anything happens to me before I can come back & get what I have hidden in your house. I'm sorry to leave without saying goodbye, but I fear that harm may come to you if I stay another hour.

You probably heard about a bunch of chinky miners that got killed in Snake River country. Me and you know those who killed them chinkys, but I promise you that I did not kill anyone.

I found some gold at Dug Bar near a shack used by them cow boys that done the shooting and when I came here from Imnaha I brought the gold with me. One of them killers is in town today looking for me & he will surely kill me if he can.

I guess if you are reading this it is because he caught up with me, so I want you to have the gold. It is worth a fortune. You will find it in the place where I was working, which I do not need to write down here. You will remember the place.

Omar

When I finished reading, I got my camera and took several photos of the note, using different exposures.

"Do you think this is real?" I asked.

"Well, sure, I don't see any reason to doubt it. I don't know very much about Carlton's family," Jill explained. "But to my knowledge, no one in the family had ever come into big money, so I'm guessing that this note was never seen until Carlton found it in 1994."

This was the final link. It proved that Carlton knew about the Chinese gold and explained how he knew it was hidden in the Applegate house. The one thing he didn't know was where Omar had been working in the house—only Rebecca and Jeremiah would have known that.

The dilemma I now found myself facing was the possibility of Jill's complicity in Tara Foster's murder. We might soon know if she had been aboard John Prescott's boat, but would her presence there necessarily mean that she participated in or even knew about the murder? The fact that she had brought this new discovery to me was pretty strong evidence of innocence.

I decided to go with my instincts and dismiss her as a suspect.

"What do you know about the gold miners who were killed?" I asked.

She shrugged. "Not a thing. I've never heard of it."

I went to my bookshelf and pulled out my copy of *Massacred for Gold*.

"This book tells the whole story. I first learned about it during my investigation into the death of the woman who was rolled up in the carpet—you remember that, last fall?"

Looking confused, she just nodded.

"Her name was Tara Foster. She worked for the historical society," I said, gesturing in the general direction of the museum. "Prior to her disappearance, she'd been researching that event. There's no way to know what she found out, but I think it's quite possible that she discovered the connection that this note describes."

"I don't get it. What connection?"

"You said that Carlton found this Bible when he and his cousin were cleaning out Aunt Clara's house after she died, right?"

"Yes, but…"

"Do you know the name of Carlton's cousin?"

"I probably heard it, but he was such a distant relative we never heard from him after that."

"His name is Thomas Foster. He was Tara Foster's husband."

Jill stared at me.

"I just found that out a few days ago," I explained, "and I'm still trying to figure out how or if it has any bearing on the Foster murder."

"My god," she whispered.

"Tara Foster was helping Carlton. He matches the description of a museum patron who was frequently seen with her. Tom Foster has confirmed that he introduced them."

"I'm sorry, I still don't get it."

"What do you think Carlton might have been thinking when he first read the note?"

Hesitantly, she said, "Well, you can bet that the mention of hidden gold would have caught his attention. He was always hoping to stumble into a fortune. I can't begin to guess how much he spent on lottery tickets."

"The 'fortune in gold' would capture just about anybody's attention. But at first, he didn't even know who Rebecca and Omar were. That's probably what took him to the museum. He probably went there and asked if anyone ever heard of an incident where Chinese miners had been killed in Snake River country."

"And maybe that's where Tara Foster got involved."

"When I talked to the lady at the museum, she showed me a copy of a 1967 magazine article about the incident written by a former Forest Service employee named Gerald Tucker.[3] It's quite possible that Tara Foster showed the same article to Carlton.

It told of two or three dozen Chinese miners gunned down in Hells Canyon by a gang of horse thieves in May of 1887. It was said that gold dust estimated to be worth between five thousand and ten thousand dollars was taken in the massacre. The article gave the names of the horse thieves: Carl Hughes, Hiram Maynard, Robert McMillan, Frank Vaughan, Titus Canfield, Blue Evans, and *Omar LaRue*."

Martha, who had been listening, quietly spoke up. "Carlton would have immediately noticed the name of Omar LaRue, because the note in the Bible was signed by Omar. That would have told him that he was on the right track."

"And that much gold would have been worth three hundred thousand to six hundred thousand dollars in 1994," I added.

"And a lot more than that today," Martha said.

I continued. "Next, Carlton would have to figure out who Rebecca was. She could have been a girlfriend, wife, relative, or just an acquaintance, but Carlton could reasonably guess that the Bible where he'd found the note had belonged to Rebecca. Why else would Omar have chosen it as the place to hide his note?

The old tradition of passing the family Bible from one generation to the next implied that Rebecca might have been one of Clara Shedd's ancestors. Clara was born in 1896, so it was fair to guess that Rebecca was her mother. Proving that in the days before the internet and Ancestry.com would have been a difficult task."

---

3. Gerald J. Tucker, "*Massacre for Gold,*" Old West (Fall 1967): 26-29.

Martha handed me a copy of the family tree that she had printed from Ancestry.com.

Thinking on the fly, I speculated how Carlton might have gotten the same information. Aunt Clara had lived in Redmond. I would have gone to the Deschutes County records office to look for documents that would reveal Clara's maiden name, *Applegate*. That's a fairly common name in Oregon, but even if Deschutes County had nothing to indicate who Clara's parents were, Carlton could have gone to the Oregon State Library in Salem, where a mountain of old civil records are stored.

"Suppose he found Clara's birth certificate. It would have shown her birthplace, Oregon City, and her mother's name, Rebecca LaRue Applegate. With that information, he'd have known to search old Oregon City records for the Applegate family home, probably at the museum—with Tara Foster's help."

"And that's how he found the Jeremiah Applegate house," Jill concluded.

"I'd bet on it," I said.

"Once he knew the address, Carlton drove down to Canemah, and there it was. When the dive company sold all of these old houses in 1993, Chuck Hampton bought the Applegate House and the vacant lot next door. Chuck renovated the old house and was building a new one on the vacant lot—that's Kaylin's house now."

"I can only imagine how badly Carlton would have wanted to buy the old Applegate House."

"I remember how he hung around and got to be Chuck's drinking buddy. When Chuck was ready to move into his new house, Carlton made him an offer on the old house. Then shortly after we moved in, he started tearing the house apart, claiming that he needed to fix things that Chuck had done wrong in his renovation—he called them Chuckisms. Now I know what it was really about."

"I remember him talking about Chuckisms."

"Over the years, he became totally obsessed. He tore open the walls, the floors and the ceilings throughout the house."

"I always thought he was doing that to replace the wiring and plumbing," I said.

"So did I. But all along he was looking for hidden gold," Jill lamented.

"And you think that this may have something to do with Dave Blodgett's disappearance?"

"I know it sounds crazy, but suppose Dave found something in the house? Carlton wouldn't just let it go, not after all the years he spent looking for it."

I had already reached the same conclusion.

"Do you think that Carlton is actually capable of that? Killing Dave?"

"It sounds impossible, when you say it out loud—but Carlton did a lot of crazy things because of that gold."

"Have you told any of this to the police?"

"Oh heavens, no! It's so far-fetched. I mean, who would believe it?"

"So why are you telling me about it?"

"I heard that you were working for Carrie Blodgett."

"Hmm. Who told you that?"

"Actually, it was Colleen, my daughter. Her friend Trisha heard you talking with her parents over on Miller Street."

There is no such thing as confidentiality among teenagers.

"Well, I do appreciate you showing that to me," I said. "You need to put it in a safe place. A lot of people have died because of that gold."

"I was hoping you could put it in your safe."

"I'd be glad to do that. Did you find anything strange in Carlton's house?"

"Strange? Like what?"

"Odd chemicals—stuff that you wouldn't normally have around, like acids or unidentified powders."

"I didn't notice anything like that. You think he was running a meth lab or something?"

"No, nothing like that."

We chatted for a few minutes before Jill finally moved toward the door.

"Just one more question," I said. "Has Carlton ever used the name Calvin?"

She gave me a puzzled look and said, "Calvin? Not that I ever heard. Why?"

"It's nothing," I said.

Well, it always worked for Columbo.

After Jill left, I turned to Martha and tabulated with my fingers what I had just confirmed.

"Here's what Tara Foster would have known. One, Carlton McDermitt had approached her asking about Chinese miners murdered for their gold. Two, Omar LaRue was believed to have participated in the Snake River killings in 1887. Three, Omar LaRue's sister was Rebecca Applegate. Four, Jeremiah and Rebecca Applegate built a house that was still standing in Canemah. And five, Carlton McDermitt bought the Jeremiah Applegate house after learning all of this."

Martha said, "Unless she was a complete dunce, Tara would have put it all together. She would have had every reason to believe that Carlton thought the Chinese gold was somehow hidden in that house."

"So what might she have done to cause Carlton to kill her on John Prescott's boat? And who did he have along on the boat that day?

52

Tuesday, August 5

"**W**ith Omar's letter to his sister, we have a solid motive for Carlton to kill Tara Foster," I said to Kim after breakfast. "That ought to be enough to close the books on it."

"It'll close the books on Foster, but what about the gold?" she asked.

"That has me stumped," I admitted. "Jill hasn't found it in Carlton's house, so either he hid it really well, or maybe he already sold it."

"Where would he sell that much gold?"

"I know the guy up at Oregon City Coin and Jewelry. Darren buys and sells a lot of gold. Let's see what he can tell us."

"**S**elling gold dust isn't as easy as most people think," Darren said. "There are huge variations in the purity of raw gold. Gold dust is nearly always contaminated with sand, glass, and even silver. Ten to twenty percent of the weight might be worthless."

"So would you buy it that way?" I asked.

"Sure, but I'd discount it pretty severely, at least 50 percent, to cover the cost of refining it and to hedge against the expected loss to impurities."

"What's it take to get the impurities out?"

"I can do it in small quantities, an ounce or two, in a little kiln that I have in the back room. It's what I use to melt down old jewelry."

"Is it something that an amateur could do?"

"Anyone could do it, as long as he's willing to spend s few grand on the kiln and associated equipment. But most people who process gold at home use a combination of nitric and hydrochloric acids, because that process doesn't require any special equipment. That's how they recover the gold out of old computer circuit boards, but you'd be talking quantities measured in grams, not ounces."

"The quantity I'm thinking about is more like twenty or thirty pounds."

"That's a lot of gold, Corrigan. Are you just talking, or is this real world?"

"It's out there, and someone's going to try to move it."

"I would think that anyone who could find that much gold would know what to do with it."

"Not if he stole it."

"Why haven't I heard anything about it?" he challenged. "If somebody stole thirty pounds of gold, it would make the news."

"It will," I assured him. "But in the meantime, I want to know about anybody trying to refine or sell a large quantity of gold dust."

"I have a list of people in the area who can refine gold in that volume. I can email that to you."

"Thanks. And if you hear of anybody trying to move a large quantity of gold dust, I'd appreciate a call."

Kim was ready to leave by the time I got off the phone, but she paused long enough to ask, "Could that be what Carlton was doing with the torch?"

"The idea crossed my mind. But number one, except for the weight-belt molds, there was none of the paraphernalia he'd have needed for smelting gold, and number two, there was no gold anywhere around. The truth is, we don't know for certain that Carlton ever actually found the gold. All we know for sure is that he believed it was there."

"That's good enough to prove motive for Foster, but what about that worker—Blodgett?" she asked.

"Wheeler told me that they're going to bring Yamhill County's dogs down here to see if they can pick up anything around the Applegate house. If Dave's in the bottom of the old well, you can bet that it's because of the gold—whether Carlton actually found it there or not."

Right after she left to drive to the sheriff's dock in West Linn, Kim phoned to say that there was a Yamhill County Search and Rescue SUV at the Applegate house. I found my shoes and headed up Water Street to watch the search for Dave Blodgett.

The search-and-rescue team's SUV was parked on Water Street, and a Clackamas County Sheriff's Office cruiser was parked behind it. As I approached, a middle-aged lady in blue workman's coveralls was attaching a leash to a dog in the back of the SUV. The cadaver dog was the size and shape of a German shepherd, but he was almost completely black instead of the normal shepherd colors.

I introduced myself to the Clackamas County deputy, whose name badge said "Greg Bingham," and we exchanged business cards.

"I've been working with Michael Wheeler on a related matter, and I passed along the tip that there might be human remains buried on this property," I explained.

"I assume your information is pretty solid, or none of us would be here," Bingham said.

"The man vanished without a trace. This was the last place he was seen."

"There has to be more to it than that."

"We know that an individual believed that there was a substantial cache of stolen gold hidden somewhere in the house. At the time he disappeared, Dave Blodgett was digging up the cellar floor, and we know that the suspect showed an unusual interest in the excavation."

"So you figure Blodgett found the gold and the suspect killed him."

"Right. On the day Blodgett disappeared, he uncovered an old water well beneath the original slab. We think that's where the gold was hidden, and we think that's probably where we'll find Blodgett."

I led Bingham to the side of the house adjacent to where the old well was located.

"I saw the well before it was covered. It's about two feet inside the foundation wall. I'd guess that the bottom of the well is about twenty feet below ground level. Right here," I said, pointing to a spot near the corner of the original foundation.

Bingham nodded and said, "Okay. Now let's stand back and see what the dog thinks."

The handler let the dog lead the way. With his nose to the ground, he walked methodically back and forth across the lawn, working his way up the side yard between the Applegate house and Kaylin Beatty's fence. In one spot, near the foundation in the area of the well, he paused and looked interested.

After a few seconds, he moved on. Twice, he came back to the same spot. I held my breath waiting for him to lie down as he was trained to do when he identified the scent of a decaying body. But he didn't. He proceeded to scan the entire yard and perimeter of the house.

"He seems to be interested in *something*," the handler said, "but he isn't sure about it. It might be something as innocuous as a dead mouse. Or it might be exactly what you suspect—just not strong enough to be sure."

With some reluctance, Barry Walker unlocked the door and allowed the dog and handler to go inside the house. He led them downstairs and to the utility room in the corner where the well was located. The dog's ears immediately perked up, and he went to the side of the room. Poking his nose down next to the base molding near the corner of the room, he started getting excited.

Pacing back and forth along the side wall and wedging himself between the new furnace and water heater, he started making a whining sound. At last, he picked a spot and settled into a crouch with his nose almost touching the baseboard. He was lying directly on top of the well.

"You can take that to the bank," the handler said. She rubbed the dogs head and gave him a treat from her pocket. "There are human remains under here. I think he picked up the scent outside but not strong enough to be sure. Now he's sure."

Back outside, while the lady put the dog back into the SUV, Deputy Bingham talked with Barry about what had to be done.

"I don't want you tearing the house apart," Barry complained. "We just spent over two hundred grand remodeling it, and we need to get it onto the market."

"Having a corpse under the basement floor isn't going to help it sell," Bingham pointed out. "In any case, we have to dig it out."

I repeated what I'd earlier told Michael Wheeler. "An excavator told me that he could dig a hole next to the foundation and then tunnel laterally to the well. He wouldn't have to touch the house at all."

Immediately interested, Barry asked, "Who's the excavator?"

"It's Kaylin's son, Justin Beatty. Of course, it'll destroy the lawn," I said.

"Will the county pay to fix the damage?" Barry asked.

Bingham said, "Not likely, but your insurance might."

Barry just shook his head. "Let's just get it done. The sooner, the better."

"Okay," Bingham said. "Let me get a search waiver for you to sign. I'll go back to the office and get this thing started."

I handed Bingham the excavator's business card that Kaylin had given to me, and then I walked back to my place, anxious to get out of the sunshine, which was still very uncomfortable on my arms.

Martha was busy on the phone with one of the people on Darren's list of gold assayers. When she finished the call, I started to tell her what had happened at the Applegate house but was interrupted by the phone. Caller ID indicated that it was Michael Wheeler.

"I just got back from Tacoma. I met with John Prescott last night and went through the photo-spread exercise. The results are okay," he reported.

"Okay? Just okay? You mean he didn't make a positive ID on the new photos?"

"This time, he's 'almost sure' about the male. Regarding the female, she's the only one in the spread that he picked out, but the best he could say was 'maybe' she was the one on the boat."

"Yeah," I said, "I've about written her off as a suspect anyway. She brought me some new information yesterday that I don't think a guilty person would have wanted me to see."

"What is it?" Wheeler asked.

"It's a handwritten note that she found in an old family Bible from McDermitt's house. I sent you a picture of it. Check your email when you have a minute. It pretty convincingly shows what the motive was."

"I'll check it out. But if McDermitt's wife wasn't involved, who was the woman on Prescott's boat?"

"I don't have any ideas on that," I admitted. "But let me tell you what has just happened down here. Deputy Bingham was here with Yamhill SAR. The cadaver dog is sure. Dave Blodgett is buried at the bottom of the old well."

I could hear Wheeler let out a long breath.

"Bingham's getting the search waiver signed right now. You won't need to get a warrant."

"Nice work, Corrigan. Lousy timing, but nice work."

I knew what he meant by lousy timing. Jury selection was going to start in the morning for Alan Blalock's trial for the murders of Jessie Devonshire and Randy Mendelson under Judge Gerald O'Brien. The trial could go on for weeks—maybe even months, if it followed the course of O. J. Simpson's murder trial. And throughout the trial, the sheriff's office would be on standby to provide testimony or to investigate new evidence introduced by the defense.

53

Wednesday, August

"They're here," Martha said when she brought in the mail. She pointed up Water Street toward the Applegate house. "They're unloading a tractor right now."

"Want to watch?" I asked.

"No way! I want to be as far away from that as possible. Yuck!" she finished with a shiver.

Leaving Martha to run the office, I walked over to watch Justin Beatty unload a Case 580 backhoe with an extended arm that would allow him to dig to a depth of eighteen feet. He carefully backed the big machine up over the curb onto the lawn, where it left deep ruts in the freshly laid sod. Barry Walker shook his head sadly as he watched the destruction.

Once in position, Justin worked the levers that lowered the pads and stabilized the backhoe. Another worker stood by on the driveway with a Bobcat front loader to move the excavated dirt out of the way. The first scoop tore into the perfectly tended lawn, leaving a ragged hole a foot deep. Barry couldn't watch. He got into his pickup and drove away.

It might have been an easy dig, except for the remains of the monster bay laurel tree that had been taken out back in March. With about every third scoop, Justin would hit another thick root that would have to be cut before he could continue. The assistant would park the Bobcat and take a chain-saw over to the hole and cut away the roots, which were as much as ten inches thick.

Bud showed up with a beer and leaned against the fence where I was staying in the shade. "If I knew you were here, I'd a brought another. I could go get one," he offered.

"No thanks," I said. It was barely eight in the morning.

"Too bad about the lawn."

"Too bad about Dave Blodgett."

By eleven, the hole was just about as deep as the back hoe could reach. Water seeped up from below, making muddy puddles in the bottom. I remembered seeing the water standing in the bottom of the old well, so I knew that we were at the right depth. Nobody talked about the unpleasant odor rising from the hole. They didn't have to.

Justin used the backhoe to lift aluminum box frames into the hole. These were attached together and braced against each other and the foundation of the house to prevent the sides of the hole from collapsing.

"I think I'm done for now," Justin told Deputy Bingham when the bracing was finished.

"Good. Hang around, in case we need you," Bingham said.

"I'll be next door," he said, pointing at Kaylin's house.

David Elkton, the CSI criminalist assigned to the case, lowered an extension ladder into the pit. He smeared a generous amount of Vicks VapoRub below his nose before putting on a disposable respirator mask. He tossed the VapoRub to his assistant.

"It doesn't help much," he said, "but everyone expects us to use it."

"Summer cold going around?" Bud asked.

"No. They use the VapoRub to block out the smell," I explained.

"That's enough for me," he said. "I'm going home."

At the bottom of the ladder, Elkton directed his helper to start cutting into the side of the pit. Using a shovel and a small pick, he started scraping a hole toward the old well. At first, he dug pretty aggressively, but as the tunnel got deeper, he slowed down. There were two reasons for that. First, he didn't want to accidentally damage any evidence, but equally important, he needed to be careful not to have the tunnel collapse on top of him.

"OSHA would shut us down if they ever caught us digging a tunnel like that," Justin told me.

"It's not a job I'd want," I said. "In fact, I've seen about all I want to see. I'm going to go back to my office and leave this to people with stronger stomachs than mine."

"How's it going over there?" Martha asked when I sat down at my desk.

"They're almost there. I didn't want to stay around."

"Want to know what I've found out about processing gold?" Without waiting for an answer, she continued, "Nobody in town has processed anything close to the amount of gold dust we're talking about. And they all agree that there's no way Carlton—or anybody else— could do it at home."

"I wonder if he could have found someone who would buy it as raw gold dust."

"I asked about that. Some of the foundries will do that, but nobody has seen anywhere near twenty or thirty pounds at once. They say that they rarely see as much as one pound."

"Okay," I said slowly while I considered what came next. "There's someone out there somewhere who would buy black market gold dust. There's a black market for everything. We need to figure out how to find it."

"Carlton wouldn't have had any more idea than we do," Martha pointed out.

"That's a good point. He'd have had to ask around. Start calling pawn-shops and gold buyers. See if any of them will admit to having talked to anyone about a large amount of gold dust."

"Would they tell me if they did?"

"Not if they are black market gold dealers. But Carlton would have almost certainly have talked with honest brokers before finding someone who'd buy what he had and not question the source."

While Martha started making calls, I searched online for any news on the Blalock jury selection. I found one report that said twenty-two out of twenty-four potential jurors had been dismissed. Only two had passed the first cut. They'd bring in a fresh pool tomorrow and keep trying.

Feeling restless and impatient in the middle of the afternoon, I took a walk outside and found Water Street choked with news vans. Obviously, word of the excavation had gotten out. City police had been brought in for crowd control, and nobody was being allowed near the Applegate house. I knocked on Kaylin Beatty's front door, knowing that her kitchen window was right above the pit.

"Come on in," she said. "When you start up a circus, you really do it right."

"Can you tell what's happening?" I asked.

"They put up a tarp and blocked the view. But I keep seeing more and more people over there. They're building something down in the hole. They sawed up a bunch of lumber and took it down the ladder."

"Probably shoring up the tunnel. Where's Justin?"

Kaylin laughed. "He's earning his pay."

She pointed down into the sunken living room, where Justin was asleep on the carpeted floor.

"How'd you figure out that Dave was in the well?"

"That's a really, really long story," I hedged.

"But if Dave died in the well, who did I see driving his car away?"

"Most likely, it was whoever put him into the well."

"So you really believe that someone deliberately killed him?"

"He didn't fall down the well and then bury himself under chunks of concrete."

"Oh…do you know who did it?"

"It's not public knowledge, but Carlton is the top candidate."

"Wow. That's pretty scary. All this time, I thought he was just a goofball."

"Looks like they're planning to work into the night," I said. Out the kitchen window, I could see workers unloading and assembling portable floodlights on collapsible stands.

I was interrupted by a bugle call from my cell phone—Martha's idea of a joke. She had heard me complain about the ring tone and helpfully changed it to "Brahms' Lullaby." When I griped about that, she set it up to sound like a cavalry charge. I hadn't yet taken the time to figure out how to fix it.

The screen said the call was from Leo Gilchrist, so I motioned good-bye to Kaylin and headed outside.

"Are you ready for this?" Gilchrist asked rhetorically. "The IRS has offered an out-of-court settlement."

"So the bastards finally figured out that they don't have a case," I grumbled.

"Probably. Here's the deal. The amount that they seized from your bank account is $32,817. They're now willing to settle for 10 percent of that and refund the rest, if you sign off on their offer."

"That's still thirty-three hundred more than I owe," I said, letting my irritation show more than I'd intended.

"I never said it was perfect. But it does get back *most* of your money, and it keeps you from having to go to court."

"What about the ten grand I had to give the state?"

"That's not part of the deal. Officially, the IRS is sticking with its claim that you owe the thirty-three grand, and the state will calculate its tax bill on that."

"I don't like it. What happens if I reject their offer?"

"Then things stay as they are. They hold your money and continue getting postponements on the court date."

"Okay," I said while I mentally worked through the logic. "They wouldn't have floated the offer unless they knew they'll lose in court. You and I know they can't win. So my counteroffer is that they completely drop all claims against me, notify the Oregon Department of Revenue accordingly, and pay all of my legal expenses. Anything less than that and we'll go to court, where they'll lose and pay punitive damages on top of all that."

"I understand where you're coming from," Gilchrist said, "but you should know that it is very unusual for the IRS to make an offer like this. It's very generous by their standards. And they still hold all of the power. Like I've said before, they can delay a court appearance almost indefinitely."

"You're not seriously suggesting that I accept their offer," I challenged loudly.

"No. I'm just trying to give you the whole picture."

"The whole picture is that if the IRS doesn't completely drop their claim, I'll probably never see my private investigator's license again. No deal. And that is my final answer."

54

Thursday, August 7

"The medical examiner's report just came in. Carlton McDermitt didn't die in the fire," Michael Wheeler announced. "There was no smoke in his lungs."

I was lost for speech.

"It was blunt-force trauma. He was struck in the back of the head. Probably died instantly."

"Did something fall on him?"

"Not likely. The ME says it was more like a shot from a baseball bat."

"But who—"

"Oregon City Police have a witness who saw someone running away just as the fire was breaking out."

I remembered. "Oh yeah, there was the Italian guy—Guido something—he's the one who dragged me out of the fire."

"Barcelli. He nearly hit a guy who ran across the highway in front of him."

The picture snapped into focus. Kim had been right.

"The missing gold…" I said. "McDermitt wasn't making lead weights—he was melting the gold, and someone else found out about it!"

"Who could have known about it?"

I was already trying to figure that out.

"McDermitt probably didn't know what to do with gold dust. He'd have asked around. Maybe he asked the wrong person," I speculated. "My partner, Martha Hoskins, is already canvassing the pawnshops and precious metals dealers."

Hearing myself refer to Martha as "my partner" came as a surprise. But since I was officially working under her license, I guess it was appropriate.

I continued, "Our theory was that McDermitt might have been trying to find someone who'd buy the gold dust as it was. But whether he was doing that or trying to learn about processing it into bullion, he almost certainly talked to *someone*."

"If he was looking for someone to fence the gold, he'd have been dealing with exactly the kind of people who might shortcut the deal with a baseball bat. Call off your screening. This needs to be done by someone with a badge. No offense."

"I understand. We'll stay out of the way. But I would like to know—"

"Yeah, wouldn't we all?" he concluded.

"I guess we're done," I said to Martha.

"Partner, huh?" she answered.

I stretched the truth a little bit. "I've been thinking about it for a while."

"I like the sound of it."

"I was figuring on having Gates write up some kind of contract after I get done with all of this legal crap. But we'd better drum up some more business. I think we've gotten all we're going to get from Dennis Lawen."

"Maybe there's some kind of reward for finding the Chinese gold," Martha suggested.

I remembered something mentioned in *Massacred for Gold* that had to do with reparations paid by the US government to China in compensation for the deaths of the miners. Most of the victims' names were unknown, however, so it was not likely that there'd be a reward. But clearly the gold belonged to the heirs, if they could ever be identified.

"I don't think I want to get involved in that treasure hunt," I said. "Look how many people have died because of that gold."

Changing the subject, Martha said, "I saw that they're packing up over at the Applegate house."

"They got the body out late last night—too late for the morning paper, but it'll be all over the news this afternoon. By then, they ought to have positive ID, but there's little doubt."

"What about Carrie Blodgett?"

"I called her yesterday afternoon after all the media buzzards showed up. I told her what they were probably going to find."

"How'd she take it?"

"As you would expect. Sadness. Tears. But relief that it's finally over."

But it wasn't over. The only way it would ever really be over would be when the cursed gold was recovered and returned to its rightful owners. And along the way, there would be a full accounting for all of the mayhem the greed for that gold had caused.

I let my mind ponder the question I had raised with Michael Wheeler: who would Carlton have asked about processing gold dust? Attempting to isolate the basic question from Carlton, the Wallowa County massacre and the current investigation, I asked myself who I would call if I had a question about gold mining. One name came to mind: Big Dan Barlow.

In casual conversation with Big Dan, I'd heard him talk about using a hydraulic dredge to mine creek beds in southwest Oregon. Assuming that he'd had any success at it, he would know what to do with the recovered gold. Would Carlton have gone to Big Dan?

I walked a hundred yards up the railroad tracks and spotted Big Dan on his dock, entertaining a dozen or so young people, many of whom were girls in skimpy bathing suits. Dan had a knack for attracting crowds like this to his dock, maybe because of his always-entertaining war stories or maybe because of his always well-stocked refrigerator. Except for Big Dan, nobody there appeared to be over twenty-five, and some quite a bit younger.

Finding a chair in the shaded part of his dock, I accepted the beer he offered. "Who are the kids?"

"Oh, they're friends of Red Harper's granddaughter," he said with a dismissive gesture.

"Remember last year when you were helping to dig the old El Camino out of the river?" I asked, pointing in the general direction of the West Linn boat ramp.

"Sure. What about it?"

"You were talking about the machinery you were using and mentioned that you'd done some dredge mining."

"Yeah, I've done a little bit of that."

"Did you find any gold?"

He laughed. "If I'd found very much, I'd still be doing it. But I got a few ounces."

"How'd you go about selling it?"

He shrugged. "I just melted it down with a torch and took it to a gold dealer."

"Simple as that?"

"Well, not exactly. You have to use boric acid and borax to separate the impurities, but the main thing is you have to be damn careful not to blow away your gold dust with the torch."

"So it can actually be done with a torch," I said just to be sure I understood.

"It'd be better to use a kiln—something capable of heating to two thousand degrees. But yeah, I did it with a regular cutting torch."

Now for the real question.

"Did Carlton McDermitt ever ask you about any of this?" I asked.

"Is that what this is about? Did he cremate himself trying to melt gold?"

"That's what I'm trying to figure out. Did you ever talk to him about gold?"

With a derisive laugh, Big Dan said, "McDermitt didn't have the guts to ask me about that—or anything else."

"Can you think of anybody else he might have talked to about it?"

"Well, if he wanted to know how to use a cutting torch, he'd probably ask Mike Mohler."

"Captain Alan's brother?"

"Right. I'd be willing to bet that Mike and Captain Alan have done some gold mining in their time."

He was probably right. Short of computer programming and quantum physics, I couldn't think of many things that Captain Alan hadn't done at one time or another.

I walked up to Third Avenue and found Mike outside, nailing asphalt roofing shingles to the side of his house to cover the tar paper that had been there for as long as I'd lived in Canemah. It was strange, but probably an improvement.

"Hot day for doing that," I said.

"Been meaning to do this for a while now," he answered. "Had this whole load of shingles sitting around for a couple years. Just never got around to putting them up."

"Mind if I get out of the sun?" I asked, gesturing to my still reddened hands.

"Oh, sure," he said quickly. "I heard you about got fried down there."

"Not so lucky for McDermitt."

"Yeah, I feel kind of bad about that. I let him borrow my oxyacetylene rig, and I heard that's what started the fire."

"That was *your* torch?"

"Yep. McDermitt borrowed it last week. I assumed he knew how to use it, but I guess maybe he didn't."

"Did he say what he wanted to use it for?"

"He asked if it would get hot enough to melt his old wedding ring. I got the impression that he was pissed off at his ex."

"Seems like he could've just brought the ring up and melted it here."

"Yep. I suggested the same thing. But he said he also had some scrap iron to cut up, and it'd be easier to take the torch down there."

"Hey!"

I turned to see who was shouting from the street.

Leonard Butts shouted, "Didn't you listen to what I told you last week?"

Mike groaned. "Here we go again."

"That is totally inappropriate and unacceptable in Canemah," Butts said. "Nailing roofing to the side of a historic house is a violation of city code!"

"It's *my* house," Mike said. "I'll do what I want."

"Canemah is the only National Register historic district in all of Clackamas County!" Butts said with the righteous fervor of a gospel preacher in a tent show.

"Give it a rest, Leonard," I said. "He's fixing his house the best way he can afford."

"He can't put *any* kind of siding on that house without *prior approval* from the neighborhood association and the Historic Review Board."

I approached Butts shaking my head at his strident insensitivity toward poor old Mike and saw him reach for the fish club hanging from his belt. I held up a hand.

"Take it easy," I said quietly. "He has no money and no job. He's disabled. Why don't you just mind your own business and go home?"

"We can't allow people to compromise the integrity of the neighborhood. Maybe you don't care, but we could lose our historic designation!"

He continued his sermon as I turned and headed back toward Apperson Street, and he was still preaching when I went beyond earshot.

When finally free of that distraction, I contemplated what Mike had told me. It all made sense as far as it went. Carlton had first determined that the torch was capable of melting gold, and then he'd given a plausible cover story for why he needed the torch at his place.

But the two overriding questions remained. Who killed him, and where was the gold?

55

Friday, August 8

It was a quiet evening, and I was sitting in my ski boat with Kim. It was the first time I'd taken the boat out since the fire. The engine was off, and we were drifting on the nearly imperceptible current upstream from Canemah. We'd just finished eating chicken dinner baskets from the Fred Meyer deli and were sipping a bargain-priced chardonnay from Australia.

"Someone else had to have known that Carlton had the gold," I said, continuing the discussion we'd been having for the past half-hour.

"He wasn't very good at keeping it a secret," Kim noted. "I mean, he had to kill Tara Foster because she figured out what he was up to. And then he killed Dave when he found him in the well. It just seems like he wasn't very discreet with what he knew."

"I'll agree, to a point. But as far as I know, he didn't talk to just anybody about the gold. When he talked with people about it, it was always because they had—or had access to—information that he needed."

"Okay then, what about Mike Mohler? Maybe Carlton told him more than he admitted to you."

"Mike sure as hell didn't kill Carlton," I said flatly. "The man Guido saw *ran* away from the scene. Mike can barely walk, let alone run. Anyway, he didn't act like he had anything to hide when I talked to him."

"All I'm saying is that Carlton wasn't the only one who knew about the gold."

"I keep thinking about Janet Monroe. She was in on it way back in the 1990s. She knew about the gold, and she knew that Omar LaRue had gone to Oregon City. It's entirely possible that she put it all together."

"You ought to be able to find out if she's been up here since you talked to her."

The ridiculous bugle call from my phone interrupted our conversation. I looked at the screen and didn't immediately recognize the number.

"This is Darren at Oregon City Coin. You asked me to call if anyone came in wanting to sell a large quantity of gold dust."

"That's right. What's up?"

"Well, this doesn't have anything to do with gold dust, but it's pretty strange."

"Tell me," I urged.

"Okay, I should've told you about this when you called the other day, but like I said, it wasn't gold dust, so I didn't think of it."

I switched my phone to speaker so Kim could hear.

"Anyway, all kinds of people bring me all kinds of stuff, all hoping to make some money. Last month, a couple of teenagers brought in a gold bar that they wanted to sell."

"Exactly when was that?" I asked.

"It must've been around the twenty-fourth or twenty-fifth. But it's been bugging me ever since," Darren continued. "The thing is, there's no way any teenagers should be walking around with a 160-ounce bar of gold."

"One hundred sixty ounces!"

"It's rare enough to see that much gold, but in the hands of teenagers, it's just plain wrong. It wasn't dated, but it was old. It was stamped 'US Government Property.' The hallmark was 999 from the San Francisco mint."

"So what did you do?"

"Well, you know me. I buy just about anything that comes in the door," he admitted.

I looked at Kim, and she raised an eyebrow.

"But this was just too weird," he continued. "I asked the kid where he got it, and he said his grandmother gave it to him for his birthday. My guess is that if his grandmother had anything to do with it, he stole it from her. Sure as hell, he stole it from *somebody*."

"You didn't buy it?" I asked.

"I probably could have given them a hundred dollars an ounce, and those pukes wouldn't have known any better. But then there'd a been hell to pay when Grandma found out. Know what I mean? I didn't want to get tangled up in that hairball, so I let it go."

"Let it go?"

"Yeah, I told 'em I couldn't buy US government property and watched two hundred thousand dollars go out the door. It broke my heart."

"Any idea who the kids were?"

"Never seen 'em before, but I took down a license number when they drove away. I reported it to the Oregon City Police. They said they'd check it out if somebody reported a gold theft."

"That doesn't seem like much of a response."

"I should have just bought the damn gold. But like I said, it was just too hinky. I've been thinking about it ever since, so I decided to give you a call."

"Can you describe the kids?"

"I doubt that either of them was over sixteen. One of them was rail thin, maybe five eight. And I'd bet that he was a tweaker. He had that look about him. The one who did the talking was kind of a gawky kid—you know, all out of proportion. Reddish-brown hair, taller than the tweaker and not so skinny."

"What about the car?"

"Old Honda sedan, maroon. Want the plate number?"

"Sure. Go ahead."

"YOT 922 Oregon."

After clicking off, I took a contemplative sip from my wine glass.

"Do you remember reading how Dug Bar got its name?" I asked Kim.

She shook her head.

"It was named for an outlaw named Tom Douglas, who had a cabin there. It was his cabin that the rustlers used when they attacked the Chinese gold miners."

"So?" she asked blankly.

"Historians believe that Blue Evans murdered Tom Douglas to get his hands on some gold that Douglas had stolen in a stage coach robbery in Montana. When I searched the net, I found several references to an incident that seemed to match. The gold taken in that robbery was described as three gold bars belonging to the US government."

Kim's eyes widened. "And you think…"

"What if the gold Omar LaRue took from Dug Bar was not the Chinese gold dust? What if it was the gold bars from the stage coach heist?"

"But if that's the gold that Darren saw—"

"Carlton's son, Patrick, fits Darren's description of the kid with the gold bar—the US government gold bar."

"Would Carlton really send his kid out to sell the gold?"

"Play along with me. If he did, Patrick would've reported what Darren told him—that he couldn't buy US government property. So Carlton would have thought that he had to melt down and recast the gold bars. When he borrowed the torch from Mike Mohler, Carlton never said anything about gold *dust*."

"And then this unknown subject interrupted the job, killed Carlton, started the fire, and got away with the gold," Kim finished.

"I think that's very plausible."

"There's another possibility. Suppose Patrick and his tweaker friend found the gold by accident somehow. Maybe Carlton had it hidden in the tackle box and the kids had wanted to go fishing. They could have found the gold, taken it, and put tire weights in the tackle box to give it some weight."

"But surely Carlton would have looked in the box," I argued, even while recognizing that what Kim had suggested made sense in every other way.

"And then when they learned that Carlton was just about to discover that the gold was gone, they whacked him with a baseball bat," Kim continued as though she hadn't heard me.

"I'm having a hard time imagining that Carlton was killed by his own kid," I said.

"Okay then, maybe it was just the tweaker."

"I'm going to have to find out who he is," I finally declared.

56

Saturday, August 9

I entered the license number Darren had given me into a subscription online database. The car was a 1988 Honda Civic registered to Dorothy Culver in Newberg. From another database, I learned that she was fifty-seven years old, divorced, and worked for a company that manufactured dental equipment.

Obviously, she wasn't the tweaker who had been in Darren's store, but she would probably know who he was, a relative or acquaintance.

"Yes, this is Dorothy Culver. Who's calling, please?"

"My name is Corrigan. I'm a private investigator in Oregon City."

"Why are you calling me, Mr. Corrigan?" she asked cautiously.

"I see that a 1988 Honda Civic is registered to you," I explained.

"I sold that car over a year ago."

"The registration is still in your name. Did you sell it to a family member?"

"No, I posted it on Craigslist and someone came along and bought it."

"Do you have the name of the person who bought it?"

She sighed deeply. "If I ever did have it, it's long gone now. Why do you want to know all this?"

"The driver of the car may have witnessed a crime last month," I lied, not wishing to reveal my real interest in the car.

"Well, I can't help you with that. Like I said, I sold the car a long time ago."

"Can you describe the person who bought it?"

"It was a young guy. I didn't like him much. He and his buddy looked like a couple of street-gang kids. But he paid in cash, so I signed over the title."

"You know, when you sell a car in Oregon, you're supposed to send the DMV a copy of the bill of sale with the new owner's name and driver's license number. This kind of thing is the reason for that law. Besides, if the car gets involved in an accident, you may still be held liable for damages."

"I can't do anything about it now."

"No, but next time you sell a car."

I looked again at the registration information. The tags were due to expire at the end of August. Given the descriptions from Dorothy Culver and Darren, I doubted that the tags would ever be renewed. For people living on the fringes, it is common practice to buy cars based solely on when the license plates expire.

These buyers have no intention of ever transferring the title. They look for the car with the most time left on the current tags, which in Oregon can be as much as two years. In this way, they avoid the expensive inconvenience of having to show proof of insurance. When the tags expire, they simply abandon the car and go find another.

Short of actually finding the Honda, the best chance I had for learning who drove it to Darren's shop would be through Patrick McDermitt— assuming that he was, in fact, the kid with the tweaker.

Teenage kids can be easily bluffed into blurting out everything they know. But they can also be easily panicked into doing irrational things. Recognizing that it was the second possibility that may well account for Carlton being dead, I carefully weighed my options.

I reasoned that Patrick's mother would know who her son was hanging out with, but would she talk to me if she had any idea that what she said might get her son into serious trouble with the law? Another idea was to interview other kids at Patrick's school. But that could be pretty touchy too in this age where everyone is on the lookout for "stranger danger" in schools.

What's more, there was a pretty good chance that a tweaker wouldn't even be enrolled in school. So that left me with Jill, who would never forgive me if she felt that I'd tricked her into implicating Patrick in the murder his father. It would be better, I decided, to let someone else ask the question.

I jotted Jill's phone number on a slip of paper, figuring that perhaps I could get one of Patrick's neighborhood friends to call him and ask the name of the dude with the maroon Civic. I knew just where to look for neighborhood kids on a hot Sunday afternoon.

I pulled a Coke from my refrigerator and walked over to Big Dan's place. As I'd hoped, there was a group of young people playing down on his dock. Pulling up a chair next to Big Dan, I looked around for Red Harper's younger granddaughter, Brandi.

"How're the burns?" Dan asked.

It was a rhetorical question. He could see as well as I that the formerly red skin was now peeling off in thin strips and flakes. The stinging was gone, but it was still uncomfortable in direct sunlight. I talked with Dan about things of no consequence until I felt that my social obligation was fulfilled.

The next time Brandi walked past on her way back to the diving tower, I waved.

"Say, Brandi, I have a question for you."

"Sure, Mr. Corrigan. What is it?"

"Well, here's the thing. I'm trying to find out the name of a dude who hangs around a lot with Patrick McDermitt."

"Oh," she said brightly, "that's Shane Keasey."

She started to walk away, and I called her back.

"How do you know that's who I'm looking for?"

She put her finger to her chin and said, "Well, duh, Shane's the only one who hangs with Patrick."

Sometimes things that seem to be hard turn out to be easy. I went back to my computer and did a search for anyone named Keasey in Oregon City. There were several. I wrote down the addresses and then went to Zillow, figuring that I might be able to guess what neighborhood would be the most likely home of a meth head.

The first two I looked at seemed to be solid, respectable neighborhoods. Not that good parents don't sometimes have bad kids, but I was merely looking at probabilities. If I didn't find Shane Keasey in a trashy neighborhood, then I could come back and look at the nicer neighborhoods.

But I didn't have to. I pulled up a Zillow street-view image of the apartment complex where one of the Keasey families lived, and right there in front sat a maroon Honda Civic.

Next I searched for anything I could find on the Keasey family: father, mother, and two kids—a thirteen-year-old daughter and seventeen-year-old Shane.

There had been three domestic disturbance calls to their apartment in the last year, all involving an unnamed juvenile male, almost certainly Shane. All dealt with excessively loud music, and no citations had been issued. There was one call for domestic violence involving the parents that resulted in Mr. Keasey spending the night in jail. Charges were later dropped.

Nobody in the household appeared to have a job. Both parents were collecting unemployment benefits, and together they qualified for an Oregon Trail food assistance debit card.

I leaned back in my chair, staring at the ceiling and plotting my next move. I needed photos of Patrick and Shane that I could show to Darren. If he confirmed that these were the kids who showed him the gold bar, I'd have something solid to give Michael Wheeler.

Photos had been taken on the day Carlton first brought his houseboat downriver and tied it up in front of Jill's place. I tabbed through them until I found one that showed Patrick with his sister looking simultaneously amused and embarrassed. I opened it in Photoshop, zoomed in, and cropped Colleen out. I printed a large, clear color photo of Patrick McDermitt.

Shane Keasey would be more challenging. I loaded some bottled water and a few snacks into a small cooler and put the long zoom lens on my Nikon. I drove up to Magnolia Street and located the apartment complex. At the end of Magnolia, I turned left and immediately spotted Keasey's Honda parked in an uncovered parking space. All of the parking spaces were marked "Reserved."

I backed into a covered space about fifty yards from Keasey's car. With some luck, the people who owned the space would stay away long enough for me to get the photo I needed. After prefocusing my camera, I settled back to wait for Shane to show himself.

By mid-afternoon, I was bored and impatient. I dug around in my glove compartment and found the old prepaid phone that I bought the previous year when a *Chronicle* editorial diatribe sparked a tidal wave of hostile calls on my regular phone. I was pleased to see it light up when I flipped it open.

I switched my laptop on and waited for it to boot up and log onto Verizon. I went to the mobile-phone directory search website and looked up Shane Keasey in Oregon City. Bingo. You live on food stamps and unemployment, but your kid has his own cell phone. What a screwed up world.

Focusing on the task at hand, I conjured up my best stoner impression.

When Shane answered, I said, "Yeah, Shane. Dude, there's some guy, like snoopin' around your car."

"Who is this?" Shane asked.

"Dude, like I think the guy's gonna cut your tires."

I clicked off and picked up my camera. Seconds later, Shane Keasey ran out into the parking lot. When he looked in my direction, I pressed the button and held it down for a quick series of photos. After looking up and down the parking lot, Shane went over and walked around his car, looking at the tires.

After he went back inside, I started the engine and quietly drove away.

I stopped at Darren's shop on the way home and showed him the pictures of Patrick and Shane.

"Yep. Those are the kids. No question about it. Any idea where they got that gold bar?"

"Nothing definite yet," I said, "but I'd appreciate a call if they come back here."

I had one more thing to check after I got home. Back in April, when Officer Durham was canvassing the neighborhood about Dave Blodgett's disappearance, Rosita Valensueva and her mother had complained about a car that had blocked the alley on the day Dave was last seen alive. They had described the car as a trashy, old "piece of sheet" the color of grapes.

When I knocked on the door, it was Señora Valensueva who answered. Knowing that she spoke no English, I asked for Rosita, repeating her name twice, since that was the only word the señora would understand.

When Rosita came to the door, she invited me in. I took a seat in their front room, which faced Highway 99. The room was heavily decorated with Roman Catholic crucifixes, paintings of Jesus, and statues of various saints I couldn't identify.

I showed them a photo of Shane Keasey's Honda.

"Does this look like the car that was blocking the alley?" I asked.

Rosita translated the question for her mother, who leaned in and looked closely at the photo. She had a lot to say that I couldn't understand, but the rapid nodding of her head answered my question.

Next I showed them a photo of Shane.

"Do you recognize this person?"

Rosita translated quickly, listened to the señora's reply, and answered, "No, he does not look familiar to me, and my mother does not know him either."

"I'm still trying to figure out what it all means," I told Kim after summarizing my day's work.

"Keasey's car in the alley when Dave was killed changes the whole nature of the case against those boys," she said. "It takes it from a possible crime of opportunity straight to premeditated murder."

"Yeah, I don't see any way around that, unless it was someone else's car."

"How many twenty-five-year-old maroon Honda Civics do you suppose there are in this city?"

"Honestly, I can't remember the last time I saw one before today."

"Exactly."

"Okay, so somehow Keasey found out that there was gold in the Applegate house. And he knew that Dave Blodgett was opening the well that day. About the only person who could have told him that was Patrick. He must have somehow learned about it from Carlton."

"Maybe Carlton himself told Keasey about it to get him to do the dirty work."

"It doesn't seem like he'd deliberately get his own son involved in a capital murder."

"Patrick didn't have to know anything about it at that point. Could be he didn't get into it until Dave was long gone."

I shook my head. "We're missing something."

"Okay, try this. Go back to the theory that it was Carlton who killed Dave. He didn't want the search to focus on the Applegate house, so he drove the car up to Johnson Creek."

"Yeah, we know that's where it ended up. So what?" I asked.

"He needed a ride back," Kim said jubilantly. "Carlton got Keasey to drive Dave's car while he followed along in his own."

"And in that case, Keasey is, at most, an accessory after the fact."

"Yeah, but once he knew that Dave was missing, he'd have had Carlton over a barrel."

"So you're thinking Carlton gave him one of the gold bars to keep his mouth shut."

"Why not?"

"Indeed," I agreed. "Why not?"

57

Sunday, August 10

It was a good day to sleep in, except that Kim had to go out on patrol and got up at six thirty. She probably tried to let me sleep, but some little noise woke me up, and once awake, there was no hope of getting back to sleep. After she left, I amused myself by reading the Sunday *Chronicle*, carefully avoiding the editorial section, which was generally bad for my disposition.

I heard DC demanding to be let inside, so I went into the kitchen and opened the back door. The big cat bolted between my legs, knocking me off balance and sending me crashing against the door frame. The edge of the door exploded in a shower of splinters a few inches to the right of my head, and behind me, the glass door on one of the cabinets shattered.

For a confused second, I wondered what DC had done to cause all of the chaos. But pure instinct made me duck to my left as the second shot went by, decimating a row of coffee mugs in the cabinet with the broken glass. I pushed the door shut and crawled to where I was shielded by the stove.

And there I sat for a few seconds, catching my breath, while DC calmly crunched away on his salmon-flavored kibbles.

I pulled my phone out of my pocket and touched speed dial 1.

"Hey, what's up?" Kim asked.

"I just had two rifle shots come in the back door. If DC hadn't tripped me, I'd be dead."

"Have you called it in?"

"No, I was hoping you'd do that—maybe get to the right people faster."

"Hang up and call 911," she ordered. "I'll get on the radio."

After making the call, I edged around the corner into the hall before getting to my feet. In the bedroom, I grabbed my .45 automatic. By then, sirens were screaming in from every direction.

A swarm of cars from the Oregon City Police, the sheriff's office, and the state police jammed Water Street and Highway 99 at the ends of the alley next to my place. Armed officers spread out in all directions in search of the shooter.

"There wasn't a sound," I told a deputy I recognized. "I'd bet that he had a suppressor. And it was a semiautomatic. The shots were too close together to be anything else."

I showed him where both bullets had hit the cabinet.

"Tight grouping," he said, pointing to the two holes three inches apart.

"Look for a white male, age about sixty, gray hair crew-cut. Six foot. One-seventy. Former marine, retired from Portland PD."

The deputy stared at me.

"How do you know all that? Did you see him?"

I shook my head. "His name is Richard Elgin."

"How do you know who it was if you didn't see him?"

"This isn't the first time he's tried to kill me," I said.

As we stood on my back porch next to the where I'd been standing when the shots were fired, I pointed up to Third Avenue, where a vacant bank-owned house was visible through the trees.

"That's where I'd look—in that house with the plywood over the patio doors."

Among the many officers present was the Oregon City Police chief, who took charge and formed an assault squad. Despite having been told to stay out of it, I followed the officers across the highway and up to Third. On the uphill side of the road was a pair of matching houses that were both vacant and boarded up, victims of the Great Recession.

The police approached the one that had a narrow view of my place. They broke down the door and stormed in but found nobody present. In a second-story room, they found an open window, and on the floor beneath it was a rifle.

Mike Mohler spotted me and came over to ask what was happening.

"Did you hear any gunshots, maybe ten minutes ago?" I asked.

"No. But that don't mean nothing. I'm about deaf," Mike answered.

"Did you see anybody around that house today?"

"Yeah. A few minutes ago, I saw a guy run down the steps. He got in a car and raced away."

I called the police chief over and introduced him to Mike, who repeated what he'd told me, adding detail in response to a series of questions. During this conversation, the assault squad came out of the house carrying a rifle with a sniper scope and suppressor.

At first I thought it was an M14, but the fiberglass stock indicated that it was actually an M21, the US military's semiautomatic sniper rifle in the seventies and eighties. During my investigation of Richard Elgin last year, I'd learned that he was trained as a sniper in the marine corps. It appeared that he'd taken home a souvenir.

The theory I formed was that Elgin was taken by surprise at the quick and overwhelming response by the police. He abandoned the rifle so that he wouldn't be seen with it by one of the responding officers. Mike said that Elgin drove up Third Avenue and then up the hill toward South End Road. The car was a white sedan. That's all Mike could say about it.

Two hours later, I was back home when my phone rang. The screen showed Larry Jamieson's number.

"Are you sure it was Elgin?" Jamieson asked.

"There's a witness, and his description matches," I said. "Besides, who else could it be?"

"And he drove away in a white four-door?"

"That's what the witness said. I didn't see it."

"We tried to set up a perimeter, but we were too late. Once at the top of the hill, he could have gone in any of a dozen different directions."

I couldn't stop myself. "Want to ask the DA how her deal with Elgin is looking now?"

"I hear ya," Jamieson said. "We'll keep people around your place until we find him."

Putting that aside, I said, "Hey, I need to talk with you and Wheeler about the Foster case. We've found some stuff that just ought to sew it up."

"Okay, when Wheeler gets here in the morning, we'll give you a call, and you can tell us all about it."

58

Monday, August 11

In the conference call with Michael Wheeler and Sheriff Jamieson, I explained in full detail what I knew about the Tara Foster and Dave Blodgett cases. I was well aware of the complex and convoluted nature of the evidence, a fact that was underscored by the difficulty I had in explaining it over the phone.

While we talked, Martha took notes that stretched to several pages regarding specific questions Wheeler and Jamieson had about the cases.

She would spend the next few days assembling a package of evidence and writing a full report on the conclusions we'd reached in our investigation. With that, we would be finished. The investigation of Patrick McDermitt and Shane Keasey now belonged to the sheriff's office.

As for Jill McDermitt's possible involvement in the Foster murder, that would probably remain an unanswered question. It would be nice to see all of the loose ends tied down, but in the real world of criminal investigation, that rarely happens. There are nearly always odd pieces of evidence or testimony that can't be explained. Such was the nature of John Prescott's statements regarding the woman who accompanied Carlton McDermitt and Tara Foster on the fateful boat ride.

The Tara Foster murder would be pinned on McDermitt, and the case would be officially closed. That would take my client, Dennis Lawen, off the hook—even though he was never, except in his own mind, on the hook. Jamieson promised to get the county to reimburse me for what I'd spent on the forensic examination of Prescott's boat, as well as the lab analyses of the evidence found there.

Dave Blodgett's murder would remain an ongoing investigation. Except for Señora Valensueva's statement regarding Keasey's old maroon Honda, everything pointed to Carlton. It would be up to the sheriff's office to determine what Keasey's actual role had been. I was pretty sure that it would all come out in the interrogation room.

And the gold? That was Jamieson's problem. He'd undoubtedly find at least one gold bar still in the possession of Patrick McDermitt or Shane Keasey. They probably had all three, but if they didn't, they'd find the other two hidden somewhere in Carlton's house. Or maybe there never were three bars. The history regarding the Montana stage coach holdup has never been very clear.

"The deputy who's working the Blodgett case is also assigned to the McDermitt murder," Jamieson said. "He'll probably bring in those two kids this week."

"Smart money is on the Keasey kid," I said. "I'd be looking for an Old Navy hooded sweatshirt somewhere in his wardrobe."

"We'll probably get search warrants with the evidence you're giving us," Wheeler said. "When we get the hoodie, we'll check it for McDermitt's blood."

Jamieson then said, "I've just been told that they've wrapped up jury selection for the Blalock trial."

"Last I heard they still had three seats to fill," I said.

"The process generally goes a lot faster after the lawyers have used up their peremptory challenges."

"Does that mean the trial is underway?"

"I don't have that information, but I'd expect to see opening statements this afternoon, or at the latest, tomorrow morning."

"I'm not much interested in the opening statements, but I want to be there to hear the testimony and see the evidence."

"I expect the DA's office will be giving you a call," Jamieson said. "Last I heard, the first witness will be Deputy Stayton. I assume you'll know when she's called."

As I hung up the phone, Kim parked her sheriff's office Explorer next to my front porch. She came inside carrying two freshly cleaned and pressed uniforms on clothes hangers, covered in thin transparent plastic bags.

"It starts in the morning," she said. "They're doing opening statements now."

"Are you ready to face the Big Dogs?" I asked.

The lead attorney for Alan Blalock's was Jason Hardman, who had assembled a team of specialists in criminal law known as the Big Dogs.

The Big Dogs had already made their presence known through their activities during jury selection. A consultant had provided Hardman with a profile of the people who were most likely to resist rendering a guilty verdict. As each prospective juror was interviewed, he or she was measured against the profile and accepted or rejected accordingly.

News reporters had estimated that Blalock was spending in excess of two million dollars on his defense. That was compared with the estimated three to six million that O. J. Simpson spent on his Dream Team. The Dream Team had succeeded in getting the best verdict money could buy on the criminal charges, but Simpson ultimately lost in civil court and the court of public opinion.

The Big Dogs would pour all of Blalock's resources into winning, and that meant not just in court but also in public opinion, which is the lifeblood of politicians. To do that, they would attempt to destroy everybody associated with the case against Blalock. Kim would be first.

When my phone rang in the middle of the night, I was surprised to see on the screen the Salem number belonging to Kevin Fox.

"What's happening, Fox?" I asked, assuming that he wouldn't have called if it weren't something really important.

"We have an old friend of yours in the morgue," Fox said.

After the most recent attempt on my life, I had to wonder which witness Richard Elgin had managed to kill.

"Don't keep me in suspense," I said. "What happened?"

"The stiff is Richard Elgin."

"Richard Elgin! Are you sure?" I exclaimed.

"No doubt about it. He broke into the wrong house. The homeowner took him down with five shots from a Springfield XD. Elgin was carrying a Navy MK23, but he didn't get off a shot."

I was dumfounded. "Elgin is really dead?"

"It'd be pretty hard to fake it. Especially with the back of his head gone. Believe me, he's dead."

But how did it happen?

"Elgin jimmied the lock on a patio door. Homeowner heard noises, armed himself, and went to see what was going on. From a dark hallway, he spotted the intruder in the family room, moving real slow. He saw that the perp was armed, so he put him down."

"Sounds like that homeowner knew what he was doing," I commented.

"He ought to. He spent thirty years with the CCSO. You know him. Mickey Odell."

"Odell! He's supposed to testify this week."

"So he said. He thinks someone didn't want that to happen."

"You know, Elgin took a couple of shots at me."

"Yeah, I heard about that. Anyway, this was a lot cheaper than a trial, so I guess I don't feel so bad about having to cut him loose on that deal with your DA."

"I'd sure like to know who gave him the order," I lamented.

"We found the car he was driving. It was stolen. But his phone was in it, so maybe we'll be able to see who he was talking to."

"That sounds good. Thanks for calling."

"Just thought you'd want to know."

59

Tuesday, August 12

"**P**lease describe for us the events of June 11 through 13, last year," District Attorney Denise Andrews said to Kim.

She had already been sworn in and had answered the perfunctory questions regarding her position with the Clackamas County Sheriff's Office and how she came to be involved in the recovery of Randy Mendelson's Chevrolet El Camino from the Willamette River.

The testimony was supported by a display of photographs showing the recovery of the El Camino, from the time it broke the surface of the water until it was loaded onto the truck for transport to the sheriff's office maintenance facility.

Kim went methodically through the entire process, from the initial discovery of the sunken car through its recovery, with Andrews asking a long list of questions that kept the testimony focused and comprehensive, despite many seemingly trivial defense objections intended primarily to disrupt the flow of the trial.

"Your witness," Andrews said to Jason Hardman upon conclusion of Kim's testimony.

Hardman stood and approached the witness stand. Already six foot four, the snakeskin cowboy boots he wore added about two more inches to his imposing height. He posed for several seconds before speaking."

"Miss Stayton," he began.

"Deputy Stayton," Kim corrected quickly.

"I'm sorry," Hardman asked sweetly. "Deputy Stayton, How long have you been in law enforcement?"

"Fourteen years."

"And during that time, how many murder investigations have you been involved in?"

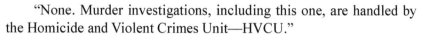

"None. Murder investigations, including this one, are handled by the Homicide and Violent Crimes Unit—HVCU."

"I see," Hardman said contemplatively. "Then can you tell us what are your qualifications for managing an underwater crime scene investigation?"

"I did not manage an investigation. I managed a recovery."

"Ah, let me rephrase the question. What special training do you have in preserving evidence in an underwater crime scene?"

"I am fully trained as a law-enforcement officer. In addition to that, I have special training in marine law enforcement, high-speed motor-craft operation, marine search and rescue, marine salvage, and I am a PADI-certified advanced scuba diver."

Feigning surprise, Hardman said, "Your qualifications are impressive, Deputy Stayton. But am I to understand that you have no training in dealing with underwater crime scenes?"

"As far as I know, no such training ex—"

"Just yes or no."

"Yes," Kim answered.

Looking genuinely surprised, he asked, "Are you telling me that you *do* have training in underwater crime scenes?"

"I'm answering the question you asked."

"Do you or do you not have any special training in underwater crime scenes?" he demanded.

"I do not."

"Thank you. Now, you have described the process used in raising Randall Mendelson's El Camino from the riverbed. Were you in the water supervising the recovery?"

"No."

"So you cannot say whether or not appropriate measures were taken to preserve the integrity of any evidence in that crime scene."

"That is not true," Kim corrected. "The recovery was performed by highly skilled professional divers with years of experience in marine salvage."

"Well, salvaging the bronze bell from a shipwreck is hardly the same thing as preserving a murder scene."

"Objection," Denise Andrews said calmly. "That is argumentative."

"Sustained," Judge O'Brien said.

 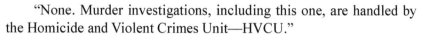

Hardman continued. "Did these professional divers have training or experience in dealing with a crime scene?"

"No."

"So what you are telling me is that neither you nor the people working for you—in fact *nobody* working on the recovery of the El Camino—had any special training or experience."

"Mr. Hardman, everyone there was highly—"

"Just answer the question, Deputy."

"Objection. Your Honor, counsel is belaboring a question that has already been answered."

"I'm just trying to get clarification," Hardman said righteously.

Judge O'Brien said, "I'll allow it. Deputy, please answer the question."

"Nobody has the kind of training you describe. It doesn't exist," Kim told Hardman.

"Well then," Hardman gloated, "how can you know that the crime scene was properly handled? How do you know that crucial evidence wasn't lost because of improper recovery techniques?"

"Objection. Argumentative."

"Sustained. Mr. Hardman, please refrain from drawing conclusions. That is the jury's job."

I could see that this was going to be a long trial. If Hardman could find this much to talk about regarding the completely uncontroversial process of raising the El Camino from the riverbed, I could only imagine what it would take to get through the actual evidence.

The next witness called was Larry Jamieson. The point of his testimony was to establish the facts about the 1980 case and its investigation. He explained how Wilson Devonshire had reported Jessie missing in the early hours of July 26, 1980, and the subsequent report that Randy Mendelson was also missing. He went on to describe the investigation's apparent inability to produce any evidence to even prove that a crime had been committed.

On cross-examination, Hardman opened with, "Sheriff Jamieson, were you involved in the 1980 investigation?"

"I was not. I joined the sheriff's office in 1992, twelve years after the event."

"Is it in fact true that nobody currently working for the sheriff's office was on the force in 1980?"

"That is correct."

"So all of your knowledge about the original investigation is based on the 1980 case file?"

"No, sir. The original case files were lost. Sometime after the investigation was suspended, the files apparently were removed from the evidence room and never returned."

"Well then, what is your source of information regarding the 1980 case?"

"A file was reconstructed from copies of the original documents."

"I see. Thank you. No more questions."

Denise Andrews next called Leslie Turner Charleston to the stand. After establishing that she was the widow of Deputy Gary Turner and that he had been one of the investigators assigned to the 1980 case, the DA questioned her about the death of her husband. The defense objected strenuously to that line of questioning, but the judge let it stand.

"Prior to his death, was your husband in fear for his life?" Andrews asked.

"Objection! Nobody can know his state of mind," Hardman said.

"Sustained."

"I'll rephrase the question. Ms. Charleston, did your late husband say anything to you that suggested that he was in fear for his life."

"Objection!"

"Overruled. The witness may answer."

"He did."

"And would you please describe that conversation?"

I saw Hardman begin to rise from his seat to object, but Judge O'Brien held up a hand, signaling Hardman to save his energy.

"He said he believed that his partner, Dick Hammond, had been murdered—"

Hardman this time flew to his feet. "Objection! That is pure speculation."

"Overruled."

"Thank you, Your Honor. Ms. Charleston, did your husband's belief that he was in danger cause him to take any precautionary measures?"

"He rented a storage unit and put all of his files related to the Mendelson-Devonshire investigation in it."

"And then what happened?"

"He was killed. It was ruled an accident, but I've never believed that. Then a few days later, someone broke into our house and tore the place apart. Every drawer, cupboard, bookshelf, and closet was tossed"

"What was stolen in the break-in?"

"At first I thought they had taken the key to the storage unit because I couldn't find it anywhere."

"Nothing else was taken?"

"Not a thing. And then a few weeks later, I found the key to the storage unit where Gary had concealed it—in a bar of soap."

"Did you use the key to open the storage unit?"

"No. I never went there. I kept the key hidden where nobody would find it. And I got a post office box because people were snooping in my mailbox and opening my mail."

"What kind of things were being opened?"

"Bills, credit card statements—anything that could conceivably reveal where Gary had put his files."

"What did you do about the storage unit?"

"Nothing. Once a year, I paid the rent, and that was it. Then last year, a private investigator came around asking about Gary's role in the Mendelson-Devonshire case. I gave the key to him."

"And who was the private investigator?"

Leslie Charleston pointed at me and said, "It was him. Mr. Corrigan."

Andrews concluded, "I have no further questions."

Jason Hardman rose and asked, "You paid the rent for thirty years on that storage unit, but you never looked inside it?"

"That is correct."

"So you don't really *know* what was in it, do you?"

"I know what my husband told me—that he put the Mendelson-Devonshire files in it."

"I see. But you never actually *saw* the files, is that correct?"

"No. I *did* see the files. For three months, they were all over the dining room table. But after his partner was killed, Gary boxed up everything and took it to the storage unit."

"But since you never looked in the storage unit, you can't *really* be certain that the files were there, can you?"

"Gary said he put them there. I have never had any reason to doubt it," Leslie asserted.

Hardman made a dismissive gesture. "I have nothing further."

Denise Andrews then called me to the stand and led me through the usual introductory questions regarding who I was and how I became involved in the Mendelson-Devonshire investigation. Then she got down to business.

"Mr. Corrigan, on June 28 last year, did you meet with Leslie Turner Charleston?"

"Yes. I did."

"What took place at that meeting?"

"We talked briefly about the Mendelson-Devonshire case, and then she gave me the key to a storage unit on Southeast Powell in Portland."

"What did you do then?"

"I drove to East Side Storage and retrieved the contents of the storage unit—two cardboard boxes containing what I recognized as copies of the official case files on the 1980 Mendelson-Devonshire investigation, plus the personal notes of Gary Turner."

A pair of assistants placed two boxes containing Gary Turner's files on the evidence table.

"Are these the files you found?"

I asked for and received permission to step out of the witness stand to go inspect the contents of the boxes. I made a show of it by leafing through the files, pausing periodically to study a randomly selected folder. When I was sure that the jury had observed my due diligence, I returned to the stand.

"Those are the files I retrieved from East Side Storage," I stated confidently.

Andrews then formally placed the boxes in evidence.

"No further questions at this time," she concluded.

Hardman stood up and paraded past the jury, flaunting his boot-enhanced stature. He studied the sheet of yellow paper he held and conjured an expression of deep concern.

"Mr. Corrigan," he intoned, "you have represented yourself as a private investigator, but I have been informed that your license has been suspended."

I did not respond, hoping that the DA would find some reason to object.

Hardman continued, "You have nothing to say about that?"

"I am a licensed private investigator and will remain so until or unless my license expires or is revoked."

"Is it not true that your license has been suspended?"

"No." Once again, Hardman had tripped himself up with his pretentious syntax.

In disbelief, Hardman said, "*No? Are* you saying that your license has *not* been suspended?"

"I answered the question you asked."

Showing his annoyance, he asked, "Mr. Corrigan, is or is not your private investigator's license currently in a state of suspension."

"It is."

"Thank you," he said with a supercilious smile. "Now would you please tell us the reasons for that suspension."

Again I waited for an objection from Andrews. There was none.

I said, "The licensing agency is investigating some frivolous accusations that were submitted to them by an anonymous informant. I have refuted all of those charges in writing and have presented proof that the accusations are without merit."

"Frivolous! Do you consider evidence tampering, false representation, and income tax evasion to be frivolous?"

"Any accusation is frivolous if it is made without supporting evidence," I said.

Hardman was a man accustomed to getting his way by intimidating witnesses. He gave me a long, cold stare. I was beginning to see why Andrews had let him run with this line of questioning.

"I see," Hardman finally said. "Are you telling the court that you have not been ordered by the US Internal Revenue Service to pay in excess of thirty thousand dollars in delinquent taxes and penalties?"

"The IRS confiscated thirty-three thousand dollars from my bank account based on an elementary mistake made by one of its auditors. I have filed suit—"

"So, Mr. Corrigan, do you consider a tax liability that is greater than the annual income of many citizens to be frivolous?"

I stared at him without comment. He waited. I continued to look him in the eye.

Judge O'Brien finally said, "Mr. Hardman, can we move forward, please?"

60

Wednesday, August 13

It was a pleasure to return to the role of spectator in Judge O'Brien's court. The prosecution introduced a succession of experts in various phases of forensic document analysis to prove the authenticity of the Turner files.

Except for Turner's handwritten notes, most of the documents were made on an office copying machine. A paper chemical analyst testified that the paper used in making the copies was at least twenty years old, based on the acid content of the fibers.

Bleaches and acids are used in manufacturing the paper for all plain-paper copiers. Because of the huge increase in the use of copying machines during the 1970s and early1980s, the acids became an increasing environmental problem. More recent paper is made using an alkaline-buffered method that greatly reduces the acid content in the paper. The relatively high acid content in the paper from the Turner files proved that it was made before the alkaline method was adopted.

On cross-examination, the witness stated that his testing did not prove when the copies were made. It proved only when the paper was made. While a low acid content would have been conclusive proof that the copies were made after Gary Turner's death, the high acid content proved only that the paper was made in the right time period.

In his flamboyant manner, Jason Hardman triumphantly proclaimed, "So anybody with a supply of old paper could have made these copies last year rather than three decades ago, is that correct"

"From the standpoint of the paper, that is correct," the witness admitted.

But if Hardman was hoping to make the case that I had falsified the evidence, the next witness set things straight. He had performed an analysis of the chemical composition of the toner used to make the copies. The relative coarseness of the carbon particles definitively proved that the toner was made in the right era. So not only would I have had to have found thirty-year-old paper, I'd also have had to have used thirty-year-old toner if I had fabricated the evidence.

After that came an expert in copier forensics. He testified that variations in the mechanical tolerances in the paper-feed and toner-application mechanisms cause imperfections in the output that are unique to each machine. The nearly imperceptible banding pattern on the Turner copies, together with the composition of the toner itself, were consistent with a late-seventies model 9200 Xerox copier—the precise make and model of the copier used in the sheriff's office in 1980.

Furthermore, by comparing copies from the Turner files with copies from other files of the era found in the evidence room, the expert was able to state with 99 percent certainty that all were made on the same machine, to the exclusion of all others.

Two handwriting analysts testified that the handwritten notes in the Turner files conclusively matched known samples of Gary Turner's writing. When asked by Denise Andrews if the notes could possibly be forgeries, the analysts both said it was out of the question.

Yet another expert testified that the ballpoint ink used in Turner's notes was thirty to forty years old, based on the solvent content of the samples. The solvents evaporate as the ink ages, and the amount that remains indicates the age of the writing.

The first witness on Thursday was George Haines, who had been a deputy with the Clackamas County Sheriff's Office at the time of the 1980 investigation.

The district attorney asked, "Mr. Haines, were you in any way involved in the 1980 investigation into the disappearances of Jessie Devonshire and Randy Mendelson?"

Haines shook his head and said, "No. I listened to the talk around the office, but that's as close as I got to it."

"Do you remember who was in charge of that investigation?"

Haines said, "Well, Barrington himself was in charge."

"Sheriff Ralph Barrington?" Andrews clarified.

"Right. Yeah, he was pretty close with Mr. Blalock, so he took charge, because, you know, Devonshire worked for Blalock."

"Do you recall anybody else who worked on the case?"

"There were two deputies. Gary Turner and Dick Hammond."

"Did you know them personally?"

"We were acquainted—I mean around the office, but I didn't actually know them socially."

"What became of Turner and Hammond?"

"They died."

"Do you know anything about the circumstances of their deaths?"

Looking uncomfortable, Haines said, "They had accidents. I don't remember the details."

The questioning continued, but Haines had nothing to say that contributed to the case. The next witness was Brent Buxton. When I'd tried to talk to him a year earlier, he had slammed the door in my face without saying a word.

Andrews opened with the same question she'd asked Haines.

"Mr. Buxton, were you in any way involved in the 1980 investigation into the disappearances of Jessie Devonshire and Randy Mendelson?"

"I did some canvassing of the neighborhood around Devonshire's house during the first couple of days."

"What was the result of your work?"

"Nothing. I didn't find anyone who saw anything."

"And then you were taken off the case?"

Buxton shrugged. "There was nothing to investigate."

"Mr. Buxton, we have two boxes of documents related to that investigation. What makes you say there was nothing to investigate?"

"I don't know anything about what's in those boxes."

"Did you know Gary Turner and Dick Hammond?"

"Yeah, I knew them."

"What can you tell me about their deaths?"

Jessie Hardman said, "Objection. That is not relevant to this case."

Andrews said, "Your Honor, the deaths of the only two deputies working the case—within two weeks of one another—resulted in the suspension of the investigation. That may very well have had some bearing on the present case."

Judge O'Brien said, "I'll allow the question. Objection overruled."

"I'll repeat the question, Mr. Buxton. What can you tell me about the deaths of Gary Turner and Dick Hammond?"

"Hammond was a junkie. He took some smack from the evidence room and overdosed. Turner drove off the road into a canyon."

"Did you find anything suspicious about those deaths?"

"Objection. Calls for speculation."

"Your Honor, I am trying to establish the mood around the sheriff's office at the time of the original investigation."

"Find another way to do it then," the judge admonished. "Objection sustained."

Andrews continued to spar with Buxton but was unable to elicit anything of value from him. I believe that she was attempting to demonstrate through Buxton's stubbornness just how strongly the investigation was resisted. Unfortunately, as I scanned the jury, what I saw looked like boredom and impatience.

Eventually, the DA went on to her next witness, Mickey Odell. Odell was what could most politely be called old school. He was coarse, tough, and abrupt. After the perfunctory questions regarding Odell's direct involvement in the investigation, Andrews got to the point.

"Within a few days of the disappearance, only two detectives were left working the case, Deputies Turner and Hammond. Is that normal?"

"Hell no, it ain't normal! Barrington pulled everyone else off the case because he wanted to keep tight control over the investigation."

"Objection! The witness cannot know what the sheriff was thinking."

"Sustained. The jury will disregard the answer."

"Deputy Odell, did you ever have a conversation with Sheriff Barrington about the Mendelson-Devonshire investigation?"

"Sure. We talked about it a lot—off the record, like."

"Did he ever express to you the desire to suppress the investigation?"

"Objection. That calls for hearsay."

Judge O'Brien said, "Counsel, the district attorney is asking for the recollections of this witness. That hardly constitutes hearsay. Overruled. The witness may answer."

"He said that lots of times. He said it was not healthy for people to ask too many questions about it."

"What did he mean by that?"

"Objection!"

"Sustained."

"What can you tell us about the deaths of Detectives Hammond and Turner?"

"I can tell you that they weren't no accidents, that's for sure!"

"Objection. The prosecution has presented no evidence to support that conclusion."

"Your Honor," Andrews pleaded.

"Overruled. Proceed."

"What was the effect of their deaths on the Mendelson-Devonshire investigation?"

"It was the end of it. Nobody was ever reassigned to the case. And everybody on the job knew better than to say anything about it."

"Deputy Odell, you stated earlier that you had a lot of off-the-record conversations about this case with Sheriff Barrington. Did he ever mention any specific suspects in the disappearances of Jessie Devonshire and Randy Mendelson?"

Hardman started to rise, but the judge motioned for him to stay seated.

"Your Honor," Hardman begged, "I object to this whole line of questioning. It is irrelevant, and speculative."

"Anything else, Counsel?"

Hardman threw his hands up in frustration.

"Overruled. Proceed."

Andrews repeated the question.

Odell said, "We talked about Wilson Devonshire and Alan Blalock."

People throughout the courtroom sat up straight. The jury showed an abrupt renewal of interest.

"You talked about them as suspects?" Andrews clarified.

"Yeah. It was plain as day. One of them done it."

"Was that what Barrington said?"

"Yeah. He said it lots of times when we were alone."

"Only when you were alone?'

"That's right. Me and him were tight. We talked about stuff that couldn't be said, ya know, on the record."

"So you had a special relationship with Barrington."

"We had an understanding. He knew I could be trusted."

"Trusted to do what?"

"Well, to keep my mouth shut, for one thing."

"Anything else?"

"He sometimes had me do special favors—things off the grid, as they say."

"Can you give me an example of the kind of 'special favors' you did for Sheriff Barrington?"

"Yeah. One day he told me there was a load of smack in the evidence room—"

"You mean heroin?" Andrews interrupted.

"Yeah. Heroin. He wanted me to take it out of there and get rid of it."

"Barrington asked you to remove a package of heroin from the evidence room and get rid of it?"

"That's right."

"Did he say why he wanted you to do that?"

"Nope. And I didn't ask."

"What did you do with the heroin?"

"I got rid of it, like Barrington told me." Odell's sly smile implied an inside joke.

"What happened after that?"

"Few days later, Dick Hammond was dead of an overdose. Barrington announced that Hammond had taken the stuff out of the evidence room. End of story."

When I got back home that afternoon, I saw the sheriff's Marine Unit boat tied up at my dock. I got my boat keys and went down to the beach where Kim was lounging in the sun.

"Glad to see you," she said. "I need to take my boat over to the sheriff's dock."

I made a show of craning my neck to see her boat. "Yeah, okay. Sure, go ahead."

She threw a sandal at me.

"I was afraid I was going to have to swim back across if you hadn't shown up," she said.

"Oh," I said brightly. "What'll you give me for a boat ride back?"

"You're in grave danger, buster. I'm armed and dangerous."

"You don't scare me," I said as we walked down to the boats.

After securing the patrol boat, we idled back out from the canal onto the open river. I pushed the throttle forward and steered upstream. A few minutes later, we stopped at the public dock in Willamette Park. We tied up and walked over to Twelfth Street on our way up to Willamette Falls Drive.

"It's nice to just take an evening stroll," Kim commented.

"It's ironic," I said. "This is the precise walk that Alan Blalock took in the middle of the night after sinking Randy's car in the river."

"Nice of you to point that out."

"I wish we could get things moving in the trial," I complained. "I worry that the jury is going to get bored with all of this background testimony."

"This isn't Denise Andrews's first trial," Kim reminded me.

"It's her first with *me* involved."

"Trust her. She knows what she's doing."

"Of course, but—"

"The pathologist's report came in yesterday on Dave Blodgett," Kim said. "He died of a single gunshot to the head. A lead slug was recovered from inside the skull. The absence of an entry wound suggests that he was shot in the eye. The preliminary ballistics analysis indicates that it was a .32 caliber bullet. There was what appeared to be a defensive wound to his right hand, so they think he saw it coming.

"Wow. The use of a gun makes a pretty good case for premeditation. Any sign of a matching weapon in the search of Carlton's place?"

"No, but all that proves is that he might have been smart enough to dispose of the gun after the crime. In fact, the search was a total bust. No weapon, no gold, no evidence."

"Sure, but Jill and the kids had already gone through the house before it was secured," I pointed out. "They could have removed anything."

"All true. It's pretty worthless as a crime scene."

"What about Patrick and Shane? Either of them have access to a .32?"

Kim shrugged. "It's too soon to say. The detectives are going to build their case carefully and quietly before alerting the suspects. Right now, they're focusing on finding out what the kids did with the gold."

"It's hard to imagine a couple of teenage stoners walking around with half a million dollars worth of gold."

We arrived at LaFiesta Mexican Kitchen and took a table on the sidewalk out front. With margaritas served and dinner ordered, we sat back to enjoy the warm evening.

"We should do this more often," Kim said wistfully.

"Drink margaritas?"

"No. Walk and talk."

"Oh, right. Long walks on the beach at sunset, that kind of thing."

"You're teasing me."

"Would I do that?"

"Yeah, you would. But I was being serious."

"Cool. I love it when you get serious."

She gave me her squinty-eye look.

"Like last month," I continued, "when you suggested going to Reno and getting married."

"I never suggested that!"

"That's okay. I don't like Reno all that much anyway. We can get married here. And after that, it's Aloha!"

"You mean you'll take me to Hawaii?" she asked brightly.

"No. Aloha—Aloha, Oregon. I can't afford Hawaii right now.

"What the hell would we do in Aloha, Oregon?"

"Same thing we'd do in Hawaii, but without the beaches, the ocean, and the palm trees."

"Corrigan, you're impossible!"

"Difficult maybe, but definitely not impossible."

After a long pause, I asked, "So it's all set?"

61

Friday, August 15

David Elkton took the stand and described in detail the condition of the El Camino when it was delivered to the maintenance garage. Possibly because of Hardman's cross-examination of Kim regarding her expertise in recovering the car, Denise Andrews took special care in her questioning of Elkton.

"Did you observe any indication that the vehicle had been damaged during its recovery from the riverbed?" she asked.

"No. A special framework was constructed beneath the vehicle so that it could be lifted without compromising the structure," Elkton explained. "All of the glass was intact, the doors were closed, and there was no sign of rust-through."

"Would it be safe to say that no evidence from the El Camino was lost or compromised prior to the beginning of the forensic examination you conducted?"

"That is correct. The cab of the El Camino was packed full of mud, almost to the roof. None of it had been disturbed until we removed the doors."

Probably because of the way Andrews handled the direct examination, Hardman declined the opportunity to cross-examine Elkton. Carrie Silverton was the next witness. She went through the entire process of washing the mud, layer by layer, out of the cab.

"What steps were taken during the removal of the mud from the interior of the vehicle to ensure that no evidence was lost?" Andrews asked.

"We placed screens beneath the door sills so that all of the silt washed from the cab was strained. It is the same procedure used by archaeologists."

"What did you observe as you rinsed away the mud?"

"The first thing that I uncovered was a human skull, later identified as that of Randall Mendelson. It was on the driver's side, against the rear window. It was removed and placed in a tub of distilled water for transport to the medical examiner.

As the mud was washed from the car, the clothed skeletal remains of two individuals came into view. The victim in the driver's seat was subsequently identified as Randall Mendelson, and the victim on the passenger side was identified as Jessie Devonshire."

"You mentioned that the victims were clothed. Would you please describe the clothing?"

"The male victim was wearing a black and orange Oregon State University t-shirt, blue jeans, and work boots. The female victim was wearing a pink satin robe and a lace-trimmed pink babydoll lingerie set.

"The female victim was lying sideways on the seat with her head toward the driver. The skeletal remains of both victims were removed as the excavation progressed. When we got to floor level, we uncovered a firearm later identified as a Ruger New Model Single Six."

The clothing and .22 caliber revolver were formally entered as evidence. Upon the completion of Elkton's testimony, Andrews brought in Dr. Nelson Stanfield, the pathologist who examined the human remains.

After the preliminary questions, the district attorney asked, "Dr. Stanfield, will you please describe the injuries you observed on the remains of Jessie Devonshire?"

"There were multiple skull fractures resulting from impact by a heavy object. At the point of impact, a portion of the skull was shattered and pressed inward. The extent of the bone damage suggests that severe brain trauma was also incurred. It is my opinion that the victim was rendered instantly unconscious. The injury probably was not survivable.

There was also a gunshot entry wound at the back of the skull. There was no exit wound. Bullet fragments with a total weight of 2.6 grams were recovered from inside the skull. This injury would be fatal."

"You said that there was no exit wound. How do you explain that?"

"The size of the entry wound is consistent with a .22 caliber weapon. With the relatively low mass of the projectile, most of its energy is dissipated penetrating the bone at the entry wound. Typically, the bullet disintegrates, causing devastating injuries to brain tissue."

"And what did you find in your analysis of the remains of Randall Mendelson?"

"This victim sustained a single gunshot injury in the parietal region of the skull, above and behind the left ear. The angle of penetration indicates that the bullet entered at a downward angle of about forty-five degrees. As with the first victim, there was no exit wound. Bullet fragments with a total weight of 2.6 grams were recovered from inside the skull. This injury would have been instantly fatal."

"Just to be perfectly clear, Doctor, could this victim have remained conscious for any length of time following the injury?"

"Absolutely not. When the bullet disintegrates, fragments of lead and bone are propelled throughout the brain cavity, essentially turning the brain into pulp. Death is instantaneous."

"Regarding the position of the wound and the angle of entry, would you regard this as a self-inflicted injury?"

"That is very unlikely. It would be a very unnatural and difficult thing to fire a gun at yourself from that direction."

When it was time for cross-examination, Jason Hardman rose slowly from his chair, a troubled expression on his face. He made a show of studying a sheet of paper he carried.

"Dr. Stanfield, do you recall performing a post-mortem examination on the body of a gunshot victim named Spencer Dee?"

"I perform many examinations. I do not remember specific names."

Hardman showed his sheet of paper to Dr. Stanfield and asked, "Is that your signature, Doctor?"

"It appears to be. May I look at that?"

"Of course. Take your time, Doctor."

After about forty-five seconds, Stanfield said, "This was ten years ago. I don't have any specific recollections about the case, but that is my signature."

"And what did you report regarding Spencer Dee's injuries?"

Reading from the paper, Stanfield said, "The victim sustained a single gunshot wound above the right ear from a small caliber weapon. There was no exit wound. Bullet fragments were recovered from the brain, with a combined weight of 2.4 grams."

"That sounds remarkably similar to your description of the injury sustained by Randall Mendelson, wouldn't you agree?"

"It does," the doctor answered.

"Would it surprise you then to learn that Spencer Dee, who was the victim in a drive-by shooting *walked* into the hospital for treatment? And that he lived for twenty-three hours before succumbing to his injury?"

With that, Hardman picked up a file from the defense table and placed it in front of Dr. Stanfield.

After looking through the file, Stanfield said, "Well, that's a remarkable case, but not unheard of in the annals of medicine."

"But didn't you earlier state that this kind of injury would have caused instantaneous death?"

"That would be the expected result," the doctor replied.

"And yet Spencer Dee proved that a person *can* survive such an injury and remain conscious and ambulatory for a *considerable* period of time, does it not?"

"It would be extremely rare."

"But not impossible?"

"So it seems."

"No more questions."

62

Monday, August 18

The prosecution's first witness of the day was Brandon Mitchell from the Oregon State Police ballistics lab in Salem. The weapon found in the El Camino was entered into evidence and identified by Mitchell as the weapon he had examined.

In the front of the courtroom, Andrews set up a display board with enlarged photographs taken during the examination. She led Mitchell through an explanation of the position of the cylinder, with an unfired cartridge in the firing position and two expended shell casings in the two positions clockwise from there.

"This is a single-action revolver," Mitchell explained. "That means that after firing, the cylinder remains in position until the hammer is pulled back for the next shot. Pulling back the hammer rotates the cylinder in preparation for the next shot."

"So what does it mean when there is a live cartridge in the firing position, as you had found in this weapon?"

"It would normally mean that the cylinder was rotated after the weapon was last fired. But in this case, it is very likely that the cylinder was completely removed from the weapon and then reinstalled."

"How do you know that?"

"Look at the position of the firing-pin marks on the two expended cartridge casings. They are not where they should be. These shells were removed from the cylinder after firing and reinserted in the improper position."

"Why would somebody do that?"

"The only reason I can think of would be to wipe fingerprints from the shell casings."

"Thank you. Did you analyze the bullet fragments taken from the victims?"

"Yes. The bullets were too fragmented to perform any kind of ballistic analysis, but we did do an analysis on the composition of the fragments using a gas chromatograph mass spectrometer."

"And what did you determine from that?"

"The composition of the fragments was identical to that of the unfired bullets left in the weapon."

"Can you please explain to us what that means to this investigation?"

"The lead used to make bullets is never completely pure. Each batch of lead will have very slight variations in the chemical composition of its impurities. The gas chromatograph provides an extremely accurate measurement of the impurities, enabling us to state with near-absolute certainty whether two lead samples originated from the same batch of raw material. The odds against finding two bullets with identical chemical composition are astronomical unless the two bullets were made from the same batch of lead.

"In this case, because the chemical composition is identical, we can state with confidence that the bullet fragments taken from the victims came from the same box of ammunition as the unfired bullets recovered from the weapon. It follows that the fatal bullets were fired from that weapon."

Hardman's cross-examination was brief and perfunctory. He succeeded in getting Mitchell to admit that there was a statistical possibility that the fatal bullets had been fired from a different weapon, although the witness managed to emphasize that the chances of that were minuscule.

Following the noon recess, Denise Andrews introduced her next piece of evidence, an enlarged print of Gary Turner's photograph of the entry hall of the Devonshire's residence on Rosemont Road, along with the original print from which the enlargement was made.

"Now that we've established *how* the victims died, we will move forward and establish *where* and *when* they died," Andrews said.

She then called Mark Adair to the stand, introducing him as a forensic document analyst specializing in photography. She led him through a series of questions establishing his expertise and experience and then handed him the original 3 ½" x 5" photograph.

"Have you seen this photograph before?"

"Yes. It was submitted to me for analysis by your office."

"What were you able to determine in your analysis?"

"This print was made from a 35 mm negative on Kodak paper in a high-volume C-41 film processing machine of the type commonly used in the photo kiosks in parking lots where today you find espresso vendors. The batch number of the paper indicates that it was manufactured in May 1980."

"Can you tell when the print was made?"

"Yes and no. While it is conceivable that a print could be made at any time on paper from old stock, the fact that this print was made in a machine that is functionally obsolete makes that extremely unlikely. What's more, the dyes in the print show fading typical in prints that are at least twenty years old."

"What do you mean when you say that the machine that made this print is functionally obsolete?"

"High-volume automatic photo processors are no longer in use. Very few people use film cameras, so their film today is processed manually in small labs. It is not economically viable to operate an old C-41 machine."

"Given all of that, what would you conclude about the age of this print?"

"It was almost certainly made within a few months of the time the paper was manufactured. It is extremely unlikely that it is any newer than, say, 1985."

On cross-examination, Hardman said, "Mr. Adair, would a person today be able to purchase Kodak paper manufactured in 1980?"

"If you had the time, I think you could find it. There are often leftover materials found in old storerooms that are marketed to aficionados of old school processing."

"Would it also be possible to artificially fade the dyes to make a print look older than it actually is?"

"Yes. It could be done by using exposure to heat and light."

"Thank you. I have no more questions."

On redirect, Andrews asked, "Could this photo be a recent print made to look old?"

"Absolutely not. Like I said before, the print was made by a machine that hasn't been used in at least ten years."

"What about the artificial aging of the dyes?"

"The heat required to do that would bake the paper in addition to fading the dyes. There is no evidence that this paper was exposed to the kind of heat it would take to artificially age the dyes."

Next, Andrews re-called Sheriff Jamieson to the stand. After the judge reminded him that he was still under oath, Jamieson took his seat on the witness stand.

Andrews handed him the 3 ½" x 5" photograph.

"Please tell us the source of this photograph."

"This was found in one of the boxes removed from Gary Turner's storage locker, which were given to us by private investigator Corrigan on September 26 last year."

"Can you tell me where and when the photograph was taken?"

Predictably, Hardman jumped to his feet and loudly said, "Objection! This witness cannot have any knowledge of when or under what circumstances the photo was taken."

"Your Honor, we are prepared to provide supporting evidence for Sheriff Jamieson's testimony," Andrews countered.

"Proceed. Objection is overruled."

Jamieson answered, "This photo was taken on July 26, 1980, by Deputy Richard Hammond in the entry hall of the Devonshire home at 1525 Rosemont Road in West Linn."

"How do you know that?" Andrews asked.

"The photo is part of a witness contact report that Hammond wrote on that date when he interrogated Wilson Devonshire, which was included in the 'murder book' from the Turner files."

"I call your attention to the large reddish-brown stain visible on the carpet in the photo. Based on your experience as a homicide detective, what would be your immediate interpretation of that?"

"It looks very much like someone made an unsuccessful attempt at cleaning up a large bloodstain."

"At the time this photo was taken, what explanation was given regarding the stain?"

"Wilson Devonshire told Deputy Hammond that the stain was caused by spilled paint. He said that he had painted his front door the previous evening, July 25, and had accidentally spilled paint on the carpet."

"Was that ever confirmed?"

"The only way to confirm it would be to do a chemical analysis of the stain."

"Was such an analysis done?"

"Not to my knowledge."

"Would you say that was an unusual oversight, given the circumstances?"

"It is beyond unusual. It is extraordinary," Jamieson said.

"**P**rosecution calls Barbara Devonshire to the stand."

The last time I'd seen Mrs. Devonshire, she was still recovering from the death of her husband and the total destruction of her home in the fire that nearly took her life. As she took her seat on the witness stand, she appeared composed and determined. Andrews directed her attention to the enlarged copy of the entry hall photo.

"Does this scene look familiar to you?"

"Yes. That is the entry hall in the home where we resided at the time my daughter disappeared."

"Did you ever see that stain on the carpet?"

"Yes. I saw it the day after Jessie disappeared, when I returned home from a trip to the coast. My husband told me that he had spilled paint there."

"Didn't you wonder about the timing—a blood-colored stain appearing on the carpet on the very day your daughter disappeared?"

"At the time, I was too distraught to think clearly. But over the years, that has been one of the things I've wondered about."

"What became of the stained carpet?"

"Wilson had it taken out and replaced a couple of days later."

"What did he do with the old carpet?"

"I don't know. I suppose he simply dumped it into the trash.

The final witness of the day was Lila Mendelson. The mother of Randy Mendelson testified that Dick Hammond and Gary Turner communicated regularly with her during the course of their investigation. She cited a conversation with Turner where he had told her of his interest in the carpet from the entry hall.

"What did Detective Turner say about the carpet?"

"He was suspicious because Devonshire had removed and disposed of it."

"Did he say anything else about the carpet?"

"He thought that he might be able to find it, but he died, and nothing ever came of it."

63

Tuesday, August 19

Judge O'Brien said, "I remind you, Mr. Corrigan, that you are still under oath."

The district attorney picked up a piece of wood and carried it to the witness stand.

"Mr. Corrigan, do you recognize this piece of wood."

I said, "Yes I do. It is a piece of flooring from the entry hall of the former Devonshire home in West Linn."

"How did you come into possession of this?"

"It was given to me by the current owner, Sara Huntington."

"What was your interest in the board?"

"It was taken from the floor in the entry hall at the location where Deputy Hammond's photograph shows the stain on the carpet. I obtained it with the idea of submitting it for analysis to determine what caused the stain."

"And did you have that analysis done?"

"Yes. I submitted the board to a private lab in Portland, where an ABO test was conducted, confirming the presence of human blood in the tongue-and-groove portions of the board. The blood was identified as B positive, the same blood type as Jessie Devonshire. On that basis, I had the board sent to a DNA lab in Seattle for genetic profiling."

Andrews entered the board into evidence and then proceeded, "Mr. Corrigan, a DNA profile by itself is of limited value without a profile to compare it with. How did you go about obtaining a sample of Jessie Devonshire's DNA?"

"I did not have access to the victim's remains, and because her family members had not at that time been excluded as suspects, I had to look elsewhere. I located one of Jessie Devonshire's friends, Melissa Vale, who possessed a Christmas card sent by Jessie in 1979. DNA samples were obtained from the flap on the envelope."

"And the result of the DNA analyses?"

"They were a match. The blood on the floor was from the person who licked the envelope."

Showing me the report from Seattle DNA lab, Andrews said, "Jessie Devonshire. Mr. Corrigan, is this the DNA lab report confirming that match?"

I confirmed that it was, and she entered it as evidence.

"Thank you. No further questions at this time."

Hardman got straight to the point. "Mr. Corrigan, did you personally remove the board from the floor of the former Devonshire house?"

"No. It was removed by the current owner during a remodeling project."

"So you have no direct personal knowledge of the board's origin?"

"The current owner—"

"A yes or no answer, please."

"Yes."

"Yes?" he asked. And then he figured it out. "You mean yes, you have no direct knowledge of the board's origin."

"Yes."

I could see his annoyance at being once again confused by his own cleverness, and it took a special effort on my part to avoid smiling.

Hardman then set out to use the strategy that proved successful in the O. J. Simpson trial by setting the stage for a claim that the DNA sample on the board was contaminated through improper handling so that the results were irrelevant.

"Mr. Corrigan, when did you obtain this board?"

"July 3, last year."

"Nearly thirty-two years after Jessie Devonshire's disappearance?" he asked, feigning surprise.

"That's right."

"During that thirty-two-year period, were precautions taken to preserve the sample?"

"I do not know."

"Thank you. Now regarding this envelope, you say this was given to you by a friend of the victim, is that correct?"

"Yes."

"The postmark says December 17, 1979, nearly thirty-three years ago. Can you tell me what precautions were taken to preserve the integrity of the DNA on the envelope flap?"

"No. I have no knowledge of that."

He turned his back and said, "That's all," as he walked back to the defense table.

Andrews called Sara Huntington and showed her a photograph of the entry hall taken during the remodeling. A large brownish stain was clearly visible on the oak flooring.

"Mrs. Huntington, did you take this photograph?"

"Yes. It is part of a before, during, and after series that I shot during the remodeling project."

Andrews then held the photo next to the enlargement of Deputy Hammond's photo of the Devonshire entry hall.

"Would you say that these two photos were taken in the same location?"

"Yes. You can tell by the electrical outlet on the wall above the stain."

"Why did you remove the boards from that location?"

"They were too badly stained to refinish. The varnish was badly worn, so the stain penetrated into the wood. We were able to find matching wood, so it was easier to replace the stained wood than to salvage it."

Hardman's cross-examination pursued the same path he'd taken with me, attempting to discredit the DNA evidence based on the history of the board. The witness conceded that she and her husband had taken no special care to preserve the DNA samples.

The next witness was Melissa Vale, who explained the origin of the envelope. Hardman's cross-examination was like an instant replay.

"The prosecution calls Dr. Thomas Kent."

Kent was the analyst who performed the tests at the DNA lab in Seattle. Once he was sworn in, Andrews led him through a series of questions establishing his identity, credentials, and connection to the case.

"Now, Dr. Kent, the defense has expressed concern that the DNA specimens may have become contaminated or otherwise rendered invalid due to the length of time involved or the way the samples were stored. What assurances can you offer regarding the validity and accuracy of your testing?"

"DNA chains are remarkably stable. They might deteriorate under conditions of extreme heat, but the temperatures required would have destroyed the substrate material, so we can conclude with absolute certainty that that didn't happen. As to external contamination, it would be evident in the profile, whether it involved mixing with other DNA sources or deterioration of the sample from chemical exposure."

"Did you observe any evidence of deterioration or contamination?"

"The samples taken from both items were clean, and the results were quite good."

"And what was that result?"

"Both samples were from the same individual."

Hardman put on a troubled expression as he stood for his cross-examination of Kent.

"I see in your report that you performed more than one test on the envelope."

"That is correct. We performed two tests."

"Why did you perform the second test?"

"The result of the first test was not 100 percent conclusive."

Raising his eyebrows, Hardman said, "I think the word you used in the report was 'ambiguous,' wasn't it?"

"The test was ambiguous on one of the thirteen markers. The sec—"

"Now let me ask you, Dr. Kent, are you able to tell in your analysis exactly how old a DNA sample is?"

"Not using DNA analysis. There are other tests that can estimate the age of the sample, but those tests were not done on these samples."

"I see," Hardman mused as though deep in thought. "So even if that was Jessie Devonshire's blood, you cannot say when it got onto the floor board."

"That is correct."

After adjournment for the day, a young lady I recognized as an assistant from the district attorney's office caught up with me on the courthouse steps.

"Mr. Corrigan, do you have a few minutes?"

"Sure. What can I do for you, Miss…"

"Dillard. Monica Dillard. I'm with the district attorney's office. Can you join me over there?" she asked, indicating the Verdict Bar and Grill across the street.

Occupying the oldest building in downtown Oregon City, the Verdict is a business that takes clever advantage of its location. In addition to offering discounts and making special accommodations to jurors and others involved in courthouse proceedings, just about everything about the Verdict plays on the trial theme. The main area is called the Hearing Room, and side rooms are called the Holding Cell and the Jury Room, while the restrooms are called the Judge's Chambers. Happy hour is called Abatement Hour, and the menus are called Writs.

Monica and I took seats in the Holding Cell and were soon joined by Sheriff Jamieson.

Monica started by saying, "Tomorrow is when we start tying Alan Blalock to the crime. We'll start with witnesses who will testify to Blalock's history with underage girls. It's been a struggle to find victims who are willing to testify, but we have what we need.

Once we've established what Blalock's so-called internship program was all about, we'll bring in Barbara Devonshire to testify as to how Jessie got involved. That will lead directly into the discussion of her lingering suspicions in the days, weeks, and years after Jessie disappeared."

I spoke up, "But she suspected that it was her husband, not Blalock, who was responsible."

"While it's true that she suspected her husband was involved—which he was—she also believed that Blalock was at the heart of it," Monica explained. "That's what she'll say on the stand. After Mrs. Devonshire, we had always planned to bring in Richard Elgin to testify as to his knowledge of Blalock's affairs—how he drove the mayor and his 'interns' to motels and stood by while the 'advanced education in city government' took place. And then we intended to finish with his account of the events of July 25, 1980."

"Will the court allow his recorded statement to be used instead?" I asked.

Sheriff Jamieson said, "We're probably not going to be able to do that."

I turned to Monica and asked, "Won't this jeopardize the whole case?"

"It won't *help* it," she said. "But we'll work around it. We have other witnesses who will make the same points. I just wanted to keep you up to date."

64

Monday, August 20

Denise Andrews called her first witness, Alicia Jefferson, to the stand.

"Mrs. Jefferson, are you familiar with the name Richard Elgin?"

Alicia gave a contemptuous laugh. "I was married to Richard Elgin for four years, from 1981 to 1985."

"Who was your ex-husband's employer?"

"The Portland Police Bureau. He was a police officer."

"What were his duties with the police bureau?"

"He had only one duty. He was the driver for the mayor."

"And who was the mayor?"

"It was Alan Blalock until 1984. Then it was Bud Clark."

"What can you tell me about Richard Elgin's RTE Consulting Company?"

"Richard set it up so that he would have a way to bill the city for special favors he did for important people in city government."

"Including the mayor?"

"Of course. The mayor more than anybody else."

"What kind of things did he do to earn this money?"

"Mostly, he earned it by keeping his mouth shut."

"Objection. The witness cannot know that."

"Sustained. Strike that from the record. The jury will disregard the answer."

"Did Richard Elgin ever confide in you regarding things he did for Mayor Blalock—things beyond driving his car?"

"Many times."

"Did he ever tell you about the mayor's sexual activities?"

"Objection!" shouted Hardman.

"I'll rephrase the question," Andrews said quickly. "Mrs. Jefferson, did your husband ever tell you about driving the mayor to hotels during the day."

"Yes. That was a fairly common event."

"Did he say who accompanied the mayor on these hotel visits?"

"He said they were young women—or girls."

"Objection! This is hearsay."

"Your Honor, the witness is testifying about a conversation in which she participated. It is not hearsay."

"Overruled."

"What did your husband tell you about these young ladies?"

"He called them starry-eyed groupies. He said they were 'clueless.' That was the word he used."

"Did he indicate how old these 'starry-eyed groupies' were?"

"He said they were schoolgirls. He always called them kids."

"Did your husband ever mention the girls' names?"

"He did, but I don't remember them. It was a long time ago."

"Did your husband ever talk about the Jessie Devonshire disappearance?"

"Yes. It was a very current topic during the time we were dating. He was personally acquainted with Jessie Devonshire and her stepfather, Wilson Devonshire, who was the mayor's top aide at the time."

"What did he tell you about Jessie Devonshire?"

"He said he couldn't talk about it, but he made it quite clear that he had some inside knowledge."

The next witness was someone named Charlotte Holland. She was small, probably less than five feet tall and under one hundred pounds. She had an emaciated look, with sunken eyes and thinning hair, and yet her face was hauntingly pretty. Her hands trembled as she was sworn in. She appeared to be in her mid-fifties.

Alan Blalock leaned over and whispered something to Jason Hardman, who raised his hand in a calming gesture. Blalock became visibly agitated and gripped the attorney's arm while whispering. Hardman patted his hand and seemed to offer some kind of reassurance.

"Your Honor, we object to the introduction of this witness," Hardman said.

The judge then had the jury escorted from the room. Once they were gone, she allowed Hardman to continue.

"This trial is about the Devonshire and Mendelson murders. Unless this witness has knowledge of that event, her testimony can only be prejudicial to the defendant."

Andrews said, "Your Honor, this witness will help show a pattern of behavior on the part of the defendant that led directly to the murders of Jessie and Randy."

"Mr. Hardman, I'm going to allow the witness. Return to your seat."

After the jury returned to the courtroom, Andrews asked, "Ms. Holland, are you acquainted with the defendant, Alan Blalock?"

"I knew him a long time ago," she said quietly.[4]

"What is your earliest memory of Mr. Blalock?"

"I think it was when I was seven or eight years old."

The sudden stillness in the courtroom was chilling.

She continued, "We were in a big building, maybe a hotel. We were in an elevator, and he was holding my hand. Then he led me into a big room full of people, and everyone clapped and cheered."

The district attorney showed her an enlarged copy of the front page of the *Portland Daily Chronicle* from November 1976. Under the headline "Blalock Elected Mayor," there was a photo from the victory celebration in the ballroom of the Portland Hilton. It showed Blalock approaching the stage, holding the hand of a little girl with dark hair and a wide smile.

"Is this you?"

"Yes, it is," Charlotte said, her voice cracking.

I did some quick mental arithmetic. If she was eight in 1976 when Blalock was elected mayor, she was currently forty-five. I took another long look at her. The years had been hard on her.

"How were you introduced to Mr. Blalock?" asked Andrews.

"We lived close to him, like just down the street. My parents were friends and big supporters. They helped him a lot in his campaigns. Sometimes, Mr. Blalock came to our house."

---

4. The testimony of the fictitious character Charlotte Holland in this story is derived from statements made to Portland, Oregon reporter Margie Boulé in a series of interviews with Elizabeth Lynn Dunham, who was a real life victim of abuse similar to that portrayed in *El Camino* and *Deadly Gold*. Reference: Margie Boulé, "Neil Goldschmidt's sex-abuse victim tells of the relationship that damaged her life" *The Oregonian*, January 31, 2011.

"Please tell us what happened over the next few years."

"Well, Mr. Blalock was a very important person. I knew that, even when I was little. I was very proud, because of all the little girls in the world, he had chosen me to be his friend. He used to bring me presents when he came to our house. He always gave me a hug and a kiss.

And then I remember one time when my mom took me to the mayor's office and Mr. Blalock had me sit on his lap at his big desk. It embarrassed me a little bit because I was in fifth grade and thought I was too old for that."

"How old were you then?"

"Ten, I guess. Anyway, Mr. Blalock often put his hands on me. I didn't think there was anything sexual about it. Because, you know, I didn't know anything about sex, and it had always been that way."

"When did you recognize that there was something sexual in Mr. Blalock's actions?"

"It came on gradually. At the time, it was just the way things were. So when I started, uh, developing, he kept on touching me the way he always had. But it started to change. I knew it was sexual when he started doing things like…feeling my breasts…squeezing my thighs."

"And this led to a sexual relationship?"

"Yes. The first time was in our basement. Mr. Blalock came over after school and brought a bottle of Cherry Kijafa. It was the first time I ever drank alcohol, but it was very sweet and I liked it. Anyway, we had sex. I didn't like it, but I felt like I was on top of the world."

"How old were you at that time?"

"I was thirteen—in seventh grade."

"So that would have been in about 1981?"

"Yes. I guess so."

"What happened after that?"

"Mr. Blalock made arrangements to be with me. Sometimes it was at his office. Sometimes at hotels or in parks—different places. He would send Mr. Elgin to pick me up after school, and then we'd go someplace for sex."

"How long did this go on?"

"About three years, and then I got pregnant. That's when my folks found out about it."

She shook her head and brushed tears from her eyes.

"They sent me to a doctor who did an abortion. After that, I didn't see Mr. Blalock again."

"Have you ever told this to anyone before today?"

"No."

"And why is that?"

"It was shortly after my abortion that Mr. Blalock was elected governor. Then a couple of years later, when I was eighteen, an attorney showed up with a confidentiality agreement for me and my parents to sign. Mr. Blalock gave us $350,000, and we agreed to never mention what had happened. We all signed the paper."

Denise Andrews walked over and put her hand on Charlotte's.

"I have no more questions."

"Ms. Holland," Hardman opened, "have you ever been arrested?"

"Yes," she answered, looking down into her lap.

"For what were you arrested?"

"Different things," she said.

"What things?"

"Drugs. Drunk driving. Solicitation."

"You mean prostitution."

Charlotte didn't answer.

"Ms. Holland, have you ever been treated in a mental institution?"

"Yes."

"Did you reside in a mental hospital from 1992 to 1994?"

"Yes."

"And what was your diagnosis?"

"I'm not sure," she said quietly.

"You're not sure? Maybe this will help," Hardman said, waving a sheet of paper.

"It says here that you were committed because you were unable to function in society. It says that you showed symptoms of paranoia and psychosis. Do you know what those things are?"

"Not really."

"Have you ever been in a treatment program for addiction?"

"Yes."

"Please elaborate."

"I've been treated for different drug addictions and alcoholism."

"Heroin?"

"Yes."

"Methamphetamines?"

"Yes."

"Oxycodone?"

"Yes."

"Anything else?"

"I don't know."

"Ms. Holland, is it not true that you have been treated for symptoms of dementia?"

"I don't know what that is."

"Memory loss. Have you been treated for memory loss?"

"I don't know."

"It says here that you have," Hardman insisted, still waving the paper.

When Charlotte made no comment, Hardman said, "No more questions."

Charlotte sat there crying, and it was obvious that she had no idea what she was supposed to do. The contempt I felt for Alan Blalock at that moment was unlike anything I'd ever felt toward anyone in my entire life. I looked toward the jury box and saw several jurors wiping tears from their eyes.

The prosecution then called Lisa Olene to the stand.

After the preliminaries, Andrews asked, "Are you related to Katy Olene?"

"Katy was my sister. She was three years older than me."

"Where is your sister now?"

"She's dead. She took her own life in 1979."

"How old was she when she died?"

"It was her seventeenth birthday," Lisa said.

"What can you tell us about the time leading up to her death?" Andrews asked.

"It was because of him!" she blurted, pointing at Alan Blalock.

"Objection!"

"Sustained. The jury will disregard that," Judge O'Brien said.

He turned to the witness and said, "Please limit your testimony to facts and refrain from drawing conclusions."

"Please start at the beginning," Denise Andrews said.

Lisa drew a deep breath. "Our folks had been friends with Alan Blalock for years—I don't know exactly how long. Mom worked on his campaign committee, and then after he was elected, she went to work in his office. During the campaign, we sometimes had campaign meetings at our house, and that's when Katy met Mr. Blalock."

"That was in 1976?"

"That's right. Mr. Blalock seemed very interested in Katy. After the meeting was over, he talked to Mom about getting Katy into a city council meeting, like, to watch how city government worked. She went as Mr. Blalock's personal guest."

"How old was she at that time?"

"She was in eighth grade, thirteen years old."

"Did you talk with her about her experience?"

"We used to talk about *everything*. She said the city council meeting was kind of boring, but she was really proud that she was invited to attend, and she said that Mr. Blalock treated her like a grown-up.

Then after Mr. Blalock was mayor, Katy started going to city hall to learn more about city government. That was when she was a freshman at Saint Mary's Academy, which was only four or five blocks from city hall. She would walk over after school and stay until Mom got off work."

"What did she do while she was visiting city hall?"

"Mostly she hung around in the mayor's office. I could tell that she had a real crush on Mr. Blalock. I thought it was kind of strange, but Katy was all hung up about being mature. She always tried to act older.

One day, when Katy was bragging about visiting the mayor, she got all gushy and told me that the mayor loved her and she loved him. At first I thought it was just a story, but then she showed me a package of birth control pills and said that Mr. Blalock got them for her."

"Do you remember when that conversation took place?"

"It was around Christmas time in 1977, when Katy was fifteen."

"Did your mother know what was going on?"

Lisa shook her head. "I don't think so. I think it started in the mayor's office, but pretty soon the mayor started sending a car to pick up Katy at school and take her to other places for…you know, sex."

"Did your sister say where they went?"

"Sometimes. She talked about some places like hotels or private houses. She was really on a big ego trip about it, telling me what it was like to be an adult and all. She even said that when she got to be eighteen, he was going to marry her."

"Didn't she know that Alan Blalock was already married and had two children?"

"She said that he was going to get a divorce. That was before things started to turn bad."

"In what way did things turn bad?"

"Katy came home one day in a very bad mood. She told me that the mayor had invited some other girl to visit his office. She was very angry about that and cried a lot."

"When did this happen?"

"It was shortly after school started in 1978. Things got bad pretty fast after that. Katy got really moody and wouldn't talk to me. She started ditching school a lot. I don't know where she went after Mr. Blalock stopped seeing her, but she often came home drunk.

She was in trouble at school and got into a lot of arguments with Mom and Dad. They took her someplace for counseling, but Katy hated it. And then on her birthday in April, she stole a gun from a friend's house, went into the woods, and killed herself."

"Did she leave any kind of a note?"

"Not that I ever saw. But my folks started arguing a lot after that, and I heard them say something about Katy's note once. They got a divorce, and Dad moved away. I never saw him again."

"What about your mother?"

"She continued working for Mr. Blalock as if nothing had ever happened. She worked on his first campaign for governor. After that, she stayed on at city hall and worked for Mr. Clark."

"Did you ever have any interaction with Alan Blalock?"

"There were times when he came to our house. He was always friendly to me. Once, he put his arm around my waist, which was kind of creepy. I mean, he was sleeping with my sister, and there he was trying to grope me! I pushed his hand away and threatened to tell Mom."

"How old were you then?"

"I was twelve."

Hardman's cross-examination was brief, aimed primarily at emphasizing that Lisa's knowledge of what "may or may not have" happened between Katy and the mayor was based entirely on what Katy had told her.

Following a late recess for lunch, Denise Andrews called her next witness. As she took the stand, Barbara Devonshire looked as though she hadn't slept well. She appeared nervous and unsure of herself.

"How did your daughter become acquainted with Alan Blalock?"

"She was in seventh grade, and my husband, Wilson Devonshire, worked in the city attorney's office. He helped set up a field trip to city hall for Jessie's social studies class, and they got to talk with the mayor. Shortly after that, the mayor told my husband that he was very impressed with Jessie's interest in city government.

Blalock invited Jessie to join what he called his junior internship program, so Wilson started taking her to the mayor's office once a week. Not long after that, Blalock hired Wilson to be his aide in city hall. It was a huge career advancement. I know now that it was Blalock's reward to him for bringing Jessie to him."

"Did you have any idea what was going on between Blalock and Jessie?"

"No. God knows I should have, but I didn't see what was right in front of me."

"And that was…"

"That Blalock was using Jessie for sex."

"Objection. The witness just stated that she did not know what or indeed if anything was going on between the defendant and her daughter."

"Sustained."

"Mrs. Devonshire, when did you first learn that Alan Blalock was sexually involved with your daughter?" Andrews asked.

"I wondered about it from the time Jessie disappeared. But after my husband's death, I found a letter he had left in a safe deposit box. It told the whole story."

Andrews showed Barbara two sheets of paper. "Is this the letter you are speaking of?"

"It is."

Andrews then read the letter, which told the entire story of how Blalock had recruited Jessie into his internship program and turned it into a sexual liaison. It described how for two years the mayor had used Jessie and concluded with Wilson Devonshire's explanation for what had happened on July 25, 1980.

Devonshire told of receiving a phone call from Blalock urging him to get home because something had happened to Jessie. Devonshire arrived home to find Blalock there and the bodies of Randy Mendelson and Jessie lying in a pool of blood in the entry hall. Blalock had gone to the Devonshire home to spend the afternoon with Jessie, but at some point, they had argued. Jessie left the room and returned waving a gun.

When she headed for the front door, Blalock struck her in the head with Jessie's eagle coin bank and took the gun from her hand.

Randy Mendelson was working in the yard and heard the argument. When he knocked on the door, Blalock let him in and immediately shot him. He then shot Jessie, just to make sure that she was dead.

Blalock then convinced Devonshire to help with the clean-up and cover-up. Together, they put the bodies into Randy's El Camino and came up with the idea of spilling paint to conceal the bloodstain that they were unable to remove from the carpet. Hours later, in the middle of the night, Blalock drove the El Camino into the Willamette River.

The letter concluded with a statement that proof of everything he had described there could be found in Wilson Devonshire's office.

"Did you subsequently find the proof described in the letter?" Andrews asked.

"Yes. Mr. Corrigan helped me search Wilson's office, and he finally discovered that Wilson had concealed the evidence inside a bronze eagle."

Andrews picked up the eagle and showed it to Mrs. Devonshire. "Is this the same eagle?"

"Yes."

"How did you and Mr. Corrigan determine that the evidence was concealed inside it?"

She pointed at the brass plate on the base. "It was the Latin inscription, SI VERUM TESTIMONIUM EST INTUS. Mr. Corrigan translated it. 'If you wish the truth, proof is inside,' or something like that."

"What happened then?"

"We smelled gasoline, and in a matter of seconds, the entire house burst into flames. It burned to the ground. We escaped with the eagle and Wilson's letter."

65

Tuesday, August 21

I was up first. The DA led me through some questions regarding the discovery of the letter in Wilson Devonshire's safe deposit box and the subsequent search for the supporting evidence. I told how the eagle had been in plain sight the whole time, but the Latin inscription hadn't registered.

"What did you do with the letter and the eagle after escaping from the burning mansion?"

"Mrs. Devonshire and I were taken to the hospital for treatment of cuts and burns. I kept the letter and eagle with me the whole time. Deputy Kim Stayton picked us up at the hospital, and since Mrs. Devonshire had lost everything in the fire, Deputy Stayton offered to put her up for the night. When she dropped me off at my place, I locked the evidence in my safe."

"Did you open the eagle before putting it into your safe?"

"No."

"When and under what conditions did you open it?"

"The day after the fire, I called my attorney William Gates to witness the opening. Also present were Deputy Stayton and Barbara Devonshire. My assistant made a video recording of the entire process."

"Mr. Corrigan, why didn't you turn the eagle over to the authorities instead of opening it yourself?"

"In the first place, we did not know if there really was anything inside. All we knew for sure at the time was what I translated from the Latin inscription. And my translation was far from a sure thing."

"But you suspected there was evidence inside, didn't you? Otherwise why bring in the witnesses?"

"I *hoped* there would be evidence inside, and I called the witnesses to assure a clean chain of custody in case we *did* find anything."

Andrews then played the video that showed the entire process of opening the eagle and extracting the plastic bag containing the evidence.

"Will you please describe what you found in the plastic bag?"

"There were two miniature audio cassettes, a note from Wilson Devonshire, and two credit card receipts."

Andrews showed me two pieces of paper. "Are these the credit card receipts?"

"They are."

"Let the record show that the first receipt is from the Meier and Frank department store for the purchase of a pink lingerie set matching that which Jessie Devonshire was wearing when recovered from the El Camino. The second receipt is for a prescription in Jessie Devonshire's name for birth control pills. The name on the credit card used in both of these purchases is Alan Blalock."

Andrews then introduced the two microcassettes.

"Are these the audio tapes that you removed from the eagle?"

"Yes. They are."

"No further questions."

"I must say, Mr. Corrigan, you do know how to spin an exciting yarn," Hardman said.

I just stared at him and mentally replayed his cross-examination of Charlotte Holland, getting myself into the appropriate frame of mind to deal with him.

"You *say* that you first opened the eagle in the presence of witnesses, but how do we know that you didn't first open it and plant the evidence inside?"

"Objection. Counsel is making an accusation without a shred of supporting evidence."

Hardman said, "The evidence is the collection of items removed from the eagle. We will show that every piece of it was fabricated."

Judge O'Brien said, "Mr. Hardman, you know better. The objection is sustained, and the question will be stricken from the record."

Hardman brushed off the rebuke and asked, "Is it true that from the time Deputy Stayton dropped you off at your residence until you convened your witnesses eighteen hours later, you had unrestricted access to the eagle?"

"That is not true. The eagle was locked in my safe."

"But of course you could have opened it at any time."

"My security system automatically logs an entry anytime the safe is opened. That log is maintained by the security monitoring service. If you had taken the time to look at that, you'd have the answer to your question."

He wasn't ready for that.

"Mr. Corrigan, ah…I guess we'll have to take your word on that for now. How much time did you spend searching the Devonshire mansion?"

"I was there for three days."

"Three days? And all that time was the eagle in the house."

"Yes, it was."

"And were there periods of time when you were alone in the room with it?"

"I guess it's possible, but I have no specific recollection."

"So there were times when you were alone with the eagle?"

"I didn't say that."

"Oh, that's right. Your memory fails you. I have no further questions."

Andrews next brought in the sheriff's office technician who examined the eagle after Kim turned it over to Jamieson. He told of finding traces of blood in a tiny groove around the base. The DNA extracted from the blood matched Jessie Devonshire's. A pathologist testified that the base of the eagle perfectly fit the fracture pattern in Jessie's skull.

Employees from the department store and pharmacy where the credit card receipts originated testified that they were consistent with what was being used in their stores in 1980. Hardman succeeded in getting them to admit on cross-examination that the receipt forms were identical to those used in stores nationwide and that it was conceivable that old forms could still be found, even in their own stores.

On redirect, Andrews asked what it would take to produce fake receipts matching the ones in evidence.

"Well, first you'd have to make the plate with the store information on it. You'd need the machine that presses the letters into the steel plate, and you'd need the store's information. Then you'd need the credit card— or you'd have to counterfeit one, provided you had the card number and expiration date."

"How long would all of that take?"

"I don't know. I guess if you had all of the information and equipment, you might be able to do it in a few hours, but it could take weeks or months to collect everything."

A handwriting analyst testified that the signatures on the credit card receipts were Alan Blalock's. He also confirmed that the handwriting on the note found in the eagle matched those found on papers Wilson Devonshire had written in the early 1980s. That was important because his handwriting changed after he suffered a mild stroke in 2002.

Other specialists testified regarding the two-page typed letter from the bank safe deposit box. They testified that it was typed on a Royal typewriter of the type that had been used in Devonshire's office at the time he was first appointed to the state supreme court. Unique irregularities in the type proved conclusively that it was typed on the same typewriter as old documents found in the archives in the supreme court building.

"Would it be possible to create a forgery with these characteristics?"

"It would, but you'd need to have the machine from that office."

"One just like it wouldn't do?"

"No. You'd need the exact machine that all of those official documents were typed on."

Up next were the experts who would make or break the case. They were audio specialists who had analyzed the cassettes from the eagle. A lot of the testimony was highly technical, and I wondered how much of it the jury members would understand. Three different experts testified that they were certain that the tapes were authentic.

Voiceprint analysis matched the two voices on the tapes with audio samples of the voices of Blalock and Devonshire taken from news reports between 1978 and 1982. Analysis of the bias noise in the background on the tapes precluded the possibility that the audio tracks had been edited.

The testimony about audio technology continued through the rest of the afternoon. It required intense concentration to keep up with all of the technical details, and it came as a relief when Judge O'Brien called recess at four.

"Thank goodness you got here in time," Martha said. "Jill McDermitt will be here any minute, and she wants to talk with you about Patrick."

I bit my lip and said, "That probably means that he's been interviewed about the gold. I wish I had taken some time to think this thing through."

The sound of a car out front drew my eyes to the window in time to see Jill pull up next to my porch. She hurried up the steps and knocked on my door.

"Come on in, Jill," I called.

"Corrigan, you won't believe what's happening," she began. "Patrick is in some kind of trouble. They're holding him at the sheriff's office."

Playing dumb for the moment, I said, "Please have a seat. Why don't you start at the beginning."

"A detective called me at my office this morning and said he wanted to talk with Patrick."

"What did he want to talk to him about?"

"At first, he didn't say. He just asked if he could meet Patrick for a short interview. I asked if he was in some kind of trouble, and the detective said that they just wanted to ask him about something that he and a friend tried to sell."

"Did you get the detective's name?"

"Wheeler—Michael Wheeler. Anyway, he asked if I knew where Patrick was, and I said he was at home, so the detective asked me if I could meet him there. I hurried home and got there just ahead of the detectives—two of them."

"And was Patrick there?"

"Yes. He was supposed to be mowing the lawn, but...well, you know how that goes. Anyway, the detectives started out by asking if Patrick knew Shane Keasey—which, of course, he does. And then they asked if he and Shane had tried to sell some gold to Oregon City Coin.

"Patrick looked really scared. At first he said no, but then Detective Wheeler described Shane's car and said that there was surveillance video showing Shane and Patrick in the store. Then he admitted that he had been there with Shane. So Wheeler asked him again if they had tried to sell some gold, and he said yes.

"The whole time, I was wondering where Patrick could have gotten any gold to sell, and then I thought that maybe he found some old jewelry in Carlton's house and tried to sell it, but then the other detective asked where they had gotten a *gold bar*! Corrigan, they had a ten-pound gold bar!"

I nodded thoughtfully. "What did Patrick have to say about that?"

"He finally admitted that he and Shane found it in Carlton's basement back in July—not just one gold bar, but *three*! He said that they were looking for fishing gear and found the gold in a tackle box! Corrigan, that means that there really *was* gold in our house, and Carlton found it!"

"We discussed that possibility when you found the old note in the Bible," I reminded her. "And that, no doubt, makes Carlton the prime suspect in Dave Blodgett's murder."

Jill shook her head. "That is just so hard to believe!"

I felt it best not to mention that a car matching Shane's had been seen parked next to the Applegate house the day Dave disappeared. That was for Wheeler to do, and I was sure he'd get to it when the time was right. After all, *that* was what this was all about.

"Did you tell the detective about the note in the Bible?"

"Yes. I gave him a copy of the print you made when you put the original in your safe."

I was relieved that Wheeler hadn't revealed that he already knew about the note. I'd given him a copy of it when I gave him my case file.

"Where is the gold now?" I asked.

"Patrick turned over the two bars that he had. Shane has the other one. I still can't believe that those two had half a million dollars worth of gold!"

"Have you contacted an attorney?"

"Yes, of course. My attorney is with Patrick at the sheriff's office. They sent me home and said they'll call when they need me. I didn't know what to do, so I came here."

"I'm sorry to say so, but I don't think there's anything I can do to help right now," I said. "Please bear in mind that I've been working with the sheriff on this whole thing, from the discovery of Tara Foster's body right up to Carlton's fire."

"Yes, but—"

"I could easily find myself in a conflict of interest if I do anything for you on this."

"Oh," she said. Her disappointment showed. "I was hoping you could help somehow."

"I wish I could, but you see how it is."

After Jill left, Martha asked, "Do you think Patrick and Shane put the lead into Carlton's tackle box? I mean it's hard to believe that they'd think he'd be fooled by a bunch of tire weights."

I could only shake my head. "Kids."

"You figure they killed Carlton?"

"If they found out that he was about to discover that the gold was gone, they might have felt they had to do something. But honestly, I don't see Patrick killing his own father, even for gold. Shane? Well, that might be a different story."

"What a mess."

66

Wednesday, August 22

Andrews picked up where she left off with more technical testimony. When she was confident that she'd closed the door on any possible claim by the defense that the tapes had been falsified or doctored, Andrews finally announced that it was time to listen to the recordings.

Judge O'Brien called an early recess for lunch so that the tapes could be played without interruption in the afternoon. There was a palpable sense of anticipation in the court as Andrews slipped the first microcassette into the recorder, which was connected to the courtroom's audio system.

The recording began with Wilson Devonshire explaining that he was on his way home because Alan Blalock had called to say that something had happened to Jessie. He made it clear that he was making the recording to protect himself, keeping the recorder concealed in his jacket pocket.

Devonshire had stopped the recording after his introductory comments and then switched it back on when he got home. The first thing we heard was his expression of surprise at finding Randy Mendelson's El Camino in his garage. Once inside the house, the recording documented a scene of horror in the entry hall, with Devonshire reacting in shock while Blalock tried to explain that it was all Jessie's fault.

Devonshire's confusion and panic were apparent as he tried to come to grips with the reality that Blalock had murdered Jessie and Randy in his entry hall, but Blalock pleaded with him to help clean up the scene and cover up the murder.

Blalock repeatedly said that they could get away free and clear as long as the bodies weren't found. He gradually wore down Devonshire's resistance, but the clincher was when he promised to get Devonshire a seat on the state supreme court.

Despite his ongoing skepticism, Devonshire helped carry the bodies out to the El Camino in the garage. Then Blalock paged his driver, Richard Elgin, and met him on the driveway, where he instructed Elgin to leave the car at Mark's Tavern at Twelfth and Willamette Falls Drive.

The recording continued while Devonshire and Blalock cleaned the blood from the walls and ceiling and attempted to clean the blood from the carpet. We heard Blalock coach Devonshire in wiping fingerprints from the revolver. This included the removal of the cylinder from the weapon to wipe down the cartridges and shells.

We listened to their increasing desperation as their repeated attempts to clean the stain from the carpet were unsuccessful. Finally, it was Devonshire who came up with the idea of using red paint to hide the stain. He said his wife had wanted him to paint the door, so she wouldn't be suspicious when he claimed he'd accidentally spilled the paint.

The recordings went on and on, capturing the whole event in excruciatingly painful detail. Blalock explained how he was going to drive the car to the boat ramp after midnight. He'd put Randy's body behind the wheel, put the transmission in Drive, and release the parking brake. He said it would probably go out far enough from shore before it sank so that it would end up in deep water where discovery was unlikely.

Even if the El Camino was found, Blalock argued, it would look like Randy had killed Jessie and then, after driving into the river, shot himself while the car sank. Devonshire continued to express doubts and concerns throughout the cleanup and coverup.

As the tapes played, I watched the jurors, and by the time the last tape ended, I was convinced that the case was won.

The prosecution rested.

Next it would be Hardman's turn.

The early recess gave me the opportunity to deal with the growing pile of correspondence and messages on my desk. Instead, I went to the refrigerator, got a beer, and retreated to the beach. I plopped into my Adirondack chair made out of old wooden water skis—a gift from a client who had more time than money.

It felt great to kick back and truly relax after all of the tension and anxiety in the courtroom. The evening boaters were not yet out, and the river was quiet and smooth. DC showed up and hopped up into my lap. I closed my eyes and tuned out the rest of the world.

"Corrigan! Are you there, Corrigan?" I heard someone calling.

I looked up to see Kaylin Beatty on my porch pounding on my front door.

"Down here," I called.

Kaylin turned around, and when she spotted me, she rushed across the railroad tracks and down to the beach.

"This is really stupid," she began, "but the people who bought the Fellows House last month say the house is haunted."

"So how does that involve you?" I asked.

"When they bought it, I was the listing agent, so they think it's all *my* fault. They're sitting in my living room, and they refuse to go back to their house."

"It sounds like you need an exorcist, not an investigator."

"Oh come on, Corrigan, can't you just go in and take a quick look?" Kaylin begged.

"Have *you* gone looking for their ghost?"

"Heck no! I don't want to go in there. I mean, suppose there really is a ghost? Or worse yet, an intruder? At least come over and hear their story."

What are neighbors for? Kaylin led me to her place and introduced me to Tom and Wanda Biggs and their three preteen girls.

"We moved in about a month ago," Wanda explained. "And everything was okay at first. Then about a week ago, strange things started happening."

"What kind of things?" I asked.

"We started hearing noises in the night, like someone shuffling around in the kitchen," Tom said, "but when I went downstairs, there was nobody there—"

"We started finding doors open!" Wanda interrupted. "And then night before last, we were awakened by crashing, and we found pots and pans pulled out of the cupboards and thrown to the floor—that's when I started thinking we might have a poltergeist!"

"There was nobody there," Tom said. "I looked all over."

Wanda looked accusingly at Kaylin and said, "The man who lives up the hill, Leonard Butts, told me that everyone in the neighborhood knows that the Fellows House is haunted. We should have been told!"

I caught myself looking skyward, an involuntary response to the mention of Leonard Butts.

"This is the first I've heard of it," Kaylin said.

"And then last night, at exactly midnight, we started hearing doors opening and closing downstairs," Tom said.

"I think I saw a ghost coming down from the attic!" one of the girls said.

"When I went downstairs, the door to the cellar was standing open," Tom said. "When I switched on the light, the bulb immediately burned out, so I went to find a flashlight. I could hear someone—or some*thing*— moving around down there, but I couldn't find a light.

I finally used my cell phone for light and went down the cellar steps. Everything went quiet, and I felt, like, a cold breeze sweep over me, and then I saw the eyes! Three or four pairs of glowing eyes, hovering in midair. So I got the hell out of there."

Wanda continued the story. "We packed the kids into the car and went straight to my mother's place. I'm not sure I can ever go back in there!"

Everyone looked expectantly at me.

"I'm sure there's a completely reasonable explanation for all of this," I said, wondering how many times I'd heard that line in movies.

"Will you at least go in and see if somebody is in there?" Kaylin asked.

I could see no way out of it, so I said, "Let me go get a good flashlight, and I'll look in the cellar."

The Fellows House is a magnificently preserved 1868 gothic revival facing Highway 99. It's a classic two-story wood structure with ornate gingerbread trim and a gothic arched doorway opening onto a widow's walk above the front porch. Many people consider it to be the centerpiece of the Canemah National Historic District. I'd never heard any stories about it being haunted.

I got a powerful four-cell Maglite out of my garage and then, as an afterthought, stuffed my Colt automatic into my waistband on the chance that there really were intruders—not of the spiritual kind, but perhaps of the breaking-and-entering kind. I ventured across the highway, with Kaylin and the Biggs family following behind. We went around to the side entrance.

"It's not locked," Tom told me. "We were in too much of a rush. All we wanted to do was get out! I'll tell you, something's not right in there."

I turned the doorknob and slowly pushed on the door. The old hinges let out a screech worthy of any Bela Lugosi horror movie, causing everyone else to cringe and back down the porch steps, leaving me alone to face whatever terrors lurked in the dark interior.

"It's a squeaky hinge for god's sake," I said.

"Can you see anything?" Wanda asked.

"Looks like your ghost has been playing with the pots and pans again," I observed.

"Oh my god," Tom mumbled.

"There's white powder all over the place."

"What could it be? Anthrax?" Wanda asked,

"Yes, it could be anthrax. But it's probably just ectoplasm—sometimes ghosts leave it behind."

"You don't have to be sarcastic," Tom complained.

"I don't see anyone around," I said, moving toward the cellar door, which stood open, revealing a steep, narrow set of stairs disappearing into darkness.

I tried the light switch, not expecting it to work, and it didn't. So I switched my Maglite on and shot a bright beam of light into the cellar. Immediately, I heard noises, a hurried shuffling somewhere out of sight on the other side of the cellar. On the theory that a weapon wouldn't be much good tucked in my pants, I drew my Colt and thumbed the hammer.

Ducking under the low beams of the ceiling and holding the light out away from my body, I ventured off to my left, where I could see a clear pathway through stacks of boxes. A row of storm windows leaning against the far wall startled me with my own reflection, repeated a dozen times—or however many storm windows there were. It was only my calm demeanor that kept me from drilling a .45 caliber hole through the offending windows.

Then I heard the scurrying noises again, this time higher up. I swung the flashlight to my right, just in time to catch a glimpse of a fluffy ringed tail disappearing out a cellar window. Right behind it, two more raccoons clamored up the shelving, pulled themselves up to the window sill, and bolted outside. I gently lowered the hammer and put away my Colt, feeling foolish for having brought it along in the first place. I closed and latched the window.

"I heard something!" Tom exclaimed as I came back upstairs.

"Did you see the ghost?" one of the girls asked.

"What happened down there?" Wanda asked.

"I found your ghosts," I said. "There were at least three of them, but they're gone now. And I think they'll leave you alone as long as you keep your cellar windows closed."

"Ghosts can go right through walls. It doesn't matter if the window is open or shut," another of the girls said.

"I'll bet they're vampires," the youngest girl said.

"No, they're not vampires—or ghosts," I told her. "They're just big furry raccoons looking for a place to live."

"Raccoons?" Tom and Wanda asked in unison.

"Yep. I think our local raccoon population is in a state of rebellion against humanity. You're lucky. You should've seen the mess they made over at Rosie's place last year."

"Who's Rosie?" Wanda asked.

"She's the lady who lives in the little trailer over by the railroad tracks," Kaylin explained.

"I think it's safe for you to go inside," I said.

"Are you sure all of the raccoons went out?" Tom asked. "I've heard they can be dangerous if you get them in a corner."

"I'm pretty sure they're all gone."

"Raccoons are cute," one of the girls said. "I wish we could keep one for a pet."

"Yeah," the other two girls said.

Wanda said, "Maybe we could look at getting a puppy."

The girls danced up and down and said, "Yay!"

On my walk back home, I couldn't help smiling. Canemah was still Canemah.

67

Thursday, August 23

Jason Hardman opened the day with a perfunctory motion for dismissal based on his assertion that the prosecution had failed to present sufficient evidence. Even though he knew perfectly well that the motion would be denied, Hardman put on a show of indignant surprise when the judge said so.

"The defense calls Clackamas County Sheriff William Kerby," Hardman intoned.

His first question of substance was, "When did you first become aware of the existence of the prosecution's bronze eagle and its contents?"

"Deputy Kim Stayton left a voice mail on my phone alluding to new evidence in the Mendelson-Devonshire investigation. She indicated that she was on her way to turn it over to Deputy Jamieson."

"When did you get this message?"

"I didn't get it until two or three hours later," Kerby said.

"Why such a long delay?"

"It was because Deputy Stayton didn't use my emergency number. If she had done that, I'd have gotten the message immediately."

"What was the result of the delay?"

"Nothing was done to document the chain of custody prior to the time Stayton delivered the evidence to Deputy Jamieson. He immediately turned it over to the forensic staff for analysis."

"Are you telling us that there is no documentation of the origins of this so-called evidence?"

"That is correct."

"But doesn't that automatically compromise the validity of the evidence?"

"I would say so, given that there was nothing there that couldn't have been fabricated by skilled technicians."

"The prosecution presented a video recording that purportedly showed the opening of the eagle and removal of its contents by private investigator March Corrigan. Doesn't that video prove the authenticity of the evidence?"

Kerby laughed contemptuously. "It's pure drama, and it proves nothing. We have no way of knowing what took place prior to the start of the video. We have only Mr. Corrigan's word as to where the eagle and its contents came from."

"What did you do after you saw the video and reviewed the evidence?"

"I put a hold on the forensics pending better documentation of the source of the evidence."

"What happened after that?"

"Corrigan illegally shared the contents with a number of people outside the sheriff's office, including newspaper reporters and policemen who were neither part of the investigation nor authorized to see the evidence."

"What was the result of these illegal breaches of protocol?"

"The indiscriminate release of confidential material always compromises our ability to do a proper investigation, and the publication of details about the evidence makes it impossible to screen suspects."

"What was the status of the Mendelson-Devonshire investigation at the time this alleged evidence was brought in?"

"It was essentially closed. We had identified a suspect, and we had conclusive evidence against him."

"Was that suspect arrested?"

"No. He took his own life before an arrest warrant could be issued."

"I see," Hardman said slowly. "So this new material 'discovered' by Corrigan pointed toward a different conclusion than all of the evidence accumulated over the thirty-two-year investigation?"

"That's right. It was right out of the blue."

"Sheriff Kerby, what is your theory of the crime—the murders of Jessie Devonshire and Randy Mendelson?"

"All of the evidence, except what Corrigan supposedly found in the eagle, pointed squarely at Jessie's stepfather. I have seen no verifiable evidence to lead me to believe otherwise."

"Thank you. I have no more questions."

Denise Andrews strode quickly to the front of the courtroom and looked at Kerby.

"What is your current duty status with the sheriff's office?"

"Objection!"

Judge O'Brien had the jury escorted from the room before allowing the argument between Hardman and Andrews to proceed. Hardman insisted that it was irrelevant and prejudicial, while Andrews maintained that the credibility of the witness was very relevant. The debate was heated. Ultimately, the judge overruled the objection.

With the jury back in the courtroom, Andrews repeated her question.

"I am currently on administrative leave," Kerby admitted.

"And why is that?"

Kerby looked to Hardman for help, but the topic had already been debated, and an objection by the defense would serve only to alienate the judge, so Hardman stayed seated. Andrews stared him down.

"I am on leave pending resolution of an investigation," Kerby said.

Judge O'Brien had already ruled that the exact nature of the investigation could not be discussed since it involved criminal charges that had not been adjudicated. Andrews could take the questioning no further.

Still, she refused to address him as "Sheriff Kerby."

"You told the court, sir, that you had 'conclusive evidence' that Wilson Devonshire committed the murders of Jessie Devonshire and Randy Mendelson. Will you please tell us what that evidence was?"

"There was a lot of evidence. I can't begin to list it all here."

"Give us the high points," Andrews coaxed.

"Well, first off, the murders took place in his house," Kerby said cautiously.

"How do you know that?"

"We know it because of the DNA evidence from the flooring in the entry hall."

"What else?"

"Well, there was the fact that Devonshire lied about the bloodstain and said it was paint."

"And?"

"He made statements at the time of the crime that contradicted the evidence that was recovered from the car."

"How do you know all of these things?"

"They were in the case file."

"But the original case file is missing. How do you know what was in it?"

"We know from the copy you entered into evidence," Kerby said nervously.

"Where did you get that copy of the case file?"

"It was found in a storage unit belonging to one of the detectives involved in the original investigation."

"Found by whom?"

"Corrigan."

"Who?"

"That private investigator. March Corrigan."

"Isn't that the same person who found the evidence in the eagle?"

Kerby looked like he was about to blow an artery. He grudgingly nodded.

"Yes or no," Andrews coached.

"Yes."

"No further questions."

"The defense calls Kevin Fox," Hardman said after Kerby had left the stand.

"Detective Fox, did you investigate the death of Wilson Devonshire?"

"Yes."

"Did you make an arrest in that case?"

"Yes. We arrested Richard Elgin."

"Did you have evidence that Richard Elgin was involved in the Mendelson-Devonshire murders?"

"Yes, he—"

"Did you have evidence that Richard Elgin was at the Devonshire house on the day of the crime?"

"Yes, he was—"

"Was it your belief that Richard Elgin killed Wilson Devonshire out of fear that he would testify as to what really happened to Jessie and Randy?"

Fox looked annoyed but answered, "Yes."

"It appears that there was no shortage of suspects in this case," Hardman said. "No more questions."

It was clear to me that Hardman's strategy was to create the impression that there were several suspects, any one of whom may have committed the murders—a common strategy for creating reasonable doubt. For the rest of the day and all of the next, the defense introduced witness after witness to bolster the possible guilt of Devonshire, Elgin, and even Randy Mendelson.

The DA stood and asked, "Detective Fox, you said that you had evidence of Richard Elgin's involvement in the Mendelson-Devonshire murders."

"That's right."

"Was he a suspect in that case?

"Not to my knowledge."

My impression of the whole exercise was that instead of creating doubt, it only created confusion and made the defense look desperate.

"Hey, Corrigan, how well do you know this Keasey kid?" Michael Wheeler asked.

"Never met him," I said.

I was returning a call from Wheeler after court recessed late Friday afternoon.

"He's a squirrelly kid. A stoner. And a lousy liar."

"Has he admitted anything?"

"Only the same thing the McDermitt kid says—that they found the gold bars while they were looking for fishing lures. But that probably just means they got together on the story."

"Were they tipped off? Did they know you were looking at them?"

"We tried to avoid that, but you know how it goes. We talked to people who knew 'em. There's a good chance that someone mentioned it. I don't think it matters really. We found an Old Navy sweatshirt in the Keasey kid's bedroom. And get this—there are fresh burns on it."

"How's he explain that?"

"Some nonsense about losing the ash off a cigarette."

"What about the witness—Barcelli, can he identify him?"

"Doesn't look that way. The subject who ran across the highway was wearing a hoodie, and he couldn't see his face."

"So what are you looking for from me?"

"I was hoping that maybe you or someone else in the neighborhood might know something about the relationship between the McDermitt kid and the Keasey kid."

"About all I know is what a girl from their class in school told me—that Keasy was the only friend McDermitt had."

"Well, we've had some uniforms down in Canemah canvassing the neighborhood. The fire that killed McDermitt's old man started in broad daylight. Someone had to have seen Keasey in the neighborhood."

"No luck yet?"

"There's an interesting connection with the old man."

"Carlton?"

"Right. You know what pocket bikes are?"

"Sure, those miniature motorcycles. Patrick had one."

"Yeah, well so did Keasey. And Carlton McDermitt gave it to him."

That was a surprise. It always seemed to me that Carlton was pretty tight with his money.

"Why would he do that?" I asked.

"That's what we'd like to know. But the point is, maybe they had some kind of deal going on."

"The kind of deal that might involve putting Dave Blodgett in the bottom of a well?"

"That's what we'd like to know."

68

Friday, August 31

The Blalock defense was built around two underlying themes: that the forensics were technically flawed through improper handling of the evidence and that the evidence itself could have been fabricated. By hammering away on insignificant details, Hardman intended to cultivate a reasonable doubt about the prosecution's case.

Early in the week, Hardman brought "political experts" to make the case that Alan Blalock was the target of dirty tricks by right-wing operatives.

"Really, this kind of thing is a legacy of the Watergate era," insisted Albert Malin.

Malin is a political science professor from Portland State University who makes frequent appearances as a political expert on Portland television and radio stations. While he is always characterized as a neutral, objective commentator, his personal sympathies always show through in subtle ways, with a smile or a frown or a raised eyebrow, and his commentary always favors the left.

"Political operatives of today learned from the heavy-handed tactics used by Nixon's White House Plumbers. Instead of sending burglars in to bug the opposition's offices, they now rely more on planted rumors and character assaults," Malin lectured.

Hardman asked, "Can you give us some examples?"

"Well, on the national level, there's the persistent rumor that President Obama was born outside the United States—even after his Hawaiian birth certificate has been made public. On the local level, there is an ongoing effort to convince people that there is some kind of a conspiracy between Governor Kitzhaber, his fiancé, and renewable energy producers.[5] And some people always believe that stuff, even though there's no supporting proof. And of course, they've been after Senator Blalock for many years."

"In what way?"

"Oh, like the rumors about Senator Blalock's alleged affairs. There's nothing new about that. Stories have been planted over and over, and even though they are always shown to be false, the unsupported accusations persist."

"Wouldn't it take a lot of money to conduct an effective propaganda campaign?"

"Certainly. But people like the Koch brothers and Loren Parks always jump in to finance right-wing causes and interfere with Oregon politics. They—or people like them—are motivated and capable of financing the kind of operation that could fabricate evidence of the kind we see here."

"Objection. That is pure speculation."

"Your Honor, we intend to present evidence to support that conclusion."

"The objection is sustained. Counsel, your evidence needs to precede your conclusions. The jury will disregard that last statement by the witness, and it will be stricken from the record."

Hardman brushed it off and proceeded to bring in three witnesses who claimed to have firsthand knowledge of conspiracies to undermine Alan Blalock's reputation. All three claimed to have once been insiders engaged in plots to implicate Blalock in fabricated scandals.

When asked by Denise Andrews on cross-examination to name their co-conspirators, they all testified that they didn't know the identities because code names had been used. Andrews then asked if any of them could produce any documentation to support their claims. None could.

One of the witnesses reluctantly confessed that she had been only fifteen years old at the time she claimed to have been involved in the conspiracy to slander Blalock. The other two witnesses admitted that they were registered Democrats at the time they claimed to have been operatives in right-wing groups.

---

5.   Despite substantial evidence supporting the charges against John Kitzhaber and his fiancé Cylvia Hayes, the Portland news media unanimously endorsed the 2014 reelection of the governor. It was only after he had won reelection that the media acknowledged that the allegations were true. On February 13, 2015, Governor John Kitzhaber resigned in disgrace.

On Wednesday, Hardman launched his technical assault on the prosecution evidence, starting with a former Xerox engineer who testified that it was his opinion that the copies that made up Gary Turner's files could have been made on a more recent copier using old toner and paper to make them look older than they were.

The substance of his testimony was that there are still many copiers in use that predate the introduction of laser technology, and any of these machines could be used with the coarse toner intended for earlier equipment to produce old-looking copies.

To prove the point, Hardman called another witness, who brought in copies that had been made that way from replicas of selected sheets from the Turner files.

The witness explained, "We used a typewriter like the ones in the sheriff's office back in 1980. Our typist made replicas of six different documents from the prosecution evidence. We made copies of these using toner and paper from old stock found in the storeroom of a defunct business office in Hillsboro."

"Did you have any difficulty locating the old materials?"

"No, we made a few calls. That's all it took."

"And these are the copies you made?" asked Hardman.

The witness studied the papers and pointed to his initials on the back side. "Yes. Those are the copies we made."

"How long did it take you to produce these fakes, start to finish?"

"Including the time it took to find the right typewriter, copier, and material, it took about sixty man-hours. But only about five hours were spent actually creating the documents once we had everything we needed."

"Did the process require any special skills or training?"

"No, it was pretty straightforward. Anyone could do it."

The next witness was a forensic document examiner. He testified that Hardman's copies were indistinguishable from the corresponding documents from the Turner files.

"If these fake documents had been planted in the box with all of the other files, would you have been able to spot them as counterfeit?"

"No. They are indistinguishable."

On cross-examination, however, he admitted that he had not conducted the kind of microscopic comparisons that would be needed to identify the machine that had made the copies.

"Without doing the microscopic examination, can you really call these indistinguishable from the authentic documents?"

"Well, that is a higher level of examination."

"Surely, you are aware that all of the relevant documents in Gary Turner's files were subjected to microscopic examination," Andrews challenged.

"That's not something we get into."

Hardman next brought in a series of biochemists who gave highly technical testimony about the nature of DNA, focusing on the inherent challenges to producing DNA profiles. They spoke in scientific language, using terminology that would be meaningless to most people. But Hardman did not ask them to speak in terms a layman could understand.

It was my impression that his objective was to baffle the jurors. The whole effect would be to render the DNA evidence irrelevant. If the jurors believed they lacked the knowledge to evaluate the evidence, the evidence was meaningless.

One by one, Hardman's technical "experts" attempted to demonstrate that each and every piece of evidence could have been fabricated by Albert Malin's imagined conspirators working with the unlimited resources of the Koch brothers. Late on Thursday, he got to the bronze eagle that had once been Jessie Devonshire's coin bank, a gift from United Savings Bank for opening her first savings account when she was six years old.

A forensic pathologist testified that it was impossible to connect the injury to Jessie's skull with the eagle. He went so far as to speculate that the skull fracture could have happened while the El Camino was sinking, though I couldn't see how that would in any way vindicate Alan Blalock. But the objective was to cloud the issue by interjecting a bunch of irrelevant distractions, and Hardman did it with a flair for drama, treating it each new revelation as a Perry Mason moment.

Another pathologist testified regarding the traces of blood found on the eagle. Her position was that Jessie's DNA on the eagle was irrelevant because surely she had cut her finger sometime during the seven or eight years she had the eagle. The witness went on to recount all of the possible ways Jessie's blood could have innocently been deposited on the eagle. I couldn't guess what effect this was having on the jury, but I could see Judge O'Brien showing signs of impatience.

Hardman's document experts returned to the stand to testify to the many ways Blalock's enemies could have gotten his credit card numbers to counterfeit the receipts for Jessie's birth control pills and the lingerie from the Meier and Frank department store.

A handwriting analyst debunked Wilson Devonshire's handwritten note from the eagle, saying that it couldn't be matched to any known samples of Devonshire's handwriting. This testimony directly contradicted the testimony of the two prosecution handwriting analysts.

The trial was becoming something like water torture. It was a grand relief when O'Brien granted a defense request for an early recess so that testimony from his next witness could be presented without interruption when court reconvened on Tuesday.

69

Tuesday, September 4

The centerpiece of the Blalock defense was the attack on the audio recordings found in the bronze eagle. In order for there to be any possible doubt about his guilt, the recordings had to be put into question. Hardman brought in experts in voice transformation technologies to demonstrate that voiceprint analysis is not a foolproof science.

It brought to mind the 2004 debate over the authenticity of recordings made by Osama Bin Laden after many believed he had been killed in the bombing of his hideout at Tora Bora. In the end, the authenticity of the recordings became a moot issue after Bin Laden was proven to have survived Tora Bora and was subsequently killed by SEAL Team Six.

But the debate over the Bin Laden recordings left lingering questions about the efficacy of voice identification technologies, and this is what opened the door for Hardman. His first witness was Elbert Halsey, PhD, from the Oregon Graduate Institute's School of Science and Engineering in Hillsboro.

"Dr. Halsey, will you please tell us what you do at OGI?" Hardman asked.

"I am a mathematical psychologist. I study various algorithms that enable computers to modify the vocal characteristics of spoken language."

"Why is that important?"

"Voice analysis by computers is used extensively in biometric security systems. The degree to which voice characteristics can be altered has a direct impact on the security that voiceprint analysis provides. Also, the use of voice analysis in legal proceedings like this depends entirely upon the ability of analysts to identify whether a recording is authentic or is the product of voice transformation technologies."

"Doctor, can you give us a general overview of the current capabilities of voice transformation technologies?"

"The technology is improving daily, and more and more people have access to it. It has become very difficult to determine with any degree of certainty whether a voice recording is a fake. The only way to determine the authenticity of a voice recording is to look for very subtle cues that may be left behind. There are several transformation techniques available, and they can be very difficult to detect."

"Are you involved in the creation of new voice transformation technologies?"

"I am not personally involved, but one of my research associates specializes in that, and he has developed a whole new method for voice transformation."

Hardman brought out an elaborate display with representations of various waveforms and voiceprints, which Dr. Halsey used to illustrate his explanation of voice transformation. The testimony became increasingly technical, and I again had the impression that Hardman's goal wasn't to inform the jurors but rather to confound them.

Late in the afternoon, Hardman finally said, "I have no more questions for this witness."

On cross-examination, the DA asked only one question.

"Dr. Halsey, have you analyzed the Devonshire-Blalock recordings?"

"No. We do not get involved in forensic analysis."

On Wednesday, Hardman's first witness was the research associate mentioned by Dr. Halsey. He was introduced as Gregory Kamela, PhD, from the OGI School's Center for Spoken Language Understanding.

I had to wonder what these experts' business cards looked like. The length of their titles would require an accordion-fold card about a foot long.

"Dr. Kamela, can you tell us please about your newly developed voice transformation methods?"

"Well, our goal is to effectively mimic someone else's voice. To accomplish that, we have created a voice synthesizer that is capable of replicating the fine acoustic details that make up the unique characteristics of a person's vocal cords and oral cavity."

"Can you give us a layman's overview of the process?"

"In order to replicate a person's voice, we first need *exemplars*— original recordings of the individual you want to mimic. The more exemplars you can acquire, the better your result will be. The next step is to make a recording of someone with a similar voice and accent reading the exact same text as the exemplars.

"Ideally, you would use an actor who can effectively imitate the original speaker's accent, rhythm, and dialect. Our system then analyzes both the original recordings and the fake ones and learns how to compensate for inherent differences between them. In this way, it can 'learn' how to transform the actor's speech so that it produces a voiceprint identical to that of the original subject.

"After our system has been set up this way, the actor simply speaks a new text, again using the original speaker's rhythm and melody, and the system produces a new recording that has all of the original speaker's voice characteristics.

I should point out that we are not the only ones working on this. There are other scientists who have developed their own voice transformation technologies."

"But doesn't that render voiceprint technology obsolete?"

"Voiceprint technology needs to evolve in response to new technologies in voice transformation. We know the weaknesses in our system, so we can detect when it is used. But each method of voice transformation leaves its own cues. As the number of transformation technologies increases, it may become impossible to detect a forgery."

As he had done with Dr. Halsey, Hardman led his witness into increasingly technical and arcane detail. While his purpose was no doubt to make the jurors tune out, I wondered if the actual result didn't work in favor of the prosecution. By making the voice transformation process seem highly refined and technical, he may have ended up demonstrating the extreme difficulty of the process.

Denise Andrews may have picked up the same impression, because in her cross-examination, she went straight to the practical application of the technology.

"Dr. Kamela, have you listened to the Devonshire-Blalock recordings?"

"I've listened to them, but I haven't made any kind of technical analysis," Kamela said, sounding a bit defensive.

"That's all right. I didn't expect a technical analysis. What would you say about the overall quality of the recordings?"

"They are fairly good. The voices are sometimes muted, but there isn't much background noise, and the audio level is generally good. There are some places where some clipping can be heard when one person or the other speaks very loudly, but overall, I would say they are decent recordings for analysis."

"Now, Doctor, would you be able to replicate these recordings using your new technology?"

"In theory, yes," Kamela hedged.

"What do you mean by that?"

"Well, there's a lot here. It's over ninety minutes of recording, and there are some special challenges involved."

"What challenges?"

"The voices on the recordings have a lot of emotion. It would take a very good actor to convincingly replicate that—two actors, actually, since there are two voices on the recordings."

"I see. Now as I understand your process, you need exemplars of the original voices in order to train your system how to replicate them."

"Correct."

"How does your system learn how to replicate the kind of stress and emotion that can be heard on the Devonshire-Blalock recordings?"

"That could be very difficult. Ideally, your exemplars would contain the words you intend to replicate spoken under similar conditions of emotion and stress. In this case, you probably wouldn't be able to find exemplars like that. The next best thing would be to find exemplars with similar emotion and stress levels but different words. The software would then have to learn how the subject's voice patterns change under stressful or emotional conditions. It would then interpolate how other words would sound under those conditions."

"Would all that be difficult to do?"

"Very much so."

"Could you do it?"

Kamela pondered that. "I'm not sure I can answer that question. I mean, it's theoretically possible, but it would be very challenging."

"Assuming for the moment that you wanted to make these recordings, how much time would it take to do it?"

"At least a year—maybe two or three. It would be an extremely challenging project."

"Is there any way it could be done in three months?"

"I believe that would be impossible."

I could see where Andrews was going. If the recordings were some kind of elaborate fake, they had to have been done after the recovery of the El Camino in order to make what was said compatible with what was found in the car. If they couldn't be faked in that time frame, then they couldn't be fakes.

70

Thursday, September 6

In the interest of keeping my blood pressure under control, I stayed away from the courthouse during the closing arguments. I was satisfied that the prosecution had presented a solid case, and barring some kind of jury tampering, which wasn't outside the realm of possibility, a guilty verdict seemed inescapable.

It was a cloudy day and surprisingly cool for early September. On days like this, there was really no reason for Kim to go out on the river since there would be very few boaters out. She was never thrilled about spending time in the office, but it was an opportunity to catch up on paperwork.

After she drove away, I went to work wading through my long backlog of email and phone messages. Most of them were people voicing their support, but there were also some from Blalock supporters, whose verbal attacks revealed a cult-like devotion to their leader, irrespective of anything he might have done.

Early in the afternoon, my printer returned a "Paper Out" message, and I discovered that there was no paper in the cabinet. I needed a break anyway, so I drove up the hill to pick up a few reams of paper and some groceries. On the way back home, I took the shortcut down through upper Canemah.

The tall trees shaded the narrow street, where split-entry houses from the 1970s are incongruously mixed in with small cottages and farmhouses from the nineteenth century. As I wound my way down the hill, I encountered Leonard Butts in a gray hooded sweatshirt walking his two Springer Spaniels. I had already gone past him when it registered that in large, open-face letters across the front of his sweatshirt were two words: *Old Navy*.

There must be millions of Old Navy hooded sweatshirts in the world. And yet my investigator's mind forced me to consider whether this could be the same one Guido Barcelli had seen on the night of the fire. It was just a passing thought because there was no earthly reason for Butts to kill Carlton McDermitt.

And yet there was something else—an obscure memory or a bit of related information. I couldn't quite get it to snap into focus. It was just an instantaneous flash in my memory banks of something related to the sweatshirt—or to Leonard.

When I got back to my place, I shook it off. Without question, Butts was an abrasive, opinionated, arrogant ass, but coincidences notwithstanding, he simply couldn't replace Shane Keasey as the only viable suspect in the McDermitt murder. For someone of my analytical mindset, there is a perpetual risk of over thinking things.

Martha handed me a note when I dropped the packages of printer paper onto her desk. "Call Leo Gilchrist."

I hadn't talked with Gilchrist since the IRS had made their lame offer for an out-of-court settlement on my lawsuit a month before.

When I got him on the phone, he opened with, "Are you ready for this? There's a US senator who thinks he can help with your lawsuit."

"At this point, I'm ready for *anything*," I said. "Who's the senator and why does he think he can help my lawsuit?"

"It's Leland Parkdale—a Nevada Republican. He's the one who's been trying to get a full-scale senate investigation of the IRS for targeting the Tea Party organizations in the run-up to last year's elections. You've probably heard about their fight over Lois Lerner's emails, which she claims were all lost in a computer crash."

"How does that help us?"

"Well, since the Tea Party investigation is stalled, his people are starting to look at the Washington insiders who are suspected of using the IRS to punish people they don't like."

"Blalock," I said.

"He's one. There are others. It's nothing new. But Parkdale is determined to air it out."

"What's his plan?"

"The entire focus of our effort to date has been *what* the IRS did. Senator Parkdale wants to focus on *why* they did it. He believes that your lawsuit will give him grounds to subpoena all of the IRS correspondence relating to your case. With that, he hopes to follow a paper trail back to where the order was issued."

"Won't that just piss off the IRS?"

"Listen, Corrigan, they're just people, not supervillains. When it comes down to it, it's their jobs they're most concerned about. They'll roll on Blalock as soon as they understand that there's no future in going down with the ship."

"I'd buy that if it was just Blalock, but we both know he's just a part of the inside-the-beltway establishment."

"No doubt about it, but his unique vulnerability at this point gives Parkdale a rare opportunity. If he finds proof that Blalock dumped the IRS on you, he'll uncover other cases too. Your case is hardly unique."

"Yeah, but won't all that just delay my case?"

"That's a possibility. But I think the threat of an expanded investigation might give the IRS some serious incentive to settle quickly and quietly."

"I'm all for getting it over with, but I've really been looking forward to public executions in the town square," I said.

"What should I tell the senator?" Gilchrist asked.

"Tell him I'm willing to talk about it."

As I hung up the phone, Martha scowled at me.

"So that's how things get done in politics," she commented.

"If you want some real insight into how modern politics works, study Lyndon Johnson. During his time in the senate, he pioneered hardball politics. A lot of people admired him for the way he was able to get things done, and his tactics have ruled Washington ever since."

"I'd have never figured you for an LBJ fan," Martha said.

"Believe me, I'm no fan. I despise everything about him. If you want to really learn about LBJ, try Googling 'Billy Sol Estes' sometime."

As the afternoon went by, the cloud cover moved north, and the sun came out. I loaded some things into an ice chest and went down to the beach. I was half asleep when I heard tires crunching on gravel and looked up to see Kim's Explorer. I waved, and she came down the steps to the beach.

"I was just thinking about lighting some charcoal and burning some chicken," I said.

"Do you have anything to go with it?" Kim asked. "Your refrigerator looked pretty bare this morning."

"I went shopping," I proclaimed. "We have fresh vegetables, plus all the ingredients for a great potato salad."

With a pained expression, Kim said, "Oh, I really don't feel like working in the kitchen."

"I'll tell you what—and I wouldn't do this for just anybody—I'll take care of slicing the vegetables and making the potato salad if you bring down the dishes and silverware."

I used to have a whole set of tableware just for use on the beach, but it went away with my storage shed during the flood. Now we had to borrow from the kitchen.

She eyed me suspiciously. "There has to be a catch."

"Nope. No strings attached. On the other hand, if you become overwhelmed by gratitude, we might work something out later."

"You're up to something. I can always tell."

"Nope. It's a straight-up deal."

She patted the holstered Sig Sauer on her belt.

"Just bear in mind that I'm armed," she said.

Half an hour later, she came down the steps from the house, freshly showered and wearing—well, she looked really good. She put the cardboard box containing the tableware on a chair next to the round glass-top table.

"Cooking the chicken already?" she asked, giving me an accusing look.

From the ice chest next to my chair, I withdrew a plastic tray containing a selection of precut vegetables and a tub of potato salad from the Fred Meyer deli.

"As promised, I took care of it." I grinned.

"I knew it! I knew it! I knew it!"

"I have wine, too," I said, holding up a bottle of Kendall-Jackson Chardonnay.

"Corrigan, you are beyond redemption. But I'll take a glass of that wine anyhow."

We didn't talk about the trial. We'd already said all there was to say about it, and nothing we could do would change the outcome. With dinner finished and the sun going down, we sat in front of the fire pit enjoying the ambience of the propane-fueled fire.

"The grapevine has some interesting new information about the gold from the well," Kim said. "It seems that the 'US Government' stamp might carry no weight in a legal sense."

"Are you saying that the gold may not belong to the government?"

"That very well may be the case. It seems that there are many gold bars with identical markings in private hands—relics from the days before serial numbers were stamped into the bars. Apparently, people buy and sell them routinely."

"Does that mean the government won't try to claim them?"

"Who knows? The thing is, with a large number of these things in private hands, how could the government prove that these particular ones belong to them?"

"Then whose are they?"

"That probably will have to be settled in court, but one possible conclusion is that they were part of the property—part of the Applegate House. Any ownership prior to that has gone far beyond any statute of limitations."

"Wait, are you saying the gold might belong to Barry?"

"Possibly. He was the owner of the property when the gold was stolen. If the court says that the gold was part of the house when he bought it, then it's his. But there's another possibility. The court might rule the gold personal property, not part of the house," Kim explained.

"Then what?"

"In that case, Omar LaRue's letter is the oldest provenance for the gold. In the letter, he says only that he 'found' the gold at Dug Bar. Lacking any proof of where it came from before LaRue found it, a court just might rule 'finders keepers,' meaning that the gold was his. The letter conveys the gold to Rebecca Applegate, making guess-who the natural heirs."

"Colleen and Patrick McDermitt," I said.

"Wouldn't that be ironic? If it was personal property and not part of the real estate, then Carlton may have been entitled to it all along—in which case, he killed Tara Foster and Dave Blodgett for nothing."

"Not to mention getting himself killed," I added. "Any news on the investigation into Patrick and his buddy?"

"They executed search warrants at both houses. They didn't find anything at Jill's place, but at Keasey's place, they picked up pair of Air

Jordan shoes that have what look like spots of blood. They'll be testing them in the next day or two."

"I don't suppose they found a .32 caliber pistol."

"No such luck. But they did find a baseball bat. They'll be testing it for any sign that it was used to whack Carlton."

71

Friday, September 7

I was aboard *Annabel Lee* for the first time since the trial began, looking at where I might resume work on the project if I ever got my money back from the IRS. I was feeling pretty pessimistic, and it seemed that the whole project had turned sour. My enthusiasm for sailing the world seemed like an empty pipedream.

Still, I couldn't be aboard without feeling the compulsion to do something, so I started cleaning up some of the residual mess left after all of the plumbing, electrical, and mechanical work done in the past four years. As I swept sawdust and construction debris into piles in the middle of each compartment, my outlook slowly improved.

In the engine room, while doing some routine maintenance checks on the propulsion and generator systems, I switched on the radio. The three o'clock newscast was dominated by news of the Blalock trial. The closing arguments were finished, and the judge had issued a lengthy set of instructions to the jury. The case officially was in the hands of the jury.

My phone rang. Dreading the inevitable calls from reporters, I looked at the ID screen before answering. The call was from Martha.

"It's gone to the jury," she told me.

"Yeah. I have the radio on. Now we just have to wait."

"Is there any doubt how it will come out?"

"Who knows? Everyone thought that OJ was a sure thing too."

I didn't like hearing myself sound so whiny, so I quickly added, "But Blalock isn't OJ."

Finishing my cleanup job took the rest of the afternoon. I bagged up all of the trash and carried it up to my Yukon. Before leaving, I walked through each compartment looking for anything I might have left behind.

Once clean, the project actually looked like it was worth finishing, and that made me smile.

Listening to the Eagles on CD, I drove over to the transfer station and waited in line to dump my trash into the big pit, where it would be compacted and shipped to eastern Oregon for burial. Some future archaeologist would no doubt ponder the spiritual significance of my bits of conduit and copper wire. Back home, I vacuumed and washed my Yukon before putting it in the garage. Staying busy kept me from thinking about the trial.

It was six thirty when I sat down and turned on television to catch the last segment of the evening news. But instead of the usual studio news set, I was greeted with a live broadcast from the courthouse.

A reporter said, "Many observers expected your deliberations to go on for several days. How did you reach your verdict so quickly?"

"It was not a difficult decision to make," said the man I recognized as the jury foreman. "The first thing we did was conduct a straw poll, and as it turned out, we all agreed. Then before doing the official vote, we went down the lists of witnesses and evidence just to make sure that we weren't overlooking anything."

"You had nearly three weeks of testimony to review. How did you do that in less than three hours?" the reporter asked.

"It all hinged on the credibility of the evidence, and it all pointed one direction."

The reporter looked at the camera and said gravely, "What might seem to some as a rush to judgment appears to have been a slam-dunk for this jury. Laurel?"

The screen switched to the studio set, where news anchor Laurel Porter's grave expression reflected the importance of the event.

"A stunning verdict in the trial of Senator Alan Blalock: guilty of second-degree murder in the death of Jessie Devonshire and first-degree murder in the death of Randall Mendelson."

I realized that I'd been holding my breath since turning on the news. Finally I could breathe. My greatest worry had been that Blalock's people might have found a way to coerce one or two jurors into voting not guilty, and I had put considerable effort into mentally preparing myself to deal with an acquittal.

A Channel 6 news van pulled up in front of my house, and a reporter rushed to my door while his cameraman unloaded his equipment.

"Mr. Corrigan, could we have your reaction to the verdict?" he asked.

"It's too bad that it took three decades to find some justice for the Devonshire and Mendelson families. This case could have been solved in 1980 and would have been, except for the overbearing influence of the Blalock political machine, which prevented an honest investigation from taking place."

The interview lasted for about fifteen more minutes, but the only part that made the eleven o'clock news was my answer to the first question. Reporters from the other stations arrived while I was still talking with Channel 6, and the result was a kind of press conference on my front porch. I repeated my answer about a dozen times as the reporters kept asking the same questions over and over in different ways.

My phone rang, and the screen said it was Martha calling. I excused myself and turned away from the reporters.

"I guess you know about the verdict," she said. "I thought maybe you'd want a reason to get away from the wolf pack."

In my most businesslike voice, I said, "Yes, that's correct. Thank you very much for the call."

"I do have a message that you might want to deal with," Martha said. "Since you've been all wrapped up in the trial, I set the office phone to forward calls to my cell. A few minutes ago, Senator Parkdale's assistant called. The senator would like to talk with you. Want the number?"

"Sure. Send it as a text. I don't have anything to write with. Anything else?"

"Nothing that can't wait."

To the reporters, I said, "I have an important business matter that can't wait. I hope you understand."

Without waiting for a response, I went inside to wait for the text message from Martha. When it came through, I placed the call, which was answered by a receptionist who transferred me to Parkdale's assistant.

"Mr. Corrigan, I'm glad you got back to me," he said. "Your attorney, Mr. Gilchrist, has been in contact with us regarding your lawsuit against the IRS."

"Yes, I discussed that with him yesterday," I said.

"Good. Well, the senator would like very much to meet you and talk about your difficulties with the IRS."

"I'm open to that."

"Listen, I know this is terribly short notice, but the senator is actually in Carson City right now, and if there's any way you could get down here in the next couple of days, he'll make time for you."

"Is it that important?"

"Senator Parkdale is committed to ending the practice of using the IRS as a weapon against political adversaries. He believes that your case could be the one that opens the door to a full-scale investigation."

"Let me see if I can get a plane ticket. I'll get down there if I can."

"Excellent. Get me the flight number, and we'll have someone pick you up at the airport."

I got on the computer and searched for flights to Reno. I found all of the direct flights booked solid. The best I could do was to fly to Los Angeles and then catch a commuter flight to Reno via Sacramento. I didn't even bother trying to find a return flight.

"The forecast is for nice weather over the weekend. How'd you like to do a road trip?" I asked Kim when she got home.

"I'm scheduled to work this weekend. What'd you have in mind?"

"If we get an early start, we can get to Reno in time for dinner with Senator Parkdale. Afterward, maybe there'll be time to take in a show."

"Senator Parkdale?"

"He's buying," I coaxed.

Kim pondered that for a moment.

"Well, Sammy Cushman owes me a weekend. Maybe he'll fill in for me."

"So you're up for it?"

"Sure, unless you start attaching strings to it."

"Only one," I teased.

"Oh boy. Here we go. Corrigan—"

"We take your car," I said quickly, heading off the protest. "It's convertible weather."

"Ah. Well, let me check with Sammy."

72

Saturday, September 8

MapQuest said it was an eleven-hour drive. I figured we'd do it in under ten. We packed light and hit the road before five, with the top up and a thermos of coffee close at hand. It felt good to get behind the wheel and leave behind all of the turmoil and chaos.

We stopped in Bend to fill the gas tank and buy some Egg McMuffins. Kim put the top down and took over driving, heading south on US-97, while I made a futile attempt to get some sleep. State Highway 31 took us southeast across the high desert of Central Oregon. We were making good time until we came up behind a beat-up pickup towing an old fishing boat somewhere around Silver Lake.

We were in section of road where there were few straight stretches long enough to pass, and the old guy in the truck was oblivious to the line of cars that built up quickly behind him. Plodding along at about forty miles an hour, we must have driven twenty miles before Kim finally found a place where she could get around him. As we pulled out to pass, something in the boat caught my eye.

"That's it!" I exclaimed, startling Kim into looking hastily around.

"What?" she asked loudly.

"The fish club!"

"The *what?*"

"There was a fish club in that old boat!"

We were approaching eighty miles an hour as Kim pulled back into the right lane and let off the accelerator.

"What in hell are you talking about?" she asked.

"The fish club," I repeated, realizing that further explanation was needed.

"Day before yesterday, I saw Leonard Butts walking his dog. He was wearing an Old Navy hooded sweatshirt. Something else registered, but I couldn't put my finger on it. *He was carrying a fish club!* That's what's been bugging me for two days."

"So what? He always carries it."

"Yeah, but remember what Guido Barcelli said about the guy he saw running away from the fire when Carlton was killed? He was wearing an Old Navy hoodie and carrying a kid's baseball bat!"

"That was Shane Keasey, not Leonard Butts!"

"I know, I know. But what if—"

"It has to be just a coincidence."

Another vague memory forced its way into my mind.

"Have you ever gone past Butts's place when his garage door is open?"

Kim shrugged. "Probably, but I don't—"

"I've seen it maybe a hundred times. Right there in Butts's garage sits a decrepit plum-colored Plymouth Neon."

"Yeah, so?"

"It is the color of grapes! Remember what Señora Valensueva said?"

"Yeah, but I don't remember *ever* seeing Butts drive that old Neon. It may not even run. Usually he drives a silver pickup. Anyway, why would his old car have been in the alley next to Señora Valensueva's house? I mean, he wouldn't drive *anything* to Señora Valensueva's house—it's only a couple of blocks from his place."

"It doesn't make any sense, I understand that. But that's *three* things! The sweatshirt, the club, and the old purple car. And like the old saying, one is a novelty, two is a coincidence, but *three* is enemy action—or in our case, criminal activity."

"That's pretty thin," Kim said.

I didn't have an answer for that. She was right. And yet I couldn't help thinking about it. Half an hour later, we intersected US-395, which took us all the way to Reno. We pulled up in front of the Peppermill Tower Hotel at two thirty.

The hotel is huge and overdecorated in the garish style of casinos everywhere. At the front desk, I handed the clerk my card, and she keyed my name into her computer.

"Mr. Corrigan," she said brightly. "Welcome to Reno. Your suite is ready. Is your luggage in your car? We'll have someone take it up right away."

"Uh, this is all we have," I confessed, showing my gym bag and Kim's overnight bag.

"No problem," she said.

A valet appeared from nowhere and took our meager luggage.

"Let me show you to your suite," he said.

Our suite was about three times the size of my entire house. It featured a bar and dining room with seating for four, an in-room Jacuzzi tub, and two movie-screen sized television sets—because one might not be enough, I assumed.

On the table sat a pair of Waterford crystal champagne flutes next to an ice bucket containing a bottle of Dom Perignon that undoubtedly cost more than I spent on booze in three months. I gave the valet a twenty, wondering if that was too much or too little.

The card on the table was from Senator Parkdale, welcoming us to Reno and asking us to confirm our availability for dinner in the White Orchid Dining Room at seven. Enclosed with the note were open vouchers for spa services, room service, and beverages at any bar in the hotel.

I'm not sure what I'd expected, but clearly I wasn't prepared for this.

I looked at Kim, and she asked, "What should we do first—go shopping or drink the champagne?"

"We'd better go shopping. I don't think my blue jeans will cut it."

I managed to find a relatively affordable Ralph Lauren suit and a couple of shirts and ties, while Kim got herself a pair of designer evening dresses with matching shoes and (of course) new underwear. As we rode the elevator back up, Kim looked at herself in the mirrored glass wall.

"I need some work," she said.

In our room, I opened the champagne while Kim called the front desk and asked if it was possible to get her hair done before dinner.

"Certainly. Do you have a favorite stylist here?" the clerk asked.

"Not yet. Will you pick one for me?"

I poured the champagne and said, "Victory!"

We touched our glasses and allowed ourselves the luxury of a few minutes of uninterrupted happiness, something that had been a rare thing since the day Kim pulled the El Camino out of the river. Later, while she

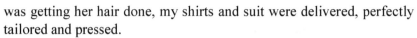

was getting her hair done, my shirts and suit were delivered, perfectly tailored and pressed.

"Ms. Stayton, you look absolutely stunning," Senator Parkdale said. She did.

"And you're the one who finally brought down Senator Blalock," he said to me. "I am very happy to meet you both."

"It's an honor to meet you, Senator," I said.

"Please call me Lee," the senator said. "I'm afraid my wife couldn't make it tonight. She had a prior engagement, but she sends her thanks for all that you've done."

We were joined for dinner by a senator from Idaho and four congressmen from surrounding states, all accompanied by their wives. We were seated around an elegantly set banquet table beneath Swarovski crystal chandeliers. The six-course dinner was simply magnificent.

"I could have sold tickets tonight," Senator Parkdale said. "Everyone wants to meet you. Overnight, you've become the most famous man in America."

I groaned. "I'm not ready for that. All I did was follow the evidence."

"Oh, it was a bit more than that," he said with a wave of his arm. "You defied the big boys. You refused to be intimidated."

It was clear that he wasn't going to let me duck his praise, so I let it stand. The conversation over dinner was social and casual.

One of the wives had seen something about me on television and was fascinated by *Annabel Lee*.

"You're the first person I've ever met who owns a sailing ship!" she said.

Everyone was greatly amused by the story of how I'd accidentally won the ship in a bankruptcy liquidation auction, and they at least pretended to be interested in the whole process of restoring her into a yacht capable of sailing around the world.

When someone asked about the rescue of Martha Hoskins from the brink of Willamette Falls, I welcomed the opportunity to give full credit to Kim.

"Deputy Stayton is the one who did that. All I did was tie a knot. She backed the boat through a swift crosscurrent at the edge of the spillway so that I could get a line attached to Martha's boat."

Then I sat back and admired Kim as she took the spotlight off of me. It gave me cause to reflect on just how fortunate I was to share my life with this beautiful, charming lady who kept a room full of some of the most sophisticated people in the country entertained for most of the next hour.

It wasn't until after dessert that the topic of the IRS lawsuit came to the table. In fact, it was treated almost as an afterthought, even though I understood that it was the whole reason we were there. I explained how I'd found phone records for calls from Senator Blalock, Wilson Devonshire, and Richard Elgin correlating with the start of my troubles with the IRS.

Parkdale explained how his investigators were using public document requests and subpoenas to obtain records of communication between the IRS and as many as two dozen well-known congressmen and senators.

"Most of them, like your Senator Blalock had a go-between who provided a buffer against investigations like ours. What you found out about Blalock was crucial in showing how they do it."

It was about ten thirty when the dinner party finally broke up, with a personal invitation from Parkdale to join him for brunch in the morning. I took Kim to the Terrace Lounge, where we finished the evening with dancing and cocktails until we both knew that we were going to have to stay in Reno for at least another day.

73

Sunday, September 9

"Yes, yes. Of course you can stay another night," the desk clerk said in answer to my question.

He continued, "You are Senator Parkdale's guest, and he made it clear that you can stay as long as you wish. And he has instructed me to transfer all of your charges to his account."

I didn't know it at the time, but later I would find out that he'd managed to intercept the billing for our little shopping trip in the hotel boutiques. A person could get to like this kind of thing.

Over brunch, the senator and his aide gave me some legal forms.

"You'll want to run all of these past your own attorney, of course, but what they do is define precisely what will be your standing in our lawsuit."

"I just want my money back," I said.

"You'll get it and, I daresay, a lot more."

After a leisurely brunch, Parkdale excused himself and said that he had to catch a plane back to Washington, but not before urging us to stay as long as we wanted and enjoy ourselves at his expense.

The conviction of a United States senator for murder was big news, and even though my cell phone number was tightly restricted, a few reporters had somehow managed to get through. To each of them, I recited a carefully worded statement minimizing my role in the successful prosecution and giving full credit to the sheriff's office and district attorney.

Kim and I were making a sightseeing tour of the Peppermill complex when my phone again rang. When another unrecognized number appeared on the screen, I was ready to fire off my ritual speech.

"Is this Corrigan, the private investigator?" asked the voice on the phone.

Assuming it was a reporter, I prepared to vent my annoyance that she had somehow gotten my cell phone number.

"Yes, this is Corrigan," I said cautiously.

"Mr. Corrigan, this in Janet Monroe. We spoke a couple of months ago."

It took a moment to shift out of my anti-reporter mindset and grasp who it actually was.

"Sure, I remember. How are you?"

She ignored that and said, "You've been in the news—that whole thing with Senator Blalock."

With no idea why she'd called, I said, "Well, that's all over now, thank goodness."

"Anyway, I'm not calling about that. Fox News did a profile on you this morning—I guess you know that."

Actually, I didn't. I'd been carefully avoiding television.

Janet continued, "Part of the story said that you recently tried to save a man by pulling him out of a burning building."

"I was a bit late," I said, not wanting her to mistake me for any kind of hero.

"They said that. But I think they said his name was Carlton McDermitt. Is that true?"

"It is. Why do you ask?"

"Well, you remember I told you about a strange man who came into the museum sometimes? That was his name—Carlton."

"Excuse me?" I asked, trying to keep up.

"Yes. It stuck with me because we used to make jokes about 'Carlton the Doorman,' you know, from the old TV show. Anyway, I was surprised when you started talking about the killing of those Chinese miners in Hells Canyon because that's what Carlton was interested in. As I remember, he had some kind of family connection with someone involved in the massacre."

Remembering how difficult it had been to get her to talk the last time I was in Reno, Janet's willingness to talk now was perplexing. I didn't comment, preferring to let her lead the conversation.

"And now he's dead, and they say someone murdered him."

"That's right," I said simply, hoping to keep her talking.

"Do you think it had something to do with the Chinese gold?"

"What makes you ask that?" I asked, knowing that the sheriff's office had not said anything to the media about the gold.

I waited while she decided what to say.

"If it was the gold, I think my ex-husband might have had something to do with it. He was pretty determined to find that gold back then. It became a kind of obsession with him."

"How so?" I asked, suddenly very interested.

"Um…I don't like talking about this on the phone. Is there any way you could come back down here. I promise I'll tell you the whole story."

"The fact is, I'm in Reno right now. I could meet you this afternoon."

Kim gave me a look that suggested that I'd just overstepped my authority in social planning.

"Really?" Janet said, her voice cracking a bit. "What time? Where?"

"We're at the Peppermill. What time works for you?"

"I can be there in an hour."

"Okay, can we make it four at the Banyan Bar?"

"I'll see you there."

"Who was that?" Kim asked when I disconnected.

"Janet Monroe—the museum worker I came down here to talk with back in July."

"What does she want?"

"She says she knows who killed Carlton."

Kim just stared at me.

I introduced Kim to Janet Monroe. We had been there for some time before she arrived, so we already had tropical cocktails in front of us. I urged Janet to order what she wanted.

"I'm afraid this place is out of my league," she said sheepishly.

"Don't worry about it," I urged. "Senator Parkdale's picking up the tab.

"Huh? Why would he—"

"It has nothing to do with you. Just enjoy it."

When we finally got down to business, she said, "Remember I told you that my husband and I went to Wallowa County on vacation? That was when I went to the museum there and found those old letters."

"I remember all of that," I said.

"Okay, what I didn't tell you was that my husband spent the whole week down at Dug Bar with a metal detector, looking for the gold. And then when I showed him the letters I'd found at the museum, he got angry because the letters said that the gold wasn't down there where he'd spent all week looking."

"I don't recall them saying that."

"No, they didn't. Not directly. But they said that Omar LaRue had gone to his sister's place in Oregon City and later that Blue Evans had shown up there angry and looking for LaRue. My husband had done a lot of research into the Evans gang, and he figured that the only reason for Evans to go all the way to Oregon City to find LaRue was that he must have taken the gold."

Of course, we'd already reached that conclusion, but I let her talk.

"How does any of this relate to Carlton McDermitt's death?" I asked.

"Well, Leonard knew all about McDermitt's interest in the massacre because I told—"

"Excuse me, who did you say?"

"Leonard, my ex-husband. I told him all about the things we looked up for Carlton McDermitt."

"Wait. Wait. Is *Monroe* your married name?"

"No. It's my maiden name. I never took my husband's name. I mean, who'd want to be called Mrs. Butts?"

"Your husband was *Leonard Butts*?" I asked loudly.

"Well, yes. I thought you knew that."

I glanced over at Kim, and she was shaking her head in shock.

"Uh no, I didn't. So how much did Leonard know?"

"I don't know if I can remember all of the details. We—Tara Foster and I—had helped McDermitt figure out that the Applegate house had belonged to his ancestors. And we knew that the McDermitts had bought the house awhile later. But we didn't make the connection. Not then.

"But when Carlton kept coming in to find out more about the Chinese gold miners' massacre, we thought it was a pretty interesting piece of history. Then when I told Leonard some of the things we were finding out, he got really interested. He thought he could find the gold. That's why we spent our vacation over in Wallowa County.

"As soon as Leonard read the letters I found in the museum, he got the idea that the *gold* was the whole reason McDermitt bought the

Applegate house—because he thought that the gold was hidden somewhere in it."

"When did all this happen? When was your trip to Wallowa County?"

"I don't remember what year it was. Maybe 2000 or 2001," Janet said. "It was in springtime—April or May."

"Was Tara Foster still alive?" I asked.

I saw Janet look suddenly uncomfortable.

"Yes," she said. "It was before...all that."

"She was killed in June of 2000."

Her eyes suddenly filled with tears, and she whispered, "I know."

I waited for her to continue.

"I shouldn't have come here," she finally said.

"Janet, you have to tell us what you know," I urged. "It's all going to come out, regardless what you do."

"I always knew it would."

It suddenly occurred to me that it had been *Janet* on board John Prescott's boat with Tara Foster and Carlton McDermitt. She fit Prescott's description perfectly. It was never Jamie and Calvin. It was Janet and Carlton!

"You were on the boat that day with Tara Foster," I said gently.

"I never saw what happened to her. I didn't know," Janet said forcefully. "I went to bed early. I had nothing to do with it. In the morning she was gone. That's all I ever knew...except..."

"Except what?"

"Except, when she didn't come to work on Monday, *then* I knew. But Leonard told me not to say anything about being on the boat. He told me not to say anything to anybody. I always thought the guy who took us out on the boat would spill the whole story, but he never did."

"So you just kept quiet?"

"I got divorced and moved out of state. But I always knew it would come back to me."

"But if you thought Carlton had killed Tara, why not say so?"

Janet stared at me. She looked confused.

"Carlton?"

"We know he was on the boat," I said.

"*Carlton*?" she repeated, only louder. "Carlton wasn't on the boat. Where'd you get that idea?"

"We know—"

"It was *Leonard!*" Janet almost shouted. "*He* was the one on the boat. *He* was the one who killed Tara Foster, not Carlton!"

"Leonard? Are you saying *Leonard Butts* killed Tara Foster?"

"Yes!"

"Hold on. You'd better tell me the whole story," I said.

"After we came back from Wallowa County, I showed Tara copies of the letters I'd found. They were historically interesting."

"How did that lead to the boat ride?"

"The boat ride had nothing to do with the letters. John invited Tara to take a ride down to the Rose Festival in Portland. She was excited about going through the locks at the falls, and when I said it sounded like fun, she got him to extend the invitation to us—Leonard and me. The gold had nothing to do with it."

That corresponded with what Prescott had said.

"So what happened?"

"Everything was fine until we got stuck in the locks. We didn't get out until dark, so we had to tie up in West Linn. John wouldn't go upriver in the dark.

"We ate snack food because that's all we had aboard, and we drank a lot of wine and beer. John went to bed early, said he had a headache. So the rest of us started playing cards. Pretty soon, Tara started talking about the Chinamen's gold. That's when she said that she thought it was in the Applegate house."

"How'd she figure that out?"

"Well, the same way Leonard did, I guess. Anyway, she'd told Carlton what she thought and suggested that they get some X-ray equipment into to his house to find it. Tara had the idea that the gold should go to the descendents of the murdered Chinamen.

That started a big argument with Leonard. He was drunk, and he was smoking pot. He could get pretty obnoxious."

"He still can," I agreed.

"I got sick of listening to him, so I went to bed. When I got up in the morning, Tara was gone. Leonard said that she'd walked over to the restrooms and made a phone call and then someone came and picked her up. Only thing is, I *knew* that wasn't true, because earlier I'd tried to use that phone, and it was out of order."

"Was there anything else that made you suspicious?"

"I thought it was really strange that the carpet was gone. There had been carpet on the rear deck where we were playing cards, and in the morning, it was gone. Leonard said he'd set it on fire while trying to light a joint and had to throw it overboard.

"Then last year I heard how they found Tara all rolled up in a piece of carpet. It made me cry for days just thinking about it."

"Did Leonard ever use a name like Calvin?"

"*Calvin*? Heck no. Why?"

"It isn't important. Never mind."

I explained to Janet that when we got home, Kim and I were legally bound to turn over the information she'd shared with us. I spent some time assuring her that she wouldn't get into any trouble over it, but I recommended that she get an attorney just the same.

"You have a couple of days. But you'll probably hear from Deputy Michael Wheeler by the end of the week. And please don't say anything about this to anyone other than your attorney. The last thing we need is for this to get back to Leonard Butts."

"Don't worry about that. I've kept quiet for thirteen years."

After Janet left, I looked at Kim and shook my head.

"One is a novelty, two is a coincidence, but *three* is criminal activity," she said.

"Let's go have a nice dinner," I suggested. "And then go to bed early. We have a long drive tomorrow."

"Aw, you just want to *sleep*?" She pouted.

"I never said that."

74

Monday, September 10

We didn't get up early. We had room service bring us eggs benedict for breakfast. I kept giving twenty-dollar tips on the theory that even if I'd stayed at Motel 6 and had all of my meals at McDonalds, I'd have spent more than I'd handed out in tips over the last two days.

"We should have gotten married while we were here," I lamented as Kim drove away from the hotel. "We'll never be able to afford that kind of honeymoon again."

"Yeah," Kim said wistfully. "Maybe we should have."

"You're a terrible tease, you know that?"

"Yeah, I know that. Is it a problem?"

"I guess not. Let's go home."

First thing Tuesday morning, I called Larry Jamieson and told him the news.

"Not again," Jamieson groaned. "How many times have you wrapped up this case now? Three? Four?"

"I think it's just three," I said. "Unless you're talking about McDermitt, in which case it's just two. Same with Blodgett. But the nice thing is that it's all one suspect, and he's still alive."

"Okay, let's hear it," he said tiredly.

He got Deputy Wheeler on the line, and then I went through the whole explanation on how I came to believe that Leonard Butts was responsible for all three murders.

"But what about the two kids, Patrick and Shane?" Wheeler asked.

"Looks like they just made the mistake of being kids," I said.

"With Janet Monroe's testimony, we may have Butts dead to rights for Foster, but there's a lot of work to do to make a case against him for Blodgett or McDermitt," Jamieson commented.

"My theory on Blodgett is that Butts had been watching the Applegate house pretty closely throughout the remodeling project—just like McDermitt and for the same reason. They both believed there was gold hidden in there. And then when Blodgett found the old well under the cellar floor, they both reached the same conclusion—that the gold was hidden in the well.

"Remember old Bud was out chasing his runaway dog in the middle of the night and saw lights in the basement of the house? That could have been Carlton in there searching the well. We know that he found the gold, so it almost had to have been then. Of course, Butts didn't know that, so he probably was watching the house that day, waiting for Blodgett to go to lunch. As soon as Blodgett left, Butts drove his old car down and parked in the alley."

"Wait. Why didn't he just walk?" Wheeler asked.

"He'd done the arithmetic. He knew that if he found the gold, it'd weigh thirty or forty pounds, and it would be difficult to carry on foot. I imagine also that he figured there wasn't much chance of being identified in the old Neon because he never used it.

But Blodgett tripped him up by bringing his Happy Meal back to the house instead of staying at McDonalds and eating it there. Blodgett probably found Butts in the well, and in the ensuing confrontation, Butts killed him. Maybe you'll be able to find the weapon in his house."

"That's a whole lot of speculation," Wheeler pointed out. "The only direct evidence is the witness who saw the car, and she's already said it was Keasey's. That sure as hell won't get us a search warrant."

"No," I agreed, "but we're in a lot better shape on McDermitt. We have the witness, the sweatshirt, and the weapon. And we have the motive."

"Sounds good when you say it," Jamieson said. "But I don't know if we can sell that to a judge."

Martha came in just as I was concluding the phone call, so I had to repeat the entire story for her.

"The first thing I'd like you to do is find some pictures of Leonard Butts. Look through the photos you gathered up when you were looking for pictures of Carlton. I want to see if John Prescott will recognize him."

"I have a question," Martha said. "I can see how Butts would have concluded that Carlton had the gold. But how could he have known that he was about to melt it down?"

"That's the proverbial missing link, isn't it?" I confirmed. "The ironic thing is that Carlton never did need to melt the gold. Apparently, he thought that he had to get rid of the government markings on the bars."

I leaned back in my chair and pondered the sticky details. Butts must have had just enough time to search the well before Blodgett came back with his lunch. He had to assume that Blodgett had beaten him to the gold. Maybe Butts had anticipated that possibility, and that's why he had the gun.

And yet for Butts to actually *use* the gun, he must have felt some certainty that the gold had actually been removed from the well. I couldn't imagine anyone, even Leonard Butts, killing someone just because gold *might have been* in the well. He had to have been pretty sure. But how?

Carlton must have left something that tipped off Butts—maybe a visible hole where the gold had been or muddy footprints. *Somehow*, Butts was able to conclude that there had been gold and that someone got to it first. He probably threatened Blodgett, trying to make him give up the gold. But of course, Blodgett knew nothing about it. By then, Butts was committed. He had to kill him.

It was the middle of the day, so he had to cover up the crime pretty quickly, since someone could walk in at any time. He dropped the body down the well and shoveled in some dirt to conceal it. Then he drove Dave's car to an area of high crime and caught a bus or cab back. His mistake was leaving his own car in the alley all afternoon.

At that point, he could have just given up. Or he might have figured out that Carlton had recovered the gold. He easily might have heard Bud's comment about seeing lights in the house the previous night. But if he knew that Carlton had the gold, and was determined to get it, why did he wait until Carlton was ready to melt it? Over three months had passed; during which time, Butts could have taken the gold at any time.

So on August 1, what made Butts confront Carlton in his garage? He had to have learned something or seen something. The torch—it had to be the torch. And then I remembered my conversation with Mike Mohler a week after the fire. But it wasn't what Mike said. It was what Butts said: "Didn't you listen to what I told you last week?"

That had to be it.

"I'm going to take a little walk," I told Martha. "I'll be back in a half an hour."

I walked up to Mike Mohler's place and found him chopping away at English ivy vines that were climbing up the trunk of a tall fir tree in his yard.

"This stuff will choke the life out of a tree," he said.

"Yeah, and it's damned difficult to kill."

"It's an ongoing fight. The ivy's bound to outlast me in the long run."

Getting to the point of my visit, I said, "Hey, I was wondering about the day Carlton McDermitt borrowed your cutting torch."

"It's all taken care of. He had insurance that's going to get me a new torch."

"That's great. But what I was wondering was whether anyone else was around when Carlton came up to borrow it."

"Oh. Well, yeah. Leonard Butts was there with those two big dogs. That was when he started preaching about my shingles. You know, he's filed a complaint with the city, the meddling bastard!"

"Do you think he heard what Carlton said—like the reason he wanted to borrow the torch?"

Mike shrugged. "Well, sure. I mean he was standing right there."

"So he heard Carlton say he was going to melt some gold?"

"It was just his ring, as I recall."

"Right. But Butts heard that?"

"Sure. Unless he was too busy lecturing me about preserving history to hear anything else."

So now we knew. Butts heard Carlton say that he needed to melt some gold. He'd have known on the spot that it was the gold from the well. I went back to the office and reported to Martha what Mike had told me.

"I have a question, then," Martha said. "If Butts went down there to take the gold, why didn't he take the gun he used on Blodgett?"

I shrugged. "Maybe he was afraid someone would hear it. Or maybe he disposed of it after he killed Blodgett."

Martha pointed out the window. "I'd bet that he tossed it into the river, right out there."

75

Wednesday, September 12

I looked at the photos of Leonard Butts that Martha had found. They were freeze-frames from video recordings made of city commission meetings where Butts had used the "citizen comment" time to browbeat the city planning department for approving plans for a new house on Fourth Avenue.

Using Photoshop, I cropped and enhanced the best of the images. In his initial interview, John Prescott had described "Calvin" as having a bushy mustache, but for as long as I'd known him Leonard Butts was clean shaven. So I looked through photos of Carlton McDermitt until I found one with the same angle as my photo of Butts. I copied Carlton's mustache and pasted it onto the image of Butts.

I attached the modified photo to an email to John Prescott and added a photo of Janet Monroe that Kim had taken while I was talking with her in Reno. I asked if these could be the people who were on his boat.

I wasn't worried about contaminating the witness, because we already had Janet Monroe's statement that she had been there with Butts.

About twenty minutes after I hit the Send button, my phone rang.

"John Prescott here," he said when I answered.

"I guess this means you got my email," I said.

"Those are the people. No question about it."

"Okay, but there is one thing. You said that their names were something like Jamie and Calvin. Remember that?"

"Sure. What about it?"

"Her name is Janet."

"Yeah, that's it! Janet."

"And his name is Leonard."

"Right! Janet and Leonard. I remember now."

"But you said it was something like *Calvin*."

"Well, it is. Calvin. Leonard. They're both nerdy kind of names. See what I mean?"

Once again, I reminded myself that no two people see things the same way. All along, I had assumed he was talking about the word structure when he was talking about the word connotation. To him, Calvin and Leonard were similar. I shook my head thinking of all the hours we'd spent looking for someone named Calvin.

Later in the day, I made a couple of roast beef sandwiches and carried them down to the new dock in front of the Applegate house, where Kim was supervising a pair of divers using an underwater metal detector to search for a gun. The riverbed sloped down sharply from shore to a depth of about thirty feet below the outboard edge of the dock.

"How's it going?" I asked, handing Kim a sandwich and a Coke.

"Thanks. There's no shortage of metal down there," Kim said. "Lots of railroad spikes. It's a pretty difficult search."

"Well, it's a long shot, at best. We don't know that he actually threw a gun out here. It just seemed like something he might do under the circumstances."

"I know. But on the other hand, what would these guys prefer to do? Get in the water and play with expensive toys, or hang around in an office doing paperwork?"

I paused to look at the array of items the divers had brought up. In addition to innumerable railroad spikes, there were rusting hand tools, including hammers, wrenches, pliers and screwdrivers of all description, plus a circular saw. There were three bicycle frames, an old outboard motor, and several twisted and torn pieces of thick iron plate that may have come from the boiler of the steamboat *Gazelle*, which blew up here in 1854 with the loss of two dozen lives.

"How long are they going to stay at it?" I asked.

"As long as they're having fun, I suppose."

One of the divers broke the surface and handed Kim a line. She tugged on it, and when it became clear that something big was on the other end, I pitched in, and together we brought up a motorcycle frame— one of the expensive aluminum alloy frames.

"Makes you wonder what happened to the rest of the bike," I commented.

"Sent to Mexico as a basket of parts," Kim said. "Then sold back to Americans on the internet."

I was walking back up the ramp with the empty Coke cans when I heard a shout from one of the divers.

"We've got it!" one of the divers called out.

I hurried back down to the dock and watched the diver swim in. He placed a muddy revolver next to the motorcycle frame. Kim and I knelt down to look at it. It was a six-shot H&R .32 swing-cylinder revolver with pearl grips. The lack of rust or corrosion indicated that it hadn't been in the water very long.

Kim handed me the keys to her Explorer.

"There's an evidence kit in the back," she said.

I went and retrieved a Tupperware tub, a gallon of distilled water, a roll of evidence tape, and a Sharpie felt-tip marker. By the time I got back to the dock, the divers were climbing up the ladder onto the dock. I handed Kim the tub, and she carefully placed the revolver into it. Then she filled it with distilled water and snapped on the lid.

The divers started peeling off their wetsuits, and I was about to carry the motorcycle frame up to Water Street when movement in my peripheral vision caused me to look up. There on the railroad tracks with his two brown and white dogs stood Leonard Butts. How long had he been watching?

"That's Butts," I said to Kim. "He *has to* know what this is about."

She called out, "Mr. Butts, please stand right there."

He froze for a moment, and I could see the fear and indecision in his eyes as Kim started up the dock ramp. He looked rapidly left and right.

"Stay where you are," Kim ordered.

He dropped the dog leashes and bolted up onto Water Street, running left, toward Miller Street.

"He's running!" she yelled. "Come on!"

The divers were still barefooted and unable to help, so I started after Kim.

"Stay with Butts," she said. "I'll get my rig."

When we got to the pavement, Kim ran right and I ran left. Ahead of me, I heard a ruckus, and as I rounded the corner onto Miller Street, a black sedan with engine racing and tires spinning fish-tailed out onto the highway. There was a woman sitting on the pavement next to the curb.

"He took my car! Stop him! That man just took my car!" she yelled.

I helped her up and asked if there was anyone else in the car. She shook her head. At that moment, Kim came around the corner in her SUV. She screeched to a stop, and I scrambled into the passenger seat.

"He went up the hill toward town," I told her. "He 'jacked that lady's BMW."

Kim switched on the overheads and touched the siren button on the floor, creating enough of a gap in the traffic to get us onto the highway heading north. She drove up the center lane, passing cars that were slow to get out of the way.

The traffic signal at the top of the hill turned yellow, but Kim kept her foot on the gas, clearing the intersection with her siren. We caught just a glimpse of the black car going into the tunnel at the bottom of the hill, brake lights on and tires smoking.

"What the hell's he doing?" I wondered.

"Panicking," Kim said.

The scene in the tunnel was chaos. Two cars were stopped at crazy angles at the other end, blocking most of the highway. Kim aimed for the gap on the right-hand side. As we came out of the tunnel, I looked to the right, up Railroad Avenue, and saw the BMW blow the stop sign and slide into the left turn onto Seventh.

A confused driver stopped in front of us, blocking our way. The old man froze when Kim flashed her headlights and hit the siren. At the same time, she was on the radio reporting the chase and calling for assistance. The man finally got the point and edged over toward the cars parked on the right, creating just enough of a gap for Kim to squeeze through.

We turned onto Seventh and spotted the BMW on the old arch bridge about 250 yards ahead. Traffic was heavy and moving slowly across the bridge. There were about eight cars between us and the BMW, but no place for them to pull out of our way.

When we finally got across the bridge, we saw the BMW caught in traffic at the next signal. A West Linn Police car approached from the other direction, its blue and red lights flashing. The signal changed, and Butts lurched ahead, but we had closed to within fifty feet.

He turned onto the I-205 freeway ramp, squeezing past cars that were lined up for the ramp signal, sideswiping a couple of them and scraping the concrete barrier. The Explorer was too wide to follow, so we had to slow down and wait for people to get out of the way. I kept my eye on Butts as he got past the bottleneck and onto the six-lane bridge.

He stomped on the gas, engaging the twin turbochargers, and 330 horsepower came abruptly to life. Butts was utterly unprepared for that, as his rear tires spun, throwing up a cloud of dirt and smoke in front of us. The car slipped to the left, and just as the tires hit the raised pavement markers, a loaded dump truck in the next lane sounded its air horn.

Butts overcorrected and swerved sharply to the right, then overcorrected again and completely lost control of the BMW, which rammed into the front corner of the Kenworth dump truck. The impact spun the BMW across the right lane into the concrete barrier.

At about seventy miles per hour, the car turned sideways and went into a series of irregular high-speed flips that ended when the car went over the barrier. Kim skidded to a stop where the BMW disappeared. For a few chaotic moments, while traffic piled up behind us in multiple rear-end collisions, we didn't dare to get out of the Explorer.

It's about 120 feet down to the Willamette River. By the time we were able to look over the railing, there was no sign of the BMW other than a widening ring of waves on the surface of the river. A couple of fishermen raced toward the scene in their boats, but any thought of rescue was futile.

As Bud would later observe, "No ifs, ands, or Butts."

76

Tuesday, December 31

"I told you there wouldn't be a lift line over here," Kim said.

We'd just arrived at the Northwest Express chair, having worked our way around the mountain from the Sunrise Lodge, where I'd parked. We used three different chairlifts on the way over to Northwest, and there had been long lines at each.

"When you're right, you're right," I conceded. "I just hope that the teeming masses don't know something that we're about to find out."

"Too late to chicken out now, Corrigan," Kim teased.

"We'll see who chickens out."

The sun was starting to break through the cloud cover, making the fresh layer of snow sparkle. Every little breeze would dislodge loose snowflakes from the branches of the fir trees, creating dazzling rainbows in the sun.

At the top of the lift, we skied off to the left. Pausing at the top of the run ominously called Devil's Backbone, we looked out over the panoramic view of the Cascade Mountains.

"I'll wait for you at the bottom," I said as I pointed my skis over the edge.

"In your dreams, Corrigan!"

In reality, we both took a somewhat cautious approach on our first pass since there was no telling what was underneath the new snow. As it turned out, except for some ice in a few narrow chutes, the run was perfect.

We'd gotten in on a last minute three-for-two deal at Mount Bachelor Village, lift tickets included, and it gave us the perfect opportunity to end the year on a positive note. And actually, we had a lot to celebrate.

Under Measure 11 rules, former senator Alan Blalock was given two consecutive life sentences with a minimum of twenty-five years to serve on each. He would die in prison. His attorneys would file appeals until the money ran out, but his conviction was solid and wouldn't be undone.

In the aftermath of Leonard Butts's spectacular departure from life, all of the pieces came together. The revolver from the river was registered to Butts. One of the six bullets in the cylinder had been fired, and the composition of the lead in the remaining cartridges matched the lead taken from Dave Blodgett's skull.

Traces of Carlton McDermitt's blood were found on a pair of shoes in Butts's closet and on the sleeve of his Old Navy hoodie.

His study was filled with books, pamphlets, and articles relating to all aspects of historical preservation. But there was one shelf reserved solely for material about the Hells Canyon Massacre and the search for the stolen gold. In the end, Butts might have been just another among thousands of unsuccessful treasure hunters.

Instead, he was an unsuccessful treasure hunter and a triple murderer. Kim still believes that Butts intentionally wrecked the stolen BMW rather than face trial. We both saw the same thing, though, and I think he was too panicked to have a rational thought. He didn't think about facing trial. He didn't think about getting away. He just ran. And he was a lousy driver.

The lingering question of why Carlton hadn't tried to sell the gold when he first found it was answered when it was discovered that he was in the process of filing bankruptcy. He apparently didn't want his new-found fortune to be wasted on old debt, so he hid the gold bars in the old tackle box. Unfortunately, Patrick and Shane decided to go fishing.

After we'd completed ten runs, we skied over to the Pine Marten Lodge, where we took a break for a massive plate of nachos and a generous dose of Black Butte Porter. In the middle of lunch, my phone rang.

"Hey, Corrigan," Leo Gilchrist said, "you want to end the year with something to celebrate?"

"It sounds like you're about to deliver some good news," I said.

"Could be. The IRS has made a pretty generous offer—all your money back, a cash settlement that will pay both of us pretty well for our trouble, and a formal and official letter of apology. What do you think of that?"

"What do they want in return?"

"They want you to drop all legal action currently in progress and agree to refrain from future litigation on anything related to this issue."

"So that includes Parkdale's suit."

"That's right. Everything."

"Okay. I want to talk to Parkdale before I do anything. Last I heard, their subpoenas had been issued but not executed. I need to know if it'll damage their position if I drop out. How much time do I have?"

"They didn't put a deadline on it, but I wouldn't wait too long. You know how fast the wind can change in politics."

"I'll put in a call. Probably won't be able to talk to him before Thursday, though."

"Good enough. Let me know what you decide. And Happy New Year."

"It isn't Dom Perignon, but it'll do," I said as we lifted our glasses.

"Here's to a whole new year," Kim said.

Snow was falling around us as we sat in the hot tub sipping a California sparkling wine from plastic cups. In the distance, we could hear people in the lounge counting down the last seconds until midnight and the New Year.

"This year, let's do something we've never done before," I suggested.

"Do you have something in mind?"

"Yep."

Also by Ken Baysinger

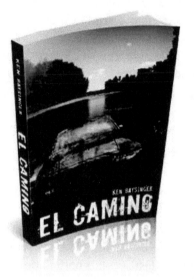

El Camino

The Mendelson-Devonshire case was legendary. It was also political dynamite. In 1980 the disappearance of Jessie Devonshire and Randy Mendelson had been Portland's biggest news story of the year. It remained the region's most notorious unsolved case.

It couldn't even be properly called an unsolved crime, because it had never been proven that a crime had been committed. All that was known was that fifteen-year-old Jessie Devonshire had vanished without a trace and that Randy Mendelson, a twenty-year-old landscaper, had disappeared at the same time.

Everyone had a theory, but nobody had an answer to the mystery. The one fact that everyone knew was that Jessie Devonshire was the stepdaughter of Wilson Landis Devonshire, who was an official in the Portland Mayor's office and a rising star among Oregon's political elite.

The case that lands in the lap of a private investigator named Corrigan had been the biggest hot potato in Clackamas County law enforcement for at least ten years following the disappearances. At least three careers had ended because detectives had been unable to provide the answers that the politically powerful principals in the case demanded.

ISBN: 978-1-947491-98-4 ©2017
Yorkshire Publishing   392 pages $19.99

www.kenbaysinger.com

Also by Ken Baysinger

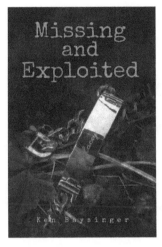

Missing and Exploited

A car collector looking for a place to store his vintage Studebakers stumbles across a name carved in a wooden beam from a century-old building. Just a quarter-mile away, the skeletal remains of a young woman are found outside a homeless camp.

The investigation that Corrigan starts as a favor for his old friend quickly becomes a nightmare beyond anything he could have imagined. As the body count rises, the mystery becomes ever deeper, until it takes on a life of its own.

For three decades, children have been vanishing without a trace, until Corrigan uncovers the terrible truth. And nothing comes without a cost.

Relationships are torn apart, and at times even nature works against Corrigan and his small team of investigators as they chase down obscure clues from the cold case files. Chasing leads across five states over six months, Corrigan faces the greatest challenges of his investigative career.

ISBN: 978-1-5245-5269-5   ©2016
Xlibris   390 pages $19.99

25% of the author's first year royalties for *Missing and Exploited* will be donated to the National Center for Missing and Exploited Children

www.kenbaysinger.com

CPSIA information can be obtained
at www.ICGtesting.com
Printed in the USA
LVOW07s1921240817

546255LV00012B/71/P

obtained

0019B/468/P